YANK

By

Norman Ferris

ISBN: 1-4033-0797-0

This book is printed on acid free paper.

1stBooks - rev. 05/24/02

This book is a work of fiction. Names, characters, places and incidents are products of the author's imagination and are used fictitiously. With the exception of occasional references to well-known public figures like Harry Truman and Lyndon Johnson, resemblances to actual persons, living or dead, are entirely coincidental. The author and publisher have neither liability nor responsibility to any person or entity with regard to any loss or damage alleged to be caused, directly or indirectly, by the opinions expressed or information provided in this book.

For Henry and Eleanore Galant

With Great Affection,

And with Fond Recollections of

Jim and Gerie Davis,

Bell Wiley,

And Kit and Charlie Kellogg,

The Best of Friends

Who Live On

In Grateful Memories

CONTENTS

CHAPTER 1
CULTURE SHOCK

"I have news... We're moving to Texas." His father's unexpected announcement jolted sixteen year-old Loren like a hammer blow. He felt dizzy. The familiar surroundings of the dining room—the large mahogany table at which the four Temples had just sat down to dinner, the elaborately inlaid buffet and china closet—blurred into a dreamlike distortion of swirling shapes.

Moving? Leaving Winona? It couldn't be true. Surely Adam Temple, who had just returned to the table from having answered the telephone, would now burst out laughing at his son's dazed reaction to his little joke.

Loren's sidelong glance at Nan Temple's furrowed brow, however, told him otherwise. His mother sat stiffly at her end of the table next to the kitchen door, tapping an index finger against an empty coffee cup. "When?" she abruptly asked her husband.

"Soon," said Adam. "That was Ward Hatton, the editor of the Tocqueville *Endeavor* who came to Chicago last week to interview me. He offered me a job as managing editor. I accepted. We'll have to sell this house, find one in Tocqueville, and move. All in less than one month."

"That will be difficult," objected Nan. "Especially since the boys have two more weeks of school before their summer vacation. Can't we take a little longer to get ready?"

"Hatton wants me on the job by the first week of July," declared Adam. "I gave him my word."

"All right," replied Nan. "I'll do my best."

"As will Loren and Tommy," said Adam. "Won't you, boys?"

"Sure, Dad," said Tommy, surprisingly sanguine.

Loren reluctantly nodded. Tommy was only thirteen. The full significance of losing their comfortable home and being parted from their friends had not yet hit the youngest Temple. Once he gauged the impact of the dislocation, Loren imagined, Tommy would join him in pleading with their parents not so terribly to disrupt their lives.

Such pleas were unlikely to succeed. Loren's father had told his sons repeatedly that as the "head of the family" he would be the one to decide what was best for the four of them.

Loren excused himself from the dinner table and went outdoors to think.

* * *

He plodded head down along the cracked concrete sidewalk, breathing deeply, almost gasping, his mind crowded with troubling thoughts. Above him gray squirrels leaped through the leafy canopy provided by massive elm trees. Somewhere a bird burst into song. Oh, shut up, thought Loren.

Turning at the corner, he headed for the village green, passing a huge house surrounded by an immaculate lawn and lush shrubbery, the home of a slender blond cheerleader whom Loren yearned to date. In his shyness, he had not yet approached her, but he had been hoping soon to summon the courage to speak. Now, however, that intention had been squelched by his father's abrupt announcement.

Sitting on the steps of the marble monument to Winona's war dead, vaguely conscious of the large American flag flapping overhead in the evening breeze blowing westward off Lake Michigan, Loren felt tears dripping down his cheeks. Wiping them away with a shirt sleeve, he began to reminiscence about a less complicated time of life.

* * *

During the late nineteen-thirties, the Temple family had lived in the village of Corner Creek, Virginia, not far from the nation's capital. Loren had been a lively, curly-headed little boy with no worries and plenty of books to read. Blissful in the comfortable solitude of his bedroom, he had spent countless hours adventuring with *The Swiss Family Robinson, Black Beauty, Smoky*, the *Oz* people, and the *Wind in the Willows*. At school he had learned easily and received high grades. His father, an editor on a Washington newspaper and a village councilman, was his special hero, ranking slightly higher than Prince Valiant of the Sunday comics.

His mother was irrepressibly cheerful. She discerned good in everyone and in every situation. She delighted in her occasional dinner parties, her weekly card games with neighbor women, and helping out at the Corner Creek Little Theatre. Returning home with Adam after an evening play rehearsal, Nan would pay the sitter and wish Loren and Tommy pleasant dreams with a good night kiss. She radiated a blithe warmth that sweetened her world, like the delectable pastries she concocted in her kitchen domain.

Leaning back on the Winona war monument, Loren recalled how during the Corner Creek years his father would bring his big black Hupmobile to life with an arm-wrenching tug on a crank that jutted out below its radiator grill, like a thin cigar from a toothy grin. Loren also remembered seeing an even larger vehicle zoom past his front yard, from the rear window of which a smiling lady waved at him—a lady whom his mother matter-of-factly identified as Mrs. Roosevelt, the wife of the popular President. He recollected tugging at the tunic of an army officer who was visiting next door, trying to rid it of its ribbons as they playfully wrestled on the thinly carpeted floor of the Eisenhower sun porch. And Loren recalled the shining sight of airplanes climbing into the sky from the Arlington airport, and the elongated shadows stretching across the Temple lawn when a large blimp sailed silently overhead, bound for the navy base on the Potomac River.

He remembered lying in the weeds watching the antics of tadpoles in a frog pond located in the dark woods next to a desolate intersection called "Seven Corners," over which loomed a grassy mound on which fortifications had been hastily thrown up during the War Between the States. This was the phrase invariably used by several old men who liked to sun themselves on a bench in front of Blake's hardware store and spit tobacco juice on the sidewalk as they reminisced in cracked voices about their respective roles in what Adam insisted was really the American Civil War.

Then, in 1940, when Loren was only eight years old, his idyllic life had abruptly ended. His mother, without warning, had suffered a heart attack and almost died. Still in her early thirties, she had been whisked away to a hospital. Her two small sons had been packed off to live with strangers on a farm in the Shenandoah Valley where Adam had assured them they would love the rural life that he had enjoyed as a boy.

Loren had hated that farm. The elderly pair who owned the place were grumpy and grim. They tried to persuade him to perform unpleasant chores that he feared were dangerous. And he had missed his mother.

That summer had seemed endless. And Loren's unhappiness had increased when he learned that his mother had returned home from the hospital only a few days after he and his brother had been farmed out. Why then, he had wondered, had they been kept away from her until the start of school in September?

During that summer Loren had begun to wet his bed almost nightly, accidents that produced punishments and shame that further eroded his declining self-confidence.

At the end of the following school year, Loren had anticipated a happy summer at home. Instead, he and his little brother had been exiled to another isolated farm, this one in central Michigan, where Adam's aunt and her surly husband informed Loren that they put up with him solely because his father sent them money. His only solace was receiving weekly letters from his missing mother.

Had she suffered another heart attack? Surely not, because she had written not from a hospital but from home. Loren had not understood why she had permitted the separation from her children to last so long, this time for almost a year. He began to shrink from contact with other people, lost his spontaneity, and took refuge in prolonged daydreams. Alone, vulnerable, he waited…

*   *   *

Eventually, during the summer of 1941, Adam reunited his family in the sedate surroundings of Winona, Illinois, within commuting distance of his new job at the Chicago *Star*. Known widely for its affluence and for its progressivism in elementary education, Winona seemed the perfect place to raise children. Tommy, adaptable like his mother, made the adjustment easily. For Loren, however, the sudden shift from the solitude of Michigan farm life to the hectic pressures of suburban society was difficult. For many months—all through sixth, seventh and eighth grades—he remained on guard.

Over time his wretched shyness was gradually alleviated by his success in athletics. Quick, strong, and well-coordinated, he had become the starting second baseman, when only a fourteen-year-old freshman, on the Winona Country Day School baseball team. Then, the following fall, he had displayed considerable talent at football. By his junior year he was starring at both sports.

Slowly he made new friends. Still reticent and sensitive, he had nevertheless been tentatively emerging from his cocoon when his father suddenly proclaimed the family's imminent departure for a new life in Texas.

* * *

Loren tried half-heartedly to resist. "Do we have to go?" he asked his mother.
"I'm afraid so," she replied.
"Why?"
"Your father lost his job and had to find another one."
"But why Texas? Couldn't he have found work in Chicago?"
"Possibly. But there is another reason we're going to Texas."
"What's that?"
"My health. My heart may not be able to stand another Chicago winter. Dr. Rosenwald says that if I'm going to live much longer, we'll have to relocate to a much warmer climate."
"Oh." Loren could think of nothing more to say. He went to his room. Looking longingly at the four walls papered with pictures of baseball players and at the piles of books and magazines that represented a decade of voracious reading, he began to estimate how many cardboard cartons it would take to box the lot. At least the move to Texas would not deprive him of these treasures.

* * *

Not long after proclaiming the Temple family's pending departure, Loren's father surprised him by offering him an option. "I've checked with your headmaster," said Adam, "and you can live at Country Day, in the house where they keep boarding students. You'll have to room with another boy. But Mr. English assured me that you'll be well cared for. Your mother agrees with me that we can afford to pay room and board if you want to stay in Winona until you graduate from high school."

At first Loren was elated to hear his father's offer. But he soon realized that without the comfort and convenience of his own room, and especially without the privacy to cope unobserved with his nocturnal incontinence, he would be vulnerable to unendurable embarrassments. He let his anxieties dictate his choice. He would not stay in Winona.

At sixteen, he had a very limited knowledge of the world. Nothing in his experience had prepared him for Tocqueville, Texas, or for the dangers he would soon encounter in that perilous place. Had he known all that he would encounter there, he would definitely have decided not to leave Winona.

* * *

On the evening of Monday, June 28, 1948, darkness had already engulfed Tocqueville when forty-seven year-old Adam Temple steered his battered brown 1939 Hudson into its northern outskirts and proceeded along a corridor of flickering neon toward the shadows of a quiet residential district. For three days while Adam drove, Loren had sat beside him and navigated, tracing their journey on a succession of wrinkled road maps. Tommy, meanwhile, had squirmed uncomfortably in the back seat, squeezed among suitcases and piles of clothing which his father had been unable to cram into the trunk. Both boys had tried to shorten the hours by reading, but the swaying and bouncing of the car over rough highways had jolted their books, and Adam's incessant epithets hurled at offending drivers, along with his disdainful observations about their surroundings, numbed their brains. In the car's confinement Adam's aura seemed to swallow space.

Nan had taken a train to Texas a week earlier to find and purchase a house. She was unpacking boxes when the Hudson's headlights flashed across the still uncurtained front windows, as Adam steered the vehicle into the driveway. At once Nan hurried out the front door and down the porch steps to greet her husband and sons. While Adam brushed his lips against her upturned pucker, Loren stretched his stiff muscles and stared about. Dimly in the darkness he could discern strange shapes. An unfamiliar aroma like that escaping from a high school Chemistry lab assaulted his nostrils. He shivered, briefly overcome by an inexplicable feeling of fear. Then he hugged his mother and followed his parents up the front steps of his new home.

After devouring three sandwiches and two glasses of milk, Loren found his way to his new bedroom. There, on the bare wooden floor, sat a World War II surplus army cot covered with fresh white sheets, an empty chest of drawers, and a stack of unopened cartons resting against the inner wall. He missed the thick woolen carpet and the double bed with the massive mahogany headboard that had helped to make his Winona room so comfortable a refuge.

In a corner he spotted the small toy chest in which, for as long as he could remember, he had kept his most cherished possessions. Now it was empty, as was the small red bookcase that in Winona had held his Rover Boys books and the tattered volumes of the Harvard Classics. Soon its shelves would be replenished. But he missed his walk-in closet in Winona, where he had stretched out on the floor, sucked a Green River soda fetched from his hidden hoard, and poured over his cherished collection of baseball record books. In Tocqueville the closet was merely a cranny.

While preparing to leave Winona, Loren had watched intently to make sure that the movers packed his books and photographic equipment, as well as accumulated mementos, including dozens of Wrigley Field scorecards and hundreds of autographs of old-time baseball players. In the Hudson he had brought a metal box crammed with photographic negatives, many of which had been produced by his Ciroflex camera, a gift from his parents on his thirteenth birthday. The pinhole camera with which he had begun picture-taking a decade earlier still survived, a backup to the more sophisticated Ciroflex. Loren planned to continue improving his photographic skills in Texas.

He pulled the top sheet off the cot, shed his outer clothing, and lay down in his damp underwear. Despite a steady breeze drawn out of the darkness by a roaring attic fan, he continued to perspire. Through a screened window came the chirruping of crickets and an occasional swish of automobile tires on the nearby street. Not long after he fell asleep, an enormous cockroach crawled onto his pillow near his open mouth and waved its feelers in what might have been a gesture of welcome.

CHAPTER 2

CRAVINGS

Unpacking boxes in his room on the evening of Wednesday, June 30, Loren decided that he needed some companionship. He turned on his radio. As he twisted the dial searching for something stimulating, his pajama-clad younger brother padded on dirty bare feet through the open bedroom door. "Say," exclaimed Tommy, "whaddya think of th' neighbors?"

"I don't know," said Loren. "I haven't met them yet."

Tommy laughed. "The women," he said, "are a strange lot. Mom had Mrs. Moo Tun, Mrs. Kaplan, and Mrs. Pryor over for coffee yesterday. I could see and hear them easily from my room. It was a disaster. Mrs. Moo…"

"Mouton," corrected Loren. "She's a Cajun, according to Mom. French."

"That explains why she talks funny," said Tommy. "Anyway, all the while they were here Mrs. Mouton kept glaring at Mrs. Kaplan. Who, by the way, is one sexy woman. And Mrs. Kaplan wouldn't say a word to either Mrs. Mouton or Mrs. Pryor. Just ignored them and talked only to Mom. And Mrs. Pryor kept her prominent nose in her coffee cup and frowned the whole time without even looking at the others. It looks like our closest neighbors detest each other!"

"I gather the party didn't last long."

"It hardly got started," said Tommy. "They left after the first cup."

"Poor Mom."

Tommy snickered. "Yeah, but you know our mother. Always looking on the bright side. She likes Mrs. Moo—Mouton; so after the others were gone she took the coffee pot and two cups next door. She took me with her. I hoped to meet the youngest Mouton girl but she wasn't there."

"And?"

"We both got an earful, although I don't think they knew I was listening behind my magazine. Mrs. K's husband's a pediatrician and is away a lot, either at his clinic or at the hospital. No children. She's bored. Mrs. M thinks she plays around. Before they got hitched she was some kind of show girl in New Orleans. Probably married Dr. K for his money. She talks about him as if he were a rich uncle, not a husband. She reads romance magazines, shops for expensive clothes, and disappears for days at a time to visit 'relatives.'"

"I saw her yesterday sunning herself in the back yard," said Loren. "Nice body. I wonder why she has no children."

"Maybe Dr. K can't get it up," said Tommy. "With a woman like that you'd think it would be easy."

"Yeah," agreed Loren, thinking guiltily of how he had nearly creamed his jeans watching out his window as Mrs. K emerged from her back door, her yellow bathing suit stretched tightly across her buttocks, her red curls cascading over her freckled shoulders.

"As for Mrs. Pryor," continued Tommy, "her husband's the minister of that big Baptist church on Austin Avenue. I guess you've seen it: a brick building with a high steeple and a sign out front with Bible quotations?"

"So that's his church? Religion for the rich. I bet they pay well."

"According to Mrs. M," said Tommy, "the Pryors are loaded. Look at that huge house. And the Cadillacs and Packards parked outside. I think they play cards."

"Or plan charitable work?"

"Ha! Those people? Cushioned pews, a great big organ, and air conditioning. Probably not more than an occasional prayer for the poor."

"Cynic," accused Loren. "I've seen their charities mentioned on the society page of the Endeavor. Let's give Mrs. Pryor the benefit of the doubt, as Mom would say."

"She would."

"What about the Moutons?"

"Well, Mom says they're crazy about square dancing. Every weekend th' old folks gather up their two daughters and their son—he's an assistant attorney general with an office in the Court House—and they all go to a Catholic Church and dance to fiddle and accordion music. It must be sweaty stuff. When Mrs. M spoke of square dancing, and about how her family has never missed Sunday mass for umpteen years, she got excited and started spouting French."

"What did Mom think of that?"

"She just watched th' woman's hands. 'They translate,' she said."

"Curious," said Loren. "I wonder..."

"What?" asked Tommy.

"Nothing," said Loren. He decided not to share his hope that his Mom would also make friends with the fascinating Mrs. Kaplan.

"Time for bed," announced Tommy. He slipped across the hall to his own room, which was not much larger than a walk-in closet. Through the two open doors Loren watched his brother tumble into bed. Hardly more than a minute later, the little guy's chest rose and fell rhythmically, and Loren knew he was asleep.

Tommy's ability to put himself to sleep almost as soon as his head hit the pillow had always amazed his brother. "It's simple," the younger boy had explained. "I jus' do th' ol' relaxin' bit."

"What's that?" Loren had inquired.

"First I tell my toes to go limp; then my ankles; then my calves; my knees; my thighs; and so on, right up to my head."

"Your brain is last?"

"Nah. After I tell my scalp to go to sleep, I say to my tongue to go limp in my mouth, and when that happens, I'm gone. I never remember anything else."

Loren had tried his brother's technique a few times, but he had never been able to make it work. Now he lay on his damp cot and tried to think of something soothing. Instead, as usual when bedtime came, he brooded, remembering Winona.

He had recently suffered a considerable embarrassment there. He had been invited by the slinky daughter of a millionaire to his school's junior prom, held at a local country club. Shy, self-conscious (especially about his acne which nightly squeezing in front of the bathroom mirror had only exacerbated), and painfully aware of his ineptitude at small talk, he had felt ridiculous in a shiny second-hand tuxedo and tight black patent leather shoes. Worried that his clip-on bow tie would at any moment tip askew, and that his tentative dancing would produce sarcastic behind-the-hand remarks from his more polished schoolmates, he had nervously endured the evening ordeal.

Only the gossipy chatter of his garrulous date had kept them from foxtrotting in silence. And when the orchestra began to play faster music and they sat, Miss Aletha Carson had eventually had to ask him to fetch her punch and cake, or he would never have thought to do so. Finally, when the party had ended and Loren had driven his now taciturn companion back to her family's mansion, he had guided his father's car home in a fog of despair.

At the Country Day School, which he had attended on a full scholarship, Loren's grades were good, although he sometimes had to force himself awake before five in the morning to struggle with Latin or Algebra. But his studies were less important to him than athletics. According to one of the sideline mothers, overheard by Nan Temple (who habitually turned her back toward the field whenever Loren carried the football), he had played the gridiron game "like a big cat." And the crusty coach of the baseball team, who had played professionally, had been heard to mutter that Loren was "one hell of a hitter." Away from the playing fields, however, he was clumsy and tongue-tied, and had found it almost impossible to look directly into the eyes of anyone who was looking at him. One day, passing head down through a cluster of girls near the rear entrance to the upper school building, he had overheard a popular blonde harshly query a companion: "Just who does he think he is?"

Trivial as this incident might have seemed to others, it had produced in Loren an increased sense of isolation. The more he ignored his female schoolmates, fearing ridicule, the more they had seemed to react resentfully. He actually wondered whether, through some occult intuition, they might be able to read his mind and thereby uncover the unseemly urges, the gross appetites, of his secret self. Although he had never kissed a girl's lips, he had several times awakened from wet dreams in which he had apparently coupled with willing women, although the exact details of what had happened were never quite clear. And so he had wondered whether he would ever be a normal male: swaggering, cussing creatively, and poking pretty girls proprietarily, like the actor Errol Flynn, whom Loren had envied with a palpitating intensity.

Once he had discovered inside his father's newspaper a brief account of a court trial in which Flynn had been accused by two teen-aged girls of statutory rape. Included in the otherwise circumspect story was the allegation by the younger of the two that when the movie star had escorted her aboard his yacht, he had asked her to lean forward to enjoy the view through a porthole. When she had innocently complied, she testified, he "stuck" her. Loren and several friends had been so intrigued by that tale (tail!) that they had formed the ABCDEFGHI Club, an exclusive organization whose members proudly, if covertly, rooted for Flynn to evade jail for his escapade. In any true history of Winona, Illinois, one of Loren's friends had declared, some mention should appear of the American Boys Club Defending Errol Flynn's Great Honorable Intentions.

Loren's own carnal impulses had been kept in check by society's conventions and by his own insipid inhibitions. But every time he had felt an aching yearning, as the soft flesh hardened, he could only wonder wistfully whether he would ever reach the promised land. Meanwhile, as the years of his adolescence passed, he had suppressed such cravings by crashing through clutching bodies on the football field, or by thrusting his left hand into the soft leather of a fielder's glove, wrapping the long fingers of his right hand around a baseball, and making the dust fly from a crouching catcher's mitt with a satisfying smack as he mystified a lunging batter. Here no enchantress intruded. Here fulfillment beckoned. Here Loren would at last enter the adult world.

Sports were safe. Girls were not. Holding fast to this thought, Loren slept.

CHAPTER 3

THE NATIONAL PASTIME

On July 1, Adam decided to make his first visit to the Tocqueville *Endeavor*. He invited Loren to accompany him. They arrived immediately after lunch, when most of the editorial work on the afternoon paper would be completed, but before the staff dispersed. Anticipating being left to himself while his father visited his new colleagues, Loren clutched a 1909 Spalding baseball guide, containing the statistics for an exciting season that had ended with a world championship for his beloved Chicago Cubs. There had been a playoff victory over the hated Giants of John McGraw and Christy Mathewson, after which had come the World Series wherein the Cubs had humiliated the Detroit Tigers and their nasty-tempered batting champion, Ty Cobb. Although Loren had practically memorized the major league portion of the volume, he never tired of leafing through its wrinkled pages and imagining how exhilarating that season must have been for the famous trio of Tinker, Evers and Chance, and for the fabulous Three Finger Brown, the Giant Killer, whose devastating curve ball had enabled him repeatedly to triumph over the great Mathewson.

Baseball was Loren's passion. Its rules and rituals provided security; its contests produced excitement and suspense; and its endless opportunities for strategic thinking and skill produced heroes to admire and, for an aspiring young ballplayer, to emulate. Above all, the game offered inexhaustible hope. For the faithful, no game was irrevocably lost until the last batter was retired. And no season was a failure until a team ran out of time to sustain a string of victories, such as the season-ending twenty-one game winning streak that had produced a pennant for the 1935 Cubs, or the rapid rise from last place to the top of the standings of the 1914 "miracle" Braves. If a guy's favorite team finished this year at the back of the pack, there was always next year.

Moreover, there was the staggering symmetry of the game, as if some divinity had handed down its dimensions from on high. What human agency could have foreseen that four bases set ninety feet apart in a square would almost always produce a close play on a ground ball? And what mortal mind could have anticipated that a distance of sixty feet, six inches between the rubber slab on the pitcher's mound and home plate would be perfect for insuring a desperate duel between the best throwers and the most accomplished sluggers? Any further apart and the pitches would lose so much speed and be so difficult to curve that batters would have everything their own way; any closer together and there would not be enough opportunity for the hitter to see the ball in time to swing or to evade an inside pitch directed at his head. Beanballs, whether intentional or merely the result of wildness on the part of some erratic hurler, were part of the game, and every good player knew how and when to jerk his cloth-capped cranium back and down from a high inside fastball; but the decision to do so had to be made instantaneously while the hard horsehide hurtled plateward, sometimes at more than ninety miles an hour.

Three outs an inning, Loren reflected, were perfect for allowing fielders the opportunity to toss their gloves triumphantly onto the grass behind them and hustle in for their turn at bat without the score having reached obscene proportions. Four outs would have endlessly prolonged some innings; two outs would have made it hard to score at all.

Four balls delivered to a batter outside the strike zone (a virtual rectangle imagined vertically in the air above home plate, stretching from the the hitter's armpits to the middle of his kneecaps), and that young man could toss away his warclub and trot to first base. Three strikes, balls directed into the strike zone at various speeds and with different kinds of spin that altered the trajectories of the sphere in confusing ways, if unmolested by a batter, meant that he was out. Back, defeated, to the bench. With only two strikes, few batters would have succeeded in getting on base; more than three strikes would probably have produced cricket-like scores—tedium with tea. How ideal the dimensions of the game, Loren mused; how fine its formulae.

Even the numbers and locations of the major league teams were just right. Eight clubs in each league insured enough variety to keep fans interested. More than sixteen teams would have created confusion and discernibly diluted the available talent, which already required replenishing each spring, usually with several rookies per team from the high minor leagues. So at the start of every season the fans enjoyed the comforting feeling of familiar faces in the lineups, but also the anticipation that one or more of the newcomers might provide the magic to propel their teammates to a championship.

From 1903, the year of the first World Series, the same cities had been represented in the two leagues. Five of those urban areas, Boston, Chicago, New York, Philadelphia, and St. Louis, had one team in each league, thus insuring ribald rivalries. Frightening events might shake the world—devastating wars, economic chaos, or social upheavals—but during the first half of the twentieth century there remained for all baseball fans a single certainty: the same teams would always start and finish their seasons attached to the same cities, and after one hundred and fifty-four games, eleven at home and eleven away with each league rival, the two pennant winners would play each other in the World Series in October. And then would come the hot stove league, with fans across the nation debating during the winter months who were the best players at each position, compared with the stars of the past, while speculating about the marvels to come.

To Loren, one of the most appealing facets of major league baseball was the amazing variety of the participants. There were lanky string beans like Lefty Grove; sawed off muscle men like Hack Wilson; midgets like Wee Willie Keeler; Adonises like larruping Lou Gehrig; or fat fellows like Freddie Fitzsimmons. Players were Irish like John McGraw; Polish like Stan Coveleskie; German like Frank Schulte, Jewish like Hammering Hank Greenburg; Italian like Tony Lazzeri; French like Napoleon Lajoie; Russian like Lou Novikoff; and Anglo-American like Rogers Hornsby. But not Negro, except for the mercurial Jackie Robinson, who had broken the color line the previous season with the Brooklyn Dodgers, helping them win a National League championship. Several other Negroes were trying to launch big league careers, it seemed, but resistance was still fierce, while in the minor leagues traditional living accomodations for ballplayers were almost everywhere off limits to Negroes. Loren wondered if this unjust situation would ever change.

A few major league players were college educated, like Frankie Frisch, the Fordham Flash; and some were illiterate like Shoeless Joe Jackson; but most had begun playing professionally just out of high school. Some stars were vicious like Ty Cobb, hated even by their own teammates; others were mild mannered like Smilin' Stan Hack, Loren's special favorite. Some were natural clowns, like Casey Stengel; others were unfairly labeled as such, like Babe Herman. And some were so smoothly efficient as to approximate perfection, like Charley Gehringer, the mechanical man; while others, like Stinky Stanky, erstwhile Cub, were marginally talented, but stayed in the majors through unceasing opportunism and relentless effort.

Besides the eleven urban centers, from Washington D.C. northward to Boston and westward to St. Louis, where major league baseball had been played for almost half a century, innumerable cities, towns, and hamlets all over the United States had their own teams, professional, semi-professional, amateur, and school—from the elementary level through college. Many young men who did not themselves play the game were devoted to following it—at the ballpark, on the radio, in periodicals, or through conversations with like-minded devotees. Indeed, for most American males of all ages, baseball remained the national pastime.

On summer mornings millions of readers would open their newspapers directly to the sports pages to study the box scores before turning to page one. During the hot afternoons, radios could be heard through open windows all over the nation broadcasting play-by-play accounts of either major league or minor league games, which in the larger cities drew crowds of people for a single game that it might take months for a movie theater to equal. The fascination of the game was elemental, Loren mused, partly because it was earthy, not artificial; unrestrained by time, yet encompassed by well understood rules; and while satisfyingly symmetrical, totally unpredictable. A smart player like Fred Merkle would neglect to touch second base and thereby cost the Giants a flag. Bill Wambsganss would all at once contrive an unassisted triple play in the 1920 fall classic. Or the mighty New York Yankees, having won the American League pennant seven out of the past eight years, would inexplicably give way to the lowly St. Louis Browns, who in 1944 would capture their one and only league championship. With baseball, never despair.

In Winona, Loren's bedroom walls had been papered with pictures of players, some ripped from magazines, others taken by newspaper photographers crouched along the foul lines at Wrigley Field and Comisky Park, and afterwards discarded in the darkroom at Adam Temple's newspaper office. A wooden cigar box stuck in the bottom shelf of Loren's bookcase had been packed with postcards bearing the scribbled signatures of famous former big leaguers: Hans Wagner, Cy Young, Grover Alexander, Tris Speaker, Pie Traynor, and many others. And Loren's collection of baseball books had included the old Spalding and Reach guides issued during the first decades of the century, all of the major publications of the *Sporting*

News and, additionally, an entire shelf of team histories, players' reminiscences and miscellaneous volumes about various facets of the game. Which explained why Loren had so readily agreed to accompany his father to the *Endeavor* newspaper office. For there would probably be baseball books used for reference purposes in the office of the sports editor—perhaps some he had not yet encountered.

* * *

Both the *Endeavor* and the *Gazette*, the morning paper, were housed in a dingy two-story brick building surrounded by workshops and warehouses near the river. Ward Hatton, the *Endeavor's* executive editor, met them in the news room on the second floor. His hand was clammy and his grip limp. Loren had overheard Adam tell Nan that Hatton had been made editor shortly after he married the spinster daughter of the paper's wealthy owner. As host, he led Adam and Loren from desk to desk throughout a large room lighted from the east through huge dirty windows. Amid clouds of cigarette smoke they pressed the flesh with curious sub-editors, reporters, and proof-readers.

Hatton paused outside a large private office at the rear of the building. With a look of distaste he excused himself and left Adam and Loren alone to push open a door marked "Sports." Inside, a corpulent, red-faced man of about fifty rose from behind a cluttered desk. He held out his hand. "Douglas Mason," he said in a guttural voice accompanied by a slight wheeze, "but everyone calls me 'Bitsy.'"

"Glad to meet you, Bitsy. I'm Adam Temple, the new managing editor. My son, Loren."

Bitsy waved them to heavy wooden chairs from which they had to remove newspapers, sporting magazines, and a thick *Baseball Register*. The sports editor, obviously a potentate in these premises, noticed Loren's Spalding guide and reached out a pudgy hand. Opening the volume, he exclaimed: "Hot dawg! I've gotta buncha these things, but mine only go back t' th' twenties. Whar'd yew git this?"

"I have them all since nineteen hundred," said Loren proudly. "Dad bought them from a dealer. I think..." Shooting a sly look at Adam: "I think he felt guilty that he got rid of his own guides not long after I was born. Anyway, I shifted to the *Sporting News* record books for the nineteen-thirties and forties. They're the best."

"Yeah," agreed Bitsy. "Wanna sell any?"

"I don't think so."

"Huh. Wal then, either of yew, tell me this: who led th' National League in battin' in nineteen-forty?"

Adam looked at Loren, who quickly replied: "Debs Garms. He hit three-fifty-five for the Pirates and barely had enough at bats to qualify."

"Not bad. An' who wuz th' star pitcher fer th' Red Sox in th' nineteen-eighteen World Series?"

"Babe Ruth."

"Ah'm impressed," said Bitsy. "Do yew play ball?"

"Some."

"Loren led his high school team in both pitching and hitting this past spring," said Adam proudly.

"My, my," said Bitsy. "Whar yew playin' this summer?"

"I don't know," said Loren. "I imagine it's too late to join an American Legion team, even if they would have me."

"We only arrived in Tocqueville last week," said Adam.

The phone on Bitsy's desk rang. A chubby paw engulfed the receiver. "Whut?" he barked. Pause. "Nah. Ah ain't scorin' no nigger game. Git sumun else... Right." He slammed the phone back onto its cradle.

Directing a searching stare at Loren, Bitsy asked: "Have yew evah played semi-pro?"

"What's that?" asked Loren.

"Uh buncha local guys, th' Southside Scorpions, travel 'round on weekends playin' town teams in East Texas an' Louisiana. Some of 'em work out at th' Wisteria—that's th' big oil refinery south of heah. Th' Scorpions' manager travels durin' th' week sellin' plumbin' supplies, which is how he lines up outa town games. How old yew be?"

"Sixteen."

"That's awful young. Mosta these guys were in th' war, which means they're pushing thirty." Contemplatively, glancing at Adam: "Listen, if'n yew git uh phone call from Alfred Le Doux—everyone calls 'im 'Fats,' fer th' same reason Ah'm called 'Bitsy'—don' hang up. He'll be callin' t' invite yew t' try out wit' th' Scorpions. He tol' me las' week that they could use 'nother pitcher-outfielder."

"Thanks very much," said Loren. He meant it.

Bitsy rummaged among the papers on his desk. "Take uh look," he wheezed, and handed Loren a page torn from a newspaper. It was from an *Endeavor* sports section and headlined a recent contest between the Tocqueville and Fort Worth teams of the double-A Texas League, followed by a feature story identifying Ralph Kiner of the Pittsburgh Pirates as the only major league player ever to slam over one hundred home runs during his first three seasons. At the bottom of the page was a box score, preceded by a two-paragraph story headlined: "Scorpions Smash Lake Louis, 10-7." Loren observed that the game, played somewhere in southwestern Louisiana, had gone ten innings and that the Scorpions were credited with seventeen hits, players named Miller and Bone having had four each.

Loren said: "That must have been quite a game. I'll hope to hear from Mr. Lee Doo. By the way, is he Chinese?"

Bitsy's laugh was a deep-throated rumble. "Naw, he ain't no Chink. He's one uh them Cajuns. We got us uh buncha them 'round heah."

Thinking of the Moutons, Loren blushed. He avoided looking at his father.

Bitsy stood up. "Anythin' Ah kin do fer yew or yore son," he said to Adam, "jus' ask me." A snaggletooth smile flashed across his face so fast Loren almost missed it.

As he followed Adam into the hall, he looked back and saw the sports editor, head bent down over his desk, marking something on a proof sheet with a grease pencil. His cheek now bulged with a chaw of tobacco, some of the juice from which dripped from the corner of his mouth onto the paper.

* * *

When Loren and Adam arrived home, Nan was waiting with news. "I know how much you've wanted a summer job," she said to her son, "so I've been making inquiries. I've found one for you, part-time."

"What kind of job?"

"Mowing the lawn and taking care of the shrubbery and flowers next door," she said. "I had a visit with Mrs. Kaplan today and she was wondering if one of my boys could help her out. Her husband has a bad heart, so he doesn't like to do manual labor. You'll work over there every other Saturday morning. They'll pay five dollars, which is certainly generous."

As Loren imagined close contact with the sultry Mrs. Kaplan, his palms became moist. Bitsy had said the Scorpions practiced on Saturday afternoons and played their games mostly on Sundays. So, even if he was fortunate enough to win a spot on the semipro baseball club, he could still accommodate his neighbor, especially for the munificent sum of five dollars for a morning's work. "I'll do it," he said. "Shall I go over and tell them?"

"No," said his mother. "We agreed that if you were willing to take the job, you'd go over at nine o'clock Saturday, at which time she'll tell you what she wants you to do. I'll phone her right now to confirm."

* * *

The following evening, Loren and Tommy were playing catch on the Temples' oyster shell driveway when their father, home from his first day at work, drove up and beckoned them to follow him into the house.

"Tommy," he said, when the three of them were seated at the kitchen table and he had taken a sip of the coffee that Nan immediately set before him, "I've found you a summer job. How would you like to deliver newspapers?"

"The *Endeavor*?" asked Tommy.

"No, the *Gazette*," responded his father. "To deliver the *Endeavor* would mean that you'd be unable to engage in any after school activities. The *Gazette* comes off the press about four a.m. You'll have to set your alarm for about four-thirty, so you won't miss the delivery truck. You'll finish throwing papers by seven, I imagine, maybe a little later until you get the hang of it. We'll have to get you a larger basket for your bicycle. Well, what about it? Do you want the job?"

Tommy thought a minute. Then he replied: "O.K."

Added Adam, looking at Loren: "I have something lined up for you, too."

"What?"

"Working for a construction company. Sisti and Sampson. Seven 'till four-thirty on weekdays, with half an hour for lunch. Two hundred dollars a month."

"Wow!" Loren thought. Fifty dollars a week; ten dollars a day. More than twice what he had received working as a stock boy at a grocery store the previous summer.

"Where is this place and how do I get there?"

"Out on the Port Amberly highway. You can get there in half an hour on the bus. It's a big one-story building with corrugated metal sides and a roof to match, with construction machinery parked all around it. S and S apparently does a lot of business with the state highway department, which has a branch nearby. You can start work Tuesday. Take work gloves and a bag lunch."

While addressing the two boys, Adam had begun staring at an empty stovetop. Seeing his puzzled look, Nan said: "I forgot to mention, Dear, that a Mrs. Mason phoned this morning to invite the four of us to supper. When she said that her husband was at the *Endeavor*, I accepted. She seemed nice."

Adam looked irritated. "Why'd you do that? I only met her husband yesterday. That's short notice. Impolite."

"Honey, I think people here are more casual than they are in Winona. Besides I had a dizzy spell this morning and got behind on my work. So I would be glad not to have to get dinner."

"Oh, all right, but I'm not wearing a tie."

Nan smiled. "In that case, I won't wear one either."

* * *

The Masons, who had no children, lived in a wooden cottage shaded by massive oaks and pines. A long lot stretched back to a railroad embankment. While the Temples toured the back yard, which was surrounded by tall shrubbery and heavily planted with flowers and ferns mulched with leaves and fragrant pine needles, a locomotive pulling empty box cars rumbled past, well shielded by the greenery.

Bernice Mason was portly and pink. Clad in a tent-like flowered cotton dress and white sneakers, she wobbled about on the thickest ankles Loren had ever seen, dispensing gardening wisdom in a high-pitched tremor, punctuated by nervous giggles. Bitsy winked at Adam, as if to suggest that this was the sort of thing that men tolerated in return for three solid meals a day.

In the midst of a clump of variegated ground cover, a coiled garden hose dripped gently into a small pond. Goldfish gaped, waiting for insects, and a white kitten lay in the ferns, tail twitching, watching the fish. Behind it stood a large polished rock, set upright into the soil. Adam, who had heretofore remained silent while Nan spoke for them both, suddenly inquired: "What's that inscription?"

Loren looked. Carved into the stone was "MPKD, 1934-1947."

Mrs. Mason said morosely: "That's where our old cat is buried. She was our favorite. Mamma Pussy Kitty Dear. She lived long enough to give birth to seventy-three kittens."

Nan looked shocked. "That many?" she exclaimed.

"Yeah, she wuz uh real corker," declared Bitsy. "But she wore out." He laughed.

Mrs. Mason continued to look sad.

"All those kittens," said Tommy contemplatively. "What happened to them?"

There was an embarrassed silence. Then Mrs. Mason said: "Let's go in and have supper, shall we?"

Bitsy, as Loren had surmised, was a heavy eater. The meal was ham and yams, with peas and carrots and warm buttered biscuits. As he cleaned his plate, Bitsy entertained his guests with anecdotes derived from twenty years of covering sports for Texas newspapers. Adam, who had reported on the 1929 World Series for the *New York Times*, and had later become sports editor of the *Washington Post* while still in his early thirties, smiled superciliously. But Loren listened carefully.

"Till Ah got too fat," said Bitsy, "Ah used t' umpire in th' kiddy leagues. One of th' li'l twerps back then wuz Granny Hatcher. Yew may recall he hit two-ninety fer th' Cincinnati Reds las' year."

Actually.281, thought Loren. But he asked: "Didn't Hatcher also score almost one hundred runs?"

"That's right... Wal, anyway, Granny wuz uh big kid fer his age, but one day his younger brother, uh li'l fella who wore thick glasses an' had nevah played afore, joined th' team. Ah was callin' th' game from behind th' pitcher when he come t' bat fer th' fust time. Ah could heah his ol' man yellin' at 'im from behind th' backstop. Uh real prick tryin' t' force his kid t' play, when th' li'l fella didn' wan' any part of it. He wuz so scared he wuz shakin'.

"Wal, th' pitcher, uh big ol' fella, threw one inside. Th' li'l guy froze an' th' pitch bounced off'n his shoulder. Couldn't have hurt much, but after Ah tol' 'im t' take his base, Ah cud see 'im sobbin' as he started t' run t' fust base. He nevah got there. 'Bout halfway, he changed direction, ran past th' other team's bench an' th' people behind it watchin', mos'ly parents, an' got on his bike an' peddled away. Ah nevah saw 'im again."

"Boy, he must have been a real sissy," said Tommy with an uncharacteristic lack of sympathy.

"Maybe so," said Bitsy. "But Ah heared later from one of th' parents that th' kid had been so upset when th' ball hit him that he pooped in his pants. He wuz so humiliated that he scrammed."

"Poor little fellow," said Nan.

"Wal," observed Bitsy philosophically, "summa these momma's boys are real babies. Whut this country needs is fewer pants-poopers an' mor' daddies-doers."

Adam and Nan exchanged looks of amusement. Tommy looked bewildered. Loren said: "I read some of your columns in back issues of the *Endeavor* and I noticed that you interviewed a lot of famous big leaguers during the winter months. How did you manage to do that?"

Bitsy grinned. "Simple. Ah'd phone th' team's front office an' ask fer the home phone numbah of, say, Joe DiMaggio. An' some li'l gal would say (the fat man's voice became squeaky): 'Sorry, we don' give out that kinda information.' An' Ah'd say, 'that's too bad, 'cause Ah gotta big load of concrete mix t' deliver t' his house, an' Ah need t' know exactly whar on th' property t' dump it.'

"So she gives me th' number an' Ah gets Joe D on th' line, an' he says he don' nevah give no interviews away from th' ballpark. So Ah say, 'O.K., Ah wanted t' write this week's column on yore heroics on th' field, but Ah guess Ah kin get by writin' 'bout yore personal life instead.' An' Joe D is curious enough t' ask: 'Whut yew got?' An' Ah tells him Ah been talkin' t' a li'l ol' gal who says he's th' father of her baby.

"Nachurly Joe D protests that it ain't true; no way it could be proved.

"An' Ah says, 'well maybe so; but Ah gotta write somethin' this week an' yore it.'

"So, after givin' th' matter some thought, ol' Joe says 'O.K., whataya wanna know?' An' Ah gits mah interview."

"Do you plan to interview Satchel Paige?" asked Loren. "Some say he's the greatest pitcher who ever lived. Is it true that he's going to be in Tocqueville tomorrow?"

Bitsy snorted. "Yeah. Some nigger done come by th' paper las' week an' wanted publicity fer uh game two darky teams are playin' at Shipper Stadium t'morrah night. Ah tole him t' git out. Ah ain't writin' nuthin' 'bout no niggers, even Mr. Satchel Paige. Let th' local spades go see 'im an' his nigger frens if'n they wanna. Ah ain't goin', an' Ah ain't puttin' nuthin' 'bout it in th' paper."

The fat man pushed laboriously back from the table and lumbered into an adjoining room. Soon he returned with a large clipboard to which was clamped a pad of lined paper and several typed sheets. "See," he said, "th' score sheet, rosters of th' two teams, an' uh so-called fact sheet tellin' 'bout what them darkies supposedly dun in th' nigger leagues—prolly uh pack uh lies. Now, whut am Ah gonna do wit' this crap—sorry, Mrs. Temple—which that nigger left on mah desk when Ah wasn' lookin'? Ah may be th' official scorer fer th' Shippers, but no way Ah'm scorin' no nigger game."

Impulsively, Loren said: "Give it to me. I know how to keep score."

Bitsy looked at Adam.

"I don't see why not," said the managing editor. "Loren lives baseball. He'll do a good job."

Bitsy shrugged. "O.K." He handed the clipboard to Loren. "Jus' be shore t' hand th' score sheet after th' game t' someone on th' team that bats last. D'yew know whar t' sit?"

"Is there a press box?" asked Loren. He had joined his father in several such enclosures at baseball and football games.

"Yeah. But th' official scorer has his own spot. Right behind home plate. Yew can't miss it; couple uh chairs inside uh railing, up on uh raised platform. Jus' tell th' ushers yore fillin' in fer me."

"Thanks," said Loren enthusiastically. "I've always wanted to see Paige pitch."

"Huh. Way overrated, in mah 'pinion. No nigger kin compete wit' white guys."

* * *

Later, driving home, Adam chuckled. "That Bitsy," he said. "What a character!"

"I think he's terrible," said Nan. "Such language! And blackmailing ballplayers for stories."

"If they weren't misbehaving," said Adam, "it wouldn't work. Besides, Bitsy has to get his material in an unorthodox manner, since he's gotten so fat that he can't acquire it with legwork like a good reporter. Around the office he's notorious for being unwilling to heave himself out of his chair. They told me that one day, about a year ago, Miss Texas, who was a finalist for Miss America, arrived at the

Endeavor to drum up some publicity. She was a real knockout. While she was undulating around in a tight dress shaking her—shaking hands—one of the guys ran back to Bitsy's office and said: 'Come quick an' see th' mos' beautiful woman in th' world.' And Bitsy didn't even look up from his desk. 'Describe her,' he said."

Nan and the boys laughed. "I guess he's not entirely evil," she conceded. "As long as he's not dealing with a Negro. I wonder why he detests them so?"

"It was the same in Virginia," said Adam. "It's the guilt and shame of segregation. In order to rationalize exploiting Negroes, people like Bitsy have to dehumanize them."

Nan patted her husband's arm as he steered the car into their driveway. "I'm glad," she said, "that you are different."

CHAPTER 4
ORIENTATION

Promptly at one o'clock on Saturday, Loren rapped on the Kaplans' front door. At once it opened to reveal Mrs. K barefooted, clad in a white terrycloth robe. Her toenails were coated with reddish orange to match her hair, which framed dimpled cheeks, an upturned freckled nose, and a wet red mouth flashing a welcoming smile.

"Sorry Ah'm not dressed yet," she said in a husky voice. "Ah'm runnin' late fer uh shoppin' spree. There's th' lawnmower." She pointed to the nearby driveway, where a new machine, its reels shiny and its handle grips uncracked, awaited its first use. "Ah think it may need lubricatin'," added Mrs. K. In a small brown hand she clutched a brass oil can with a long thin spout.

Loren said: "Let me."

But Mrs. K had already leaned over to drip oil onto the green-painted reels of the mower. Her robe gaped open and Loren gasped. Cherry-like nipples protruded from big breasts the color of tapioca pudding, sprinkled with freckles like nutmeg. Beneath her robe Mrs. K was seemingly naked, but the glimpse Loren got was so brief that he could not be sure. His cheeks felt hot and his mouth dry.

Quickly she straightened up and handed Loren the oil can. "Yew may need this," she said. "Ah'm goin' t' take uh shower. Ah'll leave yore money on th' kitchen counter. Come in an' git it when yore through. Mah husband is outta town this weekend; so Ah'll prolly be late gettin' home."

Turning to go inside, she paused. "Do yew play golf?" she asked.

"A little," croaked Loren.

"Mah husband has nevah made uh hole in one," she said. "Have yew?"

"No," said Loren. "Not even close."

"Ah thought so," she said. "Maybe one of these days yew'll git lucky."

Loren perspired profusely as he pushed the mower onto the lawn and began to force it through tough St. Augustine grass that had been allowed to grow too tall. It required almost all the strength he possessed to cut it. After half an hour he stopped long enough to run next door and fetch work gloves to prevent blisters from forming on his fingers. As he returned to work, he dodged around Mrs. K's yellow convertible, top down, backing out of the driveway. She smiled and waved. She wore a straw hat with a large brim and a frilly white blouse with short puffy sleeves. Her round arms were lightly tanned. Loren could not see her legs.

* * *

That evening Loren borrowed Adam's Hudson and drove it across town to Shipper Stadium, taking care when he parked in the weedy field that served as a free parking area to leave the car well out of reach of foul balls.

Although there was still plenty of daylight, the stadium lights were already on. Loren made his way through the main gate, flashing the press card his father had loaned him, and mounted some concrete steps to the box seats behind home plate. There was the scorer's table, just as Bitsy had described it, enclosed by a railing and slightly elevated above the surrounding seats, not far from the frayed netting that protected spectators from foul balls. As Loren positioned his score pad on the desktop, he noticed that he was located so close to the diamond that he could easily hear the palaver of the practicing players.

Batting practice was over, for there was no cage at home plate. One of the colored teams, wearing gray, was taking fielding practice; the other squad, clad in dirty duds that had once been white, was lounging in and about the first base dugout.

As he strained to spot uniform numbers so that he could record them on his scorecard, Loren was momentarily diverted by an usher bearing a tray loaded with several steaming hot dogs covered with mustard and shredded green pickles, several bags of unshelled peanuts, and a large mug of amber liquid topped with white foam.

"Sorry, I don't drink beer," said Loren. "And I'm afraid I can't afford to pay for all that food—maybe some of it. How much would a hot dog and one bag of peanuts cost?"

"Nuttin. Free t' th' scorer, compliments of th' management. Mister Bitsy alwuz starts wit' two doggies an' uh cuppa beer. Howsabout Ah leave yew two warm ones an' uh sacka goobers, an' git yew uh big Coke?"

Unsure what, exactly, the man had said, Loren replied: "Sure. Fine. Thanks." This scoring business was a pretty good deal. He wondered if Bitsy would let him substitute again, maybe for a Texas league game when the Shippers were in town.

Wolfing a hot dog and sipping a coke, Loren watched the final moments of fielding practice. Although the players were all Negroes, the ritual was familiar. Grounders scooped up and whipped over to first, and then around the horn, accompanied by lots of mindless chatter and spurts of tobacco juice from pursed lips. Loren noticed, however, that the young black men seemed looser, more prone to clowning, showing off. Not as intense as whites.

Somewhere a bell rang and the field emptied of players. As he stood for the national anthem blasting from a loudspeaker hung on the center field flagpole, Loren looked around. The grandstand had been filling for the past hour. Uncomfortably he observed that, except for a few fans scattered through a small section of seats down the first base line, all of the spectators were Negroes. Most were nicely dressed and, so far, quieter than comparable crowds of whites. But where did they all come from? How had they known there was a game, with no announcement in the papers or on the radio, as far as he knew? It was at times like these that Loren realized how ignorant he was of racial undercurrents.

His thoughts flashed back to the previous summer when he had joined forty-six thousand onlookers filling every seat and crowded into every aisle of Chicago's Wrigley Field to witness the debut there of Jackie Robinson of the Brooklyn Dodgers, the first Negro allowed officially to play in the big leagues. Ever since his Dad had taken him to his first game at Wrigley in 1942 (just as Adam's father had introduced his son into the Cub cult at the old West Side Park in 1908), Loren had gone back, frequently alone, to the venerable steel stadium with its ivy-covered brick outfield walls and its huge center field scoreboard, but he had never before seen more than a handful of Negro spectators at a Cub game. Now on a sunlit May day they had excitedly packed the park—cheering Robinson's every move, and booing vociferously when the home plate umpire called their hero out with his bat on his shoulder at a crucial moment, with the bases loaded and the Dodgers behind 2-0 in the seventh inning. Perhaps the sea of white shirts in the center field bleachers, always a difficult background against which to pick up a pitch, had confused Robinson, as it might any hitter making his first visit to Wrigley Field. Nevertheless, the Bums eventually won the game, thereby moving into a tie with the Cubs for first place, on their way ultimately to the National League championship, while the bungling Bruins sank to sixth.

Loren's first impression of Robinson, verified later that season and also early in 1948, was one of vehement vitality. Once on the basepaths, the Dodger first baseman created an atmosphere of anticipation throughout the ball park. Opponents, many of them seasoned veterans, appeared to panic, throwing wildly, belatedly, or not at all, as Robinson bounded from base to base, sleek and deadly. He infused the national game with an aura of menace not experienced in the sport since the formidable Ty Cobb hung up his razor-sharp spikes twenty years back. Loren hated the Dodgers, but he admired Robinson. The man played hard but he played clean. And he was a winner.

There was no Jackie Robinson on the field at Shipper Stadium on the evening of July 3, 1948. But the Negro all stars, cavorting on the tough turf while Loren struggled accurately to record their exploits, were nevertheless entertaining and super-skilled. Especially was this true of a tall thin pitcher for the so-called "home team," who began the game by sauntering toward the mound as if he had all the time in the world, while the crowd rose as one to bestow adulation. Loose-jointedly he flung his warmup tosses, a huge left foot thrusting skyward, the skinniness of his ebony arms accentuated by ragged flapping sweatshirt sleeves. The ball seemed to accelerate as it zipped across home plate and into the catcher's mitt with a sound like a firecracker.

Peering past the black-suited umpire and the bulky receiver, Loren viewed the pitches from virtually the same angle as the leadoff hitter, who blinked as strike one blurred across the outside corner, and who flinched as "Satch" sidearmed a wicked curve that buckled the batter's knees as it swished across the inside edge of the platter. Then Loren laughed delightedly as the hapless hitter flailed belatedly at a rising fast ball that passed him eye-high and put him back on the bench.

The next batsman was cowed by two scorchers he scarcely saw. Satch then finished him off with a wobbling butterfly ball that he missed by a mile as it darted down into the dirt. The final out was equally easy: two high hard ones, and then a screwball that left a bamboozled batter back on his heels as it veered across the inside part of the plate. Nine pitches; nine strikes; three Ks scratched into his scorebook by a laughing Loren, and Satch shambled off the mound toward his team's dugout amid loud applause.

The other pitcher was not as entertaining, but he was almost equally effective. The score was nothing to nothing when Satch batted in the third inning, swinging a heavy black warclub as if it was a toothpick. He smacked the first pitch on a line over a vainly leaping shortstop and ambled to first base as if he feared he might faint from too much exertion. Pulling on a heavy red and gray high-collared jacket with black leather sleeves, he took a short lead off the bag, hands on his knees. Then, suddenly, as the pitcher delivered the ball to home plate, Satch took off, his spindly legs carrying him toward second base with surprising speed. As the opposing second baseman scuttled over to beat Satch to the sack, the batter reached out and gently poked a grounder through the vacated area, allowing Satch to coast into third base standing up. There he suddenly began to deride the pitcher with imaginative references to his alleged animal ancestry and his supposed deficiencies as a ballplayer and as a human being. Soon Satch's teammates joined in; fans followed; and all at once the ballpark was echoing with cat calls and derisive epithets. The pitcher pretended to be unaffected by this unpleasant attention, but his grin was sickly and his control became tentative. With a count of three and one, he grooved a pitch that a grateful hitter whacked into the left-field corner for a two-run double.

The score stayed at 2-0 until the start of the seventh, when the wrinkled veteran whom almost everyone there had come to see was replaced on the mound by a less talented hurler half his age. The result was a rally by the visitors and a final score of 5-3 in their favor, by which time many of the spectators had already left the park.

After adding up the columns on his scorecard and gulping the last of three six-ounce Cokes, Loren went down onto the field to hand his paperwork to a chubby Negro who claimed to be the business manager of Satch's team. Then he trotted out to the Shipper clubhouse underneath the stands down the left field foul line. When no one answered his knock, he pushed his way inside and found himself in a hot damp room crowded with half dressed and a few entirely naked black ballplayers, trading jokes, flipping towels at one another, and stepping in and out of steaming showers that could only accommodate several at a time. There were no other white people there, as far as Loren could see.

"Where's Mr. Paige?" he asked the nearest Negro.

"Ain't heah. Already dressed an' gone."

"Gone? Gone where?"

"Back t' Kansas City, whar he live."

"But I wanted to get his autograph," lamented Loren.

"Can't, 'cause he ain't heah, an' thatsa fact."

"Sorry," said Loren, "to bother you." As he turned to leave the clubhouse he stared surreptitiously at several of the naked Negroes to determine whether a certain rumor was true. As far as he could ascertain, the equipment was about average. So much for mythology.

Only after he was out in the almost deserted parking lot climbing into his father's car did he think: every one of those guys was a star player, not just Satch. Now that Robinson had paved the way, some might well make it to the majors. If he had been braver, he might have obtained their autographs, which probably few white people had. What a dope he was!

*   *   *

On Sunday afternoon, July 4, Loren celebrated Independence Day by challenging his father to a game of All Star Baseball. It was a board game, played with cardboard disks representing contemporary major league players, with the outer portions divided by lines radiating outward from the center into spaces of varying sizes, each standing for various types of hits, walks, and outs. A few rare occurrences, such as hit batsmen, were to be determined by rolling a pair of dice. With a flip of a forefinger, the "manager" whose team was at bat spun a metal needle situated in the center of the disk. Where the needle stopped determined the outcome of that time at bat. On those occasions when the needle point rested directly on a dividing line, with a hit on one side and an out on the other, spirited arguments inevitably ensued. A roll of the dice would be needed to resolve the dispute.

Loren and Adam alternated in selecting their players, with Loren having first choice. He promptly selected the formidable Ted Williams, whose home run space on his disk covered almost fifteen per cent of its circumference, more than Joe DiMaggio, Stan Musial, or any other available player. Loren, moreover, had long since realized the importance of picking pitchers who had relatively high batting averages, since each one's pitching prowess in this board game was irrelevant. Bob Feller, Johnny Schmitz, and Allie Reynolds were feeble at the plate; Schoolboy Rowe, Bucky Walters, and Johnny Sain made good pinch hitters; and Bob Lemon, Jim Tobin, Sid Hudson, and Early Wynn (what a name for a pitcher!) were also no slouches with the stick.

When the game began, with Adam opting to bat last, Loren's lineup read: Hack, Appling, Williams, Musial, Mize, Reiser, Lombardi, Doerr, and Walters. Adam countered with Vaughan, Keltner, DiMaggio, Greenburg, Ott, Medwick, Cooper, Gordon, and Rowe.

As they played, Loren attempted to distract his father by introducing a touchy subject into the conversation. "Why is it," the teenager asked provocatively, "that neither the *Endeavor* nor the *Gazette* publishes any stories about Negroes, except when they are accused of crimes against whites?"

"I don't believe that's true," answered Adam, chortling as Mel Ott followed a Hank Greenburg double with a home run. "That puts me ahead, seven to six."

"I've checked," said Loren, refusing to let Adam change the subject. "Nothing about Negroes is ever printed in the society pages, in the school pages, or (naturally) in the sports pages. There are no ads for Negro businesses, or indications of where and when they can attend entertainments, such as movies or ball games. I found nothing in the papers about the outcome of last night's game. Yet there was a big crowd there, almost all Negroes. Do they have their own newspaper?"

"Not as far as I know. The word just gets around."

"Ha!" Loren gloated, as Bobby Doerr drove in Pete Reiser with the tying run in the top half of the sixth inning. "Don't you think it's unfair to deny Negroes basic information, and at least some publicity, for things that are important to them?"

"Of course. But you must realize that here, as in Virginia, we live in a segregated society in which Negroes are treated as inferiors. You don't approve of such a system. Nor do I. But it's a reality. And anyone who speaks out against it is in for trouble."

"What kind of trouble?"

"Threatening phone calls; vandalism; being fired from their jobs; and sometimes worse. Why there was a cross burning out in Riverwood just last week. The people there moved out almost immediately."

"I didn't know that. Was there something about it in the paper?"

"No," declared Adam. "The *Endeavor* owners insist that we not print anything that might stir up racial animosity."

"That's terrible. That's almost like being an accessory to a crime."

Adam frowned. "You sound like your mother. I'll tell you what I tell her. Go against public opinion and you'll be crushed. Better to watch, wait, and keep quiet about things that can't be helped, and changes will eventually come. After all, who would have thought, even a year ago, that Negroes would be playing big league baseball? But now the Dodgers have not only Jackie Robinson but also that big catcher, Roy Campanella. And Larry Doby has become a fixture in center field for the Indians. There are even rumors that Bill Veeck is going to offer a contract to Satchel Paige."

"Really? He deserves one. I'll bet he's as good as anyone Cleveland has, except for Bob Feller."

"Speaking of Feller, my boys have been hitting him hard. Aren't you going to take him out?"

"Next inning," said Loren. "There; see? The third out. One more inning to go. And I still have the lead."

"But only eleven to nine. And my sluggers are coming up."

"I'll be bringing in Mort Cooper," said Loren. "He'll hold 'em."

With two out and the bases loaded in inning number nine, Loren left Cooper in to pitch to his brother, Walker, who dribbled a game-ending grounder. "I win again," he said.

"Lucky. Can't last."

Loren went into the kitchen and returned with a plate of pretzels and a couple of Cokes. "Speaking of luck," he said, "it looks like Truman will need a miracle to keep his job after January. I wonder if the Democrats will even re-nominate him?"

While Adam, his mouth clogged with pretzels, chewed contemplatively, Loren considered what he knew about the President of the United States. Unsuccessful in business, Truman became a prominent politician in Missouri. The faithful servant of city bosses. A United States Senator. Nationally known for denouncing crime and corruption. Feisty righteousness. As President, seemed convinced that no problem was so complex that it could not be solved by some simplistic formula, some vague conception of a historical precedent, or just plain common sense. Squinting owl-like from behind thick glasses, uttered platitudes with smiling certainty. But this conception of Truman was impressionistic, Loren acknowledged; hence he was interested in his father's insights into the subject.

Leaning back in his comfortable armchair, Adam declared: "Truman will be re-nominated. The Democrats have nobody else. Some want General Eisenhower to run. Milt, his brother, our former neighbor in Virginia, recently wrote me that Ike won't have anything to do with the Democratic party. He'll wait until nineteen-fifty-two and then possibly try for the Republican nomination.

"As for the November election, all the public opinion poll-takers have Dewey far in the lead. But the same people predicted an easy victory for Alf Landon over Roosevelt in nineteen-thirty-six. Ha! The Champ carried forty-six of the forty-eight states.

"Unfortunately, Truman is no Roosevelt. FDR convinced Americans during the depression that the Democratic party was like the faithful donkey, eager to bear their burdens and stand by them in adversity, while the Republicans were rogue elephants ruthlessly trampling ordinary people underfoot. Now we have a Missouri mule, alternately kicking both the plutocrats and the people."

"What do you mean?" inquired Loren.

"As soon as he does something decent," declared Adam, "Truman will undermine it with something odious. He persuaded Congress to fund Secretary Marshall's plan for the economic recovery of Europe. Good. Then he withdrew American support for the United Nations Relief and Rehabilitation Program, so that Asians were denied the aid we promised Europeans. Stupid. He vetoed the anti-labor Taft-Hartley Act. Good. Then, when workers suffering from poverty-level wages and runaway inflation threatened to strike, he advocated drafting them into the army.

"In February he asked Congress to pass an anti-lynching law, and he now seems about to issue executive orders ending racial discrimination in the federal civil service and in the armed forces. Good. But everyone knows that he's personally anti-Negro. He has never objected to Jim Crow or to any other social injustices resulting from the domination of American society by WASPs."

"What," interjected Loren, "are WASPs?"

"White Anglo-Saxon Protestants. Like us. H. L. Mencken said the majority of them were SOBs. He was right."

Adam ceased his sermon to catch his breath. Then he said: "But the worst thing Truman has done is to support dying European colonial empires and unpopular military dictators, like Chiang Kai-Shek of China, against the aspirations of the people they have victimized. Claiming that he is "containing" communism, Truman seems determined to ally the United States with oppression all over the world.

"The so-called Truman Doctrine is just an excuse to conduct overseas interventions. Throughout most of the world America appears to be an arrogant bully, much like the European Powers of the last century. But anyone who suggests that Americans are voracious economic imperialists will have his patriotism impugned and his job threatened. Dissent is disloyalty. Truman has laid the foundation for an era of political repression. That's the real threat to American liberty, not communist espionage or sedition.

"Truman even wants compulsory universal military service, so that the government can brainwash millions of teenagers and then train them to wage war for 'freedom.' If you are 18 to 25 years old and are overheard criticizing the government, the new draft law that goes into effect in September makes you vulnerable for induction. You recall how Truman wanted to draft strikers into the army to teach them a 'lesson.'"

"That's all scary stuff," said Loren. "Looks like the Republicans are right, that it's 'time for a change.'"

Adam shook his head. "In our two-party system," he said, "the choice is usually between the lesser of two evils. Every abhorrent step that Truman has taken as President was supported by large majorities of Republicans, and just about every good thing he's done, they have opposed. Even though Truman is a half-educated, self-righteous mediocrity, and a prime example of the adage that democracy produces government by the lowest common denominator, Dewey is worse. Why? Because he is committed to turning the government over to the Robber Barons, those plutocrats who almost ruined it before Roosevelt seized it from them and returned it to the American people. I'd rather have a Missouri Babbitt as President than a sanctimonious snob from New York. Better Main Street than Wall Street."

Loren was totally taken aback by his father's diatribe—the longest continuous statement on any subject, except for baseball, he had ever addressed to his son. Although the very passion with which he had delivered his judgments made them somewhat suspect, most of what he had said rang true. One of the benefits of being a long-time editor, Loren reflected, was the daily task of evaluating information pouring into your office from all over the world.

Loren asked: "What's a Babbitt?"

"A Babbitt," snorted Adam, "is a mush-mouthed, two-faced selfish bigot. Read Sinclair Lewis's novel of the same name. It's over there, on the top shelf." He opened his magazine. Loren located the volume and took it to his room. But his mind kept wandering from the book to the threat of the military draft.

* * *

On Tuesday, July 6, Loren walked two blocks north to Austin Avenue, where he caught a city bus downtown. There, streaming sweat in the oppressive heat, he transferred to a southside bus which eventually delivered him to a stop near the Sisti and Sampson Construction Company. Inside a pine-paneled office, he was introduced by a gum-chewing receptionist to Sidney Sampson, a large sunburned man in a gray poplin suit, chewing affably on an unlit cigar. Crunching Loren's fingers in a calloused paw, he gestured toward a younger man seated near the window, who was dressed in khaki and cowboy boots. "Meet Sam Houston Howell," said Mr. Sampson. "Roun' heah we call 'im 'Buzz,' 'cause he served durin' th' war in th' army air corps."

Buzz's handshake was firm but unaggressive, his green eyes friendly. He was darkly tanned and unobtrusively handsome. His fingernails were unbroken and clean. Not used to much hard work outdoors, thought Loren.

"Do yew know who Coke Stevenson is?" asked Mr. Sampson. Loren shook his head. "Whut 'bout Lyndon Johnson?" Same response. "Do yew foller politics at all?" Believing it prudent to feign ignorance, Loren mumbled: "Not really."

After a moment of silence, Mr. Sampson said: "Ah spose that's jus' as well. "Yore job, Loren, will be t' accompany Buzz, prolly till th' end of August, an' help him put up posters an' distribute campaign literature fer Congressman Lyndon

Johnson, who's runnin' fer th' United States Senate. Yew'll be paid at uh rate of two hundred dollars uh month. Any problem wit' th' nature of th' work or th' pay?"

"No Sir," said Loren. He had never even seen one hundred dollars, at least not all at once.

"Wal, then," said Mr. Sampson, looking at his watch. "Git movin'."

Loren followed Buzz into the shell-covered parking lot, where they climbed into the cab of a dust-covered brown pickup truck. "Th' signs are back in th' bed," said Buzz, "an' th' pamphlets an' matchbooks we're sposed t' hand out are behin' th' seat. Ah see yew brought yore lunch."

"Yeah."

"No need," said Buzz. "Mr. Sampson will reimburse us fur whutevah we spend fer uh noon meal. Ah'm partial t' Dairy Queen, mahself."

"Fine with me."

"Ah think we'll git along," said Buzz. He headed the truck out onto the highway and turned south, toward Port Amberley.

After a while he asked Loren: "Do yew know whut uh helicopter is?"

"Sure. Whirlybirds. They use rotors instead of wings to fly. And they don't need runways to take off or land."

"Right. Congressman Johnson is campaignin' in one. An' he's scheduled t' be in Port Amberley th' day after tomorra.

"So heah's th' plan. We hit th' highways an' places of business 'round Port Natchez an' Neverland t'day an' t'morra. That'll take us t' Port Amberley by Wednesday. Soun' all right t' yew?"

"You're the boss," said Loren. "So what do you want me to do?"

"Ah'll show yew. It's easy, as long as th' cops or th' utility people don' happen along."

"Why's that?

"It's unlawful," said Buzz, "t' nail posters on utility poles. Somethin' 'bout interferin' with th' claws that linemen wear on thar shoes t' climb th' poles t' git t' th' wires. But all th' campaigners nail thar posters onto th' poles, anyway, 'cause they provide th' best location t' catch th' eyes of people drivin' by. An' they're on th' public right-a-way; not on private property." He braked the pickup truck and stopped on a narrow shoulder, almost in the ditch. "Hurry," he said. "Nail one of th' Johnson posters onta that light pole ovah near th' fence. Th' hammer an' roofin' nails are back near th' tailgate."

Loren jumped the ditch and waded through tall weeds, watching for snakes. "Put it up as high as yew kin reach," yelled Buzz. Loren did so; two nails on top; two on the bottom; and a large portrait of Lyndon Johnson was ready to stare beseechingly at passing motorists above the inscription: "Vote Your Convictions. Vote Johnson for U. S. Senator."

As they rode along, stopping every quarter mile or so for Loren to nail up a poster, Buzz patiently answered his sidekick's questions about the significance of what they were doing. "Thar are two hundred and fifty-four counties in Texas," he said, "an' we're right now coverin' Hennings County. We're also responsible fer portions of three adjacent counties. Johnson has people all ovah th' state, doin' whut we're doin'. There's big money bein' spent in this campaign. Ah saw uh check fer one thousand dollahs on Mr. Sampson's desk this mornin,' an' it wasn't fer road buildin'. If yew turn on th' radio in th' evenin', Johnson'll be comin' on, sooner or later, no matter which station, wit' uh campaign spot. He's workin' lak mad. Th' primary is nex' Sat'day."

"What's a primary?" asked Loren.

Buzz stared at him. "Yew don' know?" he asked incredulously.

"I don't believe we had them in Illinois," Loren replied defensively. "If we did I never noticed. I won't be able to vote until nineteen-fifty-four."

"Wal, uh primary is an election that determines who'll be th' candidate of uh political party in th' general election," explained Buzz. "Johnson is runnin' in th' Democratic party primary. Th' Republicans have one, too, but thar ain't many Republicans in this state. So, if Johnson gets ovah half th' votes on July twenty-fourth, it'll be all ovah. He'll win big in November. But that's a big if."

"What's to stop him from winning the primary?"

"Fust of all, there are uh buncha candidates runnin,' which makes it almos' impossible t' obtain uh majority of th' total numbah of votes cast. An' secon', one of Johnson's opponents, th' favorite in fact, is former governor Coke Stevenson, who looks an' talks like Gary Cooper. People call 'im 'Mr. Texas.'

"When Stevenson announced las' New Year's day that he was runnin,' 'most everyone thought that wuz it—that he wud win easily. Johnson waited till mid-May t' file his candidacy, which put 'im far behind 'gainst prolly th' most popular politician in th' history of this state. An', though Johnson has been workin' his head off, it still looks like Stevenson may top fifty percent. Our job is t' help keep him below that figure; so that Johnson kin get him into uh runoff."

"You mean a second primary election?"

"Right. Mr. Sampson says his buddies in Dallas believe Johnson kin take Stevenson in uh one-on-one contest. Ah'm not so sure. But Ah folla orders. Have yew evah heard of Brown an' Root?"

"No."

"That's whar th' real power is. Big money. State an' federal contracts fer highways an' military bases. Oil leases. Everythang that produces profits. These are th' people who decide who gits elected governor an' who represents us in Washington. An' it seems that they're backin' our candidate."

"So he should win; right?"

"Ordinarily, yes," said Buzz. "But Stevenson is very popular, and he's known all 'cross th' state fer havin' been governor; whereas Johnson is not well known, 'cept in his own congressional district. In politics, name recognition is everythang. Prolly twenty percent of th' voters will cast ballots fer th' candidate whose name they best recognize, even though that may be th' only thang they know 'bout him. When yew consider that mos' elections are settled within uh margin of ten or fifteen points, th' candidate wit' th' greatest name recognition mos' always wins. Lessen thar's sum negative factor attached, such as bein' repeatedly accused of bein' uh communist."

"You hear that more and more," observed Loren. "That fellow out in Californina, what was his name, who called Congressman Voorhis a communist and won? What slime!"

"Say, yew do know somethin' 'bout politics," said Buzz.

"My father talks politics a lot," said Loren, "and I listen. He liked Congressman Voorhis, whom he said had been voted by Washington journalists the most capable member of the House of Representatives. Now he's out; ousted by smear tactics."

"So far," said Buzz, "neither Johnson nor Stevenson are slingin' mud. But th' race ain't ovah. It'll be interestin' t' see who does it fust."

"Do you think it'll happen?"

"Shore. Ah'd bet mah bottom dollah that afore this election campaign is ovah yew'll heah th' word communist many times ovah. Wait an' see."

* * *

On Friday night, after four days of leaping over roadside ditches, brushing away gnats and slapping at mosquitoes, Loren was virtually exhausted. Soon after supper he collapsed on his cot and slept.

During the night he awakened, his bladder demanding relief. Thank goodness his sheet was still dry, except for the usual perspiration. Groggily, he swung his bare feet over the edge of his sagging mattress and felt with his toes for a rag rug that his mother had laboriously sewn together for him when he had been hardly more than a baby. His clock showed 2:45.

He felt his way down the dark hallway to the toilet, where he relieved himself, flushed, and then made his way underneath the rumbling of the attic fan back to his bed. He was about to close his eyes, when a light shining outside his window drew his attention in that direction. Something was happening at the Kaplan's.

He padded over to the window and quietly drew the shade down to the sill. A small tear in the fabric permitted him to see out, with little chance of being spotted from outside. Through a ragged opening in a tall privet hedge he had a clear view of a window next door. Its top sash was covered by heavy curtains, but the bottom portion had been removed and replaced by a large box fan. When that appliance was turned off, as Loren had previously ascertained, nothing could be seen inside. But now, with the blades whirling, he could see into a dimly lit bedroom.

Visible was the lower half of a double bed. A woman lay there on her back, uncovered. Her lower limbs protruded from a green chiffon chemise which barely reached her thighs. Mrs. Kaplan.

A second figure appeared at the foot of the bed. Visible was a brown back above white buttocks and coca-colored muscular legs. Definitely not Dr. Kaplan, who was a pudgy pallid little man. Sinewy hands began stroking Mrs. Kaplan, gradually working upward from her toes. As the stranger's fingers reached the gauzy gown and crept underneath, Mrs. Kaplan entangled her scarlet-tipped fingers in the stranger's dark curls.

While Loren stared, tense and tingling, Mrs. Kaplan's bedroom light suddenly went out. In the dark he could only discern pulsating shadows. After a few minutes more he could see no movement at all.

When he returned excitedly to his cot, Loren was still wondering: who was the mysterious visitor, and where was Dr. Kaplan? Did such encounters occur often? If so, might he not slip outside next time and hide in the hedge, a place perfect for peeping? Even more daring, he thought, would be to try to capture such a liaison on film, to be studied afterwards at his leisure.

Never had he seen a completely naked woman; much less two people engaged in the sex act, which was apparently what had just happened. The more intense his curiosity about such matters, the less he had been able to satisfy it. In Winona he had known a boy who had a summer job as a projectionist at a Chicago movie theater. Jimmy Harper sometimes gave private showings at his home when his parents weren't there. Loren particularly remembered one afternoon when he and several other classmates, girls excluded, were seated in Jimmy's darkened living room, a large projector whirring behind them, and the beginning scenes of the notorious movie, *Ecstasy*, flashing on a white sheet hung on the opposite wall.

The film had reached the moment when the slender German actress, Hedy Lamar, was beginning to strip off all of her clothes, prior to swimming naked across a river, and emerging frontally in all her splendor on the opposite bank. Having already been briefed about what to expect, the boys were staring transfixed, when the front door abruptly opened, and Jimmy's mother appeared in the front hallway, holding a heavy paper sack of groceries. As she stood smiling in the hall, calling out greetings to her son's friends, Jimmy quickly clapped his hand over the projector lens. Could she get the boys something to eat? What about drinks? No, Mrs. Harper, we're fine. Really, we are. May we help you with your groceries? Anything to move her out of the room.

All the while, nude Hedy flickered unseen on the palm of Jimmy's hot hand. By the time that Loren and one of the other boys had hurried outside and helped Mrs. Harper carry the rest of her groceries from her car to the kitchen, and then returned to the living room, the movie was mundane, the German speech unintelligible, the plot unfathomable, and their own eagerness to see more of it unsustainable, particularly in view of Mrs. Harper's insistence on popping in and out of the room with food and drink, and her growing curiosity about what they were watching.

"Mom, this movie's not one anyone ever heard about and, anyway, we're tired of watching it. We're going to the back porch to play hearts."

Several weeks later. After Jimmy made sure his mom was gone for the day, Loren got a glimpse of Jane Russell's fleshy boobs bouncing about inside her loose blouse while she rode a galloping horse in Howard Hughes's *The Outlaw*. But the sight was more tantalizing than enlightening.

For Loren, at age sixteen, sex remained largely a mystery. Schoolmates' dirty jokes at which he felt obliged to snicker, and the cheesecake pictures that celebrated firm thighs and curvy cleavage in the pages of *Life* and *Look* magazines, were far from fulfilling.

Prompted by his lurid yearnings, Loren had used his penknife to cut a hole through the wooden partition between the men's and women's dressing rooms in the bathhouse at Winona's main public beach on Lake Michigan. As he squinted through the small opening, a young woman had come into view, still dripping from her shower, her torso wrapped in a fleecy white towel. Apparently a mirror was located on the wall directly over the hole through which Loren breathlessly stared, for his quarry advanced toward him, holding her towel with one hand while she stroked her long black tresses with a hairbrush held in the other hand. As Loren silently prayed "Please, drop the towel," his penknife slipped from his grasp, clunking on the bare wooden floor. As he bent to retrieve it, he heard a rasping sound. Looking up, he saw the sharp point of a nail file protruding from his peephole.

"Take that, you filthy bastard," came a muffled soprano shout from the other side of the wall. Stunned, Loren had thrown on his street clothes, snatched his wet bathing suit and towel, and rushed outside. Diving into some shrubbery, he struggled up a steep hill to his bicycle, on which he pedaled rapidly home. For several weeks thereafter he swam and sunbathed at another beach, and whenever he recalled his near encounter with the nail file, he involuntarily blinked.

CHAPTER 5
LOREN'S REFUGE

Saturday, July 17. 10 A.M. A heavy dew had left a film of moisture on the Kaplans' lawn mower, which Loren found waiting for him next to their front porch. As he forced the whirling reels through the top layer of the wiry green turf, he perspired profusely, tense with anticipation at the thought of another encounter with his red-headed neighbor.

Dr. Kaplan had apparently vanished on one of his frequent trips out of town. His black Buick was missing from its usual spot, just outside the two-car garage located at the rear of the large lot. Mrs. Kaplan's yellow Cadillac convertible remained there, topless, awaiting its owner.

By noon Loren had finished mowing. A single knock and Mrs. Kaplan opened the back door, smiling, her tight green jersey and matching silk shorts clinging to the contours of her freckled frame. Loren felt his face reddening and his hands growing clammy. Uncertain where to let his eyes linger, he finally settled on staring at her bare pink toes. Didn't she ever wear shoes?

"Yew look hot," she observed. "Ah bet yew could use uh soapy shower. Would yew lak t' take one heah?" She pointed to a hallway, down which Loren saw an open door to a bathroom.

"I guess not," he stammered. "I have to do some things at home first."

"Suit yoreself," she said. Then he felt her hand on his right bicep. "My, whut muscles!" she exclaimed. "Ah bet all th' gurls git in line t' date yew."

"Not really. I don't date much." He wanted to stare boldly at her but could not get his eyes to cooperate. They kept straying, to the kitchen appliances, to the dirty dishes piled in the sink, through the doorway to the hall, down which was not only the bathroom but also her bedroom.

As if she could read his mind, she said: "Cum wit me t' mah room an' Ah'll give yew yore money."

His jeans had become too tight for comfort. He hesitated, wondering whether it wasn't time to depart through the nearby back door and try to get his money some other way. But a real man, he thought, wouldn't miss such a chance. Tremulously, he trailed her into the room with the fabulous fan, which now sat silently in a shaded window. The white sheets on Mrs. K's unmade bed were wrinkled and a deep impression in the pillows piled against the headboard held a single strand of red hair. She had apparently been reading a women's magazine, which lay on a bedside table open to an advertisement for skimpy lingerie.

Loren could not help thinking about what had happened in that bed hardly more than a week earlier. The recollection produced an unseemly bulge beneath his belt. Before he could turn away to hide it, he realized that Mrs. K was staring and smiling. She moved closer. Her perfume seemed to surround him, making his head swim.

He heard a rumbling sound, faint at first and then growing louder. A car had entered the driveway. "Damn," exclaimed Mrs. Kaplan. "Mah husband's home." She grabbed Loren's arm and pulled him over to a large closet crowded with brightly colored feminine clothing. Pushing some dresses aside, she shoved him inside. "Try not t' git yore sweaty body 'gainst mah clothes," she instructed. "Not uh sound. Ah'll let yew know when th' coast is clear."

As the folding doors closed upon him and left him in total darkness, Loren began quivering with fear. What would happen to him if he was discovered there? Trying not to step on any of the shoes strewn around the closet floor, or to rustle any of Mrs. Kaplan's dresses, he shifted his position slightly, in order to press an ear to the thin crack where the double doors met. Her scent surrounded him, emanating, he realized, from her clothing. It mingled with his own body odors, which he hoped would not be strong enough to give away his presence.

He heard Mrs. Kaplan call out a greeting to her husband, who asked: "Did that kid show?"

"Yeah. Came an' went." If only, thought Loren.

"Didja invite 'im inside?"

"Jus' briefly, t' give 'im his money."

"Then whut's this fi' dollah bill doin' on your bed?"

Dr. Kaplan was in the bedroom now. Loren could almost feel the heat of his hairy body.

"That's money fer shopping." A slight quaver had infected her husky voice.

"Uh huh. Ah bet. Ah know yew too well. So yew paid 'im wit sex instead, yew damn slut!"

"That's not true! An' don' call me that," she said indignantly.

"Ah'll call yew whutevah Ah wan'."

There was a scuffling sound. Loren heard Mrs. K cry out: "Git yore hands offa me! Yore hurtin' me!"

"Listen, yew bitch. Ah've had it wit' this marriage. Ah'm sending yew back t' New Orleans. Maybe that dancer Ah rescued yew from will take yew back."

"Yew'd really divorce me?"

"Damn right."

"Yew bastard!" Her cry came dimly through the closet doors. They must have gone out into the hall, thought Loren. He could barely make out Dr. Kaplan's shouted reply: "Sure, take uh bath. Scrub away whutevah yew do when ah'm outa town. An' prepare t' git served wit' divorce papers. Soon." A door slammed. Then silence.

Loren waited a few minutes more. He could hear only the radio and the buzzing of the fan in the hall ceiling. Carefully he slid out of the closet and tiptoed over to the bedroom door. He could now hear someone splashing. She's in the bathroom, he thought, naked. In the other direction, through the kitchen window, he could see Dr. Kaplan sitting on the patio sipping from a tall glass of amber fluid, a newspaper spread out on the table before him. Faced with a similar situation, Loren thought he knew what Errol Flynn would have done.

But he was not Errol Flynn. Sighing, he headed for the front door. As he passed the bathroom, its door opened. Mrs. Kaplan stood on the tile floor, her red hair stringy on her fleckled shoulders, hugging a large yellow bath towel around her with both hands, a puddle forming around her bare feet. On a shelf above the bathtub a small brown radio vibrated to the beat of country music.

"Ah'm sorry 'bout this," she said softly. "Ah wuz jus' havin' some fun an' it got outta hand. Please don' hold it 'gainst me."

Loren remained silent.

"Come back in 'bout an hour," she said. "Please. Ah really need you t' trim mah hedge afore yew quit fer this week. Ah'll pay yew 'nother two dollahs."

Loren realized that he had yet to collect what he was already owed. He thought about asking for his five dollars on the spot. Then, seeing that the towel was beginning to slide downward from her shoulders, he decided that wasn't a good idea. "All right," he blurted. And then he fled—out the front door and around the high privet hedge, to the safety of his own yard.

*　　*　　*

Later, after taking a cold shower and putting on fresh clothes, Loren summoned up his courage and returned to the Kaplans' back yard, trying to act nonchalant. Mrs. Kaplan, wearing orange shorts, was weeding a flower bed at the rear of the property. Dr. Kaplan was still on the patio, sitting in the shade with his paper. He nodded but did not speak and seemed disinterested when his wife, noticing Loren, went into the garage and came out with hedge clippers. "Cut it about five feet off the ground," she instructed, "just above the top of the fence."

The work went quickly. Before an hour had passed Loren had worked his way along the entire north and rear perimeters of the back yard. Wiping the sweat from his forehead he looked for Mrs. Kaplan, to ask if she wanted him to begin cutting back the privet hedge dividing their lot from that of the Temple's, but she was nowhere to be seen. Dr. Kaplan, however, had remained in his chair. He was now holding a book.

"Sir," Loren stammered, "can you tell me where I can find your wife? She has my money."

Dr. Kaplan looked up from his reading. Grinning faintly, he stared silently at Loren, who began to feel very uncomfortable. Then he said: "I'll take care of the money. How much was it: ten dollahs?"

"Seven," said Loren.

"Let's make it ten. I've been watching. Yew've wuked hard." He rose and took Loren's elbow in a clammy paw. "Come. I want to show you something."

Reluctantly Loren accompanied him into the shadowy garage. There Dr. Kaplan reached into a front pocket of his rumpled shorts and pulled out a checkbook.

"Yew'll take uh check?"

Loren nodded.

Removing a fountain pen from his shirt pocket, Dr. K scribbled something. Then, tearing the check from its companions, he suddenly poked it into the front of

Loren's jeans, thrusting it down behind the belt buckle. Loren was shocked to feel his testicles being fondled.

"How d'yew like that, young man?" whispered Dr. K. His shiny bald head glistened with perspiration as his insistent fingers tightened on Loren's penis. With a sudden surge of indignant energy, Loren tore himself loose and rushed out into the daylight, heading home. He had never felt so contaminated. From now on, he resolved, he would stay well away from both Kaplans.

* * *

At supper that night, Loren's mother noticed that he seemed distracted. Later she came to his room and asked: "What's the matter?"

"Nothing."

"Come on, Loren. I'm your mother. Remember?"

"Yeah, I know... Let's just say... I don't want to cause any problems between you and Dad and the Kaplans, but I'm not going over there any more."

Nan looked puzzled. "Why not? Did they say something that bothered you?"

"Did something."

"What?"

"Well, Mr. Kaplan is just too friendly, is the problem."

Nan stared at her son for a moment. "Oh, I see. That's awful. I'll phone Mrs. Kaplan right now."

"Please, Mom, don't do that. It's not necessary."

"Maybe not for you, but there may be others. She needs to be warned."

"Mom, I think she knows."

Nan considered. "You are probably right. Well, then, I'll just tell her that you won't be back any more to cut her grass. And I'll advise her in friendly fashion not to employ any other adolescent boys when her husband is around. That should do it."

"O. K., Mom; if you think that's best. But... it's embarrassing."

"I know. People like that are all around us. As long as they leave others alone, they can be the nicest people you'll ever meet, but... Anyway, we can't let the Doctor Kaplans of the world blight our lives." Patting his cheek with a soft maternal hand, she left to make her phone call.

Loren was glad he had failed to mention Mrs. Kaplan's familiarity. His feelings about her were unresolved. He was beginning to have second thoughts about his resolution not to visit her again.

* * *

In the kitchen, the day's dirty dishes waited. While Loren scrubbed them in hot soapy water, Tommy rinsed, dried, and put them away in the pantry. As the boys were finishing, Nan stuck her head in the kitchen door and said to Loren: "I made my call and everything is fine. Try to forget it ever happened."

"What's she talking about?" inquired Tommy.

"Oh, nothing important. A small misunderstanding"

Tommy did not pursue the subject, for which Loren was grateful.

*　　*　　*

During the week that followed, Loren could not help wondering whether Dr. Kaplan really intended to divorce his wife, and whether she would continue to invite her lover into her bed whenever her husband left town. Just in case, Loren planned to load his camera with fast film. Photos of Mrs. K in action might enable him to learn more about sex, such as what women like her sought from involvement in that activity.

Wondering whether his fascination with his neighbor was natural, he decided to consult Buzz. He seemed like a guy who had been around. As they took their lunch break under a huge live oak tree, its lower limbs draped with tendrils of gray Spanish moss, Loren slurped his Dairy Queen milkshake and asked if Buzz had ever figured out what women wanted.

"Whataya mean? Are yew askin' whut they wan' from men?"

"I guess so."

"Wal, Ah think mos' of 'em wan' us t' protect 'em an' support 'em an' be partners an' considerate lovers."

"About that last part…?"

Buzz stared silently at his young companion. Loren felt his face getting hot. Buzz grinned. "Are yew familiar wit' th' Kinsey Report?" he asked.

"What's that?"

"It's uh book of ovah eight hundred pages written by some professor at Indiana University. It's uh best seller. Th' mor' th' preachers condemn it from thar pulpits, th' mor' people buy it. It's fulla interestin' stuff 'bout sex."

"I never heard of it."

"Yew oughta git hold of uh copy. Fer one thang, Kinsey says that young men 'tween sixteen an' twenty are mor' sexually active than at any other age, despite th' fact that few of them are married."

"That seems impossible."

"He cites scientific proof. An' he maintains that so-called nocturnal emissions an' even masturbation make up only uh small fraction of teenage sexual activity. Mos' of it takes th' form of sexual intercourse. Which is all th' mor' strange in view of his statement that adolescent females are only 'bout one-fifth as active sexually as boys of th' same age."

Loren was astounded. Could Buzz be pulling his leg? No, his partner in politics was obviously serious. No wonder he was obsessed with sex. Millions of guys his age were out there throughout the country, consumed by the same yearnings and embarrassed by the same urges. But it appeared that most of them were somehow getting satisfied. That was the rub. Then another question popped into his mind.

"Why," he asked Buzz, "does there seem to be a perpetual war going on between the sexes?"

"War? Whut yew talkin' 'bout?"

"Guys are always boasting about banging some babe, giving some girl a poke in the ass, as I heard one fellow put it, like it's some kind of conquest." Loren noticed that Buzz looked amused. Nevertheless he continued: "Warfare. Strategies for getting an advantage. Tactics for blasting through defenses. Victory the object. All's fair in love and war, as if they were the same thing."

"Yew don' have uh sister, do yew?" asked Buzz.

"No."

"How would yew feel if she wuz th' object of th' kinda war yew described?"

"Furious. I'd want to bop any guy who even looked cross-eyed at her."

"Natcherly. Yore right that many males are predators. They view gals as soft flesh in which t' sink their seeds an' git relief from their tensions. An' it's also true that some gals are willin' t' be dominated by men. They even enjoy it. But, again, yew should ask yoreself: if'n yew wuz uh gal, would yew like t' be forced t' be some man's meat?"

"No, I guess not."

"Then is it O. K. fer us males t' force ourselves upon th' weaker sex?"

"No. But I still don't understand how to act around girls."

"Th' best advice Ah kin give yew is t' empathize wit' them. Talk t' them, an' listen t' whut they say. Sum of it will be nonsense; gals have their own jargon. But friendships wit' gals kin be even more rewardin' than those wit' guys."

"Huh. I never had a real girl friend."

Buzz looked incredulous. "How old are yew now? Eighteen?"

"Seventeen in November."

"Yew bin missin' out. An' Ah'm not talkin' 'bout sex. Thar are other kinds of guy-gal relations. An' wit'out complications like gettin' sum filly pregnant or catchin' uh deadly disease. Yew need someone t' teach yew. Uh sister is ideal. Too bad yew don' have one. Uh mother can't do it 'cause of th' Oedipus factor…"

"What's that?" interrupted Loren.

"Read Sophocles. It's all thar. Uh Greek myth that influenced modern psychology. Un lotta truth t' it."

Loren made a mental note. Buzz was much better educated than he had previously imagined. Where had he learned such things?

"Whut yew need," his companion continued, "is uh nice sisterly gurl fren, one wit' whom yew kin talk wit'out worryin' 'bout havin' sex wit' 'er. An' if'n yew feel yew need t' rub yore balls an' bat on some babe, consider Ben Franklin's advice t' find an older woman. She'll know how t' make it fun. An'—Ah 'specially like th' way he put this—they're so grateful."

At once Loren thought of Mrs. Kaplan. But Buzz's reference to balls and bats offered a safer subject for consideration. While Buzz puffed contentedly on a cigarette and listened rapturously to the whining and howling on his truck's radio, Loren meditated on his favorite subject—baseball.

*   *   *

Unlike the temporary tingle derived from certain passages of classical music, or the spasmodic satisfaction produced by certain books, the pleasures Loren obtained from involvement in the national pastime were infinite and unceasing. He *knew* the game: its rules, its lore, its subtleties. Ask me anything about it, he thought, and I'll give the right answer. What pitcher threw three shutouts in the 1905 World Series? What outfielder won four American League batting championships in odd-numbered years during the nineteen-twenties? What club won more pennants during the decade 1929-1938 than any other major league team except the Yankees, who won the same number during that time period? Loren could rattle off the answers without a second's hesitation. Christy Mathewson. Harry Heilmann. The Chicago Cubs.

But baseball's historical statistics were without meaning if one lacked the imagination to visualize boisterous apple-cheeked rookies growing wrinkled and tentative as the years went by. Or vicariously to experience the touch of baggy woolen flannel knickers, caked with dirt and sometimes stained with dried blood, against one's sweat-soaked thighs. Or to conceive of the tickle radiating from hands to shoulders as ash kissed horsehide. Or to imagine the satisfaction produced by the smack of a hard liner into the outstretched leather glove of a desperately diving infielder. Or to savor the smells of Wintergreen rub, of Neetsfoot oil, of rancid socks stiff with sweat, and of hairy bodies packed into a small locker room impatiently listening to a manager or coach talk tactics.

The perpetual drooling of tobacco juice; the mindless chatter; and the surreptitious scratching of an itchy crotch. The elaborate incantations of the coaches, as their gnarled fingers flashed signals to intently staring batters and baserunners. The superstitions—avoid stepping on the chalked foul lines; watch carefully that none of the bats laid on the ground in front of the bench are allowed to cross; don't say one word to a pitcher who has a no-hitter in progress. And the dashing, dodging, diving; the stretching, sliding, spitting—all integral to the playing of the game.

Loren cherished many memories of days on the diamond. Crouching in the traditional stance, hands on knees, for the final pitch of the half-inning; being elated by the booming "stree-yike th-reee!" as the black-clad right arm thrust skyward; tossing his glove backward onto the soft green grass; and trotting toward the bench with mingled elation and foreboding, as he anticipated being next to bat.

Memories of Chicago's Wrigley Field. Of Big Bill Nicholson gloving a carom off the ivy-covered wall in the right field power alley and gunning a perfect one-hop throw to second base to douse a double; of Ewell Blackwell blowing away batters with snarling sidearm slants; of Whitlow Wyatt snapping off a crooked curve; and of Rip Sewell launching his notorious blooper that arched high above the field before dropping, after an excruciating wait, almost vertically through the strike zone. Precious memories.

Baseball players were like soldiers, recruited while still young and impressionable; weeded out during basic training in the low minors; the survivors struggling through advanced instruction at the double-A level, until a fortunate few were ultimately ordered into major league action. An interval that passed all too quickly, before they reluctantly yielded to their precocious successors, eager to up the ante until they too were shot down by Father Time. Billy Hamilton, born in 1866, played regularly from 1889 until 1900 and hit .344. Sam Crawford, born in

1880, played regularly from 1900 until 1916 and hit .316. Harry Heilman, born in 1894, played regularly from 1916 to 1930 and hit .342. Wally Berger, born in 1905, played regularly from 1930 to 1939 and hit an even .300. And Dom DiMaggio, born in 1917, played regularly from 1940 up to the present year of 1948 and thus far was batting .293 and improving.

Almost sixty years and five generations of able athletes had created revered records that would live in the recollections of millions long after the remains of the players were deposited underground. How long would it be before some eager rookie would begin a distinguished big league career just as Joe DiMaggio's little brother was hanging up his spikes? How many more generations of big league ballplayers would follow? And would a sixteen-year-old with acne and agility, and the talent to throw a ball anywhere in the strike zone nine times out of ten, achieve his dream some day to mount the mound in Wrigley Field and pitch for the Chicago Cubs? Loren's ambition had become an obsession. To him it seemed the most important thing on earth.

CHAPTER 6
THE CANDIDATE

On Wednesday, July 21, the fog was thick on the narrow asphalt highway. Vehicles hurtling northward from the direction of the Gulf of Mexico loomed up suddenly, swooshing by in an instant, vanishing as quickly as they had appeared. Buzz kept the old pickup truck's headlights on low beam and periodically shattered the silence with quavering toots from its antiquated horn. Frogs croaked in the steaming ditches, beyond which grey Spanish moss hung in the live oak trees like lank tendrils on the sepia skulls of old crones. Huddled passively in the passenger seat of the rattling truck, Loren wished he had stayed home, curled up with a book.

Loren flinched as the driver of a passing behemoth answered Buzz's honk with an ear-shattering blast. It was only seven a.m. and his armpits were already wet. The blistering heat and lack of rainfall during the summer of 1948 had produced the worst drought in the recorded history of the region. Reinforcing the morning fog was a vast blanket of blue smoke that drifted southward from wild fires that crackled in the pine forests north of Tocqueville. Day after day, thermometer readings nudged or exceeded one hundred degrees.

Eventually the haze began to lift. Loren could now make out petroleum storage tanks as high as three-story buildings on both sides of the highway. Beyond were refinery towers stretching skyward like huge silver candles topped by flaming flares and connected by varicolored pipelines snaking in all directions. The humid air was heavy with sickening odors that reminded Loren of a high school chemistry lab.

By the time Buzz parked his truck near the Port Amberley waterfront, the fog had dissipated and the sun had climbed high into a cloudless sky. Loren trailed his fellow campaigner across grass so dry that it crackled underfoot, as they passed under the limp leaves of monstrous live oaks and headed towards an open area next to the shimmering bay. In the distance a hulking freighter churned its way toward the horizon. Buzz snatched a crumpled newspaper from an unoccupied park bench. "Look at this," he said.

An imposing headline dominating page one of the Port Amberley *News* announced the expected arrival later that morning of their candidate, in his "flying windmill." A sub-head announced: "It lands on roofs and in pastures!"

Looking over Buzz's shoulder, Lorne read that Lyndon Johnson's wife, Lady Bird—incredulous, he made sure he had read the name correctly—feared for the safety of her husband, flitting around Texas in a sixty-foot long Sikorsky S-51 four-passenger helicopter, landing on narrow highways near power lines and in barnyards where panicky chickens fluttered in all directions, merely so that he might shake the calloused paw of some bewildered cotton farmer or peck the sallow cheek of his frightened wife. Lady Bird had not been much concerned three years ago, according to the writer, when her man was flying in B-29s, helping to bomb one Japanese island after another into submission. But now, it seemed, she worried all the time. Loren was impressed. Johnson was a man with guts.

A hillbilly band seated on a shallow wooden platform began to play. A crowd gathered: men in shirtsleeves, women in thin cotton dresses, and barefoot children—but also a handful of anxious looking men in suits and ties, shirt collars already wilting. As more people climbed out of their automobiles and emerged from downtown streets, several straw-hatted Negroes supervised by a hulking white man in a dirty pith helmet began to unroll thick hemp ropes and pointed wooden stakes from a flatbed truck which had "Johnson for Senator" signs attached to its cab. Soon they had surrounded the speakers' platform with a rope barrier to keep the growing throng at bay.

Buzz and Loren returned to their truck. Affixing Johnson campaign buttons to their shirt pockets and taking bundles of the candidate's pamphlets from behind the seat, they mingled with the crowd and began to hand out their literature. Buzz appeared perfectly at home, slapping strangers on the back, winking at the ladies, patting children on their hot little heads. Loren confined himself to silently proffering his pamphlets, not making eye contact, shrinking a little every time someone showed any reluctance to accept his offering.

A distant murmur emanated from a dark spot that gradually grew larger in the cloudless sky, signaling Johnson's imminent arrival. As the big blue and white whirly bird swooped down toward the ground, its twenty-four-foot long rotor blades churning, the racket from its huge Pratt and Whitney engine caused the onlookers to thrust their forefingers into their ears. The candidate's advance men frantically shooed stray children away from the landing area, while parents with younger ones reached protectively for their tiny hands or lifted them up and held them tightly.

A deep voice suddenly boomed from overhead. "Hey, everyone. Come meet Congressman Lyndon Johnson from th' tenth district. He's been uh friend t' th' people of th' hill country. He got 'em roads. He got 'em 'lectricity. He got 'em jobs. He wants t' be yore friend, too. Come t' th' speakin' an' meet th' candidate."

Down came the helicopter, twisting, tipping, then righting itself, the blades of its tail rotor cutting a nine-foot swath through a rising dust cloud, its big overhead engine gulping gasoline underneath the three huge fan-like main sweeps. Scraps of paper blew around in circles as the mighty machine settled to the ground, its rubber tires compressing under its weight. Three men strapped into the big bubble, obscured by a cloud of dust and by reflected sunlight glinting off the surrounding glass, could be dimly seen waving to the crowd as the blades began to thump less stridently and the engine's roar to subside.

A door covered with the words "Lyndon Johnson for U.S. Senator" flew open, and out jumped a tall rawboned man in rumpled brown trousers, shiny black shoes, a sweat-soaked long-sleeved white shirt and a wide, brightly flowered tie. Above a high furrowed forehead his oily black hair was plastered straight back above large protruding ears and a toothy grin. He held a gray Stetson, which he promptly sailed into the nearby crowd. "Mah hat's in th' ring," he yelled. Then he strode forward and began grabbing for hands, pumping them vigorously but briefly, scattering compliments, asking for votes, letting his eyes linger longest on the prettiest women, always tugging his way forward to the next handshake and the next. Loren saw an elderly man flinch as Johnson, eagerly reaching for more hands, virtually threw him aside.

On the edge of the crowd, one of the candidate's workers could be seen talking animatedly to a small boy who had retrieved Johnson's hat and was trying to climb onto a bicycle in order to make off with his souvenir. As Loren stared, the dark-suited Johnson aide looked furtively around and then suddenly pushed the bicycle over, tearing the hat away from the fallen rider, and carrying it grimly back to the helicopter.

Meanwhile, Johnson continued to crunch fingers as he approached the small platform which the band had by now evacuated. Up he leaped to shake hands with local officials, who were guarded by grim-faced uniformed police officers. He then approached the lectern and said something into a microphone that did not emit a sound. A red-faced man in a crumpled brown suit stepped forward, grabbed the offending device, jiggled it, glared at it, and finally with a shrug of exasperation whispered something to Johnson. Impatiently, the candidate pushed him aside and stepped forward to the front of the platform.

"Howdy, folks," he shouted. "Kin yew heah me?" A few people yelled back "Yeah."

"Wal, then, Ah'm Congressman Lyndon Johnson, an' Ah'm gonna be yore next United States Senator ifn yew'll gimme yore hep. Ah'm fer peace, preparedness an' progress, an' agin' th' blood-red tide of commonism. Ah'm agin' socialized medicine an' th' federal civil rights program, which is uh shame an' uh farce—an' attempt t' set up uh po-lice state in th' guise of liberty. Ah'm fer eddication, bettah housin', farm-t'-market roads, rural 'lectrification, fifty-dollah-a-month pensions fer th' ol' folks, an' mor' funds fer national de-fense. It's yore gub-ment Ah'm talkin' 'bout. It's yore Amurica. It's yore campaign. Write me uh letter an' say: 'Lyndon, Ah'm wit' yew. Ah'm gonna vote fer yew. We gonna git th' job done!"

The candidate continued to speak, pausing only for the yells and whistles of approval from his admirers, his loud voice overwhelming them, dominating them. Buzz whispered: "Whut bombast! Lookit those dummies. They're eatin' it up."

Loren asked: "Isn't he saying what they want to hear?"

"Exactly. An' he ain't tellin' 'em anythang they don' wanna heah. Like his support fer th' Taft-Hartley act. Port Amberley has mor' union members than any other place its size in Texas. He'll blast th' 'labor bosses' in Dallas an' Houston, but not uh word 'roun' heah 'gainst th' A F of L."

Johnson was ranting about his main opponent, the popular former "cowboy" governor, Coke Stevenson. "Ol' Coke," he shouted, "is uh do-nuttin' candidate who refuses t' say whut he's fer. He's like ol' Herbert Hoover, who sat still like uh fat toad an' let millions uh people be thrown offa thar farms an' outa thar homes onto th' streets, as honest men trudged from town t' town a-lookin' fer work so they could feed th' hongry mouths at home. Ifn it hadn' been fer Roosevelt, we'd still have us uh depression; an' ifn ol' Coke gits intah th' Senate, that'll be th' end of roads an' lights an' jobs fer Texans."

Johnson grinned in wicked anticipation. "Heah's uh newspaper reporter interviewin' ol Coke," he announced. Taking a crumpled piece of paper and a pencil stub out of a pocket, Johnson licked the pencil point with a flickering pink tongue. "Now, guv'ner," he barked, staring at an imaginary interviewee, "How do yew stand on uh seventy-group air force t' fight th' commies?"

Johnson then stepped sideways and turned to face the phantom reporter. A corncob pipe wondrously materialized between his teeth and his clenched fists rested on his hips as he rocked back and forth, pretending to be deep in thought. Finally he spoke. "Ah believe in constitutional gub'ment," he intoned, while the crowd tittered.

Once again Johnson became the reporter. "Guv'ner, whatcha think 'bout parity fer farmers?"

Out came the pipe. Suck, suck. Contemplate. "Heah it comes," muttered Buzz. "Ah believe in states' rights," pronounced Johnson solemnly. The crowd roared. "Ain't he wunnerful?" asked an elderly woman standing next to Loren, giggling. "It's mor' like Coke than Coke!"

Buzz turned away. "Les go," he said. "He's nearly thru. If'n yew wanna meet th' congressman, we need t' git ovah t' th' helicopter, or he'll be gone afore yew get uh chance."

Winding up his stump speech with a few final jibes against Stevenson and the commies, who had become blood brothers, Johnson glanced at his wrist watch, jumped down off the platform, and hurried toward the roped-off helicopter, shaking more hands and slapping shoulders as he moved rapidly through the throng. Arriving at the helicopter door, the candidate turned smilingly to wave goodbye, at which time Buzz pushed Loren forward, saying: "Congressman, Ah wan' yew t' meet one of yore mos' loyal campaign workers."

Excitedly, Loren reached out for the big man's hand. God almighty, he was a monster! At six feet tall himself, Loren was not used to looking up at people. He noticed that the skin of Johnson's hand as he extended it looked cracked and dry. It felt flaky. Suddenly Johnson shouted: "Whut th' hell's th' matter wit' yew people? Ah wanted uh crowd, not a li'l scrunched up buncha yokels."

Buzz tried to speak, but Johnson continued to berate the two of them. "Yew ain't wurt whut mah people are payin' yew. Over forty thousand people in this town an' yew only git me uh couple hundred t' listen t' mah speech. Whut uh half-assed job! Ah'm wastin' half th' day here."

Buzz finally managed to break in. "Mr. Johnson, that wasn' our responsibility. Our job is t' put up signs an' distribute campaign leaflets. We've been wukin' hard at it."

"Phooey," Johnson shouted, spittle dripping down his chin. "Ah dun seen yore piss-poor wuk wit' mah signs. Yew put 'em 'long uh few main roads, uh mile apart. Ah wan' mah signs up on every road, on every light pole, everywhar people go. No gaps. Yew heah me!"

"Yessir," said Buzz. Then Johnson was gone, having climbed up into the helicopter, waving his big gray hat. He slammed the door just as the noise from the chopper began to sound like a huge egg-beater. Soon it rose, thumping, into the sky. A loud voice from above declaimed: "Don' fergit, folks, on July twenty-fourth vote fer Lyndon Johnson fer Senator. He's our fren'." In two minutes more the sky was silent. As the crowd began to disperse, Loren and Buzz walked back to their truck.

"Anyway," said Buzz, "he pays well. An' Stevenson is wus. In Texas politics it takes uh mean sonuffa bitch t' have uh chance t' win. An' Ah believe we're gonna win."

Loren remained silent. He wondered if he had made a mistake taking a job working for Johnson's election. It was something he wanted to ask his father.

* * *

As soon as he returned home, Loren started searching for newspapers in which to read about Lyndon Johnson. He was surprised at how interesting were the peculiarities of Texas politics. He also scanned stories about the continuing warfare between President Harry Truman and a hostile Congress and found them even more fascinating. He then leafed through weekly issues of *Time* and *Life* magazines which, fortunately, his father had refused his mother's pleas to discard. Piled on sagging shelves in the small room which Adam Temple called his den, these publications had previously furnished Loren with stories about sports. Now, however, he skipped over references to Joe DiMaggio, Warren Spahn and the Chicago Cubs to read political news.

Recalling his father's dinner table diatribes in Winona against all things Republican, he remembered that this year's presidential nominee of the GOP (Greedy Old Plutocrats, according to Adam) had also been their 1944 candidate against Franklin D. Roosevelt. Thomas E. Dewey had then seemed to Loren no more than a shoddy copy of Clark Gable, with a sneer for a smile and teeth like small headstones beneath the thick brush of a ragged mustache. During the post-Labor Day campaign, few listeners could have escaped hearing the Republican slogan, "It's time for a change," echoing over the airwaves, until Loren refrained from turning on his favorite program, "The Lone Ranger," fearing to hear the obnoxious chant once more.

Adam Temple had been furious when Dewey accused Roosevelt of condemning hundreds of American service men to death and most of the Pacific fleet to destruction by intentionally withholding advance knowledge of the Japanese attack on the naval base at Pearl Harbor in 1941. And Dewey's charge—which Loren was able to retrieve from an old *Time* magazine—that Roosevelt and his New Dealers, "the most spectacular collection of incompetent people who ever held office, ...little men rattling around in big jobs," were wrecking the national economy with their "tax and spend" policies, had also enraged Adam. Back in 1944, the Temple weekend dinner table conversations had been reduced to meaningless observations about the weather and mundane family activities, as Loren's mother wearily fought the rising tension by persistently changing the subject whenever politics entered the conversation.

Dewey had actually called Roosevelt the candidate of the communists and had appeared to suggest that the President and his party were to be blamed for most of the ills of the great depression and the occurrence of World War II, as he urged Americans to depart from the "nightmare" of the recent past and return to the "peace and calm" of Republican leadership. No wonder, then, that Adam could not help sputtering his contempt for that reactionary sonuffabitch from New York and his even more reprehensible running mate, Ohio senator John W. Bricker.

Loren smiled as he remembered the triumphant tone of his father's voice on election night as he called home from his newspaper office to announce another victory for "the Champ." How Adam had chortled when he showed Loren the huge headline, borrowed from the hit Broadway musical, *Oklahoma*, that he had personally placed atop page one of the Chicago *Star*. "Oh What a Beautiful Morning!" The publisher had issued a mild reprimand for the news editor's lack of objectivity, but it had been worth it.

How distant, now, seemed Chicago. And Winona. Wistfully Loren recalled how during the frigid months that followed Roosevelt's fourth election, tiny clouds of steam had leaked from the ancient iron radiators in the Temple home. How large cakes of ice had floated offshore in Lake Michigan. And how tightly he had wrapped his woolen scarf around his mouth and nose as he fast-walked to school in rubber boots on crunchy snow.

The fire department had opened hydrants to flood a neighborhood park, and Loren had risked frozen feet playing ice hockey after school and on weekends. There was also sledding on a snow-covered street extending downhill two blocks from the town community center past the Episcopal Church to crash landings on the village green. Loren and his younger brother would return home, pulling their sleds by frayed cotton ropes, their cheeks bright red, their noses running, their clothes and even their eyelids encrusted with snow, pausing in the back yard to tussle with their playful St. Bernard puppy before brushing and stomping off as much snow as possible on the back porch. Boots, coats, stocking caps, gloves, scarves, even sweaters came off there, before the boys were permitted to go inside.

In the warm kitchen Mrs. Temple, an apron tied over her dress, had been joined by Mioko Takahira, a young woman who had earlier joined the Temple household, along with her husband, Kio. The two of them were Nisei, native-born Americans of Japanese ancestry living in California, who were among the hundred thousand U.S. citizens incarcerated as potential wartime security risks. Arrested and given only a few hours' notice before being relocated to inhospitable prison camps, these innocent people, victims of the hysteria of 1942, had lost everything—homes, furnishings, vehicles, farms and businesses. Loren's mother had wept sympathetically when she learned what had happened. Later she discovered that some of the prisoners might be released into the custody of non-oriental Americans living in the interior of the country, provided the latter would sign a bond for their good behavior. She begged Adam to offer their home to a deserving couple.

In due course, the Takahiras arrived and occupied a large front bedroom. They worked uncomplainingly for their room and board, Mioko cleaning, cooking and washing up under the supervision of Mrs. Temple, while Kio went off to work six days a week in a local garage, servicing and repairing vehicles that could not be replaced during wartime. When not working, the Takahiras kept to their room, shyly refusing invitations to join in family life, but always available when needed to perform some task. When they left at the end of the war to return to California, they departed as friends, and all four Temples were sorry to see them go.

Meanwhile, Roosevelt, whom the Takahiras were less inclined to blame for their misfortune than Earl Warren, California's Republican governor, had died. The news had reached Loren on a sunny day in mid-April. He had gone to the Winona playfield to pitch for his team of twelve and thirteen-year-olds who were playing the boys from Faith, Hope and Charity, a Catholic school in a neighboring town. ("Before the first pitch they'll have faith," Loren's teammates chanted, "until the ninth inning they'll still have hope; afterwards we'll give them charity.") With a chest-high inside fast ball and a wrinkle of a curve that he kept close to the strike zone low outside, Loren was striking out batter after batter, with only an occasional pop up or a weak grounder to keep his fielders alert. The FHC pitcher was almost equally effective until the fifth inning, when Loren swung hard at an outside fast ball and managed to hit it squarely. By the time the center and right fielders had judged its flight and began to converge to cut it off, the ball had rocketed past them into the vastness of the unfenced playfield, coming eventually to rest in some bushes about four hundred feet away. Running hard, Loren crossed home plate before either fielder even reached the ball. A loud cheer went up from the small group of spectators sitting in the diminutive wooden bleachers along the third base line. Strangely, it continued after the next batter swung vainly at a pitch well above his eyes.

Loren had wondered why his home run had caused such elation among the usually quiet spectators. Sensing that something was wrong, and noticing that his father, who had delayed his departure for work to watch Loren pitch, was standing beside the left field foul line, he ran out to inquire what had happened. Adam was scowling. He said: "Roosevelt's dead. And the bastards who infest this community of privilege are ecstatic. They hated him." Then a brief smile twisted his lips. "Wait until they get a taste of Truman."

* * *

Three years later, the exultations and the disappointments of life in wartime Winona had all faded into dreamlike memories. Recollections of excitedly riding the rattling trains with boyhood friends; of being surrounded by the cozy clamor of Wrigley Field, its distinctive brick outfield walls covered with English ivy; of returning, victorious, to the shady streets and quiet affluence of Winona; of stretching out on his bed endlessly studying baseball picture magazines and record books. Such recollections now seemed merely a fantasy. Tocqueville, Texas, had become Loren's new reality.

CHAPTER 7
EXIT DOCTOR K

As the tall weeds beside the highway shriveled in the late afternoon heat, Loren stumbled back and forth between Buzz's truck and a succession of utility poles and fence posts, pounding roofing nails through cardboard posters, of which there seemed to be an endless supply. It was Friday, July 23, the day before the primary election, and Loren was sick of Lyndon Johnson's face.

His mind kept shifting from his labors to speculation about what might happen that night on the other side of Mrs. Kaplan's fan. Leaving for work early that morning, he had seen Dr. K toss his black medical bag and a large leather suitcase into the trunk of his Buick and drive off without a word to his wife, who stood in her bathrobe, expressionless, just inside the front door.

By six-thirty that evening, Loren was in his room, stretched out on his cot listening to "The Lone Ranger." The familiar introduction, "From out of the West came the thundering hoofbeats of the great horse Silver," invoked images of a world in which truth triumphed and scoundrels succumbed, a predictable world in which the masked man would inevitably disarm his quarry with a single silver bullet and answer the villain's complaining cry with the admonition "You're not hurt." Loren took pleasure in the background music that one of his Winona friends had told him was from Franz Liszt's *Les Preludes* and Gioacchino Rossini's *William Tell Overture*, and he wondered whether Tonto, the Lonely Stranger's Faithful Indian Companion, realized what his name meant in Spanish.

At seven, Loren cast a wistful glance through his open window at the twilight outside and picked up a book, A. T. Wright's novel, *Islandia*, in which he was soon engrossed. The hours raced by while the mysterious magic of the volume held him spellbound. At ten-thirty the light went out in his parents' bedroom. The Temple house, except for Loren's own room, was entirely dark. Marking his place near the end of the novel, he rose, blinking his tired eyes, and moved across the room to switch off his bedroom ceiling light and pull down the shade over his window. He peered through a small opening. Nothing.

Keeping the volume low, Loren tuned his radio to one of the four Tocqueville stations, all of which broadcast dance music during the pre-midnight hours. He knew a couple of the bandleaders, Woody Herman and Harry James, by name, but what they produced were not his favorite sounds. Nevertheless, he accepted romantic dance music as next best to classical symphonic or operatic music, even though he detested dancing.

In Winona, Loren's mother had encouraged him to learn to trip the light fantastic, enrolling him at considerable expense in a dance school for junior high schoolers taught by a former Rockette in the basement of the Winona Women's Club. Awkwardly he had stumbled through the prescribed steps, while the wrinkled woman shouted "one, two, three; one, two, three," and he tried to ignore the feel of the flexing muscles in his partner's back underneath his hand, resting tentatively on the soft fabric of her dress. "One, two, three" chanted the instructress, while her burly spouse stood guard, arms folded, at the exit, and a dozen young couples glided over the shiny linoleum floor. Several of the boys, including Loren, were unable to keep their eyes off their shuffling shoes; others (to Loren's chagrin) slid smoothly, limber bodies erect, smiling serenely, their female partners putty in their possessive paws.

One evening the girls had brought box suppers to be auctioned by the dance instructor's husband. The boys had been asked to bid, starting at ten cents, to determine which girls would be their principal partners for the evening. Naturally Loren had forgotten to bring enough money to be competitive. Fingering the change in his pants pocket, he had estimated that, at most, he possessed fifty cents. Not that it mattered, because he had also failed to observe, as the girls entered, which box belonged to each.

Several of the other boys, opportunists, had appeared early and stationed themselves near the entrance. With smug smiles, they had calculated their bids. Loren had felt lost as he stood at the rear of the crowd gathered around the dance teacher and watched the boxed suppers, one by one, find new owners, as boys and girls paired off. Once he had half-raised his hand, but another boy had immediately bid higher and got the box, which proved fortunate when it was revealed that it belonged to a corpulent young lady with a perpetual pout.

Next to be auctioned was a shoe box covered with pink tissue paper and topped with a pink ribbon. At fifteen cents, Loren's was the only bid. When the owner of the goodies emerged from a group of gigglers, he realized his mistake. For his "date" for the evening was to be Margaret Plummer, plain and very shy. Her appearance had at once reminded him of the saying "Boys don't make passes at girls who wear glasses." Together they had gnawed cold drumsticks, sour cole slaw and hard baking powder biscuits, and had drunk orange pop, sitting silently on hard metal folding chairs surrounded by chattering couples. Once Margaret had smiled slightly when he offered his handkerchief to wipe the chicken grease from her slender hands. Her mother, it seemed, had not thought to supply napkins, unless, of course, Margaret had herself prepared the meal.

Loren had been trying to think of something to say when the music on the Victrola began. Belatedly he had realized that he was supposed to ask Margaret to dance. Fervently hoping that someone would cut in, he led her out onto the floor to fox trot. She had seemed very thin. He remembered fearing that if he held her too tightly, she might break. But she had surprised him: she had turned out to be a strong dancer, easily following his awkward steps. But saying nothing.

As the evening progressed, Loren had decided that he was stuck with the loneliest and certainly the most silent girl at the dance. And he realized that she probably considered herself trapped in the same predicament. Resolving to make the best of his situation, he had begun to relax somewhat and let the sound of the music dictate his movements, except when waltzes were supplanted by jitterbug rhythms, at the first notes of which he had led Margaret over to a chair and had gone to fetch her punch and cookies.

During one such break, Willie Walker had beckoned to Loren and whispered "Cum'ere." Willie had been a classmate in sixth grade but had disappeared thereafter into the massive maw of Winona Junior High, only to re-emerge in the dance class. He had a reputation for devilment. Curious to learn what mischief he contemplated, Loren followed him into the boys' cloak room, where three other boys huddled amid the jackets and hats hanging on hooks, awaiting the end of the evening. "What's up," Loren asked.

A boy called "Henry," last name unknown, said: "Now that we've eaten and given the babes a thrill, we're bustin' out."

Puzzled, Loren asked: "How?"

Henry answered by striding over to the cinder block basement wall next to the two toilet stalls and reaching up to unlatch a small window. Shoving it up until he could fasten it to a hook in the ceiling, he summoned Willie to stoop beneath it, after which he climbed upon his accomplice's back and crawled out into the frosty night. Two other boys followed, until Loren and Willie were the only two left. "You're taller than I am," Willie said, "so let me stand on you, and after I get out I'll reach down and haul you through."

Loren hesitated. But the alternative of returning to the dance floor, where he would have to explain what had occurred in the cloak room, was not an attractive one. He bent over and briefly felt Willie's weight on his back. In another moment his companion had made his escape. "Hurry," Willie whispered, extending both hands. Reaching as high as he could, Loren seized them and dug the toes of his shiny shoes into the mortar between the whitewashed cinder blocks as he scrambled upward.

Just then he was startled by a loud shout from the cloak room door. "Hey, kid; whatcha think you're doin'?" It was the voice of the "bruiser" husband of the "mad matron," as the boys called them. Desperately Loren struggled to haul himself through the window before he could be reached from behind, but just as his head and shoulders emerged outside the building he felt two strong hands gripping his ankles, trying to pull him back. Kicking and clinging tightly to Willie and Henry, who had gleefully joined in the tug of war, Loren heard a cry of "Shee-it!" from below, as one foot pulled free, and several seconds later the other one was also released, but only because the shoe that had encased it had come off in the grip of the cursing consort, who held it like a trophy as he rose from a seated position on the floor.

Following the other boys out into the late evening silence, Loren despondently limped along cold concrete sidewalks, his unshod foot rapidly becoming numb. Henry recommended that they visit their school to kill some time before going home. After entering the gym through an unlocked door, they found a basketball underneath some bleacher seats and played two on three in their stocking feet until Willie, looking at his watch, said: "The dance must be over by now. Time to go."

It was past eleven when Loren tiptoed through the Temple front door. He almost succeeded in sneaking undiscovered up the stairs, but a creaking step was his undoing. "Loren," his mother called from the back bedroom. "Is that you?"

"Yes, Mom," he answered half-heartedly.

Emerging into the hallway clad in her robe, Nan asked: "How was the dance, dear?"

"Just fine."

"Did you have a good time?"

"Pretty much," he muttered.

"Well, you'd better take this upstairs with you," she said, withdrawing from behind her back his missing shoe.

Loren slowly descended to the hallway and relieved her of the offending object, unable to look her in the eye. His mother said nothing more, but he felt her disapproval as he fled back up the stairs to bed.

* * *

A light flashing through Loren's Tocqueville bedroom window suddenly restored reality. Feeling for the camera at his bedside, he peered out. A false alarm. Must have been a passing car. Mrs. Kaplan's bedroom remained dark.

Only three radio stations were still on the air. One was broadcasting music from a movie that featured Ginger Rogers, who reminded Loren of his next door neighbor. Also in the same movie was Fred Astaire. Now, *there* was an entrepreneur. Loren shuddered as he recalled his own association with the famed male dancer. After his mother had withdrawn him from the Winona dancing school (or he had been expelled; he had never discovered which), she had dressed him in a new mustard-colored sports jacket and driven him, protesting, to a nearby university town, in which she located a Fred Astaire dance studio. Here Loren was to be taught by qualified professionals how to dance. His strong-willed mother had made up her mind. She knew what was required to survive in Winona society.

While Nan waited patiently in the anteroom, Loren followed a young woman named Ellen, a college student, into a small room with a single window, a phonograph, and an alarm clock, which the instructor set to go off in thirty minutes.

The music was a fox trot, which Loren thought he knew how to do. It quickly became apparent, however, that his previous instruction had been cursory, and that Ellen had more sophisticated moves in mind. One of these involved bending her backward, with only one of his arms keeping her from falling to the floor. As she coaxed him to try this gambit, assuring him that she trusted him to hold her safely, she called him "handsome" and complimented him on his strength.

She was very pretty, with regular features, shoulder-length brown hair, sparkling green eyes, and a dazzling smile. As they danced, Loren timidly, Ellen confidently, she hummed to the sound of the music and the room seemed to start spinning. When she threw herself backwards onto his left arm, her eyes closed, a vein had throbbed in her creamy neck and her breasts bulged against her tight wool sweater.

Loren felt his male member swelling. Stop, he commanded. Don't, he pleaded. In vain. Worried that she would look down at the front of his trousers, he moved closer to her as they continued to dance. But feeling her torso pressing lightly against him only made matters worse. "Now you're getting it!" she exclaimed. Little did she know.

The music stopped. The record had finished playing. What to do? Loren's stiff shaft had begun to press so tightly against his pants that he feared that his fly would pop open. At any moment she might see it. Then what? A snicker? A cry of revulsion? A call for help?

As Ellen turned to move the phonograph needle back to the beginning of the record, Loren quickly stepped over to the window, pretending to be fascinated by something down in the street, two stories below. He felt her close behind him. "Come and dance," she said.

Wordlessly, he shook his head. His mouth was dry and he felt feverish.

"What's wrong?" she asked. "Are you all right?"

Again Loren shook his head. He had no idea what to say or do... At this moment the alarm clock buzzed. Hallelujah! As Ellen went to turn off the alarm, he slid past her and out the door into a hallway, at the end of which was a men's room. Inside, he consumed almost ten minutes shrinking his misbehaving appendage down to civilized size.

In the waiting room he encountered his worried mother. "Are you all right, dear?" she inquired. "The young lady said you seemed suddenly sick."

"It was nothing," Loren declared. "Just an upset stomach. I'm fine now."

"In that case, let's go home. I've reserved this same time for the next two Saturdays. Is that all right with you, dear?"

Loren thought: no way I'm coming back here. But it was not the time to argue about it. So he said: "You're th' boss, Mom." Later he would think of a reason not to return.

His father, as usual, had the final word, which was what Loren had hoped would happen. Asked by his son to intervene, he said: "Why does the boy need to learn all those fancy dances? Master one today; it's out of fashion tomorrow. A few of the basics, which he says he already knows, should be enough."

Nan's voice had been sugary sweet. "And he'll turn out to be a hit in society, just like his Dad." She awaited her husband's reaction, but Adam seemed to miss the sarcasm. She then asked: "By the way, darling, do you know why everyone calls Fred Astaire?"

From behind his paper, Adam replied: "Because that's his name."

"No dear. Because he has so many steps."

Lying on his cot in the hot bedroom of his new Tocqueville home, Loren laughed out loud as he pictured his father's face, watching his wife march, stiff-backed, into her Winona kitchen. A mixture of chagrin and pride had flashed across Adam's features. A complicated thing, marriage, thought Loren.

*   *   *

A faint glow on his window shade signaled that a light had been switched on in the bedroom next door. Peeking, he could see through Mrs. K's whirling window fan to the bottom half of her bed. Several maddening glimpses informed him that the occupant was moving around the room in her panties and brassiere. She seemed to be changing the sheets and pillow cases.

He reached over to his bedside table for his camera, almost knocking it onto the floor in his eagerness to begin taking pictures. He reminded himself that restraint was required, because the roll of film had room for only eight shots. He had to make every one count.

To provide clarity he had previously removed his window screen. Now, as he steadied his camera on the sill, he felt a sharp prick on one shoulder. Unable to resist slapping the mosquito, he hoped that the noise of the window fan next door would drown out the sound. Then he realized that he now had unimpeded access to the outdoors. Hanging his camera by its strap around his neck, he hoisted himself over the window sill and dropped to the ground. It took only a moment for him to wedge himself through a small gap in the privet hedge that divided the two properties, suffering several scratches in the process. Creeping across the Kaplan driveway, he shrank into the shadows directly under Mrs. K's window. Now, with any luck, he could both see and hear.

The first sound he heard was that of the opening and closing of a door. Mrs. K apparently heard it too, because a slight smile spread over her face and she turned toward the bedroom door, reached behind her back, and dropped her brassiere onto the floor. Loren reflexively snapped the shutter of his camera, not only once but twice, only afterwards thinking: no, wait for the fireworks.

Abruptly, the expression on Mrs. K's face changed from one of welcome to one of loathing. Following the direction of her stare, Loren saw her husband standing naked in the doorway, sneering malevolently, his jutting male member pointing directly at his surprised spouse. "Don't come near me, yew repulsive animal," she shouted, so loudly that Loren flinched.

Dr. K's reply was unintelligible, but it looked to Loren as if he had mouthed the word "bitch," as he tried to push his resisting consort onto the bed. He grimaced as she slapped him hard across the face, and then he hit her so hard with his fist that she fell back, whimpering, onto the mattress, out of Loren's view.

The action had taken place so suddenly and had been so shocking that he had neglected to record any of it on film. Stupid. Now, what? Some sort of struggle was going on: he could hear sounds of sobbing and what might have been grunting and cursing. Loren wondered, should he try to intervene? Was there anything wrong with a man forcing himself on his wife? He did not know the rules of marital behavior.

While Loren dithered, Dr. K apparently finished what he had intended to do and reappeared at the foot of the bed, his porcine body red from his exertions and shining with perspiration. As he exited, Loren saw what looked like ten vertical scarlet streaks down the middle of his back. Behind him, his wife yelled: "Greaseball, Ah'll kill yew fer this!"

Loren managed two quick clicks of his camera's shutter as Dr. K turned in the hall to direct an obscene gesture at his wife. Mrs. K was once again in full view, her damp red hair pasted to her forehead, her mouth twisted into a snarl, and her fingers curved like claws. Loren noticed that she was a redhead all the way. Then she slammed the bedroom door with a report like a gunshot and leaned against it, tears streaking her cheeks.

Suddenly Loren realized that what he was doing was wrong. Ashamed, he turned away from Mrs. K's window. It was time to scramble back to his room. Anyway, the show appeared over for the current evening. On impulse, however, he took one last look, and was startled by what he now saw.

The bedroom light was now off, but the door, once again open, offered some slight illumination. Mrs. K was lying on the bed. Seated beside her was someone who was not Dr. K. Although Loren could not see the face, he was positive that this was the same visitor he had seen welcomed to Mrs. K's bedroom two weeks earlier. On neither occasion had Loren heard any sounds coming from an automobile or from a doorbell or a knocker. Here was someone who had probably come on foot and who had easy access.

Mrs. K was still sobbing. There was something strange about her visitor, who was trying to comfort her. It was not the clothing: a bulky sweatshirt with ragged sleeves, blue jean shorts, and sockless sneakers. Ha! He had it! The intruder's muscular brown legs were smooth, as if shaved. Loren recalled how some of his high school teammates had kept their legs free of hair to avoid the pain that would result from ripping off several feet of adhesive tape after every game and practice session. Mrs. K's companion must be an athlete.

As the visitor followed Mrs. K out of the bedroom, one consoling arm hugging her shoulders, Loren snapped a quick picture. Intent on getting it, he caught only a blurry glimpse of the visitor's face in the ground glass screen of his camera, but he thought that the film might well have captured the countenances of both Mrs. K and her friend, both of whom were now, Loren apprehended, going to confront Dr. K.

What happened next, however, was bewildering. Suddenly all of the lights in the Kaplan house blinked out, and the window fan gradually slowed and stopped. Loren could hear nothing; nor could he now see inside. Nevertheless, after a few minutes the back door creaked open and, and from his position crouched in the shadows beside the house, Loren could dimly discern two figures dragging something through the darkness of the back yard. As they pulled their burden across the turf, he heard Mrs. K say: "Jus' uh little further an' we'll be ridda this bastard." Into the open garage they hauled what Loren now knew was Dr. K. One of them snapped on a ceiling light, which the other instantly jumped to extinguish, but not before Loren had, with two quick clicks of his camera, filmed the entire tableau: two furtive figures and, lying on the concrete floor between them, the limp form of Dr. K.

To get a clear shot he had ventured dangerously close to the back of the house, which meant that if any light, like the headlights of a passing car, should shine behind him, he could easily be seen from the garage. Realizing this, he sank back into the shadows just as Mrs. K returned to the house, passing within a few feet of where Loren lurked. Soon she re-emerged with what looked like a coil of heavy rope, which she took to the garage. It was too dark for Loren to make out what was happening inside, but something strange was occurring. He heard Mrs. K say "Ouch;" and "Hol' tight, while Ah cut it" and "Oh, mah poor hans." But he heard no sound at all from her visitor.

Shortly thereafter, two indistinct figures returned to the darkened house, in which, after several minutes, lights came on and the bedroom window fan began once more to revolve.

When Mrs. K re-entered her bedroom, she was alone. She carried a short length of hemp rope, which she stuffed into her clothes closet. She then turned off the light. All was quiet. Her visitor had vanished.

Unable to remember how many photographs he had taken, and thus whether he had already used up his allocation of eight shots, Loren had nevertheless clicked Mrs. K holding the snake-like rope before it disappeared from view. The next step would be to develop and print the pictures in the Temple bathroom, after everyone else in the family had gone to bed. This was the best he could do without a regular darkroom. Certainly these were not pictures that should be entrusted to a drug store or a photo shop.

Keeping the very existence of these photos a secret, he thought, might be vital to his own welfare. For it was likely that he had managed to acquire evidence that would implicate two people in a crime of some kind. Maybe murder. After returning to his room, he removed the small roll of film from the back of his camera and shoved it into the top drawer of his bureau behind his underwear.

He yawned. He was very tired.

* * *

Loren slept fitfully the rest of that night, repeatedly awakened by disturbing dreams. Twice he padded into the bathroom to empty his bladder, the second time at sunrise. He felt woozy. Rubbing his crusted eyelashes brought tears to his cheeks, which he wiped with the back of his hand.

Fresh air, he thought, that's what I need. Silently, he slipped out the back door in order not to awaken the other family members and found himself drawn in the dim dawn to the hedge between the Temple and Kaplan back yards. He had to see what was in the garage next door. Careful not to be visible from the Kaplan house, he pulled some privet branches apart so that he could see into a side window of the Kaplan garage. And there it was—the scene created the night before by Mrs. K and her mysterious visitor—one that Loren had hoped would turn out to have been merely a nightmare. Instead there appeared before him a grisly spectacle that made him momentarily sick.

The naked corpse of Dr. Kaplan hung stiff and silent, like the carcass of a dead hog. A mass of twisted hemp bulging from the left side of his neck like a huge goiter had forced his head forward until his chin almost touched his hairy chest. His swollen tongue protruded pinkly from lavender lips; and his eyes seemed to stare blankly back at Loren, who shrank from the sight.

Forcing himself closely to scrutinize the scene, Loren observed that underneath Dr. Kaplan's fat feet dangling above the concrete floor a rusty metal bucket rested on its deeply dented side and had apparently been positioned to suggest that he had hanged himself.

As Loren fled from the fearful but fascinating sight, he noticed that a faint trail had been scraped in the dew that still lingered on the Kaplan's lawn, signifying that some heavy object had been dragged over the turf. Taking refuge in his room, he considered whether to tell his parents what he had seen. His father would of course immediately telephone the police, who would ask questions. His mother could always tell when Loren was not telling the truth, even if others could not. The entire situation was so threatening that he decided to keep his own part in it secret. Let the proper officials deal with it.

* * *

Later that morning, while Loren was in his driveway throwing a baseball back and forth with Tommy, a strident scream sounded from next door. "What in the world was that?" exclaimed Tommy.

"Probably nothing to worry about," said Loren. "Mrs. Kaplan may have encountered a mouse in her flower bed. Or perhaps a snake."

"Boy, she sure yells loud," said the younger boy. "Made the hair stand up on..."

"It's your turn to pitch," interrupted Loren. "Here, hand me the catcher's mitt. And try not to bounce your curve ball. My shins are bruised enough already."

Two police cars soon arrived next door. The boys ran over to the hedge to investigate. Red roof lights flashed, radios cackled, and three uniformed officers stood with a tearful Mrs. Kaplan at the entrance to the garage, looking at the body. Tommy ran to fetch Adam.

By the time the boys had followed their father next door, one of the policemen, holding a pencil and small notebook, was trying to make sense out of what a sobbing Mrs. Kaplan, wearing a short bathrobe over some kind of nightgown and seated in a lawn chair, was trying to tell him. When she shifted her position and re-crossed her bare legs, the cop dropped his pencil on the flagstones, which broke off its lead point, causing him to ask sheepishly if anyone had a pen knife.

A young man, his wrinkled suit coat open and his tie loosened, was closely scrutinizing the rope around Dr. Kaplan's neck, contemplatively running his fingers over the knot. Taking several steps backward, he raised a small camera, which flashed brightly as he took a picture. He followed with a photo of that portion of the garage floor on which rested the overturned bucket. With a slight smile of satisfaction, he headed for the new widow, now being consoled by a couple of solicitous policemen, one of whom was trying to look down the front of her robe.

"Gawd!" said Tommy. "That's the awfulest thing I ever saw. He's dead, isn't he?"

"Looks like it," replied Loren. He had noticed that the dew had evaporated from the grass in the Kaplan's back yard, but that there seemed to be still a few bent blades, if one looked very closely. He thought he saw the civilian who had just emerged from the garage stare briefly at the ground, as if he, too, was aware that it offered enlightenment. "Let's get outa here," he said.

It was lunchtime. Loren was not hungry, but he knew his mother would ask questions if he declined to eat. While he and Tommy had sandwiches, they told Nan what they had seen next door. "That poor woman!" she exclaimed. "I must go over at once." First visiting the bathroom to check her makeup, and then making a quick phone call to Mrs. Mouton, she was soon out the door.

Soon Mrs. Mouton came fluttering past the kitchen window, heading for the Kaplans.

* * *

The boys were still seated at the kitchen table, Tommy speculating about the meaning of the scene next door and Loren maintaining a nervous silence, when their father appeared in the driveway, accompanied by the fellow they had seen in the garage examining the body. Adam introduced him as Mr. Mouton, an assistant district attorney.

"Emile," said the stranger, smiling. "Ah grew up nex' door. Mama says good t'ings 'bout yew people." His handshake was firm and he looked directly into Loren's eyes as if they were windows into his mind.

"Ah'd like t' ask yew boys uh few questions," he said. "Any objections?"

"No," said Loren and Tommy together.

"Have yew seen or heard anyt'ing that would clarify whut happened las' night?"

The brothers considered the question. "I can't think of anything," said Tommy, "except..."

"Yes?" encouraged Mr. Mouton.

"Well, this fellow who drops off my newspapers—I have to deliver them early in the morning—once told me to stay away from Dr. Kaplan. When I asked him why, all he would tell me was that he liked young boys, whatever that meant."

"Whut's de name of yore fren?" asked Mr. Mouton.

"Billy. I don't know his last name, but the people down at the *Gazette* can probably tell you."

"Loren, whut 'bout yew? Yore father says dat yew've been ovah dare once or twice t' help wit' yardwork."

Loren realized that he would be unable to conceal the incident about which his mother, at least, knew—that of having been groped by the dead doctor. Briefly, eyes on the ground, he related that portion of his experiences at the Kaplan's, while Mr. Mouton took notes, and Adam seethed, as he apparently obtained his first knowledge of the matter.

"An' dat's all?"

"Yes," said Loren.

"Did yew evah see or heah de two Kaplans havin' some kinda dispute?"

"Not really... They did seem kind of distant... cold, with each other. Not like my parents."

"Or mine," said Mr. Mouton. "Thank yew, boys. Whut yew've tol' me confirms whut Ah've already heard elsewhar an' gives us an obvious motive fer Dr. Kaplan's death." Turning to Adam, he added: "We been gettin' information at de D. A.'s office dat th' late doctor had uh very bad habit. Unfortunately, we've had trouble findin' people willin' t' testify 'gainst 'im in court. Recently uh Mr. Sisti—dis is confidential—came forward; an' wit' his assistance—he's uh persuasive individual—we put t'gether uh strong case. Uh gran' jury indicted Dr. Kaplan jus' tree days ago. He may have learned of de indictment, although de proceedings were secret an' we had not yet officially informed 'im 'bout it."

"What would have happened to the bastard?" asked Adam.

Mouton frowned. "If convicted, he wudda lost his license t' practice medicine. An' he mighta had t' spend time in prison, although that wudda been up t' de judge." He paused, and then said: "Ah s'pose yew knew his marriage wuz on de rocks?"

"I didn't know," asserted Adam. And Nan, who along with Mrs. Mouton had just joined them, shook her head as well. But Mrs. Mouton burbled: "Oh, sure." She patted her son fondly on the shoulder. "You mus' admit, Emile, that yew heard it fust from me." (Emile let slip an embarrassed grin.) "An' Ah heard it," she continued, "from uh lady who's married t' dat poor woman's lawyer..."

Loren interrupted: "Do you mean *she* was planning to divorce *him*?"

Mrs. Mouton seemed surprised at his question. "Well, she did only marry 'im fer his money. Ah guess she finally decided dat it wasn' worth it. An' dat she could git alimony. Ah knew dare wuz somethin' wrong wit' dat marriage," she said smugly, "when Ah discovered dat they slept in separate bedrooms. An' he wuz frequently gone on weekends an' never took 'er wid 'im."

"So," Adam ruminated aloud, "the jerk was about to be prosecuted, which would have cost him his medical practice and probably put him in prison, and his wife was about to divorce him... Sounds like he had enough problems to motivate him to commit suicide." He turned toward Emile. "Is that the way you see it?"

Looking uncomfortable, Mouton said: "Not quite. It might look dat way. But somethin' else is involved, somethin' dat Ah'm not at liberty t' divulge."

"Something else? What could that be?"

"All Ah kin say is dat de Kaplans had some connections in New Orleans, whar dey lived afore dey moved t' Tocqueville. Dose relationships are of great interest t' certain law enforcement people."

"Do you mean someone might have killed him?" asked Adam incredulously.

"Dare are circumstances, an' some inconsistencies...," Mouton began. Then he shook his head. "Ah can't tell yew anyting' else at dis time."

"How much of this can we reveal in the *Endeavor*?"

"None of it," said Mouton sharply. "Ah'm givin' yew dis information fer background only. Any publicity now might jeopardize our continuin' investigation. Yew kin print dat Dr. Kaplan wuz foun' dead at home an' dat de cause of death is as yet undetermined. Yew kin suggest dat suicide is uh possibility. Beyond dat Ah urge yew not t' go. Ah'll let yew know immediately when we turn up anyt'ing else yew kin print. O. K?"

"All right," replied Adam. "I'll have my best reporter make a few discreet inquiries, strictly secret, and we'll share what we find."

"Be careful," warned Mr. Mouton. "Dare are people involved who kin git purty rough." He turned to Loren and Tommy. "Nice t' meet yew boys. Miz Temple, its been uh pleasure." Excusing himself, he returned to the Kaplan house, accompanied by his mother, who was chattering non-stop, as she tried to match his long strides.

"He seems nice," said Nan. "And competent."

"Yes," agreed Adam. "Also ambitious. The talk at the office is that Emile Mouton wants to be the next district attorney. There will be an election in two years and already stories are floating around that the incumbent is too cozy with certain corrupt characters and needs to be replaced. 'Emile's for real.' That's the slogan some of the young lawyers and business people are whispering. I'm not surprised that he is personally investigating Dr. Kaplan's death, given what he just hinted about the man, but I can't see any reason to call it murder."

For the rest of the day Loren, anxious not to draw any attention to himself, refrained from leaving the house. He kept thinking that Emile Mouton's reference to "inconsistencies" might well have been to his own testimony. Trying to recall what he had said, he could not remember anything that would have caused suspicion. Perhaps Mrs. Kaplan had said something.

Or it could have been a reference to something that Emile Mouton had seen in the garage. Indeed, there were aspects of the ghastly scene that Loren himself realized did not jibe with a verdict of suicide. Moreover, if Dr. K really wanted to kill himself, why would he do it by hanging, when a gunshot would probably have been quicker and cleaner? And why strip off all his clothes to do it? If nudity was meant to signify something, why leave his clothes inside the house? Such thoughts, Loren felt sure, had crossed Emile Mouton's mind.

* * *

That evening was a troubled time for all four Temples. Tommy kept asking his father what he thought about the mess next door. Adam kept answering that he thought it best to leave the matter to the authorities. Just don't worry about it. And Nan sat rigidly in an ancient wooden rocker, its unpadded rattan seat and slatted back offering minimal comfort, and stared into space. Occasionally she directed a troubled glance at her oldest son, who pretended to be deeply engrossed in reading a book. He had become aware some time ago that his mother only sat in that particular chair when she was upset. It was a special piece of furniture, having crossed the great plains a century ago in a covered wagon. In it Loren's great grandmother had rocked his infant grandmother, who had sat in it years later holding his mother. And she in her turn had cuddled her two boy babies in that same rocker, while she soothed them to sleep. The chair was one of two cherished remnants of pioneer days in Utah; the other being an old mantel clock which now, in the absence of a fireplace, sat by itself on a small sideboard in the dining room. It still worked. From where Loren sat he could see the pendulum moving back and forth, and every quarter hour hear the clock chime. As it did now. Ten chimes. With a sigh, Loren said good night and went to bed, but not immediately to sleep.

CHAPTER 8
SUNDAY AT STANLEY

When Loren entered the kitchen early on Sunday, Adam was already dipping buttered toast into soft-boiled eggs and sipping hot coffee. Clicking his cup on the porcelain table top, he stabbed at his newspaper with an index finger and announced: "Looks like your man managed a runoff."

Loren had been so engrossed in his predicament involving the late Dr. Kaplan that he had almost forgotten that the Texas Democratic party primary had been held Saturday. His continuing employment by Sisti and Sampson doubtless depended upon the outcome. Eagerly he reached for the front section of the *Gazette* which his father passed across the table. There he read that Lyndon Johnson ha d received slightly over four hundred thousand votes for United States senator, only thirty-four per cent of the ballots cast, but enough for a second-place finish. Over four hundred and seventy-five thousand votes had gone to ex-governor Stevenson, who had thereby captured a full forty per cent of the total; short, however, of the fifty per cent needed for the nomination. George Peddy, a Houston attorney with extensive family connections in East Texas, had garnered over two hundred and thirty-five thousand votes, a surprisingly large twenty per cent of all ballots cast, with approximately eighty-three thousand votes scattered among the remaining eight candidates.

The primary runoff, scheduled for August 28, would pit Johnson against Stevenson, with most of Peddy's backers expected to support the former governor. Johnson's chance of winning, therefore, looked almost hopeless. Nevertheless, Loren could now count on another month of campaigning and another two hundred dollars in his pocket, by far the most lucrative summer employment he could imagine being offered to a guy of his age.

At seven-fifteen he finished eating his oatmeal and went to his room to fetch the worn baseball uniform that he had liberated from Winona Country Day School, when it had become apparent at the end of the school year that he would not be returning in September. He checked once more to reassure himself that his spiked shoes and fielder's glove, shining from a fresh application of Neet's Foot oil, were also inside his old brown valise. Lastly, he reached under his cot for the Louisville Slugger.

During the war years, as he was learning the game of baseball on the playfields of Winona, it had been impossible to buy bats of ash or hickory to replace those broken or lost. Coaches at the junior high school and later at Winona CDS had jealously guarded their small supplies of bats and had expressed extreme displeasure if anybody broke one. Great care had been taken to instruct each player on the necessity of keeping the maker's trademark, etched into the barrel of each warclub, out of the paths of pitches, as this was supposed to be the weak area, where breakage was most likely.

At the junior high school Loren had registered for a course in wood shop solely to obtain an opportunity, once the requisite bird houses and book ends had been constructed, to get instruction on how to use a wood lathe. He then shaped a baseball bat out of a billet of oak, the only hardwood available at the time. The heavy stick had held up well, even though any collision with horsehide resulted in a hollow thunk, like an automobile tire landing in a pothole, rather than the desired crack, like the noise of a.22 rifle.

As soon as the war was over, Loren had begun going without school lunches in order to save up enough money to buy himself a Louisville Slugger. Once he had obtained a Stan Hack model, he firmly rejected all requests from teammates to try it out in practices, even in games. It had repaid his devoted guardianship with base hits, enough to maintain a batting average well above.300 for each of his three years on the Winona CDS varsity squad. Nevertheless, he had not become a first-stringer at second base until his freshman year was half over, when he replaced an ex-soldier who had been unable to recover his prewar skills.

Although the seasons had been short (twice contests had been cancelled in April because of snow), the Winona CDS baseball team had been able to travel on weekends as far as Detroit, St. Louis, Milwaukee, and Indianapolis to play similar small schools. Loren had enjoyed the comradeship of his teammates on the train trips and especially being the center of attention when pitching or at bat.

The mind games he played with opposing batters when on the mound had been intriguing, but it was from batting that he derived the most pleasure. Most of his blows were soft liners into the open spaces in right field, in emulation of his hero Hack, also an opposite-field hitter. But, Loren had also learned, the lefty-hitting Cub third baseman had a trick, when opposing outfielders played him as exclusively a slap hitter to left field, of waiting patiently until he got an inside fast ball, which he would then smack on a line over the head of the first baseman into the right field corner. By the time the right fielder had reached the ball resting against the ivy at the bottom of the wall, and returned it to the infield, Smilin' Stan would be perched on third base.

* * *

Loren had been instructed by Bitsy to report to Davis's drug store across the street from Southside High School by eight o'clock. He entered the building through a rusty screen door that slammed shut behind him, causing five men seated around a table at the rear of a long room to turn their heads and stare. They were all smoking cigarettes, and a blue haze hung over their table.

The largest member of the group heaved himself out of his chair and lumbered forward, his right hand outstretched. With a flaccid grip he introduced himself. "A'm Fats," he said. "Th' manager of this sorry crew. These guys call themselves ballplayers." Although they did not get up when they shook hands, Loren's new teammates seemed friendly enough. According to Fats, they were, successively, "Fido," "Bobo," "Duke," and "Masher." The latter, a brawny, big-bottomed character who reminded Loren of pictures of Lou Gehrig, the Pride of the Yankees, reached for a chair next to a nearby table and dragged it over to a space next to him. "Have uh seat, kid," he said. "Fats done tole us yew played ball up nawth."

"A little," said Loren, trying not to appear timid. "Three years high school. Infield. Outfield. Pitched some."

"Say, we kin use 'nother pitcher," said Fido, a squat little fellow with a heavily freckled face and a crew cut.

"Yeah," agreed Duke, tall and handsome, with a grin like a swagger. "Those Stanley Injuns gonna whip our asses if'n we don' git someone who kin trow somethin' other than fassballs." He coughed and blew cigarette smoke out of his nostrils. "Whut kinda curve do yew trow, kid?"

"A drop, mostly," said Loren. "My regular curve is pretty much a roundhouse. Sometimes hitters back away."

"Use th' drop," advised the swarthy one called Bobo. "We ain't gonna see any better hittin' th' rest of this summer than those fellas from th' reservation. They'll tee off on uh slow curve an' lose it. Man, kin them kemosabies hit!"

"Take it from wun who knows," declared Fats. "Bobo hit ovah six hundred during his yeah at Southside High."

Six hundred! Loren looked over at Bobo, who had resumed chatting with Masher. Both men appeared past thirty. Why had Bobo played only one year in high school? Now that they were no longer in school, what did he and the others do for a living? Bobo was peculiar-looking: almost ape-like, with extra long arms, huge hairy hands, beady black eyes, and a bullet-like head with a receding hairline. His face was etched with creases, from the fine lines around his eyes, to broad canyons in his cheeks. Below a bull neck, thick muscles in his shoulders rippled powerfully underneath a thin cotton jersey. Oddly, he talked out of one side of his mouth and slightly slurred his words, so that he was not easy to understand.

Loren had begun to relax, as the conversation shifted away from him, when three additional team members arrived. Again, Fats did the introducing. "This heah's our new outfielder an' pitcher, Loren Temple," he said. "Bitsy said t' give 'im uh tryout. He played ball up nawth, but he wuz born uh southerner, so he ain't no commie." Loren couldn't tell if Fats was joking. "Loren, th' tall one who luks lak uh Texas ranger is A. C. Doucet." Fats pronounced the name as 'Doo-say.' "Th' guy who's 'mos' as fat as me is Ham. Las', an' leas', too, is Slick: watch out fer him. He's alluz makin' jokes, when he ain't chasin' wimen, or tryin' t' find his way aroun' left field."

A slender fellow with an ingratiating smile, Slick had a firm handshake. "Yew mus' feel uh li'l lost," he observed, "havin' t' meet so many strange characters all at wunct. An' th' mor' yew git t' know 'em, th' stranger they git."

"Aw cum on, Slick," protested, rosy-cheeked Ham. "We're great guys. Even yew, sometimes."

Throwing a right-handed punch that stopped just short of Ham's bulbous red nose, Slick said: "Gimme a cig." Promptly receiving a cigarette and a light, he turned his attention to the nearby lunch counter, where a frowsy woman in a dirty apron was mopping up some spills. When she turned her back, two forgotten curlers were seen protruding from her frizzy hair. A tight skirt stretched across her massive buttocks.

Nodding in her direction, Slick addressed Loren: "Yew wan' anythin' t' eat?"

"No thanks," replied Loren. "I had breakfast before I left home."

"Hey Ruby," shouted Slick. "Is th' coffee hot?"

"Yeah," she muttered. Lifting a dented metal pot from the stovetop, she sloshed some steamy black liquid into a plain white cup. "Yew wan' long or short sweetnin'?" she inquired.

"Ah believe Ah'll take short," said Slick.

As Loren watched, fascinated, Ruby picked up a pitcher of what looked like molasses and poured a sticky dollop into Slick's coffee. Then, setting the cup before him, she licked the spout of the pitcher with her pink tongue before setting it back on the counter. Unconcerned, Slick sipped the dense brew and smoked his cigarette. When the glowing tip had receded almost to his lips, he stuck it in his coffee to put it out and then laid it on the table, afterwards continuing to sip from his cup.

"Whar's mah eggs?" shouted Ham. "Mine, too," demanded A. C.

Ruby glowered. She broke a half-dozen eggs onto a griddle on which bacon already sizzled, and something that looked like patties of Cream O' Wheat were beginning to brown at the edges. As the eggs solidified, she grabbed a spatula and slammed a large cockroach that had made the mistake of crawling too close. Then she used the utensil to shovel the bacon, eggs, and patties onto two large plates, which she brought over and set down before Ham and A. C. "Ah made yore grits th' way yew like 'em," she said proudly. "Nice an' crisp 'roun' th' edges."

"Thanks, Ruby," said Ham. "Yore uh good ol' gal."

Ruby beamed.

"Hey, guys," exclaimed Fats. "Ah think th' others jus' drove up outside. Whut say we git uh move on? Th' game starts at two. If'n we wanna git in any battin' practice, we'd better git goin'."

"O.K., O.K.," said A. C., his mouth full of bacon and grits. "Keep yore shirt on. We'll be through in five minutes."

Chairs began to scrape on the linoleum floor, as the Scorpions fumbled for their wallets. "S'long, Ruby," yelled Ham. "See yew nex' Sunday."

Outside, several other players waited in an old DeSoto. They greeted those emerging from the drug store with friendly jeers and suggestions that they "git th' lead out."

"Yew kin ride wit' us," said Fats to Loren. "Duke's got room. We'll be leadin' th' way." Puffing, he heaved himself into the back seat of a decrepit white Nash convertible that stood, top down, parked halfway up on the sidewalk. Dropping his bat and valise into the open trunk, Loren found himself a place next to Fats, while Slick slipped into the front seat next to Duke, who had already started the engine with a loud roar that revealed a defective muffler. In a moment they were on their way out of town, a caravan of four vehicles headed for the Timberland highway and a journey, Loren guessed, of about three hours before they reached Stanley, their destination.

*   *   *

On the open road, Loren observed, Duke liked to drive seventy miles an hour, beating time on the steering wheel to the wail of country music. He wore a white t-shirt with the arms cut off, so that Loren could see tufts of blonde hair protruding from his armpits. Slick was perusing the sports section of the *Gazette*, and Fats was writing in the pages of a black looseleaf notebook in which he had inserted pages of printed advertisements for plumbing supplies. Noticing Loren's curious stare, he said: "That's whut Ah do weekdays—sell this stuff. Travel all ovah East Texas an' Southwest Looseeana. Visit retailers an' contractors an' take their orders back t' Tocqueville, where they git filled in uh day or two. Travelin' th' way Ah do, Ah kin contact th' local semipro people an' schedule games fer th' Scorpions. We're booked fer every weekend in August, includin' one double-header."

In the front seat Slick lowered his paper. "Say, Yank," he said, "kin yew tell me whut uh man duz standin' up, uh woman duz sittin' down, an' uh dawg duz wit one leg raised?"

"Pisses?" said Loren, uncomfortably.

"Naw," replied Slick, triumphantly. "Shakes han's."

Duke turned halfway around to grin at Loren. "Ain't Slick sumptin'?"

"Watch out!" yelled Fats. Speeding over a rise in the road, they were about to rear-end an ancient pickup truck driven by an old Negro man. In the back of the truck, which couldn't have been moving at more than fifteen miles an hour, a huge pig thrust its nose into scattered straw.

Duke clutched the glass knob containing a picture of a naked girl that was attached to his steering wheel and spun it to the left, barely in time to wrench the convertible, rocking, tires screeching, across the yellow centerline, missing the pickup by inches. A small statuette tore loose from the top of the dashboard and fell onto the floor. Duke blasted the horn twice as he pulled back into the proper lane. Hauling himself out of Fats's lap, Loren looked back to see the old pig hauler jabbing his middle finger in the air and shouting something at them. Then a curve in the road carried them out of sight.

"Damn!" said Slick, retrieving the Saint Christopher statuette from between his feet and sticking it back in place. "That ol' sonuffabitch gonna git that pig killed."

Loren was sweating profusely. "That was close," he whispered to Fats.

"Don' worry," replied the big man, with a nervous laugh. "Duke may drive fas', but we ain't crashed yet. By th' way, have yew heared 'bout Clarence, th' big fella who lives uh mile or two up ahead?"

"Who?"

"Clarence. Tallest fella in th' world. Certified. Some say he's ovah thirteen feet high. Ah imagine we'll git uh look at him when we go by. He's hard t' miss."

"Thirteen feet? That's difficult to believe. I'd like to see someone that big."

"We'll be thar in uh minute."

Roaring over another hill, they approached what looked like a narrow ridge extending across their path but which Loren quickly recognized as a railroad right-of-way. A dark opening through it marked the path of the highway.

"Thar he is!" yelled Slick and Fats simultaneously. And, as Loren's eyes searched, they fastened upon a large sign located on top of the underpass, reading "Clearance, Thirteen Feet, Four Inches." "Oh, no," he groaned, as all three teammates guffawed.

"Good ol' Clarence," said Fats. "Ah heah he's got cousins up nawth."

"Yes," retorted Loren, "but they're even taller, because everything up north, they say, is bigger and better, including the ballplayers."

Fortunately, the others laughed. Slick said: "We'll see 'bout that. Yew yankees may think yore Indians in Cleveland are hot stuff, but wait till yew play ours. All Stanley Injuns do is sit 'roun' in gubment housin' an' drink rotgut whiskey an' gorge themselves on fatty food. An' git big. It's uh good thang we're playin' them in baseball an' not football."

I can hardly wait, thought Loren.

North of Tocqueville, the Scorpion caravan entered the dense forest of the Big Woods, an area, according to Fats, still not thoroughly explored, even by hunters and Indians. On a winding road, the four cars slowed down considerably as they sped through shadows cast by loblolly and long-leaf pines, swamp oaks, beech, ash, hickory, silver maple, magnolia, and sweet gum trees, identified one by one for Loren by his back seat companion, who knew them all. The big man also pointed out the persimmon, mulberry, bay, wild plum and dogwood trees growing under the canopy of the larger ones, along with youpon brush, blackberry brambles, poison ivy, Virginia creeper, honeysuckle, and wild grape vines as thick as a man's wrist, making it unimaginable that mere men could successfully penetrate very far into the dark woods.

The cars also passed through swampy areas out of which protruded water elms and cypress trees. Under them grew clumps of tupelos, cattails, spunk weed, and sawgrass. Fats also drew Loren's attention to wild violets, Indian pinks, bluebells, and the green spikes of dwarf palmettos. And he pointed out the many dragonflies and wasps that flitted among the summer blossoms clustered in the shade beneath gray beards of Spanish moss hanging from bare boughs, and the tiger swallowtail butterflies that fluttered in the open spaces.

Loren was greatly impressed at how much the Scorpion manager knew about the natural world and at how much he seemed to appreciate it.

As Duke's convertible slowed to a crawl to rattle across a narrow wooden bridge, Loren looked down into what Fats called a "bayou," a murky sluggish stream in which he glimpsed the flat head of a mean-looking snake. A few moments later Loren also saw, back in some thick timber, several strange looking creatures scuttling in the shadows, noses to the ground.

"Are those things pigs?" he asked.

"Razorbacks," replied Fats. "They like t' wallow in th' mud holes 'long th' bayous an' root 'roun' in th' moss an' dead leaves on th' forest floor. Yew don' evah wanna git too close t' those babies. They're mean. They've been known t' charge uh horse an' rider an' knock 'em both down. Didja see them tusks? They kin slash like uh butcher's knife cuttin' up uh carcass."

"This is not a friendly place."

"Not at all. Yew got angry bees nestin' in rottin' hollow places. Yew got water moccasins swimmin' in th' streams, an' rattlers lurkin' under fallen trees, an' coral snakes hidin' in th' swamp grass. Yew got momma bear jumpin' outta th' bushes t' defend her cubs, an' yew got red wolves lookin' fer a meal."

"Wolves?"

"Yeah. Like th' deer, they hide in th' daytime. Yew kin see 'em at dusk or at sunrise 'long th' edges of th' woods. Thar ain't many of 'em left, but they're thar."

Soon the trees began to thin, and cattle could be seen grazing in open fields. The caravan passed a roadside sign that read: "Timberland. Pop. 1625." Loren noticed two small sawmills and several huge piles of creosoted utility poles and railroad cross ties awaiting shipment. A pulpwood mill belched black smoke from a tall chimney.

"Boy, Ah'm shore hongry," said Duke. "It ain't yet ten-thirty," responded Fats. "Restaurants'll be closed fer church. Ah know uh good place in Stanley. Turn left up ahead, at th' courthouse square."

As the Tocqueville autos proceeded slowly along Timberland's main street, Loren admired the slave-built houses with wide front porches, fluted Doric columns, and floor-length screened windows that appeared on both sides of the avenue as they neared the center of town. A large Baptist church released its congregation: women in soft pinks and yellows and lavenders, with matching millinery, and men in gray or white cotton summer suits and starched shirts, their tight collars squeezing perspiration from their red necks, pausing briefly to shake hands with the dark-suited pastor before dispersing to their homes.

At the central square, the bed of an old pickup truck held cardboard boxes of summer squash, okra, sweet potatoes and watermelons for sale. In front of the two-story brick courthouse was parked a dirt-streaked white Chevy, the word "Sheriff" dimly visible on its side, a red light attached to its roof. A rifle and a shotgun rested on a wooden rack hung in the rear window.

Old men sat on scarred wooden benches in the shade of the large oaks that surrounded the courthouse. Their cracked hightopped shoes scuffed the dust where grass had long ago given up trying to grow. Some of the oldsters whittled shavings from pinewood sticks with razorsharp penknives which they periodically rubbed on small stones kept in the commodious pockets of their bib overalls. A few intently watched a game of checkers played on top of an overturned trash can. Others played dominos, pitched peanuts or cracker crumbs to strutting pigeons, or dozed, chins sunk upon their faded workshirts.

Most of the stores surrounding the square were closed for the Lord's Day. In front of one, a hardware emporium, sacks of seed and animal feed piled under a ragged green canopy partly blocked the sidewalk. Beyond, at the next intersection, a bent street sign read: "Stanley, 33 miles," accompanied by an arrow pointing left. One by one, the four autos from Tocqueville made the turn and, bumping across the now unused tracks of the former Timberland and Southeastern railroad, they began to gather speed, as they hurtled through a Negro neighborhood of unpainted termite-riddled shacks resting shakily upon the red dirt under tall pines. A few of their older inhabitants sat sleepily in second hand arm chairs on sagging porches. A teen-aged girl clad in a thin cotton feed-sack dress walked barefoot in the pine needles along the narrow road. Poking his head out the car window, Slick emitted a shrill whistle and yelled: "Hey, yew wooly headed sexpot; how 'bout uh li'l miscegenation?"

Seeing the girl's downcast eyes and her obvious effort to pretend that she hadn't heard the crude overture, Loren clenched his teeth with suppressed, embarrassed fury. He doubted that Slick, skirt-chaser though he apparently was, would have addressed a white girl in that manner, even from the relative safety of a getaway car. What must she be thinking?

* * *

As the trip continued, a nervous languor took possession of Loren, who had begun to wonder whether he would ever adjust to life in Texas. Ignoring the ballplayers' byplay, he dozed, awakened only once by popping sounds, like tires blowing out. "What was that?" he inquired. "Jus' ol' Bobo, shootin' at rabbits," responded Fats. Loren swiveled on his hip and looked out the back window just in time to see a long-barreled pistol recede into the window of the car directly behind them.

These guys are crazy, he thought. But there was nothing he could do about it. He closed his eyes again and leaned back against the rough upholstery, his face not far from Fats' armpit, which smelled like something dead.

Someone shouting "Heah we are!" awakened him just in time to read a sign that announced: "Stanley, pop. 1,017." Another read: "Lions Meet at Mom's at Noon, Thursdays." There were also signs for Kiwanis and Moose and a Baptist church. The local speed limit was twenty miles an hour.

Duke slowed down to fifty. At that pace they continued past a cemetery, a drive-in theater, a root beer stand, and several stores, as well as a crowded tavern and pool hall. The buildings were dingy wooden structures, and Loren thought several might have had false second story fronts, as if they were part of a Hollywood movie set. Men with maroon complexions and prominent cheek bones shaded by straw hats sat under canvas awnings and stared wordlessly at the visiting ballplayers. The town seemed dead. No dogs barked; no birds sang; no children cried out. Only the sound of automobile engines broke the silence.

Fats directed Duke to turn right at a street corner next to a closed drug store. After they passed a large brick church and several modest white wooden dwellings, they arrived at Mom's restaurant, a large Victorian house, on which a one-story addition was the main dining area.

With their cars half-filling the gravel parking lot, once a front yard, the Tocqueville ballplayers trooped inside, passed through a reception area, and entered a large room with wooden benches and trestle tables covered with red and white tablecloths. A juke box flickered invitingly in one corner, florescent around its edges, with a green dragon leering luminously from its front. Stacks of records awaited the plunk of a nickel into a chrome slot to arouse the mechanism that would blast out a popular tune.

Ham and Slick headed for the rest room. Meanwhile Duke made his way to the juke box, into which he fed several coins. At once the strains of "You Are My

Sunshine" filled the room. Two apron-clad Indian women distributed greasy menus. One of the girls was visibly pregnant, a fact that Slick, back from the men's room, appeared unable to ignore.

"Say Babe," he said, "when's th' papoose due?"

"Ain't no papoose," she replied, glaring at him. "Swallered a watermelon seed an' it grew." As she strode stiffly in the direction of the kitchen, Masher chortled: "Hey, Slick, guess she tole yew." With a faint grin, Slick lit a cigarette.

"Gimme a cig," said Bobo, looking around him, a request soon satisfied. Before long everyone was puffing away except Loren, whose eyes began to water as the smoke curled around his head. He was pleased when their orders finally appeared and the cigarettes were extinguished. As Loren chewed his hamburger and drank his milk, a dispute broke out between Ham and Slick, the former accusing the latter of caring more about money than about honesty or friendship.

"Come on, Ham." pleaded Slick. "We didn' shake hands on that bet."

"Whut bet?" interjected Masher.

"He bet me uh dollah," Ham said, "that Ah couldn' pee wit'out stoppin' longer than it took th' toilet tank t' refill after he flushed it. An' Ah won."

"But yew cheated. Jackie tol' me that yew drank uh couple uh Lone Stars in th' car on th' way heah."

"That ain't cheatin'. Pay up."

"No. Since yew cheated, th' bet is off."

"Slick," said Ham, "yore so stingy that if yew discovered yew hadda price on yore haid, yew'd turn yoreself in."

"Come on fellas," said Fats. "Eat. It's past twelve-thirty an' we gotta game t' play."

* * *

A gravel road leading to the Alabama-Coushatt Indian reservation northeast of town eventually passed through an opening in a high wire fence. A mile or so inside, rotting barrack-like buildings squatted dejectedly on concrete block foundations, like old people too weakened by the ravages of time to change position, patiently awaiting death. One of the run-down structures was a general store, through the open door of which Loren got a glimpse of men leaning against a long counter, drinking out of brown bottles, despite what Fats had told him about a government rule against the possession of liquor on the reservation. An elderly man staggered out onto the store porch and urinated into some desiccated bushes. Loren visualized Slick offering to bet Ham a dollar that his candidate, Chief Buffalo Dick, could outlast the Scorpion champion in one-on-one competition.

The ball field was surrounded by a six-foot-high fence constructed from rusty metal roofing nailed onto unevenly spaced posts that were actually pieces of tree trunks with the bark still attached. Above the fence Loren could see the top portion of a bleacher-like grandstand. Straight ahead was an entrance next to which was a sign designating the ramshackled edifice as the "Home of the Warriors." A second smaller sign announced: "Game Today."

The Scorpion drivers parked their cars well away from the grandstand and began to haul the duffel bags and valises containing their uniforms and equipment across the weedy gravel parking lot toward the open gate. Seeing Fats struggling with a heavy canvas sack the size of a mail bag, Loren hastened to help him by lifting one end. As he did so, bats rattled around inside. From Fats' other hand hung a large black valise which, Loren surmised, held baseballs, first aid items, a scorepad, and additional useful items. During the game it would also hold the players' wallets, watches, and other valuables.

A lanky freckled fellow, whom Loren had not yet met, but who he imagined was the team's regular catcher, carried on one shoulder another duffel bag, out of which protruded part of a chest protector and the top of one shin guard. A disinterested woman sitting at a ticket window waved them past her inside the ballpark. Most of the paint had been removed from the grandstand seats by years of sun and rain and the bottoms of Stanley spectators. Behind home plate a screen made of rusty chicken wire looked too flimsy to stop a hard foul ball. The infield was yellow clay, with only a few tufts of wilted grass having survived the summer drought; and the outfield looked like a cow pasture. Attached to the fences were faded signs advertising beer, chewing tobacco, an auto dealership, and Coca Cola. Several spaces awaited ads.

The visitors' clubhouse turned out to be a small cinder block shed located underneath the first base grandstand. It stank of urine, and the concrete floor was cracked and slippery. Large nails pounded into the grimy walls served as clothes hooks, and four wooden benches completed the room's furnishings. No lockers; no chairs; no rubbing table.

Two small windows located in the back wall were open above a single dripping shower head. As the ballplayers entered the room, a small green frog hopped away from the floor drain and disappeared into a large crack where two cinder blocks had separated. It was so hot inside that Fats left the door open, to try to coax a breeze from the windows, only to discover that several giggling girls were determined to watch the players dress.

"Let 'em look," said Duke, dropping his shorts. "J'ever see one this big?" he shouted out the door, pointing to his crotch. The girls screamed and drew back a few feet but did not leave the vicinity.

Fats went over and closed the door. "We don' need no trouble wit' their mommas or daddies," he said. "Let's get dressed an' outa heah."

Across the room, Bobo sat naked, his heavy jaw clenched with concentration, the muscles rippling under the pelt of dark hair that covered his upper back, as he rubbed a black bat with a huge beef bone. Loren had heard of this practice of "boning" bats, sometimes using glass bottles, with the object of tightening the wood grain and thereby providing more punch, but he had never before seen it being done. Back and forth the bone massaged the bat, as Bobo rotated it in his huge hands, until finally he nodded with satisfaction, laid the two implements aside, and began dressing.

Nearby, Feets, the tall catcher whom Loren had seen limping in from the parking lot, rubbed liniment into the upper portion of his right arm, near a jagged scar that extended from his shoulder down across his pale chest. And Bubba, who

Loren had learned was the second baseman, wound adhesive tape thickly around his shaved legs, but not before revealing angry inflammations on both kneecaps.

Noticing Loren looking, Fats whispered: "War wounds. Feets got his nickname in Italy. His infantry company wuz under heavy fire from th' Germans fer three days in zero weather. Both feet were frozen an' almos' hadda be amputated.

"Bubba wuz tortured in uh Jap prison camp. Sometimes one of his knees separates from its socket right in th' middle of uh game. Th' pain mus' be terrific. But he gets someone t' pop it back in place an' goes on playin'. Both those guys got guts."

Loren thought: Boy, do they! He finished putting on his white wool flannel uniform with the blue "Winona" sewn across his chest and a big blue letter "W" on the front of his cap. The other players had gray uniforms with red trim, and red stirrup socks. The letter "S" decorated their gray caps.

Fats, still dressed in olive-colored work clothes but now wearing a Scorpion cap and carrying a clipboard, said to Loren: "If everythin' goes well today, we'll see that yew git wun of our outfits by nex' weekend. One of our guys from las' year, Jake Beasley, can't play this summer, an' he's 'bout yore size." Thus reassured about his status, assuming he didn't disgrace himself in the coming contest, Loren stuffed his glove into his back pocket and, clutching his bat, followed several of the other players as they made their way, spikes clattering on the concrete, out onto the field.

Slick fell in beside him. "Ah've alwuz wondered," said the slender outfielder, "why they call th' seats th' stands? Is it 'cause people up thar are alluz jumpin' up?"

Loren, amused, eased in beside Bobo to exchange warmup tosses with Slick and Ham. "Whutcha grinnin' at?" asked Bobo.

"Nothing. Just thought of something."

"Ah see yew brought yer bat," the shortstop said, spewing a brown stream of tobacco juice from pursed lips.

"Yeah."

"Then les play pepper. Yew kin hit fust."

Loren picked up his warclub and ambled nervously to a spot in front of the screen behind home plate. Bobo, Slick, and Ham, joined by A. C. and Feets, wearing his shin guards, formed a line facing him. Ham tossed a ball toward Loren at hip height, and he rapped it smartly at Bobo, who stood at the end of the line. Bobo lobbed the ball back, and Loren socked it straight at Slick, standing at Bobo's left elbow. As each player returned the ball Loren, gaining confidence and beginning to relax as he immersed himself in the flow of the action, smacked it directly to the teammate directly to the thrower's left.

"Way t' go, Yank," shouted Bobo. "Li'l pepper, guys."

The Scorpions eased apart, gradually creating spaces of several feet between each one. They fired the ball harder and harder at Loren, whose bat flashed faster and faster as he banged it back at them. Soon they began a chorus of: "Yip; yeah; hot damn; hubba, hubba..." This was the real stuff, thought Loren. He was grateful for the many occasions on which his father had gone outside with him in Winona to play pepper, just the two of them in the narrow driveway, using the garage door as a backstop. Now Loren's new teammates seemed impressed with his batting eye and his ability to place his hits wherever he wished.

When it was time for the visitors to have batting practice, Fats came over to Loren and said: "Go on out t' right field. We'll call yew in when its yore turn t' hit." Loren ran to join Slick, Duke, and a young player called "Rowdy" out by the fence. A faded sign nailed next to the foul pole read "330 feet." A. C. was already hitting the outfielders fly balls with a thin stick called a "fungo" bat, which he flourished like a magic wand as he ran them across the dry grass, unable to field his placements without breaking into a gallop.

"This one's yore's," said Slick, as another fly ball rose high in the air. Seeing that it was slicing toward the foul line, Loren raced toward the spot where the outfield fence ended at some rickety bleachers surmounted by a sign reading "Colored." Slowing as he crossed the white chalkline, he gloved the descending sphere and at once launched a powerful throw that sailed on a line over the infield and took a single low bounce into A. C.'s waiting hand.

Slick looked startled. "Nice throw," he said. Loren saw Bubba, fielding grounders at second base, turn and stare. Masher, at first base, did likewise. He had obtained their attention.

As Feets, batting, completed his allocation of five swings and two bunts, followed by a leisurely jog toward first base, Fats waved Loren in from the outfield. "Yew hit after Fido," he said. "Hurry. We only have five minutes more."

As soon as Fido finished, Loren stepped into the right-hand batter's box to face Jackie Lawson, who was also getting a tryout on this occasion, and who was therefore trying to impress with pitches far more lively than the usual straight medium speed batting practice slants. Suddenly Loren felt weak—his legs trembling under him so badly that he could hardly stand. Jackie, leaning over to pick up several baseballs off the back of the mound, seemed out of focus; indeed, everything around Loren had become blurred. And his mouth felt so dry he could hardly swallow.

Backing away from the plate, he leaned over and re-tied his right shoelace. Come on, he told himself. Don't try to think. Just see the ball and stroke it.

Stepping back up to home plate, he took two practice swings and settled into his stance, feet spread as far apart as his shoulders, his left toe turned slightly toward the third baseman, bat held high behind his right ear, his eyes fixed on the ball as it left Jackie's hand. Now, everything he saw seemed extraordinarily clear, magnified, the rotation of the white ball almost in slow motion.

Crack. He had swung easily but had connected on the sweet spot; this he knew from the absence of any tingle in his arms. The ball shot into the gap in left-center field, skipped twice on the thin turf, and hit the fence with a loud thud. Four more swings produced two line drives over shortstop, a long fly that dropped just short of the left field wall, and a hard grounder over second base that barely missed a jumping Jackie.

Apparently irritated by this last stroke, Jackie grimly served up a curve ball, which Loren, trying to bunt, stabbed at and missed. "Dunce," he muttered.

""Whut did yew call me?" asked Jackie belligerently.

"Nothing. Just talking to myself."

"Wal, talk t' this, fella," said Jackie, throwing another curve.

Loren watched it carefully as it headed toward his left hip and then bent toward the strike zone. At the last possible split second, he suddenly lifted his left elbow and limply laid his bat on the spinning sphere. Bursting out of the batter's box like a sprinter, he headed for first base, which he crossed before Jackie could reach the bunt that had stopped almost on the third base foul line. As Loren continued out to right field to fetch his glove, he overheard Masher suggest to Bubba: "Ah think we got us uh ballplayer."

"Jus' as long as he don' wanna try out fer second base," was the muttered reply.

* * *

A few minutes later, someone clanged a cowbell, and the Scorpions left the field, so that the home team could hold batting practice. The Stanley Warriors were big and boisterous, determined, as one yelled, to "stomp the Scorpions." One after the other, they hammered long drives over the outfield fences into the pine trees beyond. Indian children were kept busy retrieving the blistered baseballs and heaving them back over the fences. Loren was glad he was not going to have to pitch to these behemoths.

During the Scorpion infield practice, Loren watched intently. At third base, Ham showed soft hands and surprising agility for one so fat. His arm seemed a little weak, but Masher snatched several low throws out of the dirt with a casual flick of his big mitt. No harm done. Bobo at shortstop was reminiscent of what Loren had read about the greatest of them all, Hans Wagner, formerly a player and now a coach for the Pittsburgh Pirates. Loren's father, who had seen Wagner play, had described him as a big man, as strong as steel, with extraordinarily long arms from which huge hands hung close to the ground, like Bobo's. The Scorpion shortstop was dark skinned with a black stubble on the lower portion of his face. He had a way of lunging toward ground balls, which he dug out of the dirt and flung fluidly, with an underhanded motion, to first base, grunting like a gorilla as he guarded his territory.

At second base, Bubba was slender and intense. Trying to initiate a double play, he booted an easy ground ball and, trying to pick it up, he dropped it again. Pouncing on the ball he launched a hasty throw that pulled Masher off the bag. "Sheetass pebbles," exclaimed Bubba, spitting out the words (although Loren had seen nothing divert the direction of the grounder). Too tight, he thought. Wonder what's eating him?

By contrast, Masher was so relaxed at his position that he almost seemed sleepy. Effortlessly, he shifted his spikes so that the proper toe would stab the bag at the very instant a throw smacked into his waiting mitt. He seemed short for someone playing first base, with small hands, and feet that appeared almost too tiny to support his bulky torso, but he knew exactly how to elongate his stretch, with his forward knee deeply bent and his other foot thrust back as far as it would reach to touch the edge of the bag. He's good, concluded Loren. I'll bet he and Bobo are the stars of this team.

After the Warriors took their five minutes of fielding practice, sure-handed and accurate with their throws, and after Fats had met with the opposing manager and the two umpires at home plate to exchange lineup cards and discuss the ground rules peculiar to the local ball park, the game began. Ham led off for the Scorpions and struck out on three fast balls. The big Indian on the mound grinned. He had it today. Bubba took a quick strike and then tried to bunt, but missed, looking foolish. On the next pitch he took a called third strike. Then Bobo came to bat. Like everyone else in the Scorpion lineup he, too, hit right handed. The first pitch was a hummer and Bobo took an enormous swing, his entire body twisting in a semicircle and the thick black bat swishing malevolently through the air. Chuckling, the catcher lobbed the ball back to the mound and said something unwelcome to Bobo, who responded by pounding his bat on the plate as if trying to shatter it.

The second pitch was outside. Pitch number three was a curve ball. Big mistake. Bobo hit it on a line toward left field. It appeared still to be rising as it cleared the fence and disappeared into the pine trees beyond. After the shortstop had trotted poker faced around the bases and over to the Scorpion bench to sit down, Loren noticed that his neck muscles were protruding and there was a gleam in his eyes.

Masher batted cleanup. Shaken by Bobo's blast, the Warrior pitcher fell behind in the count, three balls to one strike. He then grooved one and Masher unloaded on it. High into the cloudless blue sky it climbed. The Warrior center fielder waited, his back almost against the fence, waited..., waited,... and then gloved the ball, as it finally descended to earth. Score: one to nothing, and the home team's turn to bat.

Although A. C. had only a wrinkle for a curve, his fast ball had plenty of zing and he knew how to spot his pitches. It did him little good. In their half of the first inning the Warriors batted around. By the time Slick caught a hard liner, hit by the pitcher, the Indian sluggers had rung up five tallies.

The game continued that way. In the third inning, Fats ambled out to the mound to take the ball from the shell-shocked A. C. and drop it into the glove of a nervous Jackie Lawson. In the fifth frame, Fats brought on Whitey Hughes, whose assortment of soft stuff momentarily caught the Warriors off guard and they actually went out in order. In inning number six, however, they began once more to pound the ball. By the time the third out was registered on a nice backhanded stab in the hole by Bobo and an accurate underhand throw that barely nipped a slow runner, the score had mounted to fifteen to two.

Seated on the bench between Fats and A. C., Loren mopped the sweat from his forehead with a sodden sleeve. "Boy, it's hot," he said.

A. C. spat into the puddle of tobacco juice between his scuffed spikes. "Hell," he protested, "this ain't hot. Why, when we played heah las' year it wuz so hot th' wax ran outa mah ears. We all 'bout died of sunstroke. Heah, try this." He reached into a metal bucket half-filled with murky water and lifted out a small wet towel, which he wrung out and handed to Loren. It was ice cold. Gratefully Loren sloshed it across his face and over the back of his neck. "That's amazing," he said. "How do you get it so cold?"

"Ammonia. Fats keeps uh li'l bottle of it in his bag. It works well, but yew don' wanna drink th' water."

Invigorated, Loren resumed his study of the game. It was now the top of the seventh, and the Warrior pitcher appeared to be running out of steam. The

Scorpions began to hit. After Whitey struck out, Ham caught a fast ball on the end of his bat and drove it to right center for two bases. Bubba, grimacing fiercely, bashed a slow curve past a diving shortstop and Ham scored. Bobo drove his second homer even further into the trees beyond left field than his first one. Masher took two low curves, one for a questionable strike, and then hammered a towering fly that the center fielder didn't even bother to turn around to watch, as it flew far over his head and out of the park.

Duke swaggered up to the plate and promptly went down on the seat of his pants, as the frustrated pitcher hurled a duster high and inside. The next pitch, however, was over the plate chest high, exactly where Duke liked it. With a delighted grin, he lashed it on a line against the left field wall for two bases, sliding flamboyantly into second base in a cloud of yellow dust.

"Yank," called Fats. "Hit fer Slick. Yew'll play right field."

Jumping up off the bench, Loren headed for the plate, swinging two bats. The Warrior catcher spurted a stream of tobacco spit from between the bars of his mask, narrowly missing Loren's feet, and said: "ol' Black Dawg out thar's had 'nough. Yore goin' down."

Apprehensively, Loren tossed away one bat and settled into his stance, telling himself to remain loose and look for a good pitch. The big Indian on the mound reared back and threw. A white blur came so fast at Loren's head that he barely had time to jerk it backward, the ball smacking into the catcher's mitt so close to his right ear that he thought the stitches might have brushed his right cheekbone.

His knees shaking, Loren stepped back out of the batter's box and leaned over to rub dirt into his sweaty hands. He was so angry that he felt feverish. He had an urge to run out to the mound and attack the pitcher with his bat. But then he had a better idea.

Stepping back up to the plate, he grimly waited for the second pitch. Sure enough, it was also a duster, which he was prepared for and easily avoided. Now he was really raging.

The third pitch was on the outside part of the plate, knee high. Perfect. With limp hands Loren gently tapped the ball down the first base line and ran as fast as he could after it, as the first baseman started in and then, seeing the pitcher come off the mound to field it, returned to the bag.

As the pitcher neared the foul line and reached down for the ball, which by now had stopped rolling, Loren hit him with a vicious body block across the backs of his knees. The big man screamed in pain as he collapsed on top of the ball, while Loren, only a bit bruised, rolled to his feet and continued on to first base.

"Yore out!" yelled the home plate umpire, who had followed the play up the line, stabbing his right thumb into the air.

"Whaddya mean?" shouted A. C. from the first base coach's box. "Th' man nevah threw th' ball."

"Yore player ran outa th' base line," responded the ump. "He's out."

Loren decided not to argue. Having had his tit for tat with the Warrior head hunter, who was still groaning on the ground surrounded by teammates, he was satisfied. Besides, the ump was right. The impact of the collision had thrown Loren well outside the lane chalked along the baseline in which batters heading for first base were required to run, in order to prevent them from interfering with throws from the left side of the diamond.

As he started toward the Scorpion bench, Loren saw the Warrior manager, who had joined the players gathered around the fallen pitcher, point at him. Immediately, several members of the group started striding menacingly in his direction. The Indians were apparently going on the war path. He wondered desperately whether he could outsprint them to an exit and find a place in these unfriendly surroundings to hide.

Before he could move, however, his teammates had placed themselves in front of him, each Scorpion flourishing a wooden bat, daring the Warrior players to come closer. But hostile spectators had begun to emerge from the stands behind them, and they were vastly outnumbered. Loren thought of Custer's last stand. He was trapped.

A loud report suddenly silenced the snarling Stanleyites. A large man dressed in an official-looking brown uniform with a shiny silver badge on his chest had fired a pistol into the air. Amid the hush, his authoritative voice rang out clearly. "Y'all know who Ah am. We ain't havin' no riots in this ball park, not while Ah'm heah." Waving his gun in the direction of the spectators, he continued: "Back t' yore seats, people. An' yew,"—turning his attention to the players—"yew got uh game t' finish. Or shall Ah declare uh forfeit right now?"

Grumbling, the Stanley players drifted back to their bench, and the Scorpions did likewise, tossing their bats onto the ground where they could easily be retrieved, if necessary. The Stanley pitcher was gently hoisted to his feet by two teammates and assisted, limping, to leave the field. A new hurler began his warmup throws.

Loren sat, still vibrating with excitement, on the bench next to Fats, who squeezed the youngster's knee and said: "Look, Yank, whut yew did took uh lotta guts, but we don' need t' be takin' on th' whole damn tribe. If'n it weren' fer that guy wit' th' gun, we all mighta got scalped."

"Sorry. I was angry. That pitcher tried to hit me in the head."

"That's part of th' game. Semi-pro ain't fer sissies." Fats hesitated. The he said: "Yew ain't no sissy, that's fer sure. Jus' pick yore fights more carefully."

"O. K.," said Loren. Good advice.

Meanwhile, the new Stanley pitcher eventually retired the side. Loren grabbed his glove and ran out to right field. The Warriors had evidently decided to take out their frustrations on the Scorpion pitcher. They began once more to bash the ball. Loren had to chase a couple of liners to the fence and make hurried throws to Bubba in order to hold the hitters to two bases. The left and center fielders also had plenty of work. Finally, with two out and a runner on first, the batter slashed a single to right. Racing toward the infield, Loren gloved the ball on the first bounce and launched a throw to Ham at third base that whizzed into his glove right on top of the bag. The sliding baserunner tagged himself out. It was the final out of the eighth inning. As Loren trotted in toward the visitors' bench, carrying his glove, trying not to react to the catcalls and threats from the first base stands, some sporadic clapping could be heard from fair-minded spectators who appreciated his impressive throw.

"Great play, Yank," shouted Ham. "Yew dun good, keed," added Bobo. "Lessee if'n we can't git uh rally goin'."

Some spirit, thought Loren. Twenty to nine and Bobo is still giving the game his best. What a guy!

The Scorpions scored twice before Duke fanned for the third out in the top of the eighth, whereupon the Warriors scored three to bring on the final inning. Once more it was Loren's turn at bat. Expecting a beanball, he was careful not to dig in. But the new Stanley pitcher had apparently been given a warning and kept the ball on the outside part of the plate. The umpire seemed anxious to get the game over and made a couple of questionable calls on pitches that Loren believed were off the corner, but three more were so far outside that the arbiter had no choice but to call them balls. With a full count, the pitcher threw one down the middle. In his excitement, Loren forgot his habitual restraint, usually restricting himself with two strikes to a short compact swing, designed to make sure he got some portion of the bat on the ball. Instead he swung with all his strength. Fortunately he connected, squarely.

As he raced down the line toward first base, he glanced out to left field, trying to pick up the flight of the ball. But he couldn't see it. As he rounded the bag he heard the nearby umpire cry out: "Foul ball!"

"No!" yelled A. C. from the coach's box. "Yore outa yore mind, Ump," shouted Fats, heaving himself up off the visitors' bench and lumbering, protesting all the way, toward the diamond. "Th' ball hit th' foul pole," he exclaimed, "an' dropped ovah th' fence. Its uh home run."

"Naw," retorted the man in black. "It hit th' pole, all right, but it bounced off into foul territory. T' be uh homer it'ud have t' had landed fair."

"Yore crazy," roared Fats. "Anyone knows that if uh ball hits uh foul line on the fly, once it passes uh base, even if'n it jus' touches it, it's uh fair ball."

"Yew call me crazy one more time," declared the ump, "an' yore outa th' game. Now siddown an' shuddup." His glare dared Fats to continue the argument.

Muttering under his breath, the manager returned to the bench. Loren went back to bat. He hit the next pitch on a line directly to the center fielder. "Too bad, Yank," said Slick, as Loren returned disconsolately to the bench. "Yew kin hit 'em, but yew can't steer 'em."

Two batters later, the game was over. The Tocqueville players trooped wearily into the clubhouse and began stripping off their sweatsoaked, dirty uniforms. "Hey!" yelled Slick, who had rushed to be first into the shower. "Thar ain't no water!" Angrily he twisted an unresponsive faucet. "Ah'll go see whut Ah kin do," said Fats.

Five minutes later the manager returned with bad news. Someone had shut off the water and nobody professed to know how to turn it back on. "Serves yew guys right," the Stanley manager had said. "Yew cost us our bes' pitcher. We ain't nevah goin' t' play yew again."

"Les git outa here," said Fats. "Wear yore uniforms if'n yew wan'. We kin shower when we git home."

Soon four cars were exceeding the Stanley speed limit as they passed out of town. Fats, seated next to Loren in the back seat of Duke's car, lamented: "Th' wors' thang is, we only made twenty-foah dollahs from th' gate money, hardly 'nough fer gas n' oil an' maybe uh case of beer."

"Fergit th' gas n' oil," said Duke. "Bring on th' beer."

CHAPTER 9
CLUES AND QUESTIONS

After returning from Stanley, Loren did not sleep well. He kept thinking about Dr. Kaplan's death. He wondered whether Emile Mouton or any of the police had noticed frayed fibers on the rope from which Dr. K had hung. The rubbed part had been located on the wall side of the rafter over which the rope had been slung, instead of on the side nearest the knot pressing into the victim's neck.

There was also the question of the bucket on which a suicide-minded man could have stood while he adjusted a rope around his neck. Looking briefly at the death scene, Loren had noticed that although the overturned container had been dented on one side, its bottom remained smooth. Was it his responsiblity to point this out to the police and thereby draw attention to himself?

Such concerns were still bothering Loren when he joined Buzz on Monday morning. After exchanging congratulations that the Johnson Senate campaign was still alive, if in critical condition, they set out in Buzz's trusty truck for a network of dusty shell roads that ran past irrigated rice fields and parched pastures south of Tocqueville, where utility poles and farm fence posts still remained undecorated with Johnson's toothy grin.

As he drove, Buzz kept glancing at Loren, who had been unable to conceal a series of yawns with a hand over his mouth. "Had uh rough weekend, huh?" Buzz asked.

"The Scorpions played in Stanley on Sunday," said Loren. "We got back late."

"Heard yew hadda busy Saturday, too."

"Oh, you mean what happened next door? Yes: it was pretty horrible."

"Was it really uh suicide?"

"I don't know."

Buzz seemed concerned. "Ah can't help being curious," he said. "Ah wuz in school wit Doctor Kaplan's wife. How's she doin'?"

"Pretty well, I think. She and her husband didn't seem happy together. I suppose that may have made the shock of his death less severe."

"Ah hope so. Ah alluz liked Della. Ah should prolly give 'er uh call... Heah's uh good place t' hang our candidate." Buzz stopped the truck at an isolated intersection and Loren reached for his hammer. He tried not to appear disconcerted by Buzz's choice of words.

* * *

That evening Tommy wanted to play catch in the front yard. He had noticed a good-looking girl of about his own age riding a bicycle up and down Magnolia Avenue, and he wanted to attract her attention. Soon after they began exchanging tosses, a young woman appeared in the Kaplan driveway, tugging on a large trash container. She was dressed in a cotton frock and sandals and was deeply tanned. Loren thought her voluptuous. "Excuse me," he called. "May I help you with that?"

Smiling slightly, she shook her head. "Ah kin handle it," she said, at the same time trying unsuccessfully to lift her burden off the ground.

"Really," Loren protested, rushing to her side and seizing the barrel. "This thing is quite heavy. You might strain something." She released her hold, and Loren wrestled her burden across the sidewalk over to the curb, where he caught one foot on a rough patch of turf and sprawled full length on the grass. The trash container overturned, the top popped off, and some of the contents spilled out onto the ground. Thoroughly embarrassed, Loren heaved the barrel back to an upright position and scrambled to scoop up gobs of rancid kitchen scraps, crumpled up papers, half a dozen tin cans with jagged edges on their still attached tops, and several wrinkled women's magazines. Belatedly, Tommy bent over to help. "What's this?" he asked. Loren saw a blown electrical fuse, its central wire blackened and separated. "Nothing," he said. "Just a piece of junk." Leaning over to drop it back into the barrel, he saw, almost buried in the remaining debris, a small brown table radio. It looked like the same one that he had noticed sitting on a shelf above the Kaplans' bathtub.

With its contents restored, and its top firmly in place, the trash container rested innocently next to the curb, while Loren and Tommy gave the grass a last look to see if they had missed any bits of dross. Seeing none, Loren turned to the young woman who had been watching them with hardly hidden amusement and said: "I'm Loren," starting to extend his right hand and then realizing its current condition, quickly jerking it back. "He's Tommy."

"I'm Olivia," she responded. "Come t' visit mah sister." With a tinge of sarcasm, she added: "Thanks fer th' help."

Watching her retreat into the Kaplan house, Loren was momentarily mesmerized by the sight of her thin dress rubbing against her tantalizing posterior, a reverie soon interrupted, however, by Tommy, who complained: "Are we gonna play catch or not?"

As they picked up their gloves and resumed tossing the ball back and forth, Loren belatedly realized that he had caught a brief glimpse of someone looking out the front window of the Kaplans' house, someone who had surely witnessed him staring lasciviously at the luscious Olivia. Mrs. Kaplan. He felt foolish. He needed to get his mind off the sexy sisters next door and start thinking clean thoughts.

After supper he returned to his room to study baseball guides before bedtime. The sight of his camera sitting on his bookcase reminded him that he had still not processed the pictures made Friday night. Opening the top drawer of his dresser, he fumbled around behind his underwear, but his eager fingers found nothing. Anxiously he cleared the drawer of all its contents; still nothing. He then emptied the other three drawers with the same result. Where was the film? Could someone have taken it? If so, why?

*   *   *

During the following week, Loren wondered frequently, each time with a feeling of panic, what had happened to his film. Had it fallen into unfriendly hands? If the police came into possession of it, would they develop it and then prosecute him for withholding evidence in a murder case? If Mrs. K and her lover had it, would they not realize that he had been a witness to what they had done? Might they then believe it too risky to let him testify? If his actions became known to his parents, what would they think about their son? Would they try to protect him, or abandon him to the merciless machinery of the law?

Brooding in this macabre manner, Loren was not good company. As he and Buzz resumed their safari, his silence began to trouble his partner. Only by drawing Loren's attention to the radio news could Buzz get his co-worker's mind off his problem, the nature of which Loren steadfastly refused to discuss.

At a broadcaster's mention of a recently issued executive order by President Truman prohibiting racial discrimination in federal employment, including the armed forces, Buzz seemed infuriated. He railed against "Hitler Harry's darlin' darkies," whom a demented chief executive wanted "t' force into white folks' jobs, schools, an' places of recreation;" even into their very homes.

Appalled by Buzz's vehemence, Loren protested: "I don't think Truman's order mandated any such thing—only equal opportunity and fair treatment."

"Shore," said Buzz, "an' if'n Truman by some miracle gits re-elected, we'll have 'nother presidential order, wit'out consultin' Congress, requirin' us t' let th' niggers eat an' sleep whar we do, an' even share our bathrooms. An' have th' right t' date our women. Lemme ask yew, would yew wan' yore sister t' shack up wit' uh nigger?"

"I don't have a sister. But if I did, I can't imagine her having a Negro boy friend."

"Don' be too sure. They say niggers have huge dinguses. Some women can't resist that sorta thing. They git curious, an' then, wham, they discover they're 'bout t' give birth t' uh li'l pickaninny."

Loren decided not to acquaint Buzz with the result of his recent inquiry at Shipper Stadium. Instead he asked: "What's so different about Negroes anyway? Seems to me they're people just like us."

"Yew don' git it. They don' think or act like white people. They're dirty, childlike, irrational."

"Buzz, I don't understand you. You've told me how you were practically raised by a Negro woman, who took care of your laundry, cooked and served your food, and cuddled you when you needed comforting. You seem to have loved that woman almost as much as your parents. And yet you call all Negroes dirty."

Buzz mumbled: "Yew wuz raised uh yankee. Yew'll nevah understand till yew live in th' South uh lot longer. An' maybe not even then." He stared grimly through the windshield at the highway.

Loren wanted to point out that he had been brought into the world at the J. E. B. Stuart hospital, named after a Confederate general, in the city of Richmond, Virginia, the capital of the Confederacy; and that he had spent most of his early years in a Virginia village, living in a house on Lee Street, not far from Lee Boulevard, and only a few blocks from Lee Highway, all named after Robert E.

Lee, scourge of the hated yankees. Only later had he resided in Illinois. But something about the way Buzz sat rigidly behind the steering wheel caused his passenger to remain silent. Loren had to leave the truck several times to put up posters before the tension in the cab began to ease, so that the two campaign workers could resume conversing in friendly fashion.

Tentatively Buzz inquired: "Didja see in th' paper that Joe Tinker died?"

"Yeah. Tinker to Evers to Chance. Short to second to first. All three in the Hall of Fame. Johnny Evers died only a little over a year ago, and Frank Chance, the Peerless Leader, died back in nineteen-twenty-four. I think his life was probably shortened by all the beanballs he received from opposing pitchers. And Harry Steinfeldt, the third baseman, probably their best batter, passed away only in his thirties, in nineteen-fourteen. I don't know why."

Buzz sat silently for a moment. Then he said: "Ah gotta admit: th' Cubs of that day were uh great team. Four pennants an' two world championships in five years. An' they almos' made it five fer five."

"Yeah," said Loren. "They won one hundred and four games in 1909, but the Pirates won more. Now those old Cubs are dying off, one by one. Johnny Kling, the catcher; Jimmy Sheckard, the left fielder; and Orvie Overall, one of their best pitchers, all died last year. And Three-Finger Brown, their ace, died last St. Valentine's Day."

"That doesn' leave many still livin'."

"Well, there's Wildfire Schultz, the right-fielder who hit a lot of home runs for them; and Jim Slagle, the speedy center fielder; and pitchers Ed Ruelbach and Jack Pfiester, catcher Jimmy Archer, and utility players Heinie Zimmerman and Artie Hoffman, of the notables. And probably a few of the subs… Notice how many were German? In a way, when they played McGraw's Giants, it was Germany against Ireland."

"Yew oughta be uh history professor. But few people t'day 'member th' ol' Cubs, who shore ain't whut they used t' be."

"That's the truth. But some day…"

For the rest of the afternoon, the two campaigners spoke infrequently, each thinking how inexorable was death and how fleeting was fame.

* * *

On the following Saturday, Loren's mother asked him to accompany her to a department store that had recently re-opened its doors in downtown Tocqueville. "To help carry my packages," she said. With the beginning of the school year only a little over a month away, she was anxious to purchase proper apparel for Loren and Tommy. Moreover, she was curious, Loren assumed, to see the inside of the block-long store, whose owners had been extolling it in full-page newspaper ads as "completely re-decorated and re-modeled." They had even added florescent lighting and air conditioning to make it modern.

While his mother shopped, Loren sat in an out-of-the-way corner and watched excited women picking over piles of clothing dumped on a large number of tables, while other females fingered dresses and skirts hanging from dozens of metal racks.

He watched sales clerks stuffing papers and coins and currency into heavy cardboard containers, which they then inserted into pneumatic tubes located conveniently nearby. There would be a faint "whoosh" and the cups would magically fly up into a network of tubes strung across the ceiling and down into the store office, visible behind a glass partition, where the transactions would be quickly recorded, with a sales slip and change rapidly transmitted rapidly back to the waiting customer. Loren marveled: What will they think of next?

As he helped Nan carry packages out to their car, she said that she needed to stop at a nearby photo shop, where she had recently left some film to be developed. Loren worried: Could his mother have found his missing roll of film and decided to see what was on it? What could be done to prevent her from finding out?

Then she said: "By the way, I just remembered something. I meant to do you a favor by bringing along a roll of film that I discovered in one of your bureau drawers not long ago, but when I looked in my purse for it, it wasn't there. I imagine it will turn up. Was it anything important?"

"Not really," said Loren. "Just some baseball stuff. Don't worry about it. But if you find it, please give it to me and I'll develop it at home."

He resented his mother intruding into his private world. He had never fully forgiven her for reading his diary several years ago in Winona, including passages in which he had ruminated about the sexual proclivities of a female classmate. On that occasion, Nan had said nothing specific to Loren about his speculations, but her disapproval had nevertheless been evident.

Now once again she had invaded his male domain. Still, Loren realized, she meant well. In the photo shop she purchased a fresh roll of film and gave it to him, "in case," she said, "the other one doesn't turn up." And she apologized for not taking better care of his missing roll.

That evening, while his mother was cooking supper, Loren slipped into his parents' bedroom and hurriedly searched his mother's bureau and clothes closet, but without finding any film. He consoled himself with the hope that the small object had somehow been thrown out in the trash and was therefore gone forever. Which was just as well. Using his camera to record snippets of the saga of the Kaplan relationship had produced unforeseen consequences. The excitement that he had derived from his snooping, he thought, wasn't worth the resulting worry and danger.

* * *

The Scorpions played at home that Sunday. The opponents were from the little town of Fisher. According to Bobo, sounding off during pre-game practice, "Doze bozos don' know th' furst ting 'bout baseball. We gonna cream 'em."

Chasing fungos under a broiling early afternoon sun, Loren looked over at the visitors playing catch along the right field foul line and thought they looked competitive. He hoped Fats would insert him in the starting lineup. As he awaited another fly ball, however, he suddenly saw nothing but colorless space, then a great glare of blinding light, and then nothing at all…

How long he lay insensible on the hot grass, he only learned later. His father, who had leaped from the bleachers to join a growing crowd of teammates around his still form, estimated that he had re-opened his eyes after about five minutes of unconsciousness. Someone had draped a towel soaked in cold water over his forehead. Groggily, he staggered to his feet and picked up his glove. Blinking, he said: "I'm all right. Let's play ball."

"Not so fast," said Fats, exchanging looks with Loren's father. "Looks t' me like yew may have had uh spell of heat exhaustion. Yew need t' rest." He led Loren past the Scorpion's bench to a spot shaded by a huge live oak tree fringed with Spanish moss, and made him sit on the grass. "Yore still flushed," he said. "Ah'm gonna keep yew outa th' game. No point in riskin' heat stroke. It kin kill people. Yew stay in th' shade, yew heah?"

A guy Loren had not yet met played right field and collected two hits during the ensuing game, but he also dropped an easy fly and made one wild throw that let in a crucial run. Slick Bangwell, pitching, walked eight batters in as many innings and was hit hard. The Scorpion batters were unable to overcome a large Fisher lead. Once again they were losers, and they were far from happy about it.

"We need t' make some changes," grumbled Ham, as he came off the diamond after having been stranded on second base with the tying run in the last of the ninth.

"Right," agreed Fido, who had played center field in the unexplained absence of Duke Daniels, and had run out a bases-empty homer in the second inning, but had struck out four times thereafter, apparently trying for another roundtripper. The entire Scorpion team had appeared unenthusiastic, with only Bubba Guidry exhibiting real spirit, chattering non-stop from his second base position.

"Dammit!" Loren overheard Bobo say, with Slick standing nearby. "We need uh pitcher who kin trow strikes an' git guys out." Maybe I ought to remind Fats that I can pitch, thought Loren.

* * *

During the next five days, Loren and Buzz traveled far to the west of Tocqueville, almost to Houston, to nail up their Johnson signs. They encountered a thick scattering of already rotting placards urging Texans to vote for their man, but it was evident that nobody had campaigned for him recently in that region of steaming swamps and towering pines. Under the relentless sun they sweated profusely as they attempted to saturate their surroundings with Johnson signs to compete with the many Stevenson posters to be seen along every road, nailed onto utility poles and farm fences.

While they worked, they talked politics, a topic of never-ending interest to Buzz, and one that Loren found increasingly fascinating. The newspapers that week were full of accusations by Republicans that Soviet espionage agents and American sympathizers with communism had thoroughly infiltrated the United States government, penetrating its most sensitive agencies during the Roosevelt and Truman presidencies.

On Monday, an ex-communist had testified publicly before a Republican-dominated headline-hunting Senate subcommittee that the communists had received extensive financial support from the movie community in Hollywood. A story simultaneously leaked from the House Un-American Activities Committee (Loren wondered aloud, "What is an 'Un-American?'"—whereupon Buzz laughed and said: "Uh liberal Democrat") quoted another ex-communist as claiming that a former administrative assistant to President Roosevelt, and a former Assistant Secretary of the Treasury, had both fed "top secret" information to Soviet agents as late as World War II. The HUAC Republicans, said Buzz contemptuously, were gearing up for a series of sensational charges against Democrats just in time to influence the autumn elections.

Over Adam Temple's heated objections, Loren later learned, the executive editor of the *Endeavor* had written an eight-column banner headline for the front page of the August third issue, saying "New Dealers Labeled As Reds." Someone named Whitaker Chambers, another ex-communist, had testified before the HUAC that four former government lawyers, including Alger and Donald Hiss, brothers who had worked in the State Department, had committed acts of espionage designed to weaken the United States government, and ultimately to "overthrow it by any and all means." Both Chambers and one Louis Budenz had testified before a Senate subcommittee that hundreds of Soviet agents still held government jobs, many of them important ones.

By the afternoon of Wednesday, August fourth, radio news programs all over the country, as well as most of the nation's newspapers, were excitedly spreading what looked to Loren like unsubstantiated accusations against reputable public servants, emanating from self-confessed traitors who seemed to be trying to deflect attention from their own reprehensible acts by hurling charges (in exchange for having been granted immunity from prosecution) against the political foes of those orchestrating the hearings. Richard Nixon, a California congressman, one of the most outspoken members of the HUAC, had accused the Truman administration's Attorney General of trying to dissuade his committee from continuing its investigation because it might smear innocent people. As if that was a valid reason not to pursue it, sneered Nixon. Although all the charges had been made previously, in detail, to the Federal Bureau of Investigation and the Central Intelligence Agency, both of which agencies were making inquiries, Republican members of the HUAC insisted upon extensive publicity, even at the cost of undermining the investigations. The American people needed to know, asserted Nixon, that some of the stolen secrets transmitted to Moscow might help the Russian communists to produce atomic weapons.

"Supposing these charges are true," said Loren to Buzz, "shouldn't they have been kept confidential while the FBI continues to gather evidence of Soviet spying?"

"Shore," said Buzz, "but Nixon an' his crowd don' really care 'bout national security. All they care 'bout is personal notoriety. Their unscrupulous mud-slinging is protected by Congressional immunity, so their targets can't hit back. It's an effective political weapon. Th' recipients of th' assaults kin nevah recover from th' damage done by th' initial offensive."

"That's disgusting."

"Ah dunno know why yore surprised. Our man Johnson has been usin' th' same tactic 'gainst Governor Stevenson heah in Texas. He can't come right out an' call Ol' Coke uh communist; people heah know th' guy too well. Whut he's been doin' is t' keep declarin' that Stevenson is th' candidate of organized labor, which t' ah lotta Texans is like sayin' th' governor has th' backin' of th' red ruskies. An' th' beauty of Johnson's tactic is that, behin' th' scenes, th' unions are workin' fer him."

"If politics is such a dirty business," Loren asked, "why do you continue to participate?"

"Same reason yore involved, Ah imagine. Fer th' money. Also fer th' entertainment. Ah git uh real charge watchin' people makin' fools of themselves."

"But these are the guys who govern."

"In uh democracy we git th' gub'ment we deserve. 'Sides, we sometimes discover, surprisingly, that we've elected uh good man t' office. Our former congressman, Martin Dies, wuz uh sonuffabitch. Th' HUAC wuz his playground an' rich reactionaries were his big backers. But our current congressman is an honest, decent fellow. Yew kin nevah tell. Sometimes yew come up uh winnah."

"Then I wish I was working for our congressman instead of Johnson. I really don't like the man at all."

Buzz laughed. "Our congressman," he declared, "don' need yore help; he's unopposed. An' Lyndon ain't so bad. He really cares 'bout workin' people. If'n he gits into th' Senate, he'll vote right mos' of th' time. Coke Stevenson oughta be uh Republican. An' he would be if'n they had uh viable party in Texas. In th' Senate he'd vote wit' th' right-wingers, th' Taft-Bricker bunch. That's why Ah'm fer ol' Lyndon. Let's git back t' wuk an' give 'im some value fer his dollah."

CHAPTER 10
BROWN

"Yore startin' in right field, t'day, Yank," said Fats to Loren, when the Scorpions assembled at Davis's drug store on the morning of Sunday, August 8. "Say, didn't yew tell me once that yew'd done some pitchin' in high school?"

"That's right," responded Loren eagerly.

"Wal, our pitchin' didn' do so good agin' Fisher. A. C. couldn' make it t'day; so if Slick has trouble wit' th' Brown Bears Ah may have t' call on yew."

"I'll do my best."

"Say Yank," shouted Duke from one of the tables near the back wall. "Come siddown an' have sum breakfast."

Loren shuddered. "No thanks," he said. "I've already eaten."

Loren watched, fascinated, as Duke proceeded to consume a pile of eggs and grits floating in bacon grease. Bobo and Ham were likewise engaged, while Slick was merely having what looked like Wheaties and milk. He gave Loren a knowing look. "Th' food heah is uh bit chancy," he whispered, "but nobody's died of it yet."

In reply, Loren rolled his eyes. He sat quietly and observed his teammates as, one by one, they arrived. Except for Jackie Lawson, who was not much older than Loren, they were all mature men who had grown up in the same neighborhood, gone to the same schools, and rendered military service during the war. There was not an intellectual among them. Even Slick seemed uninterested in anything besides baseball and women. In short, they and Loren had little in common.

Yet it also seemed that they had accepted him into their closed circle. At least he had not encountered any overt hostility or resentment. They had defended him at some risk to themselves during the fracas at Stanley. Moreover, their caliber of baseball was far superior to any he had previously experienced; and he was grateful to be challenged. He therefore considered himself fortunate to have been admitted into the redneck fraternity of the Southside Scorpions.

* * *

The trip eastward to Brown over the Baton Rouge highway led through stagnant swamps in which big-bottomed cypress stumps, shrouded in the morning mists, protruded through green slime and occasionally furnished a resting place for a snowy egret or a hungry seagull. Overhead, a few fleecy clouds drifted northward in a bright blue sky. The worn tires of Duke's convertible thumped against the ridges of black asphalt protruding from cracks in the concrete highway, providing an extra drumbeat to the caterwauling radio. After scarcely an hour of travel, the Scorpion caravan turned northward off the main road onto a narrow artery that snaked along the western side of the Sepia River, whose muddy waters lapped against the gray hulks of mothballed naval warships, mostly destroyers or frigates, with here and there the great looming presence of a heavy cruiser. Although heavily coated with grease, the ships still rusted in silent subordination to the ravages of time and nature.

Loren imagined those same ships at sea only four or five years earlier, their sharp prows cutting through ten-foot-high waves, their decks alive with spunky sailors and gold-braided officers barking commands; five-inch guns booming and machine guns chattering, as their tracer projectiles left smoky trails high in the sky where enemy planes with red circles on their wingtips maneuvered to avoid the barrage of bullets from below. Some of these ships, Loren thought, had witnessed cringes of fear, screams of pain, and almost indescribable destruction and death. He fervently hoped they would not have to be pressed back into service for his own generation to repeat the experience.

The lead car, driven by Ham, darted into a restaurant parking lot, stopping under a huge neon sign depicting a bucking bronco. Underneath were the words "Wild Horse Eatery," also in bright tubular lights. "Ah hope they got somptin' 'sides horse meat," said Duke, as he parked his convertible. He, Fats, Slick, and Loren got out, stretched, and trailed after their teammates, who were already eagerly entering the restaurant.

The building was air conditioned and so dark that Loren almost ran into a departing customer and several chairs before he found an empty space in a booth beside Fats, with Slick and Jackie sitting opposite. The ponderous flab of the manager filled most of the padded bench, so that Loren was forced to position his behind on the outer edge, almost overhanging the cracked linoleum floor.

Even though it was barely eleven in the morning, the large room was crowded and noisy with the yowling of a very loud juke box overwhelming the hum of numerous conversations. Slick stared hungrily through the cigarette smoke at a waitress who stood beside a nearby booth. Her bosom swelled sumptuously beneath her dress, partly covered by a stained apron. She was not much older than Loren, but she was already hard-looking. Her smile appeared forced—not reaching her tired eyes.

"Say," Slick whispered to Fats, "ain't that th' gal who flirted wit' me th' las' time we wuz here?"

"Ah believe so. Lessee, whut wuz her name?"

"Ah 'member," said Slick. "Everyone called 'er Clit."

"Clit?" said a puzzled Fats. "Ah don' think... He paused, studying Slick's face. "Ah 'member now," he said. "It shore is... Clit."

"Jackie, ol' buddy," said Slick. "Yore th' closest. Jes' ask cute li'l Clit t' come ovah heah an' take our order, will yew please?"

Jackie nodded. He waited until the waitress had closed her order book and stepped away from the neighboring booth, as if to start for the kitchen. "Hey, Clit," Jackie shouted. She turned toward him, looking displeased.

Jackie beckoned. Slick and Fats grinned as she approached.

"Whut did yew call me?" she asked Jackie, a clenched fist resting on one hip; the other hand tightly clutching her order book.

"Why Clit," said Jackie uncomfortably. "Ain't that yore name?"

He tried to duck but too late. A sudden blow, the resounding "whap" of which silenced all conversation around them, knocked him sprawling onto the floor. Rage contorted the waitress's face. "How d' yew like that, yew dirty jerk?" she cried. Jackie appeared dumbfounded. What possessed this girl? She looked as if she wanted to hit him again.

Just then, a yell came from the kitchen door. It was the restaurant manager, pointing at her and roaring a summons: "Marie, come heah. Come heah, Ah say, at once!"

With a final glare at Jackie, the girl headed for the kitchen. "Lemme out," said Fats. Sliding past Loren, who was beginning to realize that some kind of trick had been played on Jackie, he caught up with the girl just as she reached her infuriated boss. The three of them conversed for a few moments, the girl at first indignant, then gradually subdued, even allowing herself a slight smile when Fats slipped money into her palm; the manager glowering at the outset, then looking interested in what Fats was saying; then at the end grinning and slapping the Scorpion manager boisterously on the back before he vanished back into the kitchen.

When Fats came back to their table, Loren—embarrassed for Jackie, and conscious that other patrons in the joint were still staring curiously at them—asked: "What happened, Fats?"

"Ah finally got 'em calmed down," said Fats, hugely amused about something.

"But whut got into her?" asked Jackie. "Ah only called her over t' wait on us, an' she… she really belted me." He gingerly fingered his cheekbone, which had turned greenish purple.

"Wal, Ah guess she didn't like whut yew called her," said Fats "These French gals have terrible tempers."

"Ah called her Clit," said Jackie, "jes' like Slick tol' me to. That's her name, ain't it?"

"More like uh nickname," said Slick, his eyes fixed on the empty table top.

"Yeah," said Fats. "Whut we done forgot, Jackie, is that she really doesn' like that nickname. We shudda 'membered. Ah'm sorry she hit yew."

"Me too," said Slick. "Are yew gonna be O. K?"

"Ah guess so," replied Jackie. "But Ah wish Ah had kept mah mouf shut."

Loren was about to ask what the word "Clit" meant, when the arrival of another waitress, a chubby older woman who took their orders in a guarded manner and seemed anxious to get the process completed quickly, prevented his inquiry.

He ordered a hamburger with everything on it, hoping for lots of onions, good for combating or preventing any ailment. He then left the booth to use the men's room, the door of which he discovered was locked. While waiting for the incumbent to emerge, he overheard a conversation from the nearby kitchen. One of the cooks said: "Ah wish yew wouldn' let yore nose drip onto the burger buns. It makes me sick."

His companion said: "Wal, Ah can't help it. Ah've gotta bad cold. Don' look if it bothers yew."

The gents' door opened and a seedy looking customer came out, nodding at Loren as he zipped his fly. Loren whizzed and then turned to wash his hands, but there was no soap and the water faucet did not work. Rubbing his fingers with toilet paper, he rejoined his companions, who were already starting to eat.

No longer hungry for his burger, Loren contemplatively sipped his Coke through a paper straw. Finally he extracted the poorly cooked meat from the bun and wolfed it down, closing his eyes as he did so, and leaving the bun on his plate. Slick said: "Ah nevah saw anyone eat uh burger thataway." Loren replied: "Better check your buns. There may be mold on them."

The others gave what was left of their buns close scrutiny but found nothing disquieting. Unlike Loren, they cleaned their plates.

* * *

Arriving at the Bears' ball park at 12:30, the Scorpions had barely enough time to dress and take fielding practice before the lineups were announced. Loren was batting seventh for the visitors, with only the catcher, Feets, and Slick, who was pitching, below him in the order. He hoped for a productive afternoon, so that Fats would see fit to move him higher in the lineup.

Slick got through the first six innings with only two runs scored against him. The Brown Bears were far less formidable at bat than either the Stanley or Fisher hitters, and Slick was shrewd, mixing his pitches and their locations, sticking mostly with slow stuff when he discovered that the opponents had a tendency to overswing. Their target was a left field wall constructed solidly of cinder blocks that was located only about 210 feet from home plate. Even though it was over fifteen feet high, it was an inviting target. The Brown batters all seemed to be aiming for it, but Slick kept his pitches low and away, and the best they could do were grounders to Bobo and a couple of flies that Duke easily chased down in deep center field. In right field, Loren was entirely unoccupied.

At bat, he finally got his first semi-pro hit. It came in the second inning, a hard smash through the middle, scoring Duke with the initial run of the game. Leading off first base, Loren noticed that the pitcher was concentrating on Feets in the batter's box and not paying much attention to him. On a one-and-one count, therefore, he took off for second base and made it with a hook slide under a late tag. Although Feets popped up and Slick struck out, Ham pounded a hanging curve ball into the right center field gap, and Loren scored easily.

In the fifth inning he stepped to the plate a second time with two outs and Fido perched on first base. Hoping for an inside fast ball that he could redirect toward the inviting left field wall, he let three successive curves go by without offering at them, but the umpire called two of them strikes. One of these had been at least six inches outside. Loren had learned during the Stanley game, however, that Texas semipro umpires tended to err in favor of the home team. A fourth curve was too close to let the umpire call it; so Loren had to swing at a low outside pitch that he would normally have let pass. He managed a respectable line drive over the second baseman's head, but the right fielder, playing him perfectly, drifted over for an easy catch.

In the top of the seventh, with the score now eight to two in favor of the Scorpions, Loren was due to bat again with one out and two men on. As he started for the on deck circle swinging two bats, Fats said: "Yank, Ah'm lettin' Jackie hit fer yew. He's gonna pitch th' rest of th' game, an' Slick'll play in right field. Yew kin rest an' watch. Yew done good."

Trying not to appear disappointed, Loren returned to the bench. Jackie struck out. But he pitched well, his fast ball more effective than it might have been had the Bears not been previously fed a diet of Slick's slow stuff. A line drive captured by Duke with a running grab ended the contest, 8-3.

In the clubhouse afterwards, Loren exchanged congratulations with his jubilant teammates. As he took off his dirty uniform, he felt flattered when Slick on his way to the shower hoisted Loren's bat and said: "This thing is heavy. How in th' world do yew git 'roun' on uh fast ball?"

"Mostly," he replied, "I don't. I just try to poke it to right field."

"Lemme show yew somethin'." Slick extended his own bat, which was thicker than Loren's. "Try this."

Loren took a couple of practice swings. "Seems awfully light," he observed.

Slick laughed. "Yeah. Yew kin really whip th' sonuffabitch 'roun'. Not that Ah've had much luck wit it mahself. But Ah showed Bobo how t' fix his stick th' same way, an' yew've seen whut he kin do wit' it."

"What's the secret?"

"Ah," said Slick. "That's sumptin better demonstrated than told. When we git home, Ah'll show yew."

* * *

On the way back to Tocqueville, Duke drove shirtless, his right arm flung casually along the top of the front seat, his left hand resting limply on the obscene glass knob attached to the steering wheel. Some day, Loren thought, his grip would slip and Duke, whose idea of driving slowly was to keep twenty miles an hour above the speed limit, would plunge himself and his passengers into oblivion. Loren intended to be driving his own vehicle, purchased with Lyndon Johnson's campaign money, before that happened.

A gin bottle emerged from under the front seat, along with a Mason jar of orange juice. Duke and Bobo, sitting beside him, began taking alternate sips of gin and juice. Once, as he gulped some of the fiery fluid, Duke choked, and the car swerved. Loren closed his eyes as a telephone pole at the side of the road leaped toward them out of the growing darkness. As Duke fought the steering wheel, the right front tire caught on the edge of the cracked concrete highway, which had no shoulder, and seemed to be sliding off; then came back safely on as Duke regained control.

A few minutes later, in the car's headlights, Loren saw something startling.

"What was that?" he asked Fats.

"Whut wuz whut?"

"That thing at the side of the road—looked like a minature dinosaur."

"Naw. An armadillo."

"What is an armadillo?"

"It's uh South American animal that moved into Texas back in th' 1850s an' migrated northward. It's only ben 'roun' heah in large numbers fer three or four years.

"Armadillos live in burrows like groundhogs. They feed at night on insects, diggin' 'em out wit' their claws an' zappin' 'em wit' tongues that shoot out like uh lizard's. They tear up th' soil like pigs. In Mexico they eat fire ants, tarantulas, scorpions an' snakes, even toads. An' th' Mexican peons hunt an' eat th' armadillos. They taste like pork. They live 'bout ten years, maybe longer. As long as uh dawg or uh cat."

"I've never seen anything so strange," said Loren. "That armor looked like chain mail—like something medieval. How tough is it?"

"It ain't very hard," said Fats. "More like uh alligator's hide than uh turtle's shell. Uh large dawg kin bite through it. But th' armadillos hide in heavy brush or brambles whar their enemies can't git at 'em, an' whar thar armor protects 'em from gettin' scratched."

"Look, there's another one!"

"Yeah, they're all ovah th' place. Too many. Yew'll see 'em in th' middle of th' road lookin' like uh gray football wit' uh skinny tail. When uh driver tries t' straddle 'em, they jump straight up—they can't help it; some kinda reflex action—an' git wiped out by th' underside of th' car."

Duke was driving so fast, Loren thought, that no armadillo wandering in the highway would be likely to escape. He leaned forward to check the speedometer. Bathed in the green glow behind the steering column, the white needle hovered between sixty and sixty-five. Could be worse, Loren thought. Someone should invent seat belts for automobiles, like the ones used in airplanes. That might save the lives of a few people at the mercy of drivers like Duke.

Loren remembered with a shudder how, early that morning on the trip over from Tocqueville, Duke had kept his old Nash convertible on eighty, once swinging out to pass a station wagon with such verve that the car rocked and fishtailed. As their front bumper had drawn even with the station wagon's rear wheels, it had also swerved outward to pass a small jalopy that had been shielded from Duke's view by the larger vehicle. At that moment, suddenly appearing from the opposite direction over a rise in the road, a huge truck had loomed up like the embodiment of doom.

As Loren went rigid with fear, his mind had transformed the entire scene into slow motion, as if in a dream—the three cars squeezed together on the narrow highway hurtling toward the charging behemoth, two frightened faces peering down from the truck's windshield like the pupils of a dragon's eyes, Duke and Bobo cussing, and Fats whimpering…

And then the danger had abruptly ended, as Duke willed his car past the other two barely in time to evade the truck, which roared past with a prolonged blast of its air horn and turbulence that threatened to blow them into the ditch. Looking back behind them, Loren had been relieved to see that the station wagon, too, was unscathed, and that the third vehicle had safely turned off into a driveway.

Now, as they cut through the dusk on their way home, Loren relived the terror of that morning, and shivered in his dark corner. Next to him, Fats snored, as if he did not remain in peril…

*　　*　　*

It was not yet fully dark when the cavalcade reached Davis's drug store, where Loren got into Slick's small red Chevy convertible and rode with him a short distance to his house. Waving at a blonde woman in shorts who watched them from inside the screen door, Slick led the way to a one-car garage, crowded with male miscellany. When he turned on the light, cockroaches scuttled in all directions. Reaching for a baseball bat that was leaning against a wall, Slick laid it on a work bench and clamped it tightly in a vise. Then he took down a brace and bit and began to drill a hole into the barrel. "Th' difficult thang is t' keep it straight," he explained. "If'n it's crooked, it ruins th' bat. Some guys use uh half-inch bit, but Ah think five-eighths is bettah." Grunting, he struggled to keep the bit turning as it rammed deeply into the hard ash of the bat. "Thar. Eight inches are 'bout right," he said, as he worked the drill back and forth to clear little spirals of wood shavings out of the round shaft.

Taking a handful of small corks from a tin can and saying "Neighbor of mine drinks wine like water," he began to tamp the corks into the hole with a hammer and a wooden dowel until the opening was packed almost full, only about half an inch remaining open. He then scooped up a small amount of sawdust and some tiny shavings from the surface of the workbench and inserted them into the remaining aperture, squirting a white toothpaste-like substance that he identified as wood glue on top, and then tamping the entire concoction into rigidity. "Heah," he said, "take it; it's yore's."

"Really?"

"Shore."

"But can't you use it yourself?"

"Ah already have three. Ah won' be needin' 'nother one," said Slick. "But if yew don' wan' it…"

"Oh, I do. And thank you very much."

"Don' mention it. An' after that glue is completely dry—by tomorra mornin'—rub some fine sandpaper ovah it. Yew kin also use uh brown crayon t' make it look like th' rest of th' wood grain. Jus' uh light touch; don' ovahdo it… Ah believe that's Rhonda callin' me t' supper. Ah'll drive yew home an' see yew next Sunday at Davis's."

*　　*　　*

After Loren had finished his dinner and gone into the kitchen to help his mother with the dishes, he ascertained that his father was out of earshot in the living room and that his brother was squeaking away on his violin in his own room. Then he asked: "Mom, what does clit mean?"

"What?"

"Clit. What does the word mean?"

"Why, Loren, I'm not sure I know. What is the context?"

"One of the ballplayers called a girl Clit, and she got mad, and he didn't know why; and Slick told me to ask my sister if I wanted to get to the bottom of the matter. Since I don't have a sister, I'm asking you."

"I see." Putting the last of the dishes away and hanging up her dish towel, Nan said: "I think you'd better consult a dictionary. I suggest you use the big one in the den."

Loren hauled the huge Webster's International Dictionary off the bottom shelf of the bookcase in his father's den. It did not take long to find the word for which he was looking.

When he tried to slip unperceived past the living room door to get to his own room, his mother called out: "Did you find the definition you wanted, dear?"

"Yeah. I think so." He thought he heard his father laughing and his mother shushing him. He resolved to be very wary of Slick Bangwell in the future. The guy was generous and meant no real harm, but he was a relentless practical joker. Let someone else be his victim.

CHAPTER 11
THE AUDITION

On Monday morning, when the two Lyndon Johnson campaigners resumed what Buzz called their "poster parade," Loren wanted to talk baseball. "Did you see where Satch Paige pitched the Indians back into first place last week?"

"Yeah," said Buzz unenthusiastically. "An' didja see whar Alger Hiss an' several others went afore th' HUAC an' denied they were red spies. Whereupon Truman said that th' entire investigation was uh red herrin' t' divert attention from uh do-nothing Congress's failure to address th' country's real problems. Ol' Harry's right, y'know. That's th' Republicans all ovah: Don' legislate; investigate."

"Do you think what the HUAC is doing will affect the November election?"

"Bound tuh. Evah since uh huge influx of immigrants uh generation or two ago, th' American people have been vulnerable t' scare stories 'bout foreign influences an' plots. An' th' rich Republicans who control th' corporations that own mos' of th' newspapers an' radio stations will see that those stories git well publicized, whether thar's any substance t' them or not. If workin' people try t' improve themselves through collective action, that's uh communist plot. If niggers wan' their constitutional rights, th' commies are behin' it. If women wan' some of th' goodies that men monopolize, that's on th' red agenda. If people in other countries wit' repressive regimes rebel 'gainst them, that's part of th' Russian timetable fer world conquest. Jus' listen t' that creep Thomas, that blowhard Mundt, that slimy Nixon, an' that fascist Hebert, who comprise th' active members of th' HUAC. They all use th' same code words."

"Buzz, I didn't realize that you were such a left-winger. Suggesting that Negroes have constitutional rights!"

"As long as Ah don' have t' associate wit 'em, they kin have all th' rights anyone else has, fer all Ah care."

"You're a real softie."

"Yeah, shore. Say, speakin' of th' news, didja see in Sunday's *Endeavor* that th' Yankees are holdin' uh tryout camp in Tocqueville on Thursday?"

"Boy, I'd really like to be there!"

"Wal, why don' yew go?"

"It would mean missing two days of work."

"Don' worry 'bout it. Ah won' tell th' boss. Ah'll work th' roads by mahself, an' he'll nevah know th' difference. Go on an' give those Yankee bird dawgs uh thrill."

"Gee thanks, Buzz. I really appreciate your doing this for me."

"Ain't nuttin'. Th' Yanks kin use some new blood. DiMaggio, Henrich, an' Keller are all gettin' old."

* * *

On Thursday, August 12, Loren rushed through breakfast. Then he pulled on his Winona CDS baseball breeches and purple stirrup socks, and jammed the purple cap with the white W onto his brown curls. Because of the humid heat, he decided to omit his uniform jersey in favor of a white T-shirt. He picked up his spikes and glove and boarded his bicycle for the twenty-minute ride to Shipper Stadium. Dry-mouthed and jittery, he was determined to find out whether he was ready for professional baseball.

Passing through an open gate into the stadium and trading his tennis shoes for his spikes, Loren clattered down an aisle between the box seats to a gate near the first base dugout. There his precarious confidence began to evaporate, as he observed almost one hundred aspirants already tossing baseballs back and forth, playing impromptu games of pepper, or merely lounging near the two dugouts awaiting instructions. Several middle-aged men wearing Yankee pinstripes were conversing behind home plate, and members of the local ground crew were hauling a wheeled batting cage in from the direction of the left field bull pen.

"Hey, Yank," yelled someone nearby. It was Duke, the muscles in his sunburned arms rippling as he exchanged tosses with a freckled fellow about Loren's age. "Come an' join us. This heah's Mick. His dad drove 'im heah all th' way from Oklahoma. We got guys from all ovah."

"Hi," said Loren, reaching out his hand.

"Howdy." The grip was hard but th' voice was soft and the blue eyes mild. Loren was on the verge of asking Mick's last name when one of the Yankee scouts called through a megaphone for attention. It was time to go to work. "There are ninety-six of yew," he shouted, "an' by late this afternoon we'll narrow th' number t' forty-four. Those prospects will then be invited back tomorrow. Ah wan' all th' pitchers an' catchers t' assemble heah whar Ah'm standin'; an' th' resta yew each take ten swings in th' battin' cage in groups of four. 'Member, ten swings; no more. Earl, heah, will throw yew medium fas' balls; no curves. Afore yew take yore turn at bat, Ah wan' yew t' check in wit' me behin' th' cage; so that Ah kin git yore vital information. Heah, yew, an' yew, an' th' two of yew, start hittin'. Th' rest go shag until yore called."

Along with Duke, Loren drifted into center field and was soon chasing balls that flew off the warclubs of a steady succession of hitters, as the veteran hurler on the mound, working like a human metronome, kept firing strikes, assisted by a young boy, apparently the son of one of the scouts, who chased down the balls thrown in from the field and supplied them, several at a time, to the pitcher. Although each hitter strove to put good wood on every ball thrown over the plate, some of them could do little more than hit fouls or weak grounders. Occasionally an individual stood out.

One was the blond fellow called Mick, who stepped into the lefty batter's box, holding his waving wand high above his left ear, and announced his presence by smashing the first ball thrown to him high off the right field fence, three hundred and thirty feet from home plate. With Loren watching attentively, the Oklahoman fouled off a pitch; banged a couple of hard grounders past infielders who danced out of the way; and then really tied into one. The sound of a ball hit solidly with impressive brute strength, a report like a rifle shot, turned heads all over the stadium. The ball speedily became a small white dot high in the cloudless blue sky directly above Loren and a half dozen others standing dumbfounded near the center field wall. It disappeared over the scoreboard and landed out in the parking lot, well over four hundred feet from where it had been launched.

Flashing a hint of a grin, the burly youngster prepared for the next pitch by tugging at the brim of his cap and taking a quick practice swing. Once again the vicious cut and twisting follow through. Again the loud "crack." Again a towering drive to center field that drove both Loren and Duke back against the fence, waiting for the ball to descend. It would have hit the very top of the fence if Duke had not reached above Loren's tentative grasp and gloved it with a satisfying smack. The rest was anticlimactic: a shot through the box; a hopper to first base; a long foul fly to right; and, finally, a blistering liner into right center that shot past Loren before he could move and ricocheted off the fence nearly all the way back to the infield dirt. Watching the chief scout scribbling on his clipboard with a bemused expression on his weathered face, Loren surmised that at least one aspirant had already earned himself a further look, if not a minor league contract. If only he could impress the Yankee representatives half as much!

Loren's turn to hit came soon afterwards. First he gave a gray-haired man his name, height, weight, experience (three years high school varsity), and position (he hesitated, and then said "outfield" on the assumption that there would be less competition there). He then stepped into the right hand hitter's box to face the man in the Yankee uniform, who by this time was streaming sweat and appearing anxious to get his stint on the mound over with. From deep in center field his pitches had not looked very fast, but Loren discovered to his dismay that from sixty feet away they seemed to explode out of the hurler's hand, swooshing past him before he could get set. He barely foul-tipped the first two. Concentrating hard, he smoothly stroked pitch number three, converting it into a soft liner to center. Pitches numbers four through eight he also met squarely, without swinging hard, resulting in three more shots over the infield and two hard grounders past the pitcher, all probably base hits under game conditions. Wanting to end his time at bat with a bang, if he could, Loren lashed at a knee high submission with all the power he could summon from his forearms and watched with pride as the ball flew on a rising line along the third base foul line until it cleared the fence by about a foot, barely inside the foul pole. Although he felt like strutting back to the outfield, he maintained a poker face and a slow trot until he rejoined Duke, who said: "Nice going."

The Scorpion center fielder had earlier returned from his own time at bat, during which he had swung ten times with all his considerable strength, but failed to hit anything more impressive than a trio of easy flies; after which he had slouched sullenly back to the outfield in dark disappointment.

The hitting went on until past noon, until all ninety-six candidates had taken their ten swings, a replacement pitcher, apparently from some Yankee farm club, working on the mound for the final fifty. Loren believed that he had done as well as any of the others, except, of course, for the guy from Oklahoma, who appeared to be in a class by himself. This became even more apparent when the scouts lined up applicants in groups of ten and had them race about forty yards, timing them with stop watches. Loren ran with all the speed he could summon, but finished in the middle of his bunch. The one called Mick seemed effortlessly to outsprint those with whom he ran, finishing well ahead of all nine.

It was past one o'clock when cartons filled with brown paper bags of unshelled peanuts, Spam sandwiches on doughy white bread, and Baby Ruth candy bars, along with metal coolers containing cold Cokes, materialized near the first base dugout. Everyone sat on the parched grass to eat and drink. Loren consumed two sandwiches and then opened a bottle of cola, into which, imitating Duke, he inserted half a handful of salted shelled peanuts.

"Hey," he exclaimed. "This is good."

"Tol' ya."

"I never heard of putting peanuts into drinks before."

"Aw, yew nawtherners are jus' ignorant. Yew have t' come South t' learn how t' enjoy life."

Next came infield and outfield tryouts, conducted simultaneously. One scout hit grounders to a succession of infielders, who lined up behind their chosen positions and awaited their turns to field a dozen grass cutters and display the strength and accuracy of their throws to first. Another member of the scouting corps, expertly wielding a thin fungo bat, rapped out a steady succession of fly balls to the outfielders, massed in a group of eighteen, out in right field. Each fielder was told to chase and catch, if possible, three fly balls, and then throw to third base to nail an imaginary runner. Loren hung back near the end of the line; so that he might observe the competition before taking his turn. The fungo hitter placed his drives so that the panting candidates had to run at top speed in order to seize them on the fly. A majority, after catching the ball or retrieving it on the turf, threw off balance, with little speed or accuracy. Or, taking care to set themselves before throwing, they delayed so long that they might as well have thrown home, for all the good their heaves would have done at third base.

When Loren's turn came, he timed his catch of the first fungo fly so that he received the ball backhanded in his glove just above his right shoulder, which enabled him to use his forward momentum to make a strong overhand throw. He added accuracy by following through fully with his right hand, pointing directly at the desired destination. The ball sped arrowlike to a point about twelve feet short of the recipient, where it zoomed off the infield dirt with a puff of dust, and flew in one long low bounce into the third baseman's waiting glove about six inches above the bag.

Perfect, thought Loren. Gotta do it twice more.

Next came a hard line drive. Loren started late, as the overspin on the ball was not immediately apparent. Consequently he realized as he dashed toward the infield that he might not be able to snare the sphere before it hit the ground; yet he feared that if he pulled up to take it on one hop, he might be blamed for not trying. So he gave it all he had, careful to keep slightly to the right of the oncoming drive, in order to minimize the illusion that the ball was vibrating vertically, and also to keep his open glove out of the way of his churning legs. Leaning precariously forward, he managed at the last possible instant to reach out and intercept the sinking sphere with a fingertip catch only inches above the grass. Then, as he continued forward, he shifted the ball across his body to his throwing hand, twisted to the right, and threw. Although this time the ball took two hops to reach its destination, it was still right on target.

Unfortunately, Loren's third throw hit a dirt clod in the infield and bounced off line, pulling the third baseman several feet off the bag. Nevertheless, he believed that he had done as well as any of the others, thus far. Nor did the attempts of the final three outfielders alter his favorable opinion of his own performance.

The infielders took longer to complete their tryouts. Seeing that the muscular Oklahoman was about to take his turn at shortstop, Loren watched curiously. Somehow appearing more manly than the others, although by no means the oldest, Mick was agile and showed a strong arm. But his hasty throws lacked accuracy, one of them flying so far over the first baseman's desperate leap that it disappeared under a chair in the box seats. As he grimly went through the motions of demonstrating his abilities as a shortstop, he was obviously feeling frustrated; and when the head scout called an end to the infield activity and summoned the entire crew of applicants to cluster around him, Loren saw the Oklahoman angrily snatch up a bat (Loren hoped it was his own) and with an awesome exhibition of strength, break it into two pieces over his knee.

He would make a good outfielder, Loren thought. But he doesn't seem cut out for shortstop.

It was time to learn who would be invited back the next day. As the Yankee spokesman read off names from his clipboard, there was absolute silence. About halfway through the list, Loren heard his name, and a while later that of Duke Daniel. But over one-half of the attendees were not as fortunate. With forty-four names read, the chief scout looked up and shook his head. It was over. "Sonuffabitch," said one unsuccessful candidate, slamming his glove to the ground in a rage. Several others looked dazed, as if they had awakened from a pleasant dream back into the real world. Slowly, those not chosen drifted disconsolately out of the stadium. The scouts waited patiently. No one spoke.

Finally it was time for further instructions. "Yew men," the head scout shouted, no longer bothering to use his megaphone, "come back heah t'morra. We'll have two nine-innin' games, th' fust one startin' at nine o'clock. Each pitcher will trow three innin's. Th' resta yew will each play one full game. Th' followin' men will arrive by eight t' participate in game numba one." He read off twenty-two names, assigning each person a position in the field and a spot in the batting order. Duke was to play center field on one of the morning squads. Loren's name had not yet been called.

"Th' followin' men report at one o'clock t' play at two," roared the New York rep. Loren heard: "Temple, right field," as the lineup for the home team was read. He was to bat seventh, not a very flattering designation for an outfielder. As they all left the park, he caught up with Duke. "I may not see you tomorrow," he said. "So good luck."

"Same t' yew, Yank," said his Scorpion teammate. "Ah hope we both git contracts. If'n Ah don' git one this time, Ah'm not tryin' again. Ah'll be twenty-nine next yeah, which is too old t' begin in the bush leagues."

So is twenty-eight, thought Loren. But he merely said: "You'll make it, Duke. You're a good player."

* * *

On Friday morning Loren slept late. By twelve-thirty he was on his bicycle peddling toward Shipper Stadium.

After the usual warmups, the tryout game began promptly at two o'clock. Having no knowledge of the tendencies or abilities of the opposing batters, Loren positioned himself in right field entirely by instinct. His first chance came with two out in the second inning as a ground single was hit in the slot between the first and second basemen. It was an easy play, but to make sure that the ball did not get by him, he went down on his right knee to field it before tossing it to the shortstop at second base.

In the last half of the same inning, he came to bat with two down and a runner on first base. The pitcher, a stocky lefthander, threw him curve balls exclusively, trying to handcuff him with inside pitches. With a count of two and two, ordinarily a fast ball situation, he gambled and eased back in the box, hoping for a fifth bender. Sure enough, it came zipping across the inside corner of the plate just above his kneecaps, and his altered stance enabled him to put good wood on it, resulting in a smash that the third baseman snatched with a lucky stab as it headed on a line for left field.

In the fourth inning, Loren effortlessly gloved a towering fly ball hit by Mick from Oklahoma, who was playing shortstop for the opposition. In the fifth frame, he led off. With the score still tied at zero, his duty was to get on base. After taking a hard but futile swing at the first offering from a tall righthander, who hurled a fast ball by him letter high, he waited, crouching, while two more fast balls drifted slightly high and outside. Then, sliding his right hand down the bat handle toward the barrel at the last possible moment, and making sure that he caught the pitch well out in front of the plate, he dumped a perfect bunt halfway to third base and crossed first base a step ahead of the pitcher's off-balance throw.

Under tryout camp conditions, there were no signals for sacrificing, stealing, or the hit-and-run. Although Loren was unsure of the capabilities of his team's burly catcher, who was next up, he knew that most managers would have called for a sacrifice bunt. But the big man apparently had visions of a long ball and a resulting Yankee contract, and swung away. Three swishes later he sat down. The pitcher also struck out.

With two out, Loren decided to see if he could sneak a steal. His chance came just as the next hitter walked behind the home plate umpire to reach the lefthanded batter's box. With a lefty coming up, the opposing second baseman moved over toward the first base foul line, not far from where Loren was taking his lead. The formidable fellow from Oklahoma had drifted over toward third base to pick up a pebble from the dirt and toss it into foul territory. Seeing that his back was momentarily turned toward the pitcher, Loren pretended to stumble. Eagerly, the pitcher hurled the ball to the first baseman, trying for a pickoff.

By the time that worthy had dug the ball out of his massive mitt, set himself, and thrown it to second base, and Mick, alerted by cries from teammates, had thundered over to take the throw, Loren was nearing the bag. A hard hook slide did the rest, with his left toe contacting the canvas a split second before the shortstop applied the tag. Then, when the pitcher, seemingly rattled by the delayed steal, grooved his next offering, the hitter promptly slapped it into left center field, and Loren, starting simultaneously with the sound of bat on ball, raced around third to score standing up.

In the top of the ninth, the score was still one to nothing. Loren had gone out on a lazy fly to right field two innings earlier, and had caught two more flies himself, both routine plays. With only one out to go for a win, the pitcher faced Mr. Oklahoma. Trying too hard for a strikeout, he overthrew and buzzed a high hard one dangerously close to the blonde chin stubble of the grim faced hitter, who fell backward just in time to avert being clobbered. Intentional or not, the brushbacker was not a wise move. On the next pitch, the infuriated batter took a savage swing and drove the ball like a rocket far over Loren's head, and into the street behind the bleacher seats.

Batting in the bottom of the ninth, Loren's teammates had to face a wild fireballer. On a three and two pitch, he walked the big first baseman whose back Loren had been looking at since the game began. The next batter, however, made a miserable mess of his attempt to lay down a sacrifice bunt. He thrust his bat weakly at a high pitch that he should have let pass and tapped a popup directly to the pitcher, who gleefully doubled the runner off first base. Two away; bases empty; Loren up.

From his teammates in the third base dugout, he could hear shouts of encouragement. From the opponents came cries of disdain and encouragement for the pitcher to blow him away. Aware that the Yankee scouts were watching, he fought to remain calm. He felt his hands beginning to shake and his brain failing to function. Gotta relax, he thought; let 'er rip.

Settling himself in the batter's box with only one thought—to hit the ball hard somewhere—he waited. Came the pitch, spinning suspiciously, not a conventional fast ball. Sure enough, just as it neared the plate, it dipped and drifted low and outside. Ball one.

Taking the catcher's return peg with an impatient stab of his glove, the pitcher placed his right toe on the third base side of the rubber. Once before, during the previous inning, Loren had seen him do this. Warily he edged his front foot back several inches, and slightly turned his torso to the left. The pitch came as expected, a sidearm fast ball with a considerable fade back across the plate toward him. He swung at it with all his strength and felt a welcome tingle in his forearms that signaled a solid connection.

As he ran toward first base, Loren hoped for a miracle. Maybe, just maybe, he had hit one out. But as he galloped past the bag, he looked up in time to see the center fielder launch himself upward, his glove high against the distant fence, and the white speck that was the ball disappear into the brown leather, three hundred and sixty feet from home plate. It was the hardest Loren had ever hit a ball, a sure round tripper if he had only pulled it further into left field. Instead, with no extra innings planned by the scouts, it merely became the game's final out.

Afterwards, as the players waited hopefully, the head scout announced that he would announce the names of those with whom he wished to talk. The rest, he said, were free to leave, and thanks for coming. "Keep workin' hard," he exhorted, "an' maybe yew'll fare better next year."

Loren's name was the third one called out, and the last. Number one was that of the shortstop from Oklahoma. Number two was the pitcher who had worked the first three innings against Loren's team. After waiting until the head man had conversed with the other two, Loren stepped forward, took hold of a rough paw, and received a slight smile. "Young fella," said the Yankee rep, "yew did purty well t'day."

"Thank you, Sir."

Looking down at his clipboard, the scout said: "Yew only weigh one hundred an' thirty-five, is that right?"

"Yessir."

"Put on some weight. Work on bat speed; wit' that swing yew'll nevah make it past th' low minors. An' git some instruction on how t' run faster. Think yew kin do all that?"

"I'll try, Sir."

"Good. One more question. Are yew still in high school?"

"Yessir. I'll graduate next June."

"Well, we'd offer yew uh chance t' try class C ball fer th' rest of this summer, if yew were already outta school. But we can't, now, 'cause of th' Zoeterman rule."

"What's that?"

"Zoeterman wuz uh real prospect. He signed wit' th' White Sox while still uh junior at some small school in Chicago an' got one hundred thousand dollars t' put his John Hancock on th' contract. That's as much as they pay Joe DiMaggio or Ted Williams per season. But Commissioner Chandler ruled that th' Sox couldn't keep Zoeterman, 'cause no youngster should drop outta high school t' turn pro. Plenty of time afterwards. So we kin no longer offer contracts t' boys still in school, unless th' classes they entered wit' have already graduated. Yew got me?"

"Yessir. I remember now. I played against George Zoeterman."

The old man in the worn Yankee uniform looked interested. "Is that so? Wal, don' expect uh hundred thousand bucks, or even uh hundred bucks, fer th' privilege of signin' wit' th' Yanks. In our organization th' money comes after yew make good. Work hard t' improve, th' way Ah tol' yew, an' come back an' see me nex' summer. Name's Lowrey. Ah may have uh place fer yew in our organization."

"Thank you, Sir."

Both elated and disappointed, Loren picked up his glove and made his way under the stadium seats to recover his bicycle from the dark corner in which he had left it. Riding home, he thought about George Zoeterman, a tall blond boy who had the reputation of being the best high school player in the whole Chicago area, since Johnny Groth played for Latin. During Loren's sophomore year, Zoeterman had pitched against Winona and won the game four to nothing, striking out sixteen and allowing only two hits, one of them by Loren. With Loren on the mound,

Zoeterman, the third batter in the game, had driven a respectable fast ball high over the center fielder's head into the bushes in front of the headmaster's house for a home run.

Thereafter, Loren walked Zoeterman twice. But after the coach moved Loren to left field in order to allow a senior to pitch the last two innings, Zoeterman had greeted the new hurler with a towering shot into the cars parked on the street off campus beyond left field, a feat previously unrecorded in the annals of Winona CDS.

That autumn, Loren recalled, he had read in the sport section of his father's newspaper that Zoeterman had signed with the White Sox, but that Happy Chandler, the major league commissioner, had ruled the contract void. Loren had wondered at the time whether the seventeen-year-old Zoeterman's parents had been able to keep the bonus money. He visualized how his parents would react if a major league scout asked them to approve a contract that would make Loren a professional player, with a hefty bonus for signing.

His mother would say: "Very nice, dear. But don't you think that you should go to college first?" And his father would argue that *he* had done quite well without a college diploma. Nevertheless, if Loren should actually receive an offer to play pro ball after high school, he anticipated that it was Nan's opinion on the subject of baseball or college first that would probably prevail.

CHAPTER 12

THE LOOSE GOOSE

Sunday morning. Loren could not get his mind off the Yankee tryout camp. He was thrilled to have been chosen as a professional prospect out of so many candidates. Yet he realized how far removed he was from the raw talent of the fellow from Oklahoma. Doubtless there were many Micks and Zoetermans somewhere out in the unknown world, performing like men among boys. Hence he could not help doubting whether he had the ability to play pro. Might he not be risking too much emotional energy on an unrealistic goal? Were not the odds against him?

Nonsense, he told himself. Learn. Strive. Pursue my dream.

Today, August 15, the Scorpions were scheduled to play at Fisher, north of Tocqueville. In the absence of Duke, who had let Fats know that he was too ill to make the trip, Slick had decided to drive his red roadster, with Loren and Fats in the back seat and Ham riding shotgun.

"Now, Slick," said the third baseman nervously, "Ah've heared 'bout yore drivin,' an' Ah wan' yew t' be extra careful wit' me in th' car. Ah've got uh wife an' kids that kin't afford t' lose me."

Slick smiled. "Ah may be uh reckless devil..."

"On secon' thought," said Ham, opening the car door, "Ah think Ah'll ride wit' Bubba."

"Ah mean," said Slick, "that Ah've nevah had uh wreck."

"Oh."

"Lemme splain mah velocity philosophy."

"Whut?"

"Mah attitude toward drivin.' It's simple. Don' drive faster than th' fastest car on th' road. An' if'n yew git stopped, flash this." From his shirt pocket he extracted a silver badge that read "Deputy Sheriff."

"Whar'd yew git that?"

"From th' sheriff. Mah buddy. Since Ah've had it, Ah've nevah got uh speedin' ticket. Unlike Duke."

"Whar's yore St. Christopher doll?"

"That thang Duke has stuck t' his dashboard? Hell, Ah don' need one. Ah don' drink while Ah'm drivin.' 'Specially gin."

"Wal, that's good. Maybe Ah'll be safe wit' yew after all."

"'Course Jax beer don' count."

* * *

Soon after they left the outskirts of Tocqueville, they overtook a car traveling slowly through the pine trees ahead of them. As they neared it, Loren saw on a rear bumper sticker the words: "Honk If You Love Jesus." As Slick swung his car across the yellow center line to squeeze past the dawdler before confronting approaching traffic, he blasted his horn. From the driver's window behind them Loren, looking back, saw a fist pop out, with an extended middle finger. Having seen it, too, in his rear view mirror, Slick laughed. Loren said: "That wasn't very Christian."

"Love those fundamentalists," said Slick. He glanced at his watch. "Nine-thirty. Jus' right. Listen t' this." He twisted the dial on the car radio, and the off-key lamentations of lonely lovers were soon replaced by a bouncy hymn sung amid static by some sort of choir. Then came an oracular voice asserting that Jesus had personally spoken to the reverend somebody, Loren did not catch the name, and had delivered the good news that a cure for cancer would be revealed to him, if he would build a ten million dollar "crystal" church to glorify God. "So dew as Ah say, yew blessed Christian soldiers," he intoned, "fer Gawd has commanded yew, through me, an' therefor' yew mus' obey. Sen' me ten dollah now, an' ten dollah each month from now forward, until th' Lord's work is finished." Then he gave a mailing address.

"That's unbelievable!" exclaimed Loren.

"Not as unbelievable as that thousands of people will soon be writin' checks or stickin' ten dollah bills into envelopes," said Slick. "Now comes th' best part."

"T' show th' Lawd's gratitude fer yore contributions," the voice on the radio continued, "Ah'm authorized fer an extree fi' dollah t' mail yew an autographed picture of Jesus Christ. Yew kin be th' only person in yore neighborhood t' own one. But hurry; Ah only have uh few left. Satisfaction guaranteed."

"That oughta be illegal," said Fats. "Whar's that fella located? Tulsa?"

"Th' broadcast comes from Del Rio, right on th' Rio Grande rivah," said Slick. "Th' transmitter is ovah th' border, so th' authorities can't interfere. Ah unnerstan' that preacher's rollin' in money."

Loren wondered whether all religion was superstition based on a fear of death, which unscrupulous charlatans used to enrich themselves by conning people who were gullible or confused. Surely the enormous body of church art, music, architecture, and literature furnished evidence of something far more noble and profound than what was often embodied in the strictures of those who claimed to speak for the Almighty.

He snapped out of his reverie and looked out of the car window. The landscape had gradually become less forested. He saw cattle grazing in pastures enclosed by barbed wire strung on flimsy posts along the highway. "Lookit all them steers!" exclaimed Fats, as they passed a particularly large herd. "Mus' be at least uh hundred!"

"How can you tell that they're steers?" asked Loren.

"No udders," said Fats. "An' no balls. They've been cut. Castration alters uh bull's entire outlook, from ass t' grass. So they git fat an' make better beef. It also gentles 'em down real good; so they're easier t' handle."

"Ugh," said Loren. "Are you sure you aren't giving me a bum steer?"

"Har, har," said Slick. "He got yew good, Fats."

"Speakin' uh beef," said Ham. "Ah'm hongry. How long afore we git t'Fisher?"

"'Nother hour," said Fats. "Maybe uh li'l more."

They passed through Kurtz, formerly a sleepy crossroads hamlet, Loren was told, but now a boom town owing to the discovery of oil nearby.

"Can't we eat heah?" asked Ham plaintively.

"Too soon," said Fats, looking at his watch. "Ain't noon yet. Uh lotta people'll still be in church an' everythang'll be closed. Ah know uh good place in Fisher run by sum Chinese people. Yew'll like it."

"Ah don' know 'bout that," said Ham. "Chink food kin be purty awful. Had some when Ah wuz in th' army. K rations wuz better."

"Wal, that wuz th' war," said Fats. "These people serve good eats. Trust me."

While the others talked, Loren speculated whether a rumor, repeated by Fats, that a St. Louis Browns scout was expected at Fisher, was true. The scenery rushing past the car diminished to a blur, and the conversation dwindled to a mere murmur as he pondered whether he would be better off signing with the Browns than with the Yankees…

* * *

Fisher was hardly more than a village. Located smack in the middle of a one-block business district, consisting mainly of a bank, a post office, and several stores, was Joe Chen's Chinese Restaurant. It occupied a ramshackled wooden building with dirty front windows partly covered by faded orange drapes. Feeling slightly carsick from the long trip, Loren thought he would like some vegetables for lunch, certainly nothing greasy. And maybe a fortune cookie.

Inside, ceiling fans stirred air heavy with cigarette smoke drifting up from two bluejeaned characters wearing the customary Stetsons, sweat-stained plaid shirts and dirty cowboy boots, who were seated in a front booth drinking coffee. At the back of the room, sitting around a large table, was an oriental family, dining on hamburgers and hot dogs. Except for catsup drenching some french fries in red goo, there was not a vegetable in sight.

As the dozen ballplayers settled themselves noisily in the remaining three booths along a grimy pine-paneled wall, a young Chinese woman came forward and distributed menus so greasy that Loren's almost slipped from his grasp. When she brought water, she carried the glasses with several of her fingers immersed inside the rims. Noticing that she had filled the glasses at a rusty but seemingly serviceable water fountain located in front of the entrance to the kitchen, near signs marked "Ladies" and "Gents," Loren decided to do his drinking there.

Slick ordered two hot dogs with plenty of mustard, and also four ears of corn-on-the-cob accompanied by a slice of white bread, the last to be brought as soon as possible. With a puzzled expression, but without question or comment, the waitress dutifully wrote down his request. Fats and Ham both ordered chicken-fried steaks, fries, and house salad with Italian dressing. "Ain't got it," said the waitress. "We only got Texas dressin'. Melted lard wit' hot sauce."

"Texas," said Fats. Ham nodded.

The waitress turned to Loren, who had scrutinized the menu in vain for ethnic Chinese food. "I guess I'll have the same without the salad," he said uncertainly. Wordlessly, the waitress snatched the menus and disappeared into the kitchen.

Loren followed Slick and Fats to the rest room. Stopping at the water fountain, Fats said: "Ah believe Ah need some real cool water. That stuff she brought wuz as warm as uh whore's tush."

"Shh," said Loren, looking around to see if anyone had overheard. Apparently not. In the kitchen a Chinese cook, a middle-aged man, was working to the sound of country music from a nearby radio, which was blaring too loud for him to have heard Fats' obscene observation.

"Heah," said Slick. "Yew fust."

"Thanks," said Loren. He bent over the water fountain and jammed the handle down. Liquid spurted with surprising force into his face, wetting his cheeks, his chin, his hair, and soaking the top of his shirt.

From Fats came a loud guffaw. "We call this heah infernal machine 'ol' face-full'", he chortled. "Ah tole Slick t' let yew try it fust, so he wouldn' tip yew off."

"Nice of you," replied Loren, wiping water out of his eyes with his handkerchief. He pushed open the door to the Gents room and went in.

Seated in the only stall, after carefully spreading toilet paper on the seat, he noticed graffiti scrawled on the walls. To his left, "You son of a bitch, turn the other way." To his right: "You shit eater, turn the other way." A high class place, he thought. Incognito in his enclosure, he listened to a succession of Scorpions whizzing into the urinal, guessing their identities by the duration of their emissions. Most of them immediately departed without washing their hands. Emerging from the toilet enclosure, Loren discovered that one of the miscreants was the Chinese cook.

Back in the booth, Loren observed that the waitress had brought the salads—wilted lettuce and tough pink tomato wedges smothered in dressing that looked rancid. Noticing Loren's disgusted look, Slick said: "Th' dressin's too thin. Ah done tol' that cook he had it too thick, but he overreacted an' added too much water. Two mouthfuls when Ah distinctly tol' him one."

"Ah come on, Slick," protested Ham, reaching for the jar of hot peppers that Loren knew by now would be on each table in every restaurant in Texas.

"O. K., fergit th' salad dressing, but seein' that cook at work causes me t' wanna bring up sumptin'..."

"Hell!"

"...fer discussion. Namely, Ham, do yew think wit' all those false teeth yew got in yore mouth, yew oughta be nibblin' at those chili peppers?"

"Why not?"

"Wal, ain't yew afeared of burnin' yore bridges?"

"Damn, Slick. Ah wish yew'd stop bein' sucha wise ass."

Slick grinned and began to eat his corn. He took his knife and slavered a thick layer of yellow butter onto his piece of doughy bread, shook salt and pepper onto the butter, briefly wrapped the bread around a still steaming ear of corn, and then, removing the bread, chopped the kernels off with his teeth, two rows at a time. Loren watched, fascinated.

Quickly polishing off his last ear of corn, Slick swiped at his mouth with his napkin and sighed: "That wuz uh good start." Gesturing toward the waitress, who was approaching with a heavily loaded tray, he said: "Now that we've finished our horse's ovaries, heah comes our pieces of resistance."

Removing their salad plates and Slick's devastated corn cobs, the girl set down steaks and fries in front of Fats, Ham and Loren, and placed two fat frankfurters nestled in mustard and shredded onions on soggy buns in front of Slick, who exclaimed: "Ah really go fer chink cuisine. It's so exotic!"

"Some day," said Ham, wistfully, "Ah'm gonna be so rich that Ah kin afford t' order uh big plate of lobster wit' uh pile of caviar on top,... an' then leave half of it on th' plate."

"That's th' big time, all right," said Fats. "But how yew gonna git so rich?"

"Easy. T'day Ah gits me uh buncha base hits, an' ol' man Tobin signs me t' uh Browns contract quick, afore Ah gits snapped up by some other team. Th' Browns ain't had uh good third baseman since Harlon Clift. Ah figure inside two, three years Ah'll be makin' big bucks."

"Yore crazy," said Slick. "That scout is heah fer one reason only, t' watch me pitch. Me an' Bobo got us uh plan. We gonna fix them fishermen good."

"Bobo's going to catch?" asked Loren, looking at Fats.

"Yeah. He an' Slick wanted t' try it. He caught uh couple games las' year an' did real good."

"Who's gonna play short?" asked Ham.

"Ah'll move Bubba ovah there an' put Yank in at second base. Yank, yew'll bat leadoff. O. K. wit' yew?"

"Sure," said Loren, trying not to show his excitement at getting an opportunity to start at an infield position. And also leading off! Fats had apparently developed confidence in Loren's ability to get on base, so that the big bats could drive him in.

"Say," said Ham, continuing to display a one-track mind, "this steak is 'mos' as good as that lobster an' caviar Ah decided not t' order."

Loren said: "I never heard of a chicken-fried steak before. How do they do that?"

"Yew take uh roun' steak," said Ham, "an' pound it till it's tender; then yew beat up some eggs in milk an' dip th' meat. Then yew roll it in flour an' dip it again. Then yew roll it in crushed corn flakes, an' fry it 'bout six minutes on each side; an' yew got yoreself somethin' purty tasty."

"'Specially if'n yew substitute whiskey fer milk," said Slick.

* * *

As the ballplayers filed out of the restaurant, with Fats bringing up the rear in order to pay for their meals, they helped themselves to toothpicks protruding from a small vase on the cashier's counter. Loren studied the toothpick techniques of his teammates while they drove to the Fisher field.. Ham stuck one between his lips and seemed to forget that it was there. Slick nervously tongued his from side to side of his mouth. And Fats bit down so hard on his that it snapped in two; whereupon he flipped the two pieces out of the car window. He then removed what looked like a used plug of chewing tobacco from a stained shirt pocket and popped it into his mouth. Soon brown drool appeared on his chin, as he made notations on his ever-present notepad.

Under the splintery wooden grandstand adjacent to the Fisher High School football field, the Scorpions found a door marked "Visitor's Locker Room." Inside Loren was not surprised to observe all three shower heads dripping, the lockers padlocked, the concrete floor damp and dirty, and no clean towels.

Bobo sat on a bench next to Loren as they pulled on their uniforms. Loren's outfit, inherited from a player no longer with the Scorpions, bore a big red "7" on the back of the shirt; Bobo's sported the number "3", denoting his usual place in the batting order, traditionally given to the most dangerous slugger on a team. As Bobo laced up his spikes, Loren noticed that he was perspiring profusely, his bald head gleaming in the sunlight shining through windows located high above the lockers. It was hot in the crowded room, and Loren was already sweating, too, but Bobo was streaming the stuff. A whiff of his breath revealed why. He had apparently had a sizeable snort of something strong on the way from the restaurant.

Masher, grinning as if at some private joke, passed by on his way from the toilet area as Bobo was strapping on the shinguards he had borrowed from Feets for the day. Patting Bobo on top of his hairless head, Masher exclaimed: "Gawddamn, Bobo; that feels jus' like mah wife's ass!"

Momentarily Bobo's brow wrinkled in bewilderment. Then he grinned and ran a huge brown hand over his shiny scalp. "Sonuffabitch, Masher," he observed, "Ah'm damned if'n it don'."

As Loren, no longer shocked by anything the Scorpion players said or did, struggled to suppress a laugh, several of the others who had overheard the exchange guffawed. "Way t' go, Bobo," shouted Slick. A sheepish smile creasing his red face, Masher went out to the playing field. Five minutes later, he and Bobo were playing catch as if nothing out of the ordinary had passed between them.

The Otter baseball diamond was laid out at one end of the football field, which had produced strange outfield dimensions and some rough turf. The bases rested on grass rather than on dirt, which presented the danger of a broken ankle if a sliding baserunner caught his spikes in the thick sod.

There was no dugout. The bench provided for the visiting team was scarcely long enough to hold the bulk of Fats and the three Scorpions who would not start the game. The sun burned unmercifully from directly overhead, and there was no shade except beneath the players' caps. Loren looked wistfully at a water bucket that Fats had filled in the locker room. The advice from every coach or gym teacher he'd ever known sounded in his ears: Don't drink while you're playing. It'll make you sick. Swish a little around in your mouth, if you have to; then spit it out. You can drink all you want after the game. Boy, he thought, I wish I had drunk more water in the restaurant. I hope I don't faint before we finish.

The single umpire, standing behind the pitcher's mound, called out "play ball." As the first hitter for the visitors, Loren carried two bats up to the plate, took a final swing, and then discarded the heaviest stick before settling into the right hand batter's box. Wait him out, he told himself. Try for a walk. Gotta get on base.

The Otter pitcher, a lanky lefty, threw his first pitch over the middle, waist high. "Stree-ike one!"

The second pitch was almost a duplicate of the first one. Now Loren was in a hole. Dimly he could hear his teammates encouraging him: "Come on Yank, Babe; yore th' man; it only takes one, Babe; show 'im who's boss..."

Pitch number three should have been a teaser to lure Loren into swinging at a bad ball. Overconfident, perhaps, the pitcher chose instead to deliver another heater down the middle. Loren hardly felt the tingle of contact as he caught the pitch on the fat of his bat and sent it sizzling high over the first baseman's futile leap and into right field about ten feet fair. As he scampered down the line, he saw the outfielder, who had been playing well over toward center, fail to cut off the fast rolling sphere and begin chasing it into long grass at the other end of the football stadium.

He hit the inside corners of both first and second bases with his left toe as he flew toward the third sack where an Otter player pounded his fists into the pocket of his glove and tensely awaited the relay throw from short right field. Remembering to keep his spikes high above the grass, so that they would not catch, Loren launched himself into a modified hook slide to the outfield side of the base, his left spike ramming it well ahead of the tag. A leadoff triple! He wondered if the scout for the Browns was sitting among the several dozen spectators perched uncomfortably on the sun-scorched bleacher seats and, if so, whether that gentleman had been impressed.

From A. C., coaching at first base, came a sign: thumb on the belt buckle. Hit away. Loren knew that Bubba would be trying to steer the ball to the right side, to make it easier for Loren to beat a throw home than if a grounder was hit to either the third baseman or the shortstop. With none out, however, he would have to be cautious and stay put if Bubba hit one sharply, unless it went through the infield.

With two balls and a strike, Bubba got the outside strike he had been awaiting and smacked it on a line, directly into the glove of the second baseman. One out. Bobo up.

Swaggering up to the plate like he thought he was invincible, Bobo settled into a stance that reminded Loren of the ineffable DiMaggio, who had led the New York Yankees the previous year to their sixth world championship during the nine years he had been with the Bronx Bombers, hitting for an average of .315, bashing twenty homers, and accounting for ninety-seven runs batted in. Not a super season, certainly, but highly respectable. And everything he did—hit, run, throw, field, and run bases—was done so gracefully, seemingly so effortlessly, that it appeared as if he was somehow floating in slow motion.

Bobo, by contrast, habitually cavorted clownlike in the field and lunged at the ball when batting, his burly body appearing always off-balance, whether gloving a grounder or slashing at some southpaw's curve, which now he did, as the Otter left-hander tried to bend a mere wrinkle past his big black bat. With a crack like a rifle shot, the ball rose into the air toward left field. "Tag up," ordered Fats coaching at third. "He got under it."

The ball climbed so high into the sky that Loren lost sight of it. Crouched into a sprinter's stance, his right toe nestled against third base, he waited. The left fielder slowly moved back, then came in; his eyes wide and his feet stumbling as the ball seemed to hang forever in the sky. Finally, it plopped into the staggering outfielder's glove. Loren faked a dash for home but quickly retreated to his base. Had he tried to score, he would have been an easy out.

It was up to Masher to drive in the run. All biceps and big bottom, he had the compact swing and fluid follow through of a true cleanup hitter, one who could clear any fence if he connected squarely, yet was hard to strike out. This time, however, he swung ahead of a deceptive slow pitch on a three and two count and missed it completely. Three out, and Loren had failed to score.

As the game continued, the Scorpions lashed out a hit an inning, and coaxed an occasional walk, but the Otters played errorless ball behind their portsider and turned three double plays in eight innings, each with one out and at least one runner in scoring position. So, going into the last of the eighth, the visitors had yet to dent the plate.

The home team hitters had their chances, too, but Slick kept what he jokingly called his fast ball, which had neither zip nor movement, low and outside; so that when the Otter batters, tempted, swung, they stroked grounders to Scorpion infielders. When they laid off, Slick threw them slow curves and inside screwballs, both of which they tended to turn into lazy flies or popups. Except for one mistake, a fast ball that caught too much of the plate and was promptly deposited over the left field fence by an eager Otter, Slick managed to hold the home team down.

Slick's secret weapon was Bobo. The ape man was actually a poor catcher who constantly allowed pitches to pop out of his mitt and who dropped the only foul fly that fell within his reach. But he had a special talent, one that helped keep the game close. Nature had bestowed on him the gift of being able, at will, to emit resounding belches. These were no ordinary gas blasts. Rather were they enormous reverberations that evoked both grimaces and giggles among those within range of the pyrotechnics. Bobo could explode all at once like a bomb. Or he could give vent to short staccato bursts that sounded like a pneumatic hammer biting into concrete.

Happily the ape man saved his blue ribbon belches for special occasions, as when a dangerous Otter hitter came to the plate with a runner on third base. Ham and Bubba grinned knowingly behind their gloves. Loren, hands on knees, watched closely. The outfielders leaned forward, their ears pricked. Slick worked the corners, trying to get two strikes on the batter without yielding a fair ball. With a full count, the hitter licked his lips, certain that a cripple was coming. His eyes narrowed; his muscles bunched; and his knuckles whitened on his bat, as he held it high, ready instantaneously to whip it against the pitiable pitch.

Slick called time and asked for a new ball. The umpire looked at the one in play and refused. Feigning disgust, Slick turned his back on the batter and stared dreamily around at the outfielders, waving his ragged glove at one, who then moved slightly to one side, but took his time.

Slick then studied the baserunner as if he was a scientific curiosity. Seeing that the runner had taken several steps off third, shouting insults, Slick flipped the ball to Ham as a warning not to get too frisky.

Ham, of course, tried the hidden ball trick. While Slick stood on the mound with his spikes just off the rubber, Ham held the ball hidden in his glove and waited for the runner to step off third base, so that he could tag him out. Of course, everyone on the field and most of the people in the stands knew who had possession of the ball. Warning cries of "hidden ball" rang out from all directions.

Finally Ham gave up. Shaking his head as if trying to hide his disappointment that the trick had not worked, he lobbed the ball back to Slick. The umpire demanded that the pitcher stop stalling and deliver the ball to the batter. Slick placidly agreed to do so. He leaned forward and looked for Bobo's sign. Repeatedly he shook his head. At last he nodded and went into his windup.

By this time the batter was furious. He had stepped in and out of the box a half dozen times. He had impatiently pounded his warclub on the plate. He had swished it back and forth numerous times. He would teach those clowns not to stall around. Resolutely he prepared to administer the coup de main.

Extensive discussion and considerable practice had enabled Bobo and Slick to develop an exquisite scenario. When the pitcher finally released his offering, it was a blooper that brought a gasp from the spectators as it passed through a rainbow-like arc on its way to an almost vertical rendezvous with the strike zone. Bobo and Slick knew that impatient batters would tend to swing before such a pitch had reached home plate. Others would hold back and try to uppercut it, and either miss it entirely, or hit a weak popup or grounder. Today's slugger, however, seemed to realize that his best bet was take a natural swing that would cause the bat squarely to encounter the ball. It was for batters of this latter category that Bobo reserved his secret weapon.

As the ball dropped toward the strike zone, the catcher emitted his best burp. In the past burly sluggers had turned to jello at the sound. Once a celebrated cleanup man had actually dropped his bat from suddenly palsied hands. Some said that it was not the loud noise that turned sinews to spaghetti and weakened the will; it was the reek, like suddenly being sprayed with tear gas. But men who had spent their lives within range of gulf coast oil refineries or piney woods paper mills could not have been without some immunity to such smells—no matter how personalized. So it must have been mainly the sound.

After today's strikeout the usual argument ensued, with the opposing manager kicking dust furiously, the humiliated batter sputtering his indignation, and the umpire doggedly insisting that there was nothing in the rule book against burping, no matter how offensively. Bobo, a beatific expression of innocence on his face, played catch with Slick until the debate ended. Then, after obtaining the third out on a grounder, they sat side by side, snickering, on the bench.

Bobo's eructation against the Otters in the bottom of the eighth inning kept the score at 1-0. As the ninth began, Loren, conceding that the tactic was as legitimate as sign stealing or questioning the purity of the batter's mother or the sexuality of his sister, asked Masher: "How does Bobo do it?"

The big first baseman grinned. "DOFRB," he spelled.

"What's that?"

"Look in th' bag."

Loren slid off the bench and walked behind it up to the other end where several of the players had deposited valises containing personal possessions. Bobo had brought a large duffel bag in which to carry his catcher's equipment. Coaching at third, exhorting Jackie Lawson to get on base with the tying run, he was not looking in Loren's direction. So Loren was able unperceived to slip his hand into Bobo's bag and draw out an empty bottle that had once held Dad's Old Fashioned Root Beer. Bulges in the bag suggested more bottles inside.

Loren saw Masher looking at him and laughing. Then the big first baseman laid his forefinger vertically across his lips. Loren nodded to show that he understood. Bobo's secret would be safe with him. Besides, Jackie had struck out and he was on deck.

Kneeling in the dirt halfway to home plate, Loren watched Slick crouching in the batter's box, trying to coax a walk from the tiring Otter hurler. On a full count he was successful, as the umpire hesitated before calling out "ball" on a neck high pitch. It was up to Loren to advance a slow runner.

Waiting for a barefooted batboy to deliver Slick's Southside High School letter jacket to him at first base, Loren resisted the growing feeling of panic that was causing him to have difficulty breathing and his entire body to tremble. Hitless since the first inning, he hungered for a bingle.

Fats flashed the bunt sign. The idea was to sacrifice Slick to second base and bring up Bubba with two out and a runner in scoring position. But Bubba had not had a good day, having struck out three times following his first inning line out. Loren decided to disobey Fats in the hope that he could increase the odds for a tie, if not for an outright win. As the Fisher third baseman crept toward the plate in order to field the half-expected bunt, Loren squared around and slid his right hand up the bat handle toward the barrel, poking ineffectually at a high fast ball. "Stee-rike," yelled the ump. "Come on, Yank," yelled Fats. "Yew kin dew it." Again he gave the sign for a bunt, and again Loren held out his bat as if intending to sacrifice. The third baseman, already positioned well in toward the plate, crept closer.

At the last possible instant, Loren whipped back his bat and slashed at the high fast ball with all his might. The look of fear on the face of the startled third baseman as the ball rocketed past his ear told him he had succeeded.

As he rounded first base, he saw the left fielder pursuing the ball down the foul line and Slick approaching third base with little doubt that he would score. With all the energy remaining in his body, Loren fled like a person possessed past second base and headed for third, where Fats was holding both hands high above his head in the traditional coach's signal to stop. With the score now tied, 1-1, Loren could wait on third for Bubba or Bobo to drive him in.

As he strained for third base, however, Loren got a quick look at the Otter left fielder reaching down for the ball, preparing to hurl it to the shortstop, whose back was turned to home plate. Having once been stranded on third base, Loren was determined that it would not happen again. Still at full speed he hit the bag with his left toe and sprinted past a protesting Fats, his eyes fixed on the Fisher catcher, who was crouching in the baseline, awaiting the relay from the shortstop. As the distance between them shortened, Loren saw through the catcher's wire mask his eyes rising, then falling, as they traced the course of the ball. Then came the tensing of muscles and the backhanded reach of the big mitt for the missile arriving slightly on the first base side of home plate.

As the catcher gloved the ball, Loren launched himself into a headlong slide that carried him far to the other side of home plate, with only his left hand reaching out to scrape lightly across the rubbery surface of the platter a split second before a sweeping tag caught him on the left shoulder. The umpire's shout of "Safe" was lost in the clamor of players and fans alike, but the sight of the arbiter's spread arms, palms down, was enough for Loren. Scorpions 2; Otters 1.

Then his teammates surrounded him, banging him on the back, bellowing "at-a-boy," "terrific slide," "way-t'-go," and other expressions of praise. Amid the ruckus he caught a glimpse of Fats staring at him and, as they locked looks, the manager first shook his head disapprovingly, and then he smiled, bestowing forgiveness.

* * *

Back in their automobiles after the Otters had failed to score in the bottom of the ninth, the Scorpions stank of sweat. In their stocking feet, Slick and Ham argued over what station they ought to listen to on the car radio, commented caustically on each other's foot odors, sipped from bottles of Southern Select beer, and lamented the necessity of reporting back to work the following morning. They also grumbled that neither had spotted a St. Louis scout at the Otter game.

"Say Slick," inquired Fats from the back seat next to Loren, "Whut's that music called?"

"Sorry, Ah wasn't payin' attention. Whut did yew ask me?"

"That music on th' radio. Classical ain't it?"

"Yeah. Sunday Evening Symphony. It's from Carmen."

"Huh. Ain't that Spanish?"

"Good guess," said Slick. "It's French. By Joe Bidet." Loren stared at Slick's well-barbered neck, both amused and impressed.

"Yore too smart," said Ham. "That's whut comes from havin' gone t' college."

"True," replied Slick. "Ah done graduated, too. Jus' keep this in mind: in th' land of th' blind th' one-eyed man is king."

"An' swelled haided, too."

"Say," said Fats, "didja heah 'bout th' guy who wuz so egotistical that he wuz convinced he'd delivered hisself at birth?"

"That sounds lak Slick," said Ham. "Uh law unto hisself.

"Speakin' of such," said Fats, "Yank ran through mah stop sign t'day t'score th' winnin' run. Think Ah oughta fine him?

"Fine him whut?" asked Ham. "We ain't been paid fer uh game since we played in Alexandria."

"So Yank gits away wit' sayin' 'Ah'm th' law.'"

"Why not?" said Slick. We all do it. By th' way, didja heah 'bout th' nigger cop in Noo Yawk who thought he *wuz* th' law?.... No? Wal, he went 'round sayin' 'lawsee me.'"

"That's pitiful," protested Fats, apparently unaware that Slick had changed the subject. The car radio was now vibrating with the husky voice that Loren recognized as that of Rise Stevens. "Hey Slick," said Ham, "can't yew git somethin' else? That highbrow music makes mah haid hurt."

"Yew don' 'preciate good stuff," said Slick. "Heah's uh beautiful woman singin' up uh storm as she realizes she's 'bout t' be murdered by her jilted luvah, an' yew only heah noise. An' yew missed th' fust part, where Carmen showed how, when she goes fishin' fer uh new luvah, she knows how t' cast-a-net."

Loren shuddered and pretended not to have heard.

"Whut yew talkin' 'bout?" asked Ham.

"Yank knows. Ain't that right, Yank?"

"Sure, Slick. Say, I've got one for you. Why is a lazy ballplayer accused of dogging it?"

"Dunno."

"Because his efforts are cur-tailed."

Fats groaned. Maybe Ah shouldn' discipline yew fer runnin' thru mah stop sign," he said, "seein' that yew did score th' winnin' run. But sumptin' oughta be done 'bout yew an' Slick playin' word games wit' Ham an' me trapped in this-heah car, wit' no way to 'scape."

* * *

By the time they got to Timberland, it was growing dark outside. Increasingly apprehensive about Slick's casual way of driving, Ham decided when they stopped for gas to ride the rest of the way with Bubba, which brought Bobo into the seat next to Slick. But when his new passenger expressed a wish to stop for some supper, Slick objected. His wife, he declared, would be waiting avidly for him to return, "hot t' perform." He said to Bobo: "Yew ain't in no hurry t' git home 'cause yew ain't got nobody waitin' fer yew."

"Ah got me uh niggerwoman, who…"

"Never mind."

"She's got talent, lemme tell yew, …"

"Bobo, we don' need t' heah 'bout her. Ain't that right, Yank?"

Loren remained silent, pretending to be asleep.

Bobo turned so that he faced the back seat. "Wake up, Yank. Ah wantcha t' listen t' th' poem Ah made up 'bout Charlene. Mah gal may be black, but she gives me mah fill, an' won' turn her back, when Ah'm wantin' uh thrill."

"Shee-it, Bobo!" exclaimed Fats. "That ain't bad."

"Yeah," admitted Slick. "But whut you jus' done is t' go from bod t' verse."

Loren groaned.

"That reminds me," interjected Fats, "of th' ol' widder woman ridin' one night in uh Greyhound bus. She alwuz traveled wit' uh big ol' momma pussy cat. Th' cat wuz real old; so th' lady put an extra pillow in its basket. Didn't do no good, 'cause they hadn' gone many miles when th' cat died.

"It wuz uh real hot night, an' purty soon that cat began t' stink. Th' further they went, th' more that animal stank. Well, one of th' passengers finally went up t' tell th' driver 'bout th' dead cat. An' th' driver said he'd been wonderin' whut wuz makin' that stink on his bus. So he pulled ovah t' th' side of th' road, an' he opened th' front door, an' turned 'roun' an' faced th' passengers, who were real curious 'bout whut wuz goin' on. An' he said in uh loud voice 'Will th' lady wit' th' stinky pussy please git off'n th' bus.'

"An' then, scout's honor, five wimmen got off, an' three mor' crossed thar legs."

Loren had never in his life encountered such bawdy humor as he had been hearing since he joined the Scorpions. He felt like laughing, but he also felt embarrassed to be a party to such conversations. He could not imagine hearing anything of the kind in Winona, or any place else he had ever lived.

Suddenly he was thrown forward, as the loud screech of worn brakes filled the night air. His forehead banged against the back of Slick's seat. Then he heard Bobo say: "Man, didja see whut Ah saw?"

"Yeah!" exclaimed Slick. "Les go back."

"Go back fer whut?" asked Fats.

"Geese!"

"Whatja mean, geese?"

"Big fat gooses by th' side of th' road," said Bobo. "Man, we gonna have us uh big barbecue! Roast goose an' lotsa beer! Umm, umm!"

"That's stealin'," said Fats.

"Ain't neither," said Bobo. "It's uh public highway, ain't it? Farmer ought not t'let his birds roam. 'Sides, he's prolly got so many, he won' miss uh couple."

"Say, Slick," ventured Loren, "suppose that farmer's got a shotgun?"

"No problem," said Slick. "That fella's gotta git up an' do chores early t'morra. By now he'll have had his snootfull of moonshine an' be snorin' away. Let's git them geese."

By this time he had backed the car about a quarter of a mile and parked it on the shoulder. Getting out, he waved a flashlight at a vehicle whose headlights were fast approaching from behind them. As it drew alongside, Loren saw that it was Bubba's car, its passengers staring at the stopped automobile. "Whatsa matter, engine trouble?" came the inquiry.

"Nah," said Slick. "Look ovah thar." He pointed across the road and up a hillside where a wire fence divided the highway right of way from a pasture. Loren thought he saw a house, back in some trees. And halfway up the hill, plucking unconcernedly at the vegetation, were half a dozen large white geese.

"Ah see," said Bubba and Ham, simultaneously. "Let's git 'em," suggested Feets, excitedly, exiting the other car. Six Scorpions raced each other to see who could be first to capture a goose. Fats and Loren remained behind. "Yore smart not t' go up thar," said the manager. "Them gooses are fierce. Someun is gonna git pecked real good."

Feeling cowardly, Loren wondered why in such situations he always lacked the guts to join in. He invariably hung back, perhaps prudently, but always apart.

The other players charged into the gaggle of geese. Loren stared, fascinated, at the ensuing melee. Wings flapped, bills struck, feathers flew, and cries of "Got one!" mingled with curses and shouts of "Ouch!" Soon Feets made his way across the road hugging a struggling bird to his chest, its head enveloped in one hard hand, bill held tightly shut. Bubba followed, a flapping, hissing goose held upside down by its scaly feet at arms length for safety's sake. And Ham was close behind, empty handed, having lost his bird when it knocked him off his feet head over heels down the hill almost into the road. He opened the trunk on Bubba's car, and the two geese vanished inside, but not before Ham received a final nip. "Yeeouch!" he yelled. "Yew damn devil! Ah'm gonna eat yore livah!"

The door next to Loren flew open. It was Bobo, with a goose. "Move ovah, Yank," he said. "Me an' mah fren need some room."

"Goldurn," exclaimed Fats. "If yore bringin' that monster in heah, Ah'm leavin!" Escaping through the opposite door, he took refuge in a third car that had pulled up behind the other two.

Loren scrutinized the big bird resting in Bobo's lap. "You sure that things's safe?" he inquired.

"Shore is," smirked Bobo. "Ah got him settled down real good. He kicked up quite uh ruckus 'til Ah hugged 'im some. Then he got real peaceable."

Loren could well imagine how the poor goose felt being hugged by Bobo. The bird was probably paralyzed by fear.

As the three cars pulled one-by-one back into the highway and resumed their journey into the night, Loren looked back at the scene of action. Deep in the trees he thought he saw a light. Perhaps the farmer was pulling on his overalls and reaching for his shotgun, a victim of foul play. Loren felt sorry for him.

Loren and Bobo both settled back, the goose on the latter's lap remaining quiet. Up in the front seat Slick listened to the radio, the sound gradually fading into a dim hum, as Loren fell into a troubled sleep…

Perhaps an hour later he gradually grew conscious of lights glaring on both sides of the highway. They were passing motels, gas stations, root beer stands, and honkytonks as they entered Tocqueville. It was almost two a.m. Except for an occasional pair of headlights passing in the other direction, and one old man dozing in the window of a brightly lit gas station, the world seemed asleep.

Loren felt stiff and groggy. In the rear view mirror, Slick seemed lost in thought, staring large-eyed through the bug-speckled windshield at the road ahead. Bobo was snoring, his goose sitting on his lap with a dazed look in its beady eyes. It seemed hypnotized by the lights flashing by. Then it noticed Loren studying it. Its mouth opened. "Honk," it said and wiggled in Bobo's lap.

At once a horrible stench permeated the car. A yellow substance spread from underneath the goose across Bobo's pants and onto the seat beside him, like lava flowing from a volcanic eruption.

"Gawddamn!" Bobo was awake now, outraged. "Yew sheetarsed sonuffabitch," he shouted. "I oughter wring yur fuggin' neck." With a gesture of disgust he shoved the bird, now flapping and pecking, away from him, onto his seatmate. A hard beak left a painful dent in Loren's thigh. Then feathers flew as the goose flung itself into the front seat.

By this time, fortunately, Slick had hit the brake. In another moment he stopped the car and grabbed desperately for the goose's neck. Loren lunged forward halfway into the front seat to assist Slick. He managed to grab a foot, as Slick finally captured the bird's neck up high enough to avoid a severe peck. At last the creature was once more subdued.

Into the trunk of the car it went. Slick barely got the trunk lid down on the bird in time to prevent its escaping into the night. The four Scorpions stood beside the car, reluctant to re-enter. The odor was unbelievable.

"Whut we gonna do now?" asked Bobo. "Thar's gooseshit all ovah everythang."

Loren now noticed that his fine-feathered friend had left his mark not only on Bobo's pants but on Slick's as well. Apparently he was the only one unsplattered. Then he happened to look down at his right trouser leg. Elixir of goose. Ugh.

"All we kin do," said Slick, "is tough it out. We kin clean up after we git home." To Bobo he added: "That is, if Charlene will let yew in th' house."

When Slick turned on the heater to help alleviate the night chill, it made the smell worse. Loren was close to throwing up when the car's tires crunched on the shell driveway beside his dark house.

Bobo held the goose while Loren rescued his glove and bat, and the brown paper sack containing his street clothes, from the trunk. There was poop all over the parcel. Waving goodbye, Loren ran toward the porch, shed all his garments but his jock strap, and dropped everything into some nearby bushes. Fortunately, the front door was unlocked, and he hastened down the hall and into the bathroom, where he took a soapy shower.

His mother, rubbing sleep from her eyes, and wearing a robe and furry slippers, intercepted him as he made his way to bed. "Have a nice trip, dear?" she inquired.

"Yeah, it was O. K.," said Loren. "We won."

"That's nice," she said. "What is that I smell?"

"I don't smell anything," said Loren. "Good night, Mom. I'll probably sleep late."

"Goodnight, son. I'm glad you're home safe."

CHAPTER 13

BARBECUE

At breakfast on the Monday following the Fisher game, Loren read in the *Gazette* that the great Babe Ruth had died. The home run king, who had been in critical condition from cancer for several days, was only fifty-three. During the years immediately preceding the first World War, the Babe had been one of the two best left-handed pitchers in baseball, matched only by Hippo Vaughn of the Cubs. After the war, he had been traded from the Boston Red Sox to the New York Yankees, a team that had never won a pennant. As an outfielder the Babe had proceeded to power the Yanks to six flags in eight years, finishing his career not only with over seven hundred home runs, but also with a lifetime batting average of.342, a fantastic record that Loren could not imagine ever being surpassed.

Maybe a later star would hit for a higher average, and some husky slugger might eventually hit more lifetime home runs, especially if ball parks were rendered more hospitable to the long ball by greedy owners moving the fences in and seeing that the pitching mounds were lowered, and also if the balls became more tightly wound and hurlers handicapped by a shrinking strike zone; but in order to surpass the Sultan of Swat's homer totals, such a swinger would have to take an all or nothing approach, and would be unlikely to bat much over.300.

Take Ralph Kiner, who had bashed fifty-one round trippers the previous season, only his second in the major leagues. Kiner was a one-dimensional ball player who would never hit for a high average. Ruth had been unique, Loren proclaimed to Buzz. No one would ever match him.

"Ah don' know 'bout that," said Buzz. "If'n Ted Williams had not spent three years in th' army air corps durin' th' war, he'd be uh threat t' th' Babe's records. He could still break 'em, 'cept that he's still in th' reserves an' could be called up again."

"Why?" asked Loren. "We aren't at war. Do you mean that we might have to fight the Russians?"

"Not them," asserted Buzz, "unless th' yahoos in Congress go completely berserk. Ah look t' Asia fer our next war."

"Asia? We've just defeated Japan. What other Asian enemy is there?"

"None. But yew need t' realize how this nation sometimes gits inta wars. Do yew recall readin' how th' United States meddled in uh rebellion in th' Philippines followin' our war 'gainst Spain? How th' Russians had an insurrection goin' durin' th' fust World War, an' we sent troops there t' influence th' outcome? Heah we are again in a postwar period. Time t' intervene in someone else's internal quarrel. Ah'd guess it'll be in Korea."

"Why Korea?" asked Loren.

"Th' North and South Koreans are gonna wanna reunite their country, jus' th' same as th' Germans, th' Vietnamese, an' all th' other people in countries broken up during th' last war by foreign invasion an' occupation. Each side will wanna dictate th' terms of unification. In our arrogance we're likely t' intercede, which will mean war. Members of Congress see it coming: why else are they 'bout t' reinstate th' draft? Fer national defense? Hah. Who's goin' t' invade us, or even attack our outlying possessions? We're th' ones who'll be th' aggressors."

Loren protested: "I don't want to be forced to fight because some greedy plutocrat thinks a small war will be good for business and make him even richer than he is."

"Ah applaud yore sense of self-preservation. Although summa our Texas friends would say yew lack patriotism."

"What can I do to escape being exploited by such people?"

"Be informed, stay in school, git good grades, an' make influential contacts. Lyndon Johnson, if'n he wins, will owe us somethin'."

"Buzz, I really appreciate your advice. It makes a lot of sense."

"An' Ah 'preciate your appreciation. But there are uh lotta people heah'bouts who would dismiss mah 'pinions as communist-inspired."

"Speaking of… What's the HUAC up to? I haven't seen a thing in the papers."

"They're havin' closed hearings. But their candidate, Dewey, declared las' Friday that he intended t' make uh big fuss durin' his presidential campaign 'bout alleged communist infiltration into th' U. S. government durin' th' Roosevelt an' Truman administrations. Th' Republicans got no positive thoughts 'bout domestic or foreign policy, an' their people in Congress have now been exposed by Truman as do-nothing obstructionists, so they're goin' all out t' smear his administration as bein' fulla Russian spies. When they git 'nough gullible people believin' their idiotic charges, th' militarists an' conspiracy buffs, like th' FBI's Hoover, will be in full charge. Th' next step will be t' plunge us into another nation's civil war in th' name of patriotism."

"I'm afraid you're right. Did you see what the *Endeavor's* editor wrote in Saturday's paper?"

"No."

"Here. I brought you a clipping." Loren showed Buzz a crumpled newspaper column that he took from his shirt pocket. "It was the lead editorial, too."

Buzz studied a condemnation of the Tocqueville public library for making the magazine *Soviet Russia Today* available to its patrons. The editor of that journal, according to Ward Hatton, ought to relocate to the USSR, having been so unwise as to have published articles by such "communist" authors as former U. S. Ambassador to Moscow Joseph Davis, U.S. Senator Claude Pepper, and the journalist Edgar Snow. And the head librarian should have tossed the magazine in the trash "immediately upon receipt."

"Th' man's an imbecile. Doesn' yore Daddy work at th' *Endeavor*?"

"Yeah. He detests Hatton. But he has to keep quiet if he wants to keep his job. Still, perhaps you noticed that the headline that appears over Hatton's harangue reads 'Red-Fishing?'"

"Ah wondered 'bout that."

"I'd be willing to bet that was my father's doing. And that stupid Hatton probably didn't notice."

* * *

As the week progressed, Buzz's prediction, that the Republicans in Congress were about to charge that Democrats had facilitated communist subversion, quickly came true. As early as Monday evening, when Loren arrived home after work, his father was fuming over a huge headline that Hatton had personally insisted be placed at the top of page one of that afternoon's *Endeavor*. It read: "Editor to Face Accused Spy." The story that appeared underneath it gave notice that someone named Whittaker Chambers, who worked as an editor on the pro-Republican *Time* magazine, was expected on Tuesday to confront Alger Hiss, formerly a lawyer in the administrations of Roosevelt and Truman, at a closed meeting of the HUAC. At that time Chambers, provided with congressional immunity against a lawsuit for slander, would accuse Hiss of having been a communist spy.

"Imagine," Adam spluttered, "giving such enormous play to mere speculation. Hatton has really done it this time."

"Now, dear," said Loren's mother, who had quietly entered the living room. "Don't get excited. Surely you would have expected something of the sort from Mr. Hatton. And you know there will be more of the same, at least until the November election is over. So why not just ignore it?"

"How can I ignore such an atrocious violation of journalistic ethics?"

"It's his paper, not yours."

"His editorial, too," exclaimed Loren, looking over his father's shoulder and reading aloud: "'Aside from the Red Russians, the person with the reddest face in the United States must be Harry Truman. He labeled as 'red herrings' their congressional investigations which are turning up spies under the flooring even in the atomic bomb department in Washington.'"

Loren laughed. "'Under the flooring?' 'The atomic bomb department?' The man writes like he never got out of third grade."

"Probably flunked English," said Adam. "Any spies that have been exposed were discovered by the FBI months or years ago, and now the Republicans are giving them immunity from prosecution for their testimony, probably a pack of lies, designed to smear innocent public servants. Where the hell is ol' Harry while this is happening? He ought to be hitting back."

"I expect that he will, dear," said Loren's mother, quietly. "Your dinner is getting cold. You can study the rest of your paper afterwards."

"Study the dratted paper!" muttered Adam, as he followed his spouse into the kitchen. "I edit the ridiculous rag, except for Hatton's garbage." Sitting down at the table, he dumped a tablespoon of sugar on his salad, eliciting a covert exchange of shudders between Loren and Tommy, and began eagerly to consume forkfuls of lettuce and pineapple chunks, while a blessed silence settled over the family meal.

* * *

As the week wore on, the HUAC hearings received continuous coverage in both Tocqueville newspapers and on all four radio stations. Alger Hiss finally faced his accuser during a HUAC hearing and identified him as a former acquaintance who had rented a room in Hiss's house in 1935, but whose charge that his landlord had spied for the Soviets was "a complete fabrication."

New Jersey Congressman J. P. Thomas, who chaired the HUAC, accused President Truman of trying to keep the American people from learning that Soviet spies had been stealing "vital and secret information" from the U. S. government, and he promised more "shocking" revelations to come. But Truman told reporters at a news conference that no secrets had leaked during or after World War II and that the HUAC hearings violated basic American rights. In an editorial replete with mixed metaphors and fuzzy logic, Adam Temple's boss recommended that Truman be impeached by Congress.

Once again Adam Temple was furious. "That simpleton is a disgrace to journalism," he fumed. "The *Endeavor* will never amount to anything as long as he remains its editor."

Nan looked up from her sewing and asked: "Didn't your publisher friend, the one who talked you into coming to Tocqueville, write you recently that people he knew were going to buy the paper and make you editor?"

"Yeah, he did," acknowledged Adam. "They came last week and met with the bankers and lawyers who now control the paper on behalf of the estate of the former owner."

"What happened?"

"As nearly as I can tell, the deal is off. The locals killed it when they discovered that the prospective buyers were Jews."

"No!"

"Oh, yes. Jews, like Negroes, are never to have any influence in Tocqueville. And Hatton is one of the biggest bigots. He won't print news stories or carry columns written by Jews. Meanwhile he insists that we publish crap like Mary Hayworth's insipid lovelorn column, because Mrs. Hatton dotes on it. Here's a sample: 'You are sickminded..., your distress is obsessional... Your fallacious overemphasis on sexuality as the supposed archstone of affinity, when combined with your self-deprecating anxiety neurosis, would tend to constantly refuel a gloomy train of jealous worry.' And she goes on to assert that what the poor woman needs to realize is that every man hopes 'that his wife, by her happy example and incorruptible faith in his better nature, will expedite his growth toward moral maturity: a goal towards which all rational men yearn instinctively.' I pity the gal who wrote for useful advice and got a goody-goody lecture instead."

"It didn't sound so bad to me," commented Nan, with a surreptitious grin at Loren.

"Oh, yeah," Adam huffed. "Then what about this?" Rustling his newspaper in quivering fingers, he said: "Here's a letter from a war widow whose new fiance dislikes her long hair and wants her to cut it short before he will marry her, despite her reluctance to do so. And what is Mary Hayworth's assessment of the situation? The poor widow is guilty of 'quirkish narcissism' for wanting to retain 'her cumbersome coiffure.' If she insists on clinging to her 'frumpish hank of hair,' her suitor should recognize that, in view of her 'tomfoolery,' his 'misgivings about the advisability of marriage are seriously justified,' and 'you ought to part company.'"

"Seems like she always sides with the guy," observed Loren.

"Exactly," said Adam. "Women are put on earth only to serve and obey."

"Why, dear," said Nan, "I thought you subscribed to that very view."

Adam stared sharply at his wife. Then, seeing the sly smile tugging at the corners of her mouth, he laughed. "O. K.," he said. "Have your fun. But Hayworth is a menace. Not only because of the inane advice she gives, but mainly because she writes jargon."

"About that we agree," said Nan. "Not to change the subject, but…"

"Which means," Adam interjected, "to change the subject."

"Of course. To change the subject: before I forget, Loren, would you weed my flower bed after you do the laundry on Saturday?"

"Sure, Mom," said Loren. "I have to go somewhere that afternoon, but I can work here all morning."

* * *

On Saturday morning Loren asked: "Dad, can I borrow the car this afternoon?"

"Why?"

"The Scorpions are having a barbecue out at Ferrell Park. All the guys'll be there."

"That wouldn't be barbecued goose, would it?"

"As a matter of fact, yes; but how did you know?"

"Bitsy hears things. He told me yesterday that one of your stolen ganders committed a grand indiscretion in the back seat of your getaway car."

"I didn't have anything to do with stealing any geese. I was just along for the ride."

"Your mother said that you'd washed our bedding in the same tub with your baseball clothes last Monday, and she's been smelling goose poop on her pillow case ever since."

"Aw, come on, Dad."

"That's what she says."

"All right. I have to do some more laundry this morning. I'll do your bedding over again."

"Good. Here are the car keys. Be back by six. Your mother and I are supposed to have dinner with the Hattons at their club. I imagine it'll be an excruciating pain in the behind. You and Tommy can fend for yourselves, I suppose?"

"Sure. Tommy'll open a can of Dinty Moore stew and I'll have some cereal. I'll be full of barbecue, anyway."

Later, after he had rid his mother's flowers of a few weeds, Loren retired to the back porch and began shoving bedding into the clothes washer. He flipped a switch to excite the agitator that jutted up in the center of the tub, causing the cloth to begin writhing around it, after which he took a pen knife and scraped soap shavings into the steaming water.

While the laundry was washing, he sharpened the cutting reels on the Temple lawn mower with a metal file. This done, he began to trim the tough St. Augustine turf in the back yard. As he worked he glanced occasionally through openings in the hedge separating the Temple lot from that of the widow Kaplan. He wondered how she was doing. Having observed no late-hour visitors since the night her husband died, despite having frequently glanced over at her window, he felt deprived. Just the thought of her lying in bed clad only in a skimpy nightgown brought a bulge to the front of his sweat-soaked shorts.

It was a shame, he thought, that the grass in the Kaplan yard had been neglected for so long that it was becoming too profuse to be manageable with only a push mower. Another few days and a commercial service would be needed. Or a big billy goat.

Even as Loren considered her situation, Mrs. Kaplan emerged from her house, heading for her flashy car. She was wearing a pink dress and a matching pill box hat. Catching sight of Loren through the foliage between them, she smiled and waved. Attracted by her friendliness, he cleared his throat and said: "I've been noticing your lawn. It looks like it badly needs mowing."

"Yeah, Ah know," she replied. "Ah've had no time t' see 'bout it. Because..." Her voice trailed off.

"I'm sorry."

"It's nice of yew... It's uh difficult time fer me."

"Can I help? I'd be glad to mow your yard. And I wouldn't charge anything."

"Oh, would yew? Ah insist on payin'. Th' grass is so long, it'll be hard work. Ah'll pay double whut we agreed upon before."

"That isn't necessary."

"Ah wanna. Come ovah this evenin' an' we'll settle up."

Bestowing upon Loren another radiant smile, which made him feel slightly dizzy, she entered her convertible with a flash of flesh from a muscular thigh, started the engine with a thunderous roar, and sped away.

Loren thought: Now, what have I done? Then an exhilarating idea took root in his mind. Rushing to finish cutting his own yard, and to hang out the laundry, he pushed his mower over behind the Kaplans' house. Peering in all directions to make sure that he was not being observed, he ventured to the rear of the property, where he began closely scrutinizing his surroundings. Soon he found what he was seeking. Some flowers next to the back fence had been trampled so badly that they had died. And several of the lower wires of the four-foot-high barrier were shiny, as if the rust coating that predominated elsewhere had been scraped off by someone's shoe. Moreover, the top strand was bent slightly downward.

On the other side of the fence were some bushes with broken twigs. Beyond them stood a two-story building that appeared to be a two-car garage, with an outside stairway leading up to a second floor apartment. A single large window visible on Loren's side of the building was completely curtained, but it did provide the inhabitants, whoever they might be, with a clear view of Mrs. Kaplan's back yard and the rear of her house, as well as a similar sighting into the Temple domain.

Two hours and several incipient finger blisters later, Loren finished cutting the Kaplan yard. Returning home, he completed the morning's work by running one more tub of laundry. While engaged in this task, he contemplated the significance of his new knowledge about the demise of Dr. Kaplan.

* * *

It was past time to go to the barbecue. After showering and squeezing several blackheads out of the distended pores of his pug nose, Loren put on clean trousers and a short-sleeved shirt. He sniffed his white sneakers and decided that their odor would pass unnoticed at an outdoor affair. Pecking his mother on her cheek, he drove the Hudson out to the western edge of Tocqueville. There he entered Ferrell Park, which consisted largely of an eighteen-hole golf course snaking through a swampy area dotted with pines and pin oaks, with an adjacent picnic area. Parked cars already lined the edge of the road near the trestle tables and nearby garbage cans, above which flies hovered hopefully. Yellow jackets zoomed malevolently in and out of discarded soft drink bottles lying in the grass.

Most of the Southsiders and their families were already there. Near them the corpses of two great golden geese were skewered on spits. Hot grease dripped into sputtering fires that had been fueled with pieces of dead limbs gathered from the nearby woods. A third bird had already been carved, and little was left of the carcass. Empty beer bottles were scattered about everywhere.

Ham and a fleshy woman whom Loren took to be his wife beckoned to him to join them at their table. "Hey, Yank," said the thick-set third baseman, his florid face glowing with sweat and good cheer, "have some barbecue an' beer. We got Jax, Lone Star, Regal, an' Falstaff, or Cokes if yew'd rather."

Loren accepted a paper plate from the woman Ham introduced as Annie, "mah bride of seven years." Taking a Coke from a nearby tub of ice, he popped off the cap with an opener that he rescued from a puddle of barbecue sauce on the table top. To a soft bun from the Dreamy Dough Bakery he added a pile of gooseflesh, which he then drenched in barbecue sauce spooned from a nearby bowl. He tried not to visualize the meat in its earlier incarnation. It was certainly stringy, but the thick spicy mixture in which it rested redeemed it. Loren's chin was soon smeared with scarlet sauce as he ate and looked around.

Half-clad pre-schoolers, some dotted with what looked like chigger bites on their bare legs, tussled and shrieked as they chased each other among the tables, while wives and girl friends, one of whom looked very pregnant, sat serenely on benches and gossiped with each other, and sometimes with the men.

Ham and Annie, Duke and his girl friend Boopsie Brewster, and Masher and his wife, all seemed like contented couples, but Bubba, spouseless, sat sullenly silent. As the second baseman tossed away the butt of a cigarette and reached into a shirt pocket for a fresh smoke, his bloodshot eyes darted warily about, as if he was looking for someone. He was so gaunt as to appear almost fragile.

The sound of an argument drew Loren's attention to a nearby table. There a swarthy stranger, towering above his listeners, was animatedly holding forth. Loren overheard the words "Johnson," "sonuffabitch," and "muffafugger." Slick and Feets, both holding half empty beer bottles and grinning, were egging him on. "Hey Yank," yelled Slick, "come ovah heah an' meet our new pitcher."

Hoisting himself from his seat and nodding to Ham and Annie, Loren ambled apprehensively over to the waiting trio. Shaking a hard hand, he said: "Nice to meet you."

"Sid Tibbs. Likewise."

Slick said: "Sid's gonna start fer us agin' Dibble on Sunday. He's been pitchin' fer uh chemical company team ovah at Baton Rouge, but he done got transferred t' Tocqueville 'bout uh month ago. He's played pro."

"Really? Where?"

"Ah trew uh few games last year fer Toledo. Blew out mah arm. Had t' lay out fer uh while."

"You pitched for the Mud Hens? That's pretty impressive."

"Sid also hates Lyndon Johnson," said Slick suggestively.

"Why is that?" asked Loren.

"That shitface is a nogood liar who'd steal th' shirt offa yore back an' give it t' some stinkin' nigger."

"What makes you say that?"

"'Cause Ah know th' man. Ah grew up in th' hill country whar Johnson usta teach school afore he went suckin' up t' ol' man Kleberg an' ended up wit' th' King Ranch seat in Congress. Th' slimy bastard claims t' be uh war hero. Hell, he ain't nevah seen no combat; take it from a guy who has. Sells his vote in Congress; sucks up t' th' damn liberals who're out t' mess wit' our Southern way of life; an' seduces other guys' women."

"Supposing that's all true, is Governor Stevenson any better?" asked Loren.

"Damn right he is," broke in Bubba, who had apparently been attracted by Tibbs's expostulations, and who now joined them, clutching a bottle of Jax. "Ol' Coke is ten times th' man Johnson is. An' he's gonna beat him bad next Sat'day."

"Maybe," said Loren. "But the polls..."

"Shit-eatin' polls are crap," broke in Tibbs. "Every true Texan who knows his ass from uh hole in th' ground will vote fer ol' Coke."

"Yank, here, is workin' in th' Johnson campaign," said Slick mischievously.

Tibbs stared at Loren, eyes narrowing. And Bubba, beer dripping down his chin, burst out harshly: 'Jus' whut yew'd expect from uh damn northerner. Comes t' Texas full of yankee notions an' right off starts tryin' t' instruct us who t' elect as our senator."

"I'm not trying to tell anyone how to vote," said Loren. "Johnson's people are paying me to put up signs. That's all."

"Soun's t' me like you're uh damn commie," declared Tibbs.

"The guy who hired me is a wealthy businessman," protested Loren.

"Don' make no difference," chimed in Bubba. "Some of those sonuffabitches have been bribed or threatened by th' labor unions." He glared at Loren. "Ah'll bet yore Daddy is uh commie, too. An' yore Momma..."

"Now wait a minute...!"

"...She's one, too."

"You leave my parents out of this discussion, you pathetic red neck."

"Come on, Bubba," said Slick, grabbing his teammate by the elbow. "Let's go git some more barbecue."

"Whut did yew call me, yew yankee muffafugger?" demanded Bubba.

"A red neck. What we used to call white trash in Richmond, the capital of the Confederacy, where I was born."

Dropping his Jax bottle on the ground as he lunged forward, Bubba took a wild swing at Loren, but missed. His face, contorted with fury, had turned cherry red. As he drew back a fist to try again, Feets and Slick both grabbed him and hauled him away, trying to calm him with soothing words. Sid Tibbs walked away, too, but not before giving Loren a contemptuous glare.

As soon as he used the phrase "white trash," Loren had regretted it. He felt uncomfortably alone. Ham was dolorously shaking his head. Fats, who had also been attracted by the furor, was frowning. Loren decided that it was time for him to leave the party. Dropping his plate and empty Coke bottle into a waste can, he started for his father's car. On the way he was intercepted by Fats, who was accompanied by a chunky youngster, not appreciably older than Loren.

"Yank, Ah'd like yew t' meet George Fancher. We call 'im Deacon, 'cause he don' drink, smoke, or cuss. Hell, he don' even spit."

"Howdy. Glad t' meetcha." There was no indication of unfriendliness in Deacon's manner as he shook hands.

"Deacon played football at A & M las' fall," said Fats. "An' he got into uh few varsity baseball games in th' spring, even though he wuz uh fust year man an' also had t' go t' football practice. Since school let out he's been playin' fer uh semipro team ovah at Fort Worth, makin' real money. But he's got some family problems, so he's home fer uh couple of weeks. He's goin' wit' us t' Dibble. We kin use his big bat in th' middle of th' lineup."

"Sounds good," said Loren. "I'll look forward to playing with you."

"Thanks. Say, Ah couldn' help overheahin' yore argument. Ah wan' yew t' know Ah'm on yore side. Johnson's better than Stevenson, who's uh stubborn, narrow, ignorant man. He stopped growin' when he wuz 'bout eleven years old."

"Still, some of us red necks like ol' Coke," ventured Fats. "But we don' need t' be gettin' all stirred up 'bout politics. "Member, Yank; next Sat'day we leave Davis's at seven-thirty."

"I'll be there."

As Loren turned to go, Fats hesitated, looking troubled; then he followed until they had put some distance between themselves and the others. "Ah gotta tell yew," he said in a low voice, "afore yew showed up we hadda short team meetin', at which Ah resigned as manager. Ah've had so much t' do lately in mah plumbing supply bidness that Ah can't git t' all th' games. Ah'll stay on as bidness manager. But it's time fer someun else t' run things on th' field."

Loren felt suddenly despondent. He had to ask: "Who's the new skipper?"

"Bubba." Averting his eyes, Fats waddled away.

* * *

Loren slept poorly that night. Several times he found himself awake, worrying. He felt vulnerable and needed guidance. But his problems were not the sort with which to trouble his parents. He thought of Buzz, but was wary of consulting him. So where could he turn for support or advice? He had no idea.

CHAPTER 14
BUZZ

Soon after he awakened on Sunday morning, Loren recalled that he had been supposed to collect his pay from Mrs. Kaplan the previous evening but had forgotten to do so. Before he could make himself presentable, however, he heard the front door bell ring and his mother speaking briefly to a caller. She then appeared in his doorway holding a five-dollar bill, which she gave him. "I thought you weren't going over there any more," she said.

"Well, her grass was getting so long, and she didn't seem to know what to do about it; so I decided to help out. Just once."

"You would be well advised to stick with that resolution," said Nan, firmly.

"O. K., Mom. Say, do you still want me to go with you to church?"

"That would be nice. Your father, I'm sure, would be pleased if you'd go."

"I'll get dressed."

Loren hadn't worn a jacket and tie since they had lived in Winona. It took him a frustrating few minutes in front of the bathroom mirror to get his tie properly knotted. Tommy watched with amusement. "Outa practice, aren't you?" he observed. "What's with this sudden interest in religion? I thought churches bored you."

"Not all churches."

"The only one I remember you saying anything good about was that big Unitarian church in Chicago."

"Maybe this one will be all right. Besides..."

"Yes?"

"I've heard," Loren admitted, "that if you want to play basketball or softball in the Tocqueville church leagues you have to be a member of a participating church."

"Ah ha."

"No need to share this information with Mom and Dad."

"Mum's the word. Unless some time I need you to do me a favor."

* * *

Entering the Austin Avenue Baptist Church, Loren was struck by the luxury of his surroundings. Fresh paint everywhere. Thick cushions on the seats of the high-backed pews. Brightly colored glass in the tall windows. And an air conditioning system that caused him to shiver as he sat down next to his parents and brother, glad after all that he had worn a jacket.

As the notes of the prelude, blasted by a huge pipe organ, died away, a tight-lipped middle-aged man wearing a dark suit and tie stepped into the pulpit and issued a call to worship. Then a ruby-robed choir, women in front, burst into song—something about God "in his holy temple." Prayers, hymns, and responsive readings followed, the congregation rising and re-seating themselves in unison at the proper times. Then came the Reverend Howard Pryor's sermon, delivered in a thin voice by a thin man with thinning ivory hair slicked back from a furrowed forehead.

The subject was self-reliance, and the approach was autobiographical. From having lived in poverty in South Carolina, to having been a struggling scholarship student at several Baptist colleges, through seminary status and a succession of minor pastorates, the Reverend Pryor had persevered, until now he was proud to serve one of the most respectable congregations in the South. Throughout his rise to ecclesiastical prominence, he had always belonged to the Rotary Club and the Chamber of Commerce and promoted area business interests.

Hearing such an paean to materialistic careerism in an environment that he had expected to be spiritual, Loren soon lost interest in the pastor's message and diverted himself, as had been his habit in Winona, with rating the entertainment value of the women's hats, taking into account the relative merits of fruit, flowers, fur, and other decorative features in a highly subjective series of assessments. His own mother, he estimated, scored about five on his one-to-ten scale, and it was only the almost invisible veil hanging over her blue eyes from her lavender felt hat which enabled her to reach that level. By contrast, a large buxom woman in a loud flowered dress that looked as if it had been assembled from someone's discarded window drapes got the only nine, because of the lifelike red birds perched in the green foliage atop her big black bun pulled up stiffly from a wrinkled neck.

Afterwards, as his mother and father visited briefly with people who approached them in friendly fashion, Loren told Tommy: "I guess I can stand it once a week. But I didn't hear much Christianity this morning, at least not what I thought Jesus preached."

Tommy snorted. "Not likely with this bunch. Not bad people, most of them, but self-centered and smug. Having tithed their ten per cent, they can ignore people less fortunate."

"Then why do you keep going back?"

"It's a social thing. Like Mom, I want to get to know a lot of Tocqueville people and become part of the community. If I disagree with them, I just keep quiet. Or I say something like: 'That's something to think about.'"

"Isn't that hypocritical?"

"Listen, Loren, when you're a newcomer it's safer to be hypocritical than to be merely critical. I'm not hurting anyone. Maybe I can even do some good."

Surprised by his younger brother's vehemence, Loren lapsed into silent thought. Maybe the kid was right. He wondered if his mother and father felt the same way.

* * *

Loren decided not to wait until the following weekend, when the Scorpions were scheduled to play the Dibble Dodgers, to find out how he stood with Bubba. Now that a new pitcher and another outfielder had been added to the team, his chances of being in the starting lineup were not good, especially if the new manager was going to hold a grudge. Why blow the entire weekend on the Dibble trip if he was going to be kept on the bench?

He almost undertook his dreaded mission on Tuesday, but the first heavy rain to hit Tocqueville since the previous April, according to the radio, provided a pretext to dampen his resolution. By Wednesday evening, however, he had mustered enough courage to pay Bubba a visit. Looking up John Charles Guidry in the telephone directory, he discovered that the address was listed as 2415-B Cypress Avenue, only one block south of his own street. He could walk there. Even more surprising was finding out that Bubba's garage apartment was the very one that he had earlier discovered overlooking the back yard of the Kaplans.

Bubba was alone. Wearing his Wisteria refinery work khakis and holding a half-consumed beer, he scowled when he saw Loren at his door. Returning to his armchair, he hoisted his beer bottle to his lips, took an extended swig, and then lowered it to a small table at his elbow on which sat an ashtray overrun with cigarette stubs. Loren noticed three empty beer bottles lying on their sides on the dirty carpet, next to a crumpled newspaper.

"I came to ask you something," said Loren. "Do you plan to write my name in the lineup next Saturday?"

Bubba gave his visitor a chilly stare. "Ah may," he said. "An' then again, Ah may not. Ah'll do whut's best fer th' team."

"I'm sure," said Loren dryly. "But what I need to know is whether you plan to bench me merely because we had an argument over politics."

"Ah don' have t' 'splain t' yew, or t' anyone, why Ah play or don' play people," said Bubba. "As th' manager Ah'll pick th' starters Ah wan'. Th' others'll sit.

Loren was growing angry. "Listen," he said, "I didn't come here to question your authority as a manager. But I have to tell you that if I am not going to play, at least some of the time, I shall find another team to play for."

"Suit yoreself."

"You haven't answered my question."

Bubba rose to his feet. He thrust a forefinger in Loren's direction as if he was pointing a pistol. "Yew ain't hearin' me," he asserted in a voice that had begun to quaver. "Right now Ah'm thinkin' that mah three outfielders fer Dibble are Slick, Duke, an' Deacon. All good players. All friends. All graduates of Southside High. All white trash, like me. None of 'em stuck up yankee bastards like someone Ah could name."

Wordlessly Loren turned and made for the door. As he exited, he heard what sounded like Bubba dialing a telephone. He took his time walking home, mulling over his next move. On the kitchen table he found a note from his mother requesting that he phone Mr. "Lee Due."

Going into the hall, he dialed the number. "Whatcha want, Fats?" he asked.

For a moment there was silence. Then Fats burst out: "Fer Gawd's sake, Yank; lay offa Bubba! He's not hisself. Electin' 'im as manager wuz uh big mistake. But Ah couldn' stop it. Th' guys don' know halfa whut's goin' on."

"What are you talking about?"

"Bubba's kid brother wuz killed several weeks ago in an army truck accident in Germany an' he blames hisself. He talked th' kid into joining up. Tole 'im he wuz uh slacker if'n he didn' enlist t' help hol' back th' commies. Plus Bubba an' his missuz bin on th' outs fer uh long time. Recently she moved out an' divorced 'im."

"I didn't know that," said Loren. "But I still don't see why he should take it out on me."

"He don' like yew," said Fats. "An' that makes 'im dangerous. Don' do anythin' mor' t' stir him up. It ain't safe."

"I think you're holding something back."

"Wal, its all ovah Southside. Ah'm surprised yew ain't heared it."

"What haven't I heard?"

"Bubba knifed uh guy at work on Monday. Sliced 'im up bad. Th' guy's still in th' hospital."

"I hadn't heard," said Loren. "What did the police do about it?"

"Questioned Bubba an' then released him. Called it self-defense. Seems th' other fella hadda piece of pipe. Thang is, Bubba's on edge; an' he might do anythin'. When he got home he foun' Rose fetchin' summa her thangs an' beat 'er up bad."

"That's awful."

"Yeah. She tol' Bubba he wuz crazy t' carry 'roun' uh switchblade. Said someone might shoot him. Said she wished someone'd do it. She went an' gotta restrainin' order 'gainst Bubba. He's sposed t' move outa their apartment by Friday; so Rose kin have it t' herself."

"How do you know all this?"

"Me an' Rose are real tight. We're cousins, y'know. Her Mom an' mine were sisters. Ah've known Rose since she wuz uh baby. Didn' think back then that she'd grow up t' be such uh rambunctious young woman. She don' take no shit off nobody, an' Bubba shoulda known that when he married her. They've had an up an' down relationship th' entire three years they been hitched. Bubba's uh bastard sometimes, but Rose's got uh mind of her own—too much so fer mos' any man. Ah've heard she won' let Bubba fuck her. Only times he's been able t' do it, he's hadda use force."

"That's... That's hard to imagine."

"Yew see how 'tis. So keep quiet this weekend; stay as much away from Bubba as yew kin; an' let's ride this out. Ah'll see whut Ah kin do t' git yew some playin' time."

"Thanks, Fats. I appreciate all you've said."

"Don' mention it. Not t' anyone. Ah gotta live wit' those guys."

"I understand. Goodbye." Loren hung up.

*　*　*

The next morning, as Buzz guided his truck out of town, he began directing concerned glances at his pensive partner. Finally he asked: "Whut's th' matter?"

"Nothing much."

"But somethin'."

"Yeah."

"Whut?"

Loren hesitated. Then he said: "The new manager of the Scorpions seems scary. Last week he knifed a guy and beat up his wife. Now he seems anxious to pick a fight with me."

"Who is this guy?"

"His name is J. C. Guidry. Everyone calls him 'Bubba.'"

"Huh. Bubba Guidry. Ah shoulda guessed."

"Do you know him?" Loren asked hopefully.

"Sure. We wuz all in school together, Bubba, Rose, an' me."

"And Mrs. Kaplan?"

"Her too. 'Cept she wuz Della Duhon then. Bubba played baseball an' kept t' hisself. Rose an' Della were cheerleaders an' very popular. Ah played basketball an' tennis. We wuz fairly good students, 'cept Bubba, who had problems wit' spellin' an' gettin' words in th' right order. Other guys used t' make fun of 'im, an' he wuz alluz gettin' into fights."

"I can believe that," said Loren. "Do you think I ought to quit the team?"

"Nah. Jus' don' provoke 'im. An' ..." Buzz paused, thinking. Then he added: "An' if'n he threatens yew directly, tell 'im that yore uh good fren of mine."

"Will that do any good?"

Buzz laughed. "Let's jus' say that Bubba will know whut it means t' have Sammy Howell on yore side."

"Well, thanks Buzz." Loren felt relieved. Then he thought he'd better ask: "Say, does this mean I have to fight anyone who takes a dislike to you?"

Buzz pretended to give the question some thought. Then, unsmiling, he asked: "Do yew have uh gun?"

Loren felt a lump in his throat and a sick feeling lower down. "No," he said.

His face lighting up with a big grin, Buzz said: "Ah didn' think so. In that case, let's agree: Ah'll help yew 'gainst Bubba if'n thangs git nasty, but yew don' have t' fight anyone who goes after me. Deal?"

"Deal," sighed Loren, settling back against the torn upholstery of the truck's front seat. He was wondering whether Buzz's other life, about which nothing had as yet been said, included some strong arm activity. Certainly his determined demeanor inspired confidence in his ability to deal with troublesome situations. Glancing at the naked woman on the glass knob that all Texas males seemed to think a necessary accessory to their steering wheels, Loren was reminded of something. "You know how the *Endeavor* prints a picture of some babe in a bathing suit or short shorts in almost every issue?"

"Shore," responded Buzz. "Usually next t' some religious article."

"Yeah. Well, last Saturday they had a picture of some starlet I never heard of before, but she had some special appeal, apparently, for my father. I saw him studying her while he was pretending to read a news story on the same page."

"Uh special appeal?" asked Buzz. "Lemme guess. Ah think Ah admired th' same picture. If Ah 'member rightly, yew refer t' young Miss Mary Monroe. Big boobs; right? Her cups runneth over?"

"I believe that was it—except that her name wasn't Mary. It was... Margaret; no, not Margaret. I remember; it was Marilyn. Marilyn Monroe."

"Whutevah her name, wit' that kinda equipment, she oughta go far," said Buzz. "Providin' she sleeps wit' plenty uh thick-lipped Jew producers."

Loren flinched. Buzz, he thought, had his hangups. Why were so many Protestants and Catholics prejudiced against Jews? He remembered one Winona classmate who pretended friendship for a Jewish guy, privately ridiculing him. "Feel th' material," he would say in a heavily accented voice, rubbing his thumb and forefinger together.

Loren recalled how some of his junior high teammates referred to the Jewish clothing store owner who had generously provided them with baseball equipment as "that kinky kike." No wonder Jews appeared at times remote and clannish. He wondered why some people seemed to detest other people whom they didn't even know? What were they afraid of? Were fear and hatred two sides of the same emotion?

Such thoughts could not be shared, except possibly with his mother. She was the only person he knew who seemed completely free of prejudice—who treated everyone with courtesy and hardly ever spoke ill of them in private. His father professed to be unbiased on matters of race and religion, and would have strenuously protested any imputation that he was otherwise. But his genuine friendliness toward individual Negroes, Jews, Catholics, Southerners and New Yorkers, did not invalidate his distaste for the general run of people in all those categories, apparent from his frequent observations about their supposed peculiarities and provincialisms. Sometimes Loren thought that the only overall class of people his father felt comfortable with was that of small town Protestant Middle Westerners, exactly the same sort of people Sinclair Lewis had parodied in his well known novels. Babbitts.

Loren sometimes wondered why Nan seemed so completely devoted to Adam. Even when he appeared negligent or selfish, she would always say, "Your father is very tired from working so hard to care for us," or "Your father has a lot on his mind." With her soothing protectiveness and unfailing support, she seemed to have elevated Adam to a position above and beyond criticism. Was there not a danger, Loren speculated, that someone who was continually treated that way might in time come to feel that he was blameless no matter what he did? Or if he was immature like Loren (could his father actually be that inhibited and fearful), might not being treated as the king who could do no wrong produce even further insecurity? And wouldn't Adam get into trouble when he encountered people away from the cocoon of home who did not consider him immune from criticism?

Loren's turning to Buzz for support in his own time of need, he realized, was a sign that his confidence in his father was beginning to diminish, as Adam's foibles became progressively more evident. Still, Loren didn't doubt that his father loved him and would do his best to support and protect him, whatever the cost. Which, when it came down to brass tacks, as his mother would say, was the difference between friends and a guy's immediate family.

Both of Loren's parents had inquiring minds. That was mainly why he was reluctant to consult them about the possible consequences of what he had done the night Dr. Kaplan died. They would want to know more, and more, until the whole sordid story was exposed. And they might, while trying to help him, only expose him to greater peril than if they remained entirely ignorant of his plight. If the missing roll of film turned up in the wrong hands...! Loren shuddered.

"Whut's th' matter?" asked Buzz.

"I was just thinking... What if..., what if someone I know had taken some pictures of something really bad? And what if those pictures had disappeared and might possibly have fallen into the hands of someone who could deduce who had made them? What if that person decided that the picture-taker was too dangerous to let live? What should my friend do?"

Buzz looked troubled. He gave Loren a prolonged searching stare. Then he said: "Mind if Ah ask who yore friend is?"

"I'd rather not say. I'm not supposed to have told anyone about this, as it is."

"Ah see... Wal, Ah guess th' best course of action would be fer yore friend t' play uh waitin' game. Assume that th' criminal hasn't yet foun' out 'bout th' pictures. But why hasn't yore friend reported whut he saw t' th' po-lice?"

"If he or she did that without the pictures to back up his or her story, it might not be believed. And more people would probably find out what had happened, so that the purr...pur..."

"Perpetrator."

"Perpetrators would be even more likely to try to silence the witness for good."

"So there were several people involved in the crime?"

"Two."

"Does yore friend know them?"

"One of them. Not the other one."

"Humm. Interestin'. Ah kin see why he's reluctant t' share his secret wit' anyone, includin' th' po-lice. How come he tol' yew?"

"We're close. He or she had to tell someone."

"Mah advice," said Buzz, "remains th' same. The two of yew should keep quiet an' not tell anyone else 'bout th' pictures or whut yore friend saw, at least until th' missin' pictures turn up. An' try not t' worry. Frequently these things settle themselves."

* * *

Driving back to Tocqueville that afternoon, they ran into heavy traffic. "What's all this?" asked Loren.

"Beauregard Junior College started its fall semester on Monday," said Buzz. "Th' enrollment's way up. Johnny Creek, uh local state legislator, is goin' t' try t' get uh bill passed this year t' make it uh four-year school."

"I'll probably be going there next year," said Loren unenthusiastically.

"Wit' yore academic background, Ah'da thought yew'd go East t' college; or at least t' Rice or Tulane."

"My parents can't afford such schools. But my classmates in Winona would probably think it scandalous that I won't be going to some Ivy League college. None of them could imagine attending a public junior college."

"Ah understand," said Buzz sympathetically. "Wal, some day yew'll show 'em. Whut courses will yew take?"

"I don't know. Probably journalism classes. My father would want that. What I'd really like to do is major in baseball," said Loren, with a grin.

"Sorry," said Buzz. "Beauregard doesn't have uh baseball team—only football an' basketball. An' Ah think golf an' tennis."

"Swell," said Loren. "I suppose I could try out for the tennis team."

Buzz looked interested. "Ah played tennis at Tulane," he said. "It paid mah way thru school. How much tennis have yew played?"

"Not much. And I haven't played since we moved away from Winona. I'd like to play here, but I haven't found anyone to play with me."

"Tell yew whut. Th' Johnson campaign ends this week. Mr. Sisti will pay yew fer th' month of August on Friday afternoon. Then yew'll be through workin' fer th' summer. Right?"

"Right."

"Ah'm gonna go back t' my former job, which gits me outa town uh lot, but also gives me time t' mahself. Why don' we git t'gether, say, once or twice uh week, an' knock uh few balls aroun'?"

"Fine with me."

"Ah'll phone yew. Yore in th' book?"

"Not yet. But here's the number." Loren tore a scrap of paper from a Lyndon Johnson leaflet and wrote down the number. "Now that we're out of the college traffic," he suggested, "why don't we swing by Southside High School and put up some more posters? Someone has been tearing them down in that neighborhood."

"Good idea," said Buzz, stomping on the gas pedal to send his truck speeding through a traffic light that was about to change from yellow to red.

* * *

Concentrating on their candidate most of that week, Buzz and Loren did not discuss national politics until Friday. Early that morning, as they were saturating the vicinities of polling places where Saturday's primary election would be held, Buzz asked Loren: "Whut did yew think of th' Hiss-Chambers confrontation on Wednesday?"

"I thought it interesting," said Loren, "that the HUAC chairman warned both of them that one or the other would certainly be tried for perjury. I'm betting that it'll be Chambers."

"If Ah wuz uh bettin' man," said Buzz, "Ah'd take that wager. Th' fact that Chambers has agreed t' take uh lie detector test an' that Hiss has refused makes me wonder if'n there ain't somethin' t' th' spy charges."

"I think it's all demagoguery," declared Loren. "For publicity. Look here. Another example."

Buzz stopped the truck and Loren handed over his newspaper clipping, which bore a three-column headline reading: "Sen. McCarthy Hires Out As Harvest Hand." Accompanied by a grainy photograph of a hard-faced man flashing a humorless smile from under a sweat-stained straw hat (a picture strikingly similar to some Loren had seen of Coke Stevenson), the story quoted a local farmer as commenting: "It was a fine thing for Joe to do. I wish more of those high officials in Washington would do something like that once and see our problems at first hand. Maybe then they wouldn't let the commies pull the wool over their eyes."

"Look at that bandana around the man's neck," said Loren. "I'll bet that's the first time he's worn one in his entire life. And he needs a shave."

"Guys like that alwuz need uh shave," declared Buzz. "Him an' that Congressman Nixon. Two peas in uh pod. Did yew know that two years ago McCarthy took away Bob Lafollette's Senate seat—LaFollette th' Younger wuz prolly th' best senator Wisconsin evah sent t' Washington—by repeatedly callin' him uh communist—th' same way Nixon got into Congress."

"Why can't the voters see through these jerks?"

"Good question."

Loren and Buzz worked hard all day in the glaring sunlight, until, just after four o'clock, their posters were finally all gone. Passing by Tocqueville High School on their way to the Sisti & Sampson office, they saw purple-clad boys in pads and silver helmets hitting blocking sleds and tackling dummies, while others punted or passed and caught footballs flying in the air over the lined practice field. "Why aren't yew out thar?" Buzz inquired.

"I thought about it," admitted Loren. "Actually I didn't know that practice began before school started. At Winona there was a rule that we couldn't do that."

"It's not too late. Why don' yew go see th' head coach an' ask if'n yew kin suit up an' show whut yew kin do? Yew wanna play, don' yew?"

"Sure." Loren felt fearful, nevertheless. At Winona he had been well acquainted with all of his teammates and both of the coaches. Here he would be a complete stranger. Well, he would see...

"Les git us uh afternoon paper," said Buzz, stopping the truck at a small neighborhood grocery store. He went inside and soon emerged with an *Endeavor* already folded open to an inside page. "Heah," he said, "Lookit this."

A half-page ad read: "Peace! Preparedness! Progress! Elect Lyndon Johnson! He Gets Things Done! Thirty-Nine Years Old. Old Enough To Know What To Do! Young Enough To Know How To Do It!"

Buzz chuckled. "Ah'm surprised," he said, "that they didn' say 'Young Enough t' Still Be Able t' Do It!'"

"Do you think he has a chance?" asked Loren.

"A chance? Yeah. But Ah wouldn' put any big money on 'im. Let's go git our pay."

* * *

"Whut are yew goin' t' do wit' all that loot?" asked Buzz, as Loren nervously collected a fistful of currency from an amused cashier at the Sisti & Sampson office. Two hundred dollars for August, and another ten dollars that a smiling Mr. Sisti had told him, when he poked his head in to say goodbye, was a bonus for work well done.

Loren said: "I've been thinking that I should buy a car—just an old used one that I could get around in without having to use buses or ask my father to drive his Hudson."

"Sounds like uh good idea," said Buzz. "Whar will yew find such uh vehicle?"

"I don't know," admitted Loren.

Buzz looked at his watch. "Ah have some time," he said. "Why don' we drive downtown an' see whut we kin accomplish?"

"I'm game," responded Loren, gratefully.

They jumped out of Buzz's truck just inside the entrance to an automobile junkyard enclosed within a high rusty fence topped by barbed wire. A large dog barked at them from the steps of an unpainted office that rested precariously on cinder blocks. A Negro man in bibbed overalls emerged from the small building, told the dog to shut up, and said: "Howdy."

"Yew 'member me, Fred," said Buzz, grasping a large ebony hand. "Meet mah fren', Loren Temple."

"Howdy t' yew, Mista Temple," said Fred, tentatively extending a brown hand as if unsure whether he should, until Loren reached out and took it in his. "Whut kin Ah do fer yew folks?"

"We're lookin' fer uh reliable vehicle that Mr. Temple kin drive 'roun town," said Buzz. "Nuthin' fancy. He can't afford t' pay much. But no junk, either." Loren thought he glimpsed an unspoken message delivered and received between the two older men as they exchanged glances.

"Foller me," said Fred. "Ah think Ah got jus' whut yew want."

Passing several ranks of derelict cars, they came to a box-like black sedan, sitting by itself. "Jus' got this one in yesterday," said Fred. "Belonged t' an old man whose children got 'im uh new one. One of th' kids drove it right t' this spot fer me. Uh thirty-six Chevy. Even got uh radio."

Buzz walked around the car, leaning over to examine all four tires, and pushing both front and back bumpers up and down with stomps of his heavy boot. "Humm," he muttered. "Needs uh paint job." While Loren watched, he opened the driver's door, tramped on the running board as if testing its strength, and then hoisted himself inside. The front upholstery was enclosed in a dirty brown seat cover, which meant, Loren surmised, that underneath it was badly torn. A key protruded from the ignition. Buzz turned it, checked to make sure that the gearshift lever jutting up from the floor was in neutral, and then pushed down the starter button with his left foot. There was a sputtering sound from underneath the hood, then a chugging, and soon a roar as the engine came to life. Buzz looked satisfied. "Wanna take uh spin?" he asked Loren.

"Sure," said Loren. He boarded on the passenger side, and Buzz proceeded to drive the car out of the junkyard onto a potholed street. Passing several blocks of Negro shanties, they were soon in a commercial district in which most of the businesses were closed for the evening. The steering wheel seemed a bit stiff when Buzz turned into a side street, and he frowned when he again met resistance while making another turn. He hit the horn button and was rewarded with a reverberating quack. He switched on the radio and country music wailed loudly out of the open windows, turning heads on a nearby sidewalk, as they swung back into Fred's junkyard and coasted to a stop next to the run-down office, where the owner waited in the doorway.

"Tell yew whut, Fred," said Buzz. "We like th' car. But it needs considerable wuk. We kin offer yew maybe twenty-fi dollah fer it."

"Twenty-five?" protested Fred. "Man, yew know dat's way too low. Ah knows Ah kin git fifty."

"Come on, Fred," said Buzz. "Fer this rollin' junk heap? We might pay thirty."

"Forty. Not uh penny less," said Fred firmly, as Loren looked back and forth at the two negotiators, glad that Buzz and not himself was doing the dickering.

"Thirty-five," declared Buzz. "Done," said Fred; and they shook hands.

"Pay th' man, Loren," ordered Buzz, and Loren dug in his pocket for the money while Fred stepped back inside his office to look for a title form and bill of sale.

As they left the lot a few minutes later, Loren happily sounded the horn of his first automotive acquisition, which elicited a responsive wave and a thumbs up signal from the driver's side window of Buzz's truck. They parted company where Magnolia Avenue ran westward from downtown.

A few moments more found Loren slowing the car to a crawl as he prepared to bump over the railroad tracks that extended across the street at right angles. Apparently he had not slowed down enough, however, because the car suddenly started shaking with such vehemence that he almost lost hold of the steering wheel. Desperately he stamped on the brake pedal and at once the vibrations ceased, as the car came to an abrupt stop. Sweating, he gradually picked up speed, as he navigated the half dozen blocks remaining before he reached his own driveway.

A shimmy! He had heard about such a thing—causing the poor driver momentarily to think he had been caught in an earthquake—but he had never experienced one. It was disconcerting.

"What have you done?" exclaimed his mother, as she followed him outside in response to his suggestion that she see what was sitting in the driveway. She walked around the Chevy, gingerly touching its dusty exterior, leaning over slightly to peer inside. "What will you father say?"

"He should be happy," asserted Loren. "Now he won't have me bothering him to use his car."

"Is it safe?" Nan asked.

"Sure. It's pre-war. Not thin tin, like the post-war stuff."

"Well, we'll see what your father has to say about it," said Loren's mother, dubiously. "I have to get back inside: I have dinner on the stove." She paused. "But I hope you can afford insurance," she added.

"Insurance?"

"Of course. Someone might hit you and sue us, which could wipe us out financially." She laughed. "Not that we have enough money to make us an inviting target. Still, you'll need insurance. Ask your father about it."

As Loren proudly showed an envious Tommy how well the radio worked, their mother stuck her head out of the kitchen door. "I forgot to ask," she called out. "What are you going to name it?"

Loren had not considered that an issue. But he saw her point: people named their boats, their airplanes, or their estates, if they were rich. Now he was rich in junky autos. Why not name his new acquisition? He looked at his mother with a slight smile and said: "I think I'll call it 'Shaky.'"

CHAPTER 15

DIBBLE

During the long drive to Dibble on Saturday, August 28, Loren at first sat silently in the back seat while the others gabbed. Duke drove. Ham and Fats ragged him about his low batting average, his girl friend whom they suggested had "made th' rounds," and his happy-go-lucky attitude, never worrying about tomorrow. "Life is passin' yew by, beeg boy," said Ham. "No wife, no li'l ones, no equity in yore own house, an' uh dead-end job. Yew'll wake up some day an' realize whut yew've missed."

"Yew've got no notion of th' good life, ol' timer," retorted Duke. "Ah gotta sexy gurl fren' t' satisfy mah manly urges, one who ain't buggin' me alla time when we ain't in bed. Ah rent an ol' house someone else has t' keep up an' which Ah kin leave whenevah Ah wanna an' go somewheres else. Same wit th' job. No kids t' tie me down; no dogs or cats or goldfish. Ah'm free, man. An' Ah ain't 'bout t' give up mah liberty fer th' boredom of marriage an' uh mortgage."

"But Duke," interjected Fats, "if'n yew don' know whar yore headed, yore boun' t' find yoreself elsewhar."

"How th' hell does anyone know whar they're headed? Whut's th' point of tryin' t' make predictions, 'specially 'bout th' future?"

Speaking of predictions, Loren thought, it's election day. In the morning paper, all the pundits had predicted that Governor Stevenson would be elected to the Senate. Loren's work for Congressman Johnson would then have been in vain. Except that he had been paid almost five hundred dollars, which had enabled him to acquire Shaky. And he had made a good friend in Buzz.

Duke's car entered the Big Woods, and the trees next to the highway cast a welcome shade to alleviate the heat of the morning sun. Loren's three teammates began to argue whether "book larnin'" was more valuable than knowledge derived from "jus' livin' an' lookin' 'round," as Ham put it. Loren sensed that they were trying to draw him out of his shell into the conversation.

"Didja know," asked Fats, casting a sidewise glance at his seatmate, "that thar are only two kinds of trees—carniverous an' delicious?"

Loren couldn't keep from laughing.

Fats, pleased with himself, grinned at Loren, while Ham, perplexed, said: "Whut yew mean, Fats, only two kinds of trees? Thar's oak an' cypress an' pine an' ..."

"It was a joke, Ham," said Loren. "Like the dog that could only make one sound, 'birch, birch.'"

"Why wuz that?"

"It was the only bark he knew."

"Yore wus than Slick. Stop pullin' mah leg."

"I say, pulling your leg is no small feat."

"Shee-it!"

A long silence ensued, as Loren thought of and then discarded as inappropriate a series of puns related to various body parts—and then daydreamed, with heroic deeds on the diamond the predominant theme. Ham hummed and looked out the window; Duke fiddled with the controls of the radio and cussed the lack of what he called "real music;" and Fats scribbled in his ever present notebook.

Duke broke the silence. "Hey, Fats; ain't it 'bout time we wuz comin' into Dibble?"

"Soon," said Fats. "In yore patience, possess yew yore soul."

"Whut th' hail yew talkin' 'bout?"

"Be patient," said Fats. "Luke twenty-one nineteen."

"Dammit, how kin Ah be patient when Ah gotta pee? An' don' quote th' damn Bible at me. That's one overrated book."

"Overrated? Yew gotta be kiddin'. Th' Bible's th' Good Book. Everyone should live by it. It's fulla wisdom."

"Hail yew say. Ain't none of it original. It's like Shakespeare's stuff. Mostly quotations."

Fats gave Loren a look that said whatdaya gonna do wit' this guy? "Th' hour cometh," he mumbled. "John four twenty-three."

From snippets of conversation he had overheard earlier, Loren had formed a vague impression of the small town toward which they were heading. Founded in the eighteen-nineties by a lumber baron from Texarkana who set up a sawmill that employed over six hundred men, Dibble had remained for over half a century a fiefdom of the Turner family. Its current scion was said to own a million acres of Texas forest, more real estate than the famous King Ranch in whose employment Lyndon Johnson had begun his political career. Joe Turner was also in the paper products business and was rumored to be on the verge of investing in the publishing industry. He had recently moved into a mansion constructed to his own eccentric specifications on the edge of town. It was there that the visiting ballplayers had been invited to an afternoon fish fry, as a sort of house warming.

According to a sign welcoming visitors, Dibble contained only 2,755 people. Loren caught a glimpse of dirty wooden shacks with sagging front porches where elderly people occupied rocking chairs or rested on plain benches. Mixed-breed hounds panted in the speckled shade of pink mimosa trees or dug nests in the brown needles of loblolly pines. Some of the houses were flanked by gardens in which yellow flowers and green spikes topped okra stalks reaching toward the broiling sun.

The town's business district straddled a two-block long stretch of asphalt that was itself divided by the polished steel tracks of the Texas and New Orleans railroad. Loren noticed a post office, three churches, and perhaps a dozen stores. Next to the railroad station stood a warehouse with a sign reading: "Turner Industries." The Dibble Inn, into which Fats had booked the team, was an almost new two-story structure constructed of shiny yellow pine logs with a metal roof.

The Scorpions carried their luggage into a large lobby, eager to register and receive their room assignments. Loren was heartened to see on his left a pleasant-looking restaurant, with vases of flowers on every table cloth, awaiting guests who might not find one fish fry adequate nourishment for an entire weekend.

After the desk clerk checked what Slick and Masher had written in the register and handed them their room keys, Bobo stepped forward, and the young man pushed the registration book along the counter for him to write in his name and address. Quickly Fats reached past Bobo, seized the proffered pen and, dipping it in the nearby ink bottle, wrote "Robert Skinner," followed by a Tocqueville address; and then, still without a sound, handed the pen to Bobo, who leaned forward and laboriously inscribed a large "X" next to his name on the register, after which he received a room key and left.

Loren was assigned a room with Deacon Fancher. As they reached their door, entered from an L-shaped balcony that overlooked the first floor lobby, Deacon turned to Loren and said: "Since we're gonna be roomies, Ah wish yew'd call me George. Ah hate bein' referred to as Deacon."

"Fine," said Loren. "And my name's Loren, not Yank. I wonder why every ballplayer has to have a nickname."

"Same reason we're all supposed to babble li'l cries of encouragement when we're playin'. Say, hey; yore th' one, Babe; chuck t' me, Big Boy. Tradition."

"Less talk and better execution would be my preference, if I were a manager."

"No chance of that wit' that obnoxious pepper pot, Bubba, in charge. They nevah shoulda made 'im manager after Fats resigned."

"Well, why did they? I got to the barbecue too late and missed the election. No one had told me there was going to be one."

"Bein' new this year," said Deacon, "Ah didn' think Ah shud vote. But Ah watched. Tibbs voted fer Bubba, who voted fer hisself. Several of th' guys voted fer Feets, but not 'nough, 'specially when Feets refused t' vote fer hisself. Slick tol' me afterwards that he'd voted 'gainst Feets 'cause he wuz too nice a guy. Bubba, he said, would shake things up, make things interestin'."

"Slick," said Loren, "loves trouble."

"Yeah. It mus' be time t' head out t' th' fish fry. Les go downstairs."

Leaving their bags on the two single beds, they exited onto the balcony, Deacon shutting the door, which had no lock, behind them. Loren noticed Masher and Slick, looking furtive, emerging from a room two doors away. With Masher grinning widely and Slick nodding to them with a forefinger laid vertically across his lips, the two let themselves into a room further down the balcony, while Loren and Deacon continued downstairs, passing Ham who was coming up. The portly third baseman, always slow moving, had apparently been the last to register.

At the bottom of the stairs, the roommates encountered Fats, who was talking to a whispy little man in a green pork pie hat and a green and white striped short sleeved shirt from which dangled pipe cleaner arms and tiny hands. "Ah wantcha t' meet Pete McKay," said Fats. "Mr. McKay works fer Mr. Turner. They're sendin' over uh school bus t' take us t' th' fish fry. It'll be heah in 'bout twenty minutes. We kin wait heah in th' lobby, whar it's cooler."

As the four seated themselves, there was a loud howl from upstairs, and a few seconds later Ham appeared, wide-eyed, on the balcony. "Hey, desk clerk," he demanded. "Come up heah. Now."

The startled young man behind the desk inquired: "What's wrong, sir?"

"Ah wan' yew up heah. There's some'tin' disgustin' in mah room."

The clerk, looking worried, ascended the stairs and tentatively trailed Ham into his assigned room. Curious, Loren, Deacon, and Fats followed. They were immediately joined by Slick and Masher, strangely subdued.

Pointing with a quivering index finger, an outraged Ham shouted: "Whut th' hail is this filthy crap someone left under mah bed? Don' yew clean yore rooms?"

"Sir, we do have a maid. I have no idea how that container got under your bed. Nor do I recognize what is in it."

"Dammit, yew dunce; its shee-it! An' piss, too!"

Loren leaned forward to get a good look at the object that had inspired such consternation. It was an ancient bedpan with rusty white enamel, containing what appeared to be the excrement of the previous occupant.

"Nevah in mah life," exclaimed Ham, "have Ah encountered somethin' so disgustin' in uh rented room. Uh dirty towel, yeah. Uh used rubber in th' waste basket, maybe. But this…!"

"Heah," said Slick, "lemme see." He pushed past the hotel clerk and Ham and leaned over to take hold of the bedpan. He sloshed the contents around. "Humm," he said meditatively. Then, while his audience looked on in horror, he lifted the container to his lips and drank deeply. Next, with white foam having formed a mustache under his nose, he began to eat the light brown object that had lain in the bottom of the pan.

"Gawd!" exclaimed Deacon.

"Are yew crazy?" yelled Ham. "Yore eatin' shee-it!"

The young clerk turned pale, emitted a choking sound, and stumbled from the room down the stairs, apparently heading for the men's room. Placidly, Slick continued to chew.

Masher could no longer contain his laughter. Guffawing loudly, he tried to speak but couldn't. Finally he managed to say to Ham: "Don' worry, its only beer an' uh peeled sweet potato we brought from home. One of Slick's jokes."

Ham looked dazed. Belatedly, he realized that he had been had. Then he said: "Huh. If Ah had known whut it wuz, Ah nevah woulda pissed in that pot."

Slick, startled, immediately lowered the bedpan from his mouth. He shot Ham a look of pleading panic. Ham looked blank. Suddenly Slick dropped the pan on the bed and rushed down the stairs to join the hotel clerk in the men's room, while Loren and Deacon doubled up with laughter. Masher asked: "Did yew really pee in that pot, Ham?"

Ham responded with an enigmatic half-smile and said: "Time we all got outta heah an' had us some fish. An' Masher, Ah believe this belongs t' yew, or t' yore funny roommate. It ain't whut Ah wan' fer supper."

Loren stopped in the rest room next to the lobby to see if Slick was all right. The team's leading jokester was still inside a stall. Loren bellied up to one of the urinals. When he closed his fly and went to a sink to wash his hands, he saw Slick emerge from a stall, zip up using only his left hand, and then head for the door. Seeing Loren's disapproving look, he said: "No, Ah didn' wash off all th' shee-it.

Ah wan' this right paw still oozin' wit' it when Ah shakes hands wit' that sonuffabitch Turner."

In the bus on the way to Turner's house, Loren saw Slick glancing covertly at Ham, who merely looked smug. Masher whispered something to A. C. and Duke, and they both laughed uproariously. Slick, thought Loren, would soon be contriving more practical jokes, and the odds were that Ham would be a target. And Masher, too.

* * *

At the Turner mansion the Scorpions entered a splendid reception area under a huge crystal chandelier. Directly in front of them, across a black marble floor, was a large framed oil painting of the house's owner. Mr. Turner himself greeted each visitor with a powerful handshake and a brief word of welcome. Darkly tanned, he exhibited a thick mat of curly gray hair through a partly unbuttoned starched white shirt. What he said to Loren was "Glad yew could come," which was probably what he said to Slick, who was next in line, and who after shaking hands rubbed his right hand against his trouser leg as he and the others gathered around a buxom blonde for a guided tour of the building. The woman, someone whispered, was Turner's third wife. The ballplayers stared lasciviously at her big bottom, as they trailed her up a spiral stairway for an inspection of no less than ten resplendent bedrooms and five ornate bathrooms. Once more downstairs, they passed through a hotel-sized kitchen in which several Negro women in large white aprons prepared food, and through a dining room with a polished mahogany table that could seat twenty people. They gaped at a vast living room filled with expensive leather furniture and then visited a study with bare book shelves, a breakfast room, a game room with a full-sized pool table, and a music room with a grand piano, on top of which rested a gleaming guitar.

The house was like a parody of some pages from *Better Homes and Gardens*. Everything seemed artificial, like the blonde's hair and Turner's toothy smirk.

Outside, in a freshly sodded yard, a kidney-shaped swimming pool contained several pudgy children who splashed and screamed. Nearby were tables covered with food and drink. Loren gorged himself on fried fish and chicken, biscuits, baked beans, slaw, and potato salad, all washed down by a sickly sweet Pepsi. Nearby sat the lord of the manor, surrounded by his courtiers and grateful guests, nervously waited on by his humble dark-hued serfs. He chewed his food with his mouth wide open, dripping bits of fish down his greasy jowls into his lap while a basset hound waited expectantly on the grass beside him. Mr. Turner, it seemed, had few inhibitions. Dominating those around him with his intimidating presence, using language so rough that some of the women flinched, he was superior to all conventions or codes of etiquette. In one final flamboyant gesture before he rose from the table to shake hands with recent arrivals, he abruptly removed his dentures and held them under the table, so that his dog could lick them clean. He then replaced them between his gums and resumed his role as the genial, if unconventional, host, while Loren tore his eyes away from the medieval scene and fought to keep his dinner down. Now, he thought, I've seen everything. On second thought, considering what he had already encountered during his association with the Scorpions, probably not.

As his teammates were filing past their host to express their thanks for his hospitality, Loren whispered to Slick: "He's a crude character, all right. But why do you dislike him so much?"

"Ah wuz in th' army in th' same unit wit' his son, Joe, Junior. We wuz together on Saipan an' later on Okinawa. He tole me some of th' stuff th' Turners pulled in order t' acquire their land, an' how ruthlessly his father exploited th' workers in his mills—used them an' discarded them like garbage. Joe wuz proud of his ol' man. Said he'd learned uh lot from th' ol' bastard. Said that some day, after he inherited everything as th' only son, he wuz gonna git real rich. His father wuz only uh millionaire. He wuz gonna be uh billionaire."

"A chip off the old block."

"He'll do it, too. Right now, while his daddy plays wit' his new toys—this house that ain't uh home, an' his sexpot replacement wife—Junior is supervisin' th' clear cuttin' of 'nough timber t' rebuild alla Tocqueville. Pollutin' th' water an' erodin' th' soil; killin' th' fish; runnin' off th' animals; turnin' summa God's greatest work into uh wasteland, all t' git hold of mor' money than anyone should evah need."

Slick was palpitating with rage. Loren was amazed. The guy was a real bleeding heart. Were his puns and wisecracks and tomfoolery all a facade? As Loren tried to think of something to say, Slick turned away and took an alternate route out to the waiting bus, so that he could avoid speaking to the master of the manor. Loren, less determined, allowed Terrible Turner to crush his fingers one more time, but he could barely mumble his "much obliged" with an averted face.

* * *

Late afternoon. Fats had seen to it that their equipment was already on the bus, so they were able to go directly to the ballpark. It was a relatively new structure, probably another Turner philanthropy. Inside the visitors' clubhouse, Bubba immediately asserted himself as the new manager. As he pulled his uniform pants up over his shaved legs and shorts and laced up his spiked shoes, he looked around imperiously at the surrounding Scorpions. Planting his right foot on top of a scarred wooden bench, he leaned solemnly forward, his dangling left hand holding a lineup card, his right hand shoving his hat onto the back of his head, and shouted: "Shaddup an' listen!"

During the amused silence that followed, he read off the starting lineup. As Loren had feared, he was benched. Fido, Duke, and Deacon were to play the outfield.

Bubba then launched into a lecture on the importance of being Tough. The Dibble team was Tough. The Scorpions would have to be Tougher still. "'Member men," he admonished them, "when th' goin' gits Tough, th' Tough git goin'."

As Bubba continued his harangue, several of his teammates exchanged shrugs and covert grins. Feets, with a blank look, tugged at his knee sox. Ham rolled his eyes. Slick grinned. And Loren studied the dirty window panes, the lower ones whitewashed for privacy, and then contemplated the gray paint flaking off the cracked concrete floor. How long, he wondered, could he put up with such nonsense?

Bobo, naked except for his jockstrap, vented a reverberating belch. A nervous giggle escaped from Fats, who stood, valise in hand, near the door. Then Masher leaned forward and slapped Bubba jovially on his rigid back. "Right," he declared. "It's th' time fer Toughness. Let's take some Tough battin' practice."

The Scorpion players, all but Loren, who was trying to undo a jammed knot in a shoelace, and Deacon, who was repairing a broken strap in his glove, trotted out the door. Soon their chatter could be dimly heard, as they began to exchange their warmup tosses.

Watching out of the corner of one eye, as he double knotted his spiked shoe, Loren noticed the muscles in Bubba's jaw twitching. Then, tugging his cap over his eyes, the new manager headed resolutely for the field.

As soon as he was gone, Loren looked over at Deacon. A huge grin split the big fellow's freckled features. "Whut uh prick!" he exclaimed. "Ah nevah…"

"Shhh!" broke in Fats. "He's comin' back!"

In walked Bubba, head down in grim concentration. Reaching under a bench, he retrieved the thin black bat which he guarded fiercely and would let no other player even heft, much less swing at a ball. Giving it two violent swishes, Bubba returned to the field, but not before directing a withering warning look at Loren. "Not uh word 'gainst mah authority," it seemed to say.

By the time Loren, Deacon and Fats reached the field, the sun had disappeared behind the third base grandstand, shadowing the entire infield. But it was not until the Scorpions had finished batting practice and straggled in to watch the Dibble Dodgers take their licks that someone switched on the floodlights surrounding the playing area.

Fats had been tipped off that Dibble had loaded up with ringers for tonight's game. The town fathers, remembering the 17-4 humiliation inflicted on their local heroes earlier in the summer, had not only invested in outside talent, but also, it was rumored, had wagered large sums on the outcome of tonight's contest. If so, Loren thought, Slick had probably been busy at the fish fry obtaining a piece of the action.

A loud Crack diverted his attention to home plate. One of the Dibble players, a tall left-handed hitter, had just hammered a practice pitch into the blackness beyond the right center field fence. Crack. Another shot left the park, curling into foul territory as it disappeared from view. Crack. A puff of red dust beside a dodging infielder marked the passage of a white pellet into right field, on its way to a dimpling encounter with the tin fence.

"Who's that?" inquired Slick.

"Hamilton Jones," said Masher.

"Who's he?"

"Played fer th' University at Austin. All-conference in baseball an' all-American in basketball. Word is that th' Philadelphia Athletics are tryin' t' sign him but he's holdin' out fer uh big bonus. Heavy hitter."

"I believe it," said Loren as another shot left the park.

Bobo walked over. "Lookit that," he said, pointing at a withered little fellow standing on second base talking to a much younger player with pale features and ivory hair. "One of th' seven dwarfs. An' that mus' be Snow White."

Fats, waddling by, overheard. "Take 'nother look, Bobo," he said. "That's Hank an' Tim Samuels, father an' son, shortstop an' second base. Hank played ten years in th' bigs. He's managin' t'night an' t'morrow, on loan from uh Houston oil company team. He an' his son an' Jones musta cost these folks uh small fortune. They're out t' git us this time."

Loren remembered Hank Samuels by reputation. He had played with the Gas House Gang in St. Louis during the days of Dizzy Dean and Pepper Martin; and before that he had spent some time with the Detroit Tigers. That would make him almost fifty years old. He was still spry though, Loren noticed, watching the senior Samuels dart to his right to gobble up a grounder with a backhand stab, before flipping it smoothly to his son on second. The ball hit Tim Samuels' glove precisely in front of his right shoulder. "A real pro," thought Loren.

. After both infield practices were completed, the umpires were joined at home plate by the managers. As the four men discussed ground rules peculiar to the local ball field, Loren looked around. Under bright floodlights the dry grass looked glossy green and the foul lines appeared chalk-white against the ruddy earth. The stands were crammed with spectators, possibly as many as two thousand. If most of them had paid the usual fifty cents, assuming the standard split of sixty per cent of the gate receipts for the home team and forty per cent for the visitors, the Scorpions might take home as much as four hundred dollars as a result of the night's work. That did not include whatever money had been collected from approximately forty Negroes, who were confined to some old wooden bleachers situated separately down the right field foul line.

A cheer burst from the crowd as the Dibble Dodgers ran onto the field. Squat little Fido swung two bats near home plate as the Dibble hurler fired his final practice pitches. He was a lean lefty, who lifted his right leg, knee bent, high above the ground, toe pointing almost directly at first base, as he reared back to throw. His pitches had movement; the catcher was taking some of them on the edges of his mitt, instead of directly in the pocket.

"Play ball!" shouted the home plate umpire, and Fido stepped into the right hand batter's box, stretched out his bat to touch the outside edge of the plate, and settled into his crouch, feet spread wide apart, hands several inches up the handle.

It took the Dibble pitcher less than a dozen throws to dispose of Fido on a weak grounder back to the mound, Bubba on a called third strike, and Bobo on a long fly which the left fielder caught in the corner after a long run.

With Tibbs slated for Sunday's game, Bubba had decided to send Slick to the mound. Seemingly nervous, Slick walked Tim Samuels on five pitches. The Dodger second baseman promptly stole second base when Feets had to dig a low curve out of the dirt before making a hasty throw. Batter number two poked an outside curve on the ground to Bubba's left, which moved the runner to third.

Hank Samuels wielded his long thin bat like a wand. On the second pitch he suddenly swung around to face Slick and dumped a perfect squeeze bunt out in front of the plate. It appeared that the younger Samuels would score easily. Feets, however, had somehow anticipated the play and ventured a daring gamble. At the very moment when the ball left Slick's hand, not even waiting for it to reach the plate, Feets lunged behind the ex-big league shortstop, and across the third base line into fair territory, so adroitly that he was able to glove the bunt on the first bounce and, whirling, make a diving tag on the sliding runner.

Shocked into momentary silence, the Dibble fans soon offered homage in the form of shrill whistles and loud clapping, which Feets acknowledged with a grin. A moment later he chased down a towering foul fly off the bat of Hamilton Jones and gloved it expertly, making just the right allowance for the last minute spin of the sphere back toward the diamond. Infuriated, Jones threw his bat all the way to the Dodger bench, scattering his teammates, before stalking grimly out to first base and picking up his mitt.

In the top of the seventh, the Scorpions pushed across a single tally. With one out, Bobo drew a walk, stole second, and went to third on a perfect sacrifice bunt dropped down the line by Masher. He then scored when Ham poked a humpbacked liner into center field. Duke drew a pass, but Deacon made the final out of the inning, lofting an easy fly to the right fielder, who caught it in his tracks.

In the bottom of the seventh, a nearly exhausted Slick escaped a bases-loaded jam when a Dodger lined into a pitcher-to-first double play. It was then that Loren first began to notice the intensifying effect of the game's tension on Bubba, whose constant stream of encouraging noises as he moved nervously about in his second baseman's position, or in the first base coaching box, had become virtually incoherent. When the Scorpion manager came up in the eighth, with two out and Slick on first base, he crouched over the inside portion of the plate as if daring the pitcher to throw at him. The first pitch, an inside fast ball, barely missed his head as he fell backward into the dirt. Screaming at the pitcher, "Yew sonuffabitch muffafugger asshole, throw 'nother one of those an' Ah'll beat yore brains out," he resumed his provocative position with his elbows protruding into the strike zone. Although the lefthander probably intended to throw another duster, his offering drifted over the middle of the plate, waist high, a perfect hitter's pitch. Bubba, however, was wrongly positioned to capitalize on the error. His bat shattered as it met the ball on its thin handle, resulting in a weak dribbler. Cursing loudly, Bubba dug hard for first base, while the Dodger third baseman swooped in and picked up the ball barehanded on the run, throwing underhanded across his body as he lunged forward. From Loren's perspective on the visitor's bench, Bubba's foot hit first base a split second before the splat of the ball into Jones's mitt, as the big man stretched almost full length to shorten the distance of the throw. But the umpire saw it differently. His right thumb jutted skyward, as he shouted "Yore out!"

As Bubba, panting, returned from his desperate dash beyond the base, he advanced upon the arbiter. His eyes were wild, his chin jutted, his mouth twisted with rage as he spewed a stream of goddams. When the ump turned to walk away, Bubba seized his arm and yelled: "Ah said Ah wuz safe, yew stupid sonuffabitch."

"An' Ah said yew wuz out. One more cussword an' yore outa th' game."

"How much did th' Dodgers pay yew, asshole?" retorted Bubba. "Yore as blind as uh muffafuggin' bat."

"That's it," said the infuriated official. Leveling a forefinger at his antagonist, he roared: "Git offa th' field, now!"

For a moment Loren thought that Bubba would take a swing at the man in black, but after one more exchange of hostile stares, the Scorpion manager turned away and swaggered, muttering imprecations, over to the bench. Ordering Jackie Lawson to fetch his glove from the grass behind the second baseman's position, he glanced grimly at Loren and shouted after Jackie: "Yew take ovah second base fer me. An' Feets," he added, turning toward the catcher, "yew manage." Then he headed for the clubhouse.

In the bottom of the eighth, with two out and a runner on second because of an error by the jittery Jackie, Hank Samuels reached out for one of Slick's slow curves and stroked it over Masher's head into the right field corner. Deacon had to lumber all the way from right center field to retrieve the ball, and by the time he returned it to the infield, the Dodger manager was puffing on third base and the tying run was in.

Slick worked carefully on the next batter. With a count of two and two, however, he fed Hamilton Jones a fat pitch which the big man lambasted. The ball shot back directly at Slick, who stabbed ineffectually at the white blur, only to have it pass under his glove and smash into his left ankle, before bouncing off toward the first base line. Slick tried to pursue it, but after a couple of stumbling steps he collapsed on the grass with a groan. By the time Masher picked up the ball, Jones had reached first safely and Samuels had scored the lead run for the Dodgers.

Loren watched apprehensively from the bench as Feets and the Scorpion infielders gathered anxiously around the fallen pitcher. Carefully, Ham peeled down Slick's sock and felt the spot where the ball had hit. Slick flinched and clenched his teeth. Feets leaned over to say something to him and the wounded hurler shook his head. For a moment they argued. Then Slick fell back on the ground in capitulation. Feets beckoned to Loren.

Startled, Loren hesitated. "Who, me?" he asked.

Feets nodded impatiently and once again waved Loren off the bench. When he reached the mound, Slick was on his feet, one arm thrown over Masher's bulky shoulder, beginning to limp toward the bench. "Good luck, Yank," he whispered as they passed. "Don' mess up mah earned run average."

"Git ready," ordered Feets with a worried air. "Fats done tol' me yew were uh pitcher in high school. Hope yew ain't rusty. Take all th' time yew need." He headed back to his position behind the plate, put on his mask, and crouched to receive Loren's practice pitches.

Nothing fancy, Loren told himself. Just get the ball over the plate. The next Dodger hitter stood to one side, swinging three bats, and scrutinized Loren's style with interest. After seven straight medium fast ones, Loren nodded to Feets and backed off the rubber to reach for the rosin bag. As he dusted his sweaty fingers, the home plate umpire cried out, "Play ball."

Feets squatted and thrust his index finger between his knees. Loren stretched his arms as high as he could reach and the runner cautiously led off first base. Pushing off the rubber with all his strength, Loren fired his best fast ball. Like a starving man lunging for a plate heaped with victuals, the batter greeted it with gusto. The ball exploded off his bat with a sound like doom and flew high toward the shadows beyond the left field fence. Fortunately, it hooked foul just before it disappeared from sight.

Loren took off his cap and scrubbed the sleeve of his sweatshirt across his wet brow. No more pitches like that one. Clamping his glove under his right armpit, he rubbed the gloss off a new ball. Then he took Feets' sign for a bender.

It was a terrible curve, hardly more than a wrinkle, but it hung inside and the batter was unable to offer at it. Feets, a frown on his face, sauntered out to confer. "Mah momma coulda hit those pitches, Yank," he complained. "Yew got anythin' better?"

"I think so," replied Loren. "Let's try a drop. Show me a fist when you want it. But first, let's set him up with a couple of straight ones."

"That fust so-called fast ball stunk," said Feets doubtfully.

"Yeah, I know," admitted Loren. "But I'll throw the next two with an American twist."

"Whut's that?"

"Tennis. Trust me."

"Ain't got no choice," said a resigned catcher, returning to his post.

The next pitch went just where Loren wanted it, breaking in on the hands; so that the Dodger hitter, who timed it well, could only foul it off the handle of his bat into the screen behind the plate. Then Loren wasted a straight fast one outside.

Down came Feets' fist in front of his crotch. Come on, Feets, hold onto this one, begged Loren under his breath, as he reared back, the knuckles of his right hand digging into the seam of the ball, and flung it plateward. The batter's eyes grew wide as the pitch approached him, seemingly with nothing on it. Just as he swung, however, it suddenly dropped under his flailing bludgeon, almost straight down. Feets expertly gloved it before it hit the dirt and punched it triumphantly into the air, grinning at Loren. And the Scorpions ran off the field to take their last bats, with the score 2-1 against them.

The Dodger portsider had yielded only three singles. Four Scorpions had drawn walks, but nine had gone down on strikes. Could the lefthander maintain his almost perfect pitching for one more inning? Ham, Duke, and Deacon, all right hand hitters, were determined to prove him vulnerable.

They were too eager. The lefty cleverly switched to slow curves, which induced Ham to strike out and Duke to slap a slow bounder that Hank Samuels converted into an easy play at first. From the bench Loren shouted encouragement to Deacon, as the chubby right fielder scratched with his spikes in the loose dirt of the batter's box, in order to dig himself in for maximum leverage. He's going for a homer, all or nothing, Loren thought. I won't get to bat.

"Hey, George," he shouted. "Just meet it. A single, big boy; that's what we need."

Deacon seemed not to hear. Grimly he glowered at the pitcher, his bat back, his elbows well out from his body, and his ample belly intruding upon the strike zone. After contemptuously watching a curve break outside, he gave the second pitch his best shot. He swung so hard that he went down to one knee. The catcher picked the ball out of his mitt and waved it in front of Deacon's face. "How'd yew like that one, fat boy?" he chortled, firing the pellet back to the pitcher. "Missed it by uh foot."

Deacon remained determined. After a second curve broke outside, he shifted his stance and tried to push a fourth pitch to right field, only to foul it off.

Two and two. On the bench Loren clenched and unclenched his fingers around the handle of his bat. "Only takes one," he yelled. "Come on, big man. You're the boss; you're the one."

Deacon got a small piece of the next pitch and bounced it foul down to Feets in the third base coach's box. The Scorpion manager scooped it up with a flourish and fired it with all his strength over to the Dodger pitcher, who received it backing up and gave Feets a dirty look.

Deacon did not offer at the next pitch, a low curve. As the catcher rolled it out to the mound and he and the pitcher started off the field, the home plate umpire bellowed "ball three" and shot his left hand into the air. Loren, who had been holding his breath, let it out with a sigh. The Dodgers battery mates did not argue. Eager to get the game over with, they resumed their positions. Deacon dug in.

"Ball four!" This one was not even close. The pitcher had tried to steer his curve ball and it had gotten away from him and plunged into the dirt several inches in front of home plate. Deacon tossed his bat away and trotted down to first base.

"Time," yelled Feets, gesturing toward the Scorpion bench for a pinch runner. Out came Tibbs to replace Deacon on first base. As Feets settled himself in the batter's box, Loren advanced, swinging two bats, to the on-deck circle, where he rested on one knee and shouted: "Come on, Feets; he's losing it. Wait for a good one."

Feets was zero for three for the day. Swinging weakly on the first pitch, he knocked a two-hopper to the right of the first baseman, who backhanded it and swiveled to make his soft toss to the pitcher, covering the bag. But the lefty had tripped as he tried to recover from his follow through and was consequently slow getting over to first. It was a foot race, but Feets, running out from under his cap, straining every muscle, won it by a half-step. Now there were two Scorpions aboard.

Loren took a deep breath as he stepped up to the plate. He stole a quick look at Masher in the first base coach's box and saw no sign. The Dodger pitcher stretched and threw—at Loren's head. Shocked into temporary immobility, Loren barely recovered his senses in time to sprawl backward into the dirt as the ball thudded into the catcher's mitt. "Now, now, lefty," said the receiver derisively, "don' hit pretty boy. Yew might dent his cute li'l noggin, an' th' girls might cry."

Slowly Loren got to his feet and rubbed dirt onto his bat handle. Seething, he stepped back into the rectangle and waited. The next pitch was a slow curve, as he expected it would be. He unloaded on it with all his might. The shock that went through his arms told him that he had hit it squarely. As he flipped the bat aside and headed for first base, he sneaked a peek and saw the ball sailing high over the left fielder's head well inside the foul pole. As he slowed his stride to watch, it disappeared beyond the barrier. A home run!

The entire Scorpion squad, minus Bubba and Slick, assembled to greet him as he rounded third base and continued the last ninety feet to jump with both spiked shoes onto home plate. If he could get the Dodgers out in the last half of the inning, he would have won the game! Whoopee!

Then he noticed something strange. The opposing pitcher was not behaving as if he had just been bombed for what were potentially the winning runs. Instead, he stood on the mound, a smug sneer pasted on his face, watching the Scorpions celebrate as if their elation meant nothing. Hank Samuels was engaged in earnest conversation with both umpires out behind the mound. Then the chief arbiter trudged back toward home plate, where he was met by a puzzled group of Scorpions. "Whut's up, ump?" asked Masher. "Ain't we jus' got ourselves uh three-run homer?"

"'Fraid not, boys," answered the umpire. In a voice artificially jovial, and pointing at the other umpire, he added: "Bert heard Mr. Samuels call time out jus' 'afore that las' pitch was delivered."

"Shee-it!" exclaimed Ham. "That's crap, an' yew know it. He can't call time in th' middle of uh play."

"Bert says Lefty hadn't started his motion," declared the chief umpire. "An' therefore time wuz out. That's th' way it is."

"Atsa buncha baloney!" burst out Bobo, who had shouldered his way into the rhubarb. "Nobody heared no time out called. Yew can't steal th' game from us like this."

"Take it easy, Bobo," cautioned Feets, seizing the outraged shortstop by the arm and trying to pull him away. But Bobo, the back of his neck fiery red, remained chin to chin with the umpire, his right forefinger jamming into the arbiter's chest. "Come on, ump." he taunted. "Admit yew done been paid off t' see that we don' win."

Feets pulled harder, but it was too late. "Yore outa th' game, yew stupid ape," burst out the chief umpire. Jerking his thumb at ear level, he turned his back on Bobo and walked away, to the accompaniment of a roar of approval from the spectators.

Bobo looked as if he would follow, but Masher took hold of his other elbow, and he and Feets gradually guided him, still seething, over to the bench, where he gathered his jacket and two bats and, after kicking his glove, which someone had brought in from the field, he picked it up and vanished into the visitor's club house. Deacon and Tibbs then resumed their roles as baserunners.

As the fracas developed, Loren at first failed to understand the full implications of the ruling. At last he realized that his homer had been erased from the score book and that he must return to bat as if he had not, for the first time in his life, slammed a fair ball out of a full sized ball park during a game.

His belly felt empty; his muscles felt limp. He wanted to lie down and rest. He realized that he was now afraid to bat again, afraid he would fail. Get hold of yourself, he thought. You did it once; you can do it again. Show those lousy cheating umpires that they can't stop you; bring in that run. The enormity of the injustice inflicted on him fueled his returning anger, helped him to regain his strength. Look at that snickering pitcher. Listen to the jibes of that simpering catcher. Wipe the stupid grins off their faces. With growing confidence he settled once more into his stance.

When the southpaw tried to blow an inside fast ball past him, Loren was ready for it. A hard grass cutter left his bat, headed for the hole between the third baseman and shortstop. Confident that even if Samuels reached the ball, he would be unable to make the long throw in time, Loren dug in his spikes for the sprint to first base. He was almost to the bag when an outburst of cheering from the crowd told him that something had gone wrong. Completing his dash across the base, he turned to see what had happened.

The shrewd Samuels, making a running backhanded stab of Loren's hard smash, had realized that he had neither the time nor the leverage for a successful throw to first. He made the only play open to him, and launched a sidearm heave to his son on second base, barely in time for the force on the sliding Feets.

The game was over. The Scorpions plodded disconsolately into the clubhouse to take their showers. Dressing, Loren was glad to see that Slick, although badly bruised and limping, had nothing broken, and that Bobo had calmed down and was again his usual cheerful self. Bubba, though, remained surly. Loren overheard him complaining to Feets that he should have used Tibbs to relieve Slick, not "that gutless Yank."

CHAPTER 16
THE PARTY

Back at the Dibble Inn, Loren was relieved to see that the dining room had not yet closed. He ate a hot beef sandwich and washed down a slice of apple pie with a glass of milk. Then he went outside for some cool night air. As he strolled around the side of the building into a parking area, he encountered Slick and Masher unloading two cartons of beer and one of whiskey from the trunk of Masher's automobile. "Give us some help, willya, Yank," requested the big first baseman. "This heah's uh dry county. We gotta git this booze inside afore someun calls th' sheriff."

Slick had found an unlocked door under a sign reading "Emergency Exit Only," and each of the three ballplayers carried one heavy carton through a back hallway and up a narrow stair to the rear of the long balcony onto which the guest rooms opened. Setting down his burden inside a corner room, and noticing that someone had already dumped ice into a galvanized tub in the corner, Loren returned to the balcony.

Looking down into the lobby, he noticed that it was almost empty. The big round clock behind the desk showed almost eleven and a sign had been placed on a stand in front of the dining room entrance saying that it was closed until Sunday "Brunch" the following morning. Local people had left, and the Scorpions had all finished eating and were presumably either in their rooms or out on the town. Pushing open the door to room 202, Loren discovered Deacon fast asleep on one of the beds, his pink bulk unclothed except for a pair of skimpy white shorts.

Stripping down to his underwear, Loren turned off the overhead light, yawned, and stretched out on his own bed. He was almost asleep when someone banged on the door. Before he could whisper anything, Deacon grumbled: "Come in." Slick stuck his head inside and snapped on the light. "Hey, guys," he said, "th' desk clerk says yew've got th' only phone heah'bouts." Loren glanced at the wall just inside the door. Hanging there was an antique telephone, which he had assumed was only a decoration.

"Ah guess yew kin use th' phone," said Deacon reluctantly. "Local calls only."

Slick was swaying slightly and his eyes were bloodshot. Taking a thin directory from atop the empty chest of drawers, he leafed through it, muttering, "Turner... Turner, Joseph... Ah, ha!" He dialed a number. Someone answered. Using a quavering falsetto, Slick asked: "Is Peter P. Eater thar?... Oh, wrong numba? Very sorry." He hung up. "Thanks, fellas," he said. "Ah'll be back in uh few minutes."

Loren looked questioningly at Deacon, who wagged his head in bewilderment. They both closed their eyes but left the light on.

Less than fifteen minutes later Slick sauntered in, grabbed the phone, and dialed again, seemingly the same number. When someone answered, he assumed a thick foreign accent and asked for Peter P. Eater. Again a perplexed response elicited an apology from Slick before he hung up, grinning.

Another quarter hour passed before the door once more opened and Slick, reeking of whiskey, staggered wordlessly over to the phone, while Loren and Deacon watched. Their visitor dialed, waited a few seconds, and then in his own tenor voice said: "Howdy. Yeah, Ah know its late. This heah's Peter Pumpkin Eater. Any calls fer me?"

The explosion at the other end of the line must have been a sight to see. It brought a rapturous smile to Slick's face as he gently set the receiver back on its cradle. "Thanks a million, guys," he said. "Ah don't imagine ah'll be needin' t' make any more calls t'night."

"Good," said Deacon. "Ah jus' hope ol' Mr. Turner wasn't able t' trace th' ones yew already made."

"An' Ah hope th' sonuffabitch stays up half th' night cussin'," said Slick. "Now Ah gotta git back t' th' party 'afore Ah'm too sloshed t' stan' up. G'night."

As Slick exited, Loren could hear off-key singing and loud laughter coming from somewhere further down the balcony. Some of the voices were female. "Where'd the women come from?" Loren inquired.

"Uh car load of wives an' girl frens done drove up from Tocqueville," said Deacon. "Whut don' make sense is that Rose Guidry wuz wit 'em. Fats sez she ain't been on no Scorpion trip afore."

"Maybe it's because Bubba's now the manager."

"Naw, Ah don' think so. Ah saw her register. She has uh room by herself."

"I wonder if..." Loren's speculation was usurped by cheering and wolf whistles from down the hall.

"Noisy," observed Deacon. "Sounds like somethin' interestin' goin' on." He looked wistful. "Ah gather yew don' drink."

"No," said Loren. "I never tried it. Besides, I want to know when I'm having a good time."

"Same here." Deacon stared through the window at the blackness outside. "Mah parents were both drunks," he said morosely. "Mah dad died in uh car accident. My mom lasted till las' year. Then she had uh fatal heart attack."

"That's rough," said Loren sympathetically. "My mother has heart trouble, too. She had rheumatic fever as a child. But she doesn't drink."

Deacon made no response. His expression was sad, remembering. Then he swung his head from side to side, as if trying to clear his mind of something. "Let's look in on that party," he said. "Along wit' all that hard stuff, they mus' have some pop."

After they had put their clothes back on and traversed the balcony past several closed doors, the noise became almost deafening. Loren wondered if the Scorpions were the only guests in the inn. What did the management think of all this racket?

Someone had opened a door connecting the room occupied by Bobo and A. C. with the one assigned to Slick and Masher. The four of them, arm in arm, were warbling through an out-of-tune rendition of "You Are my Sunshine," while Feets,

Fido, their wives, and assorted others of both sexes, shouted boozy encouragement. Duke's current girl friend, a blonde with spectacular legs, cradled his head against her bosom, while dripping gin from a nearly empty bottle onto his protruding tongue. Swarthy Sid Tibbs was asleep on the floor under the window, while Bubba twitched drunkenly on one of the beds.

Lounging in an armchair was a strikingly handsome young woman whose curly brown hair was cut extremely short. Her muscular arms and legs were tanned as dark as milk chocolate and her peasant blouse, pleated skirt and sandals were all of the brightest white. A frozen half-smile seemed to shield her from any close contact with the others. An independent woman, Loren thought. She had to be Rose Guidry. Why was she here?

As Deacon and Loren joined the party, they bumped into Jackie Lawson, staggering blearily off to bed. Deacon was able to locate two Cokes on one of the dressers, and he and Loren peered though the fog of cigarette and cigar smoke in search of a place to sit down. Loren finally squeezed himself into a small space on one of the beds between Masher and Mrs. Shepard, Fido's wife, a plumpish, giggling woman with a rasping voice and a face like a pug dog. She was loudly singing along with the bibulous quartet, who had begun an off-key version of "Red River Valley." Her face was shiny with perspiration.

Although the other women wore dresses, Helen Shepard lounged lumpily on the rumpled bed clad only in her slip, her bare toes curling and uncurling in time with the music. Her husband, sitting nearby on the floor, wore only his socks and shorts, his cavernlike navel almost swallowed by the fleshy folds of his prominent belly. When the singing stopped, both Shepards tipped up their beer bottles, and Loren noticed that enough of the amber fluid had already dripped down upon their fat bodies to cause them to smell fermented themselves.

Feets, the jagged white scars of war wounds etched into his back and legs, leaned over, his buttocks sticking to his damp shorts, to put a record on the turntable of a battered phonograph. Fox trot music pealed forth. Feets pulled a gawky woman to her feet and began whirling her around the room, as the others, scrambling to get out of the way, clapped and cheered. Must be his wife, Loren thought. Duke and his girl friend, her baby face pushed against his bare freckled chest, also started to dance.

Bubba sat up on the bed, shook himself and, seeing Rose seated nearby, tried to persuade her to dance with him. When she refused, he persisted, seizing her by both arms and hauling her up out of her chair, at which point she slapped him hard in the face. Letting go, he backed away, scowling. Good for you, Rose, thought Loren.

Mrs. Shepard squirmed in time with the music, her slip riding up on her flaccid thighs. She turned to Loren and said: "How 'bout it, slugger? Shall we dance?"

In the hot room Loren was sweating all over. To his horror, because Mrs. S. disgusted him, he was conscious of an unruly stirring in the region of his crotch. "I'd like to," he told her, "but I've got to get back to my room. Maybe we can do it another time." He fled through the open door onto the balcony, with Deacon right behind him. "Saw yew were leavin'," said the big fellow. "Good idea. Too hot an' too loud. Let's git some sleep."

Stripping off his clothes, except for his underwear shorts, and dropping them into a wet pile on the floor, Loren once again stretched out limply on his bed. Deacon did likewise and was soon snoring, his open mouth exhibiting yellow dentures, souvenirs, apparently, of his heroics as a gridiron gladiator.

As Loren tried to relax, the bed sheet growing damp beneath him, his thoughts turned to Sunday's ball game. If only Bubba would cease his silly vendetta... The noise at the other end of the balcony seemed to be subsiding, except for sporadic laughter and an occasional oath. Once Loren heard someone yell: "Who put sand in th' Vaseline?" Gradually the inn grew quiet. And, finally, he slept...

* * *

Sometime during the night, Loren abruptly awoke to fearful turmoil. His room seemed crowded with sweaty people shouting obscenities. As he blinked himself to full consciousness, he could dimly make out in the subdued light intruding through the open door the naked bodies of some of his teammates, leaping and dodging and hurling wet towels and other objects at each other. Amidst the cavorting crew, he also glimpsed a naked woman, her nipples standing out stiffly, as she ducked to avoid a wadded up piece of underclothing. Something that felt like a wet balloon smacked him in the forehead.

Then he was desperately trying to fend off a pair of hairy paws that were jerking at his shorts. It was Bobo, reeking of beer and some other odor which Loren could not identify. "Hey, Yank, babe: we bin t' town an' got us some wimmen. An' in honor of yore near home run we brung yew uh certified class A whore! She's right heah, broken in, ready t' serve,... an' we wanna watch." Loren's shorts suddenly tore, and Bobo, holding a fragment of cloth, staggered backward across the room, coming to rest on top of Deacon, still half-asleep.

"Whut th' hail!" roared Loren's roomate, flinging Bobo headlong onto the bare wooden floor, as he surged indignantly to his feet and looked left and right like an angry Brahma bull. "Whut're yew crazy jerks doin' in our room?"

Loren heard Duke's voice: "Take it easy, Deacon. We're jus' havin' a lil fun."

"Fun?" shouted Deacon. "Fun? Howlin' an' throwin' yore sloppy towels an' bringin' yore loose wimmen in heah, an'... whut in Gawd's name is This!" From the floor he retrieved a small drippy object similar to the one that had earlier landed in Loren's face. "Gawd! That's too much! Yew dirty bastards! Git!"

Deacon grabbed Duke and with a tremendous heave hurled him through the doorway into a sprawling heap on the balcony outside. One by one, Loren's outraged roommate either threw or chased the others out of the room. The two naked women did not wait to be seized and flung, but scrambled for safety, emitting frightened screams.

The last visitor to depart was Bobo. The apelike shortstop weighed a muscular one hundred and eighty pounds at least, not much less than the Aggie footballer. But Bobo was stinking drunk, and Deacon was sober and magnificently angry. With a great grunt he propelled Bobo through the doorway with such force that the stupefied night caller staggered, tripped over someone blubbering on the balcony, tottered terrifyingly on top of the balcony railing, and then disappeared with a thump into the dark lobby below.

Loren waited. Amid the noises of the others scurrying back to their rooms and the clicks of closing doors, he heard no sound revealing Bobo's fate. Deacon had thrown himself back onto his bed, muttering maledictions against drunks in general and horny drunks in particular. He seemed to contemplate going back to sleep.

"What about Bobo?" Loren asked.

"Whadya mean, whut 'bout Bobo?" mumbled Deacon.

"He fell off the balcony," said Loren. "He might be badly hurt."

"Serves 'im right."

"Don't you think we should go see?" asked Loren. But no answer came back: Deacon was again snoring.

Loren sat on his bed, contemplating his torn shorts, and told himself he ought to check on Bobo. What if the poor fellow had broken his neck? Would that make Loren an accessory to homicide? He could not seem to think straight.

Finally, he managed to make his way over to the open door, intending to tiptoe downstairs to see about his teammate. In the innkeeper's office behind the registration desk, he could see a light. Half-hiding behind the door he could barely make out a frightened young desk clerk peering out into the darkness. Something that looked like a small pistol gleamed in his fist.

At once Loren drew back into the shadows of his own room. He quietly closed the door and padded back to his bed, from which he pulled sheets and pillow covers before lying down on a bare musty mattress, on which, surprisingly, he soon slept.

* * *

In the morning sunlight Loren was awakened by the sound of birds chirping in the trees outside his window. He stretched and hoped that the nocturnal commotion had been a bad dream. Below the window, which overlooked the front entrance of the inn, he saw that local couples, some with children, were beginning to stroll in from the parking lot dressed in Sunday finery, apparently intending to enjoy a leisurely brunch before attending worship services. Deacon, already dressed, was fingering his chin at the dresser mirror, apparently trying to decide whether to shave. I wish I had some stubble, thought Loren.

Then he remembered Bobo. "George!" he cried out. "Bobo went over the balcony railing last night! You threw him out and he tripped and went clear over!"

"Yew can't hurt that big lug," replied Deacon unconcernedly, zipping up his toilet kit.

"But he's still down there," said Loren. "I'm afraid he's really hurt. That's a long drop."

A frown of worry creased Deacon's brow. "Yew say he ain't come back upstairs?"

"I don't think so."

"Gawd," said Deacon. "We'd better take uh look."

Dressing rapidly, the two young men rushed out the bedroom door and leaned over the balcony railing, fearful of what they might see below. Bobo was still there.

He had fallen onto a soft sofa, and there he rested, swarthy, hairy, and stark naked, as he slept off his rampage of the night before.

Only a few feet away was the front entrance to the building and further on was the door to the dining room, already open for Sunday brunch. As Loren and Deacon looked down upon the quiet scene, a well-dressed family of four entered the lobby from outside, two little girls mincing after their elders.

All four spied Bobo simultaneously. The man's mouth went slack; the woman gasped and her face turned cherry red; and the eyes of the two youngsters widened in amazement. The husband then grabbed his wife firmly by the arm and hauled her off to the dining room. The two little girls followed, looking over their shoulders, slowing their pace, until their father seized each one by an elbow and propelled them hurriedly out of sight of the disturbing scene.

"We've got to do something," whispered Loren. "Now."

"But whut?" inquired Deacon.

"Ah know," said a woman's voice behind them. It was Rose, resplendent in a yellow dress. She, too, had been watching the little drama below and was struggling to suppress a smile.

Stepping forward, she lifted a nearly full bottle of beer and poured the contents over the railing. The liquid hit Bobo full in the face. He jerked convulsively and his eyes opened. Groaning and rubbing his nearly bald head, he heaved himself to a sitting position on the edge of the sofa. Blinking red-veined eyes, he asked plaintively: "Whut's goin' on? Hey! Don' waste that beer!"

"Psst, Bobo," whispered Loren.

Bobo's eyes turned upward. His face broke into a smile. "Hey, Yank," he said, "Whutchur doin' up thar?"

"Yew'd better git yourself up heah, too, yew big lug," admonished Deacon. "Yore puttin' on uh pretty risky show—an' on Sunday morning, too!"

Bobo looked down at his nakedness. He looked around at the empty lobby. He seemed to catch a glimpse of some more brunch-minded people coming through the front entrance. "Lord Amighty!" he exclaimed. "Sonuffabitch!" He sought cover behind the sofa.

After another well dressed family had passed, oblivious to the crouching Bobo, and vanished into the dining room, the naked ape-man leaped to his feet and bounded, two steps at a time, up the stairs to the balcony, and onward to his room. As he passed Loren, Deacon and Rose, he whispered gratefully: "Ah 'preciate whut yew done, guys. Ah coulda gone t' jail."

The truth of his observation was soon apparent when the dapper manager of the inn hurried through the dining room door, accompanied by an agitated group of guests, all gesturing furiously. Perplexed that no Bobo was to be seen, they milled about the lobby for a few minutes, eliciting from Loren and his two companions that they had seen nothing unusual below, and then returned whence they came, disconcerted victims, it seemed, of an unpunishable practical joke.

"Who's fer breakfast?" inquired Rose.

"Me," answered both Loren and Deacon at once.

"Me," said Bobo, joining them, dressed nattily in sharply creased tan slacks, a lime-green open-collared sports shirt, and well-shined loafers with green socks. He had also put on a pair of dark glasses.

"Incognito, huh," said Loren.

"Incog whut?" queried a puzzled Bobo.

"Never mind," said Loren. "Say, Bobo, you really tied one on last night. Hope it doesn't hurt your hitting this afternoon."

"Don' worry," Bobo reassured him. "Today Ah shine."

CHAPTER 17

BUBBA TROUBLE

Loren, Deacon, Bobo, and Rose sat at a table in one corner of the spacious dining room of the Dibble Inn. They ignored the curious stares of the Sunday morning regulars. "Where're th' other guys?" asked Bobo. "Still sleepin'," said Rose. "They got worn out las' night."

"Whut 'bout yew?" blurted Deacon.

"Not why Ah'm heah," she replied. To Loren's unspoken question she added, her dark eyes underneath severely plucked eyebrows probing his: "Bubba done run off wit' sumptin' that belongs t' me an' Ah aim t' git it back."

"Whut's that?" asked Bobo.

"Mah truck." She dipped slim brown fingers into a yellow purse and pulled out a set of keys. "Bubba's gonna have t' ride home wit' one of yew guys," she declared. "When he wuz conked out las' night, after he had his fight wit' Slick, Ah slipped into his room an' lifted these. Soon as Ah finish mah breakfast, Ah'm outa heah."

"Why wuz Bubba fightin' wit Slick?" asked Deacon.

"They wuz playin' poker," replied Rose. "Slick, Bubba, Masher an' that Tibbs jerk. Yew 'member, Bobo."

"Yeah, but Ah didn' understan' why Bubba started shoutin' an' cussin'."

"Yew know how Slick's alluz makin' jokes an' playin' tricks. So he done somethin' wit' th' cards, an' Bubba called 'im uh no good four-flusher. Then Slick, pretendin' t' be upset, says 'Y'mean Ah got diarrhea?'"

"Bubba says: 'Whut?' An' Slick says: 'Four-flusher; diarrhea; get it?' An' Bubba says 'Damn yew Slick; yore always tryin' t' put me down. Yore such uh fuggin' smart ass, yew make me sick.' An' Slick mumbles somethin' 'bout Bubba already bein' sick in th' head. An' Ah'm thinkin' they're gonna fight, but Masher holds onto Bubba, an' Slick leaves wit one of th' local gals. Seems he was hot t' have his own private game of poker afore he got too drunk t' enjoy it."

"Some guys have all th' fun," lamented Bobo, beckoning to a waitress.

"Yeah, as long as that gal don' git pregnant," said Rose. "Ah heared her cryin' early this mornin' through Slick's door. She wuz sobbin' an' cussin' 'cause Slick hadn't used a..." With a half smile on her face, she glanced at Loren. "Ah mean, they didn' have somethin' they needed."

A middle-aged waitress arrived to take their orders. "Whut kin Ah git fer y'all?" she inquired. Deacon and Bobo ordered ham and eggs; Loren asked for hotcakes and bacon; and Rose wanted only coffee and dry toast. "Gotta keep mah figger," she announced with a wink.

As they left the dining room, Loren looked back, puzzled. Something had happened to contradict his previous experience eating with ballplayers in Texas. Nothing was wrong with the meal.

They met Slick in the lobby. He seemed displeased with his stay at Dibble Inn. As Loren carried his things outside, he heard Slick, standing at the desk, summon the manager and then loudly tell him that he ought to rename his establishment the "Fiddler's Hotel."

"Why?" asked the perplexed proprietor.

"Jus' 'cause it's such a Vile Inn." And Slick, with a smile of satisfaction, followed Loren outside to the bus where Fats and Ham were waiting for them. Soon he was engaged in a dispute with Fats, who maintained that Slick's low batting average for the season did not qualify him to start in the outfield ahead of others who had much better marks. "Yew can't beat statistics," said Fats triumphantly.

"Nonsense," retorted Slick. "Didja heah 'bout th' statistician who drowned tryin' t' wade 'cross th' creek wit' an average depth of three feet?"

"That's different," huffed Fats. "No one can argue wit' yew 'cause yore alluz changin' th' subject."

"Listen, Fats," said Slick, "if Ah don' git t' start t'day, Ah'll jus' sit next t' yew on th' bench an' talk strategy. Th' only way we're gonna beat th' Dodgers, wit' them playin' those three ringers, an' both umpires 'gainst us, is t' have uh strategy."

"Aw, Slick," said Ham, who had been listening. "Yore ideas are alluz fulla beans. None of 'em have evah worked."

"This one is mah masterpiece. Heah's whut we do. From th' time when we go onto th' field till th' game is ovah, nobody says uh word. Not uh peep from anyone. No chatter; nuttin'. It'll drive those Dodgers bonkers."

The surrounding Scorpions looked at one another. Grins began to replace skeptical expressions. They could visualize the Dibble players so preoccupied with waiting for a Scorpion to let out a sound, any sound, that they wouldn't be able to concentrate on the game. "Shee-it," said Ham. "That's th' mos' idiotic scheme yew evah come up wit'. It's so stupid, it might work. 'Sides, Ah'll try anythin' if it'll keep us from havin' t' listen t' Bubba's babblin'."

"Yeah." "Amen." "Yew got that right." Endorsements came from all sides.

"Now, wait uh minute," protested Bubba. "Ah'm th' manager, an' Ah say Slick's idea is as crazy as he is. We'll play our usual game." He was still sputtering as they left the bus and paraded into the clubhouse.

As they put on their dirty, sweat-caked uniforms, Loren saw Slick sneak up behind Feets, as the latter stood rubbing Neet's Foot oil into his battered catcher's mitt. Seeing Loren watching him, Slick thrust a forefinger across his mouth. Then he slipped a thumbtack onto the bench where Feets was about to sit down to put on his socks and spikes. As Slick tiptoed away, however, Feets brushed his uniform shirttail against the bench and the thumbtack fell onto the floor. A moment later a howl of pain burst from the catcher's lips. Reaching down, he extracted the tack from the bottom of one foot and angrily looked around for the culprit. "Who did this?" he growled.

No one answered. Then Slick broke the silence. "These are th' times that try men's souls," he intoned. Loren shuddered. "Ah hope yew didn' feel pain," Slick added. Loren fought back a snicker. He looked around. Slick's puns had gone unperceived by the others, who merely resumed dressing. Even Feets, after hurling the offending tack against the wall and emitting a loud "Gawdamighty," did the same.

"'Ten-shun! Now heah this!" shouted Bubba. He began going over the signals for the afternoon's game. Left hand on the belt buckle for a steal; right hand in the same place for a hit and run; and a tug at the cap brim for the "take" sign. "An' heah's th' battin' order," he said. "Me, Ham, Bobo, Masher, Deacon, Duke, Jackie in left field, Feets, an' Sid, pitchin'. Les go git 'em."

As the Scorpions trotted onto the playing field, they were met with a smattering of boos and hisses from a gathering crowd, and several high pitched cheers from their own wives and girl friends. Following disconsolately in the rear, Loren noticed that ahead of him Duke was limping badly. As the Scorpions exchanged warmup throws, Duke was not his usual cheerful self. After several tosses, he approached Bubba, and Loren heard him say: "Ah hate t' tell yew this, but Ah don' think Ah kin play t'day. Maybe pinch hit. But mah right knee got twisted during th' ruckus last night, so Ah kin hardly stan' on it."

"Shee-it, Duke," complained Bubba. "Whyja have t' go an' do this t' me? We're short-handed as it is."

"Ah'm real sorry."

"Take battin' practice an' see how yew feel then. But don' do anythin' t' make it worse."

The Scorpions hit. Regulars first, then Fido, Slick, Loren, and A. C. After the Dodgers took their batting practice, with Hamilton Jones and Hank Samuels slashing liners off and over the fences, Fido began warming up Sid Tibbs in the bull pen, while the Scorpion starters returned to the diamond to take fielding practice. Duke was not among them; he remained on the bench, his hat brim pulled down over his eyes; his mouth tight with pain.

On impulse, Loren grabbed his glove and dashed out to center field. As he ran, he felt Bubba's eyes boring into his back, right through the number seven just below his shoulder blades. The manager shouted something at him, but Loren could not make out the words.

A. C.'s fungo bat cracked against the practice ball, which flew high in the air to right field, where Deacon gloved it and launched an off-line throw toward third base. Twice more they repeated the process, and twice the throws went home, where Feets each time had to move off the plate to receive them. So much for Deacon's throwing ability.

Loren waited, his hands on his knees, for the ball. A. C. whipped his slender stick and the ball once again climbed high into the sky. Over near the left field line, Jackie Lawson drifted under it, pounding his glove, until it descended into his grasp. Loren relaxed his muscles and muttered a bad word. That vomit manager wasn't going to allow A. C. to hit him any flies. The pitiful prick was going to let him stand out in the middle of the field all alone and wait for balls that would never come.

As Loren crouched conspicuously, wishing he had a hole to crawl into, Jackie completed his practice throws and ran off the field, after which A. C. began hitting grounders to the infielders, and the ball melted into a white streak as they fired it around the bases, chattering like magpies. So much for Slick's strategy of silence.

There was nothing left for Loren to do but walk, head up, off the field, carefully avoiding the eyes of any of his teammates, and slouch by himself on the bench to await the start of the game.

* * *

Loren got some silent satisfaction out of the merciless beating administered by the Samuels duo and the other Dodgers to the struggling Scorpions. Sid Tibbs got by the first two innings without allowing a run, but in the third frame the home town hitters bashed him for no less than nine bingles which, when four walks by a thoroughly flustered hurler were added, meant eleven runs in all. Two Dodgers scored when Fido, as Duke's replacement in center field, trying to throw the ball before he had it securely in his glove, dropped an easy fly onto the turf and then made a wild throw back to the infield.

In the fifth inning, when Bubba brought in Slick to pitch, the Joker was pounded almost as badly as Tibbs. In the seventh A. C. took the mound and suffered the same fate. Finally, with one out and two Dodgers on base in the eighth, Bubba himself grabbed the ball and threw a pitch that a grinning Dodger promptly deposited in the pine trees beyond the left field fence. With the aid of a lucky double play off a line drive to Bobo, the Scorpions finally got out of the inning.

In the ninth Deacon hit a home run that barely cleared the center field fence, which brought the score to twenty to four, where it stayed. It was the most one-sided baseball game Loren had ever seen. At least he had not shared in the disgrace; he was the only Scorpion other than Duke whom Bubba did not play.

Afterwards, in a largely silent clubhouse, Loren dressed in a corner by himself. Once he overheard Bobo murmur: "That was th' mos' unheard of thang Ah evah heard of." He had to agree.

* * *

During the trip back to Tocqueville, Loren dozed most of the way and pretended to be sleeping the rest of the time. Mercifully, Fats, Ham and Duke left him alone. They conversed quietly about the game—what a miserable experience it had been—and about the forthcoming Labor Day weekend, during which they had a game scheduled at a place called Jasperville. When the lamentations on Duke's favorite county music radio station were interrupted by a news broadcast, Loren learned that Congressman Johnson seemed to have lost the Saturday election to ex-Governor Stevenson, but no final announcement had been issued by the state election commission, because a large number of disputed votes were still in question. Loren would have liked to hear more on the subject, but Duke, with a snort, changed stations.

His three teammates said embarrassed goodbyes as they dropped him off at his house. Loren echoed their parting words with a sad air of finality. He did not eat dinner that evening, but stayed in his room. When his mother stuck her head in his door, he pretended that the team had stopped to eat on the way back from Dibble, and he was not hungry. To her look of concern, he said only: "I'm fine, Mom. Just have to work something out in my mind, that's all." Throwing him a kiss, his mother shut the door and left him alone.

After she departed, he buried his face in his pillow, while isolated images of revenge, retribution, and vindication surged through his consciousness. It was mental torture to think that his longstanding dream of playing big league baseball, of becoming part of modern mythology, might never be realized. He felt almost feverish with failure. A crowd in Dibble had seen his humiliation, and even now some of the Scorpions were probably gloating about it... No, not gloating. Except for Bubba and Tibbs, they were good guys. They would probably feel sorry for him. They might even miss him.

On the other hand, he realized that he had all along been so much of an outsider that it would be unrealistic to think that the Scorpions would really care whether he continued on the team. His ability had not been enough to overcome his alien status. Not because he was from the North; they had, after all, dubbed him their "Yank," and had refrained from re-fighting the Civil War in his presence. Not because he was a non-drinker, non-smoker, and shy and inexperienced; they had seemed to enjoy introducing him to the mysteries of adult existence. But largely because they were provincials from the same neighborhood, prone to stick together whenever a dispute arose between one of their own crowd and a newcomer, no matter who was in the right. The sad truth was that he was indisputably, insurmountably "foreign Loren."

The rift with Bubba had enlarged into a rupture with the entire team. It had occurred, not because of anything Loren had done, at least not to anyone other than Bubba. It had to be because of who or what he was. And because he had called Bubba "white trash."

A scene from his Winona past flashed into his mind. His mother and father were hosting one of his father's long-time friends, a former neighbor from Virginia who was staying overnight during an automobile trip. What was his name? Roy somebody.

As Loren, curled up in an armchair in a far corner of the living room, studied an old Spalding baseball guide, the adults discussed a promotion one of his father's newspaper co-workers had received. Adam deprecated the man's abilities, saying that his main talent had been ass-kissing, that he was obtuse and insecure, and always passed the tough jobs to someone else. And yet, when the time came for either Adam or his co-worker to be elevated in rank and salary, the obsequious other guy had been the one promoted.

Especially did Loren recall the fleeting hurt expression on his father's face, and his mother's equally transitory look of sympathy, before the masks of bravado were restored—while their friend, Roy, puffed his pipe and considered what Adam had confided. Then Roy told them his theory about why the most deserving people were often bypassed, while those who were more ingratiating were advanced, despite their relative lack of ability and intelligence. And why they kept getting promoted until, finally, they came to rest in positions far beyond their level of competence. Roy's theory was that these were people who did not threaten anyone. Nobody felt affection for them, but nobody really disliked them, either. They lived in a limbo of lack of real feeling, and they moved up because those higher on the career ladder realized that they could always stay at least one rung above them—that the sycophants were incapable of becoming real rivals.

Loren recalled that when Roy finished his pontification the only sound in the Temple living room had been the ticking of the mantel clock. The visitor had puffed contemplatively on his pipe; Nan had reached out and taken her husband's hand in hers; and Adam had sat rigidly in his chair, his eyes vacant, and his lips tightly pressed together. Then Nan had abruptly slid off the davenport and gone to the sideboard to replenish Roy's drink.

Memories... Long after Tocqueville had stilled in the darkness outside, Loren lay limp on a bed damp with sweat and thought about his past life—and how he had not, it seemed, been blessed with a fulfilling relationship with anyone. Especially did he regret that he had no real knowledge of any girl or woman, not even his mother—what she thought, what she valued, what she felt...

Finally, he went to sleep. When he awakened the next morning he felt better, although he realized that the wretched emptiness brought on by his latest rejection had left a scar. Another one.

None of the Scorpions phoned or came by for a visit. Ever.

CHAPTER 18
OPPORTUNITIES

In Winona, Loren remembered, the week before Labor Day would have portended the end of summer, with final visits to already chilly beaches to top off tans; wearing sweaters on cool mornings as the leaves began to change color; last minute shopping for school clothes; and an increased interest in the major league pennant races. A few impatient young men would have begun to fling footballs back and forth on the village green.

In Tocqueville, as the mercury continued to climb into the high nineties, house flies still crawled on window screens in the daytime and mosquitoes still sought entry at night. Only the thudding and grunting heard on the football practice fields at the high schools signaled that autumn was imminent.

Already missing his weeklong forays along the highways and the back roads of southeast Texas, Loren lingered listlessly at home, occasionally lured outdoors by the temptation of tossing a baseball with Tommy, but mostly reading and brooding, as he aimlessly awaited events. In the *Endeavor* on Monday evening he encountered the depressing news that registration for the first peacetime military draft in American history was to have begun that day for all young men born in 1930 and earlier. One year more and he, too, would be required to submit total control over his life to strangers with agendas foreign to his own.

Two days later, there was a panic in the press when the reality began to sink in that a communist "People's Republic" had been established in China, with its enormous population. Rumors of a "preventive" war against the "red tide" that now appeared to engulf most of Europe and Asia wafted from Washington. Loren wondered: was he doomed to die in a third world war fomented by a handful of zealots who would condemn his lack of patriotism, should he dare to resist or evade "serving his country" in a "crusade" against communism?

Another newspaper story offered more positive prospects. Someone named Rand had recently returned to Tocqueville from west Texas, where he had managed a class C baseball team that had fallen into bankruptcy. Now semi-retired and in poor health, Rand planned to scout part time for the Detroit Tigers and also to organize and manage a semipro team, the East Texas Stars, composed of the most capable local talent. The story included a telephone number, which Loren promptly phoned. A young woman answered in a husky voice that Loren momentarily thought he recognized. She recommended that Loren talk to her father in person, in order to discuss his qualifications for joining the new team.

On Thursday evening, following her directions, Loren steered Shaky northward to Tocqueville's outskirts, remembering to hit his brakes each time he crossed railroad tracks in order to avert a teeth-rattling shimmy of the front wheels. Passing through a seedy section where most of the road signs had been vandalized, he eventually came to a dirt road that he identified by a sign inscribed with the words: "Sisti and Sampson Sand Pit." Following the rutted road through a heavily wooded area, he came to an isolated clearing in which a dilapidated house trailer rested insecurely upon some broken cinder blocks, surrounded by weeds and debris. Loren hesitated: he had never been inside a trailer. What sorts of people lived in such places? Knocking on a rusty metal door, he felt fearful.

A gaunt old man wearing worn bedroom slippers and a torn undershirt opened it. A lit cigarette dangled from claw-like fingers. Unenthusiastically, he stood aside to let Loren enter and motioned him to a seat on a sagging couch. "Mah daughter," he croaked, "said yew wanna try out fer th' Stars; is that right?"

"That's why I'm here," affirmed Loren. "I can pitch, play the outfield, or cover any infield position except first base."

"Soun's t' me like yew oughter locate yoreself somewares an' stick."

"I'll play wherever you want," said Loren.

"Humm. Wal, it 'pears we could use uh third baseman. But Ah'll have t' try yew out afore decidin' whether or not t' sign yew t' uh contract. If Ah do, yew'll make twenty-fi dollah uh game, plus travel expenses when we play outa town. In Tocqueville we're gonna play in Shipper Stadium."

"I was there at a Yankee tryout camp last month," said Loren. "Mr. Lowrey almost offered me a contract. Then, when he learned that I was still in high school, he said that he couldn't do it."

Rand squinted while he scrutinized Loren as if questioning his truthfulness. Then he said: "Ol' Frenchy is uh pal of mine. If he liked yore style, yew musta showed 'im sumptin'. But don' count on Frenchy gettin' yew uh pro contract nex' yeah."

"Why not?"

"Ain't yew heared? Th' Yankees dun fired 'im, as of January fust. Cuttin' back."

"That's too bad," said Loren. "I was hoping..."

"Forgit it," broke in Rand. "If'n yore good enough, Ah kin prolly git yew sumptin' wit' th' Tigers. Mor' opportunities in that organization, anyhow. Ah'll see yew at th' Tocqueville High School diamond Sat'day at ten o'clock. Be on time." He stood up. The interview was over.

Loren had several questions he wanted to ask but decided to save them. After leaving Rand's trailer he was about to hop into Shaky when he felt someone staring at him. Looking back, he saw a young woman standing in the window of the room he had just left. She quickly ducked out of sight. There was something familiar about her.

As he drove home, he felt less depressed than he had since the debacle at Dibble. Was it because he now had another chance to play ball? Or was it the fleeting glimpse he'd had of... who?

* * *

That evening, as Loren was trying to decide whether to tell his mother and father about his impending tryout with the Stars, Adam put down his paper and said: "Loren, I heard something today that might interest you."

Loren waited.

Adam cleared his throat with a loud rasping sound, which he did when he was about to impart important information. "At the office we have what we call the wire room," he said, "which is where both the *Endeavor* and the *Gazette* share half a dozen teletype machines that deliver news from the Associated Press, United Press, Reuters, and International News Service, as well as some state stuff. The night attendant there is going into the Baptist hospital next week for an operation. She'll be laid up for two months. Earl Stoner, the publisher of the *Gazette*, is looking for a temporary replacement. They'll pay fifty a week and the hours are from four p.m. until midnight, which means that on weeknights you'd be short on sleep, but no more than Tommy with his paper route."

"The money sounds good," said Loren.

"Yeah. And the work is spasmodic; so you'd have plenty of time to do your homework. And you'd get some experience with real newspaper work."

Adam seemed anxious for Loren to take the job. Partly because of that, partly because he sensed that his mother's precarious health had created a new need for an infusion into the family finances, and partly because he was curious about what really took place at night in a newspaper office, he told his father that he would like to have the position.

Adam disappeared into his den to use the telephone. Soon he returned. "The job's yours," he said. "Mrs. Marshall's operation is scheduled for Thursday of next week; so Stoner is glad to have the matter of her substitute settled. Good thing I called him. He was supposed to interview a couple of people tomorrow."

"Great," said Loren. "When does he want me to start?"

"You go in Tuesday at four," said Adam. "That's the first day of school; so you'll have to hustle as soon as you get out of your last class. Mrs. Marshall will show you what to do. She enters the hospital the following evening, so it's your one chance to find out how the machines work and what you need to tear off for the *Gazette* editors to use in the morning paper."

* * *

On Saturday morning, Loren rested his baseball bat on his shoulder, with his spikes and glove dangling from it by their laces, as he walked the three blocks to the high school diamond. He felt fortunate. Opportunities suddenly abounded: a second chance to join a semipro ballclub; a new job that might become the portal to a profession; a new school in which to make a fresh start academically and socially; and even, maybe… He fantasized about the face in the window.

Rand was already on the baseball diamond. Wearing scuffed spikes over sagging socks under an ancient uniform that read "Cougars" on the shirtfront and had the number "1" on its back, he was rapping out grounders to a trio of middle infielders, who scooped them up effortlessly and steamed them over to a giraffe masquerading as a first baseman. Motioning Loren to the third baseman's position,

Rand hit him a series of easy bounders, which he handled flawlessly. Then, abruptly, the manager smashed a steamer just inside the bag, which Loren gloved with a backhanded stab and gunned accurately to first base. Rand then rapped a grass cutter to Loren's left, which the new recruit dove full-length to spear in the webbing of his extended glove, following which he pegged a perfect throw to first from his knees. "Ah've seen enough," said Rand. "Grab uh bat."

The manager beckoned a skinny righthander to the mound. He threw hard but not hard enough to prevent Loren from smacking liners into diverse sectors of the outfield. After about ten minutes observing this, Rand said: "O.K., th' job's yours. We play in Bowie, Louisiana, next Saturday. Th' bus'll leave from Shipper Stadium at eight. Then he shouted to the other players, his cracked voice quavering, his wrinkled wattles wiggling: "Pitchers run laps. Outfielders hit. Infielders and catchers shag. Move yore asses!"

When Loren, sweaty and tired, arrived home late that afternoon, he gazed wistfully over at Mrs. Kaplan's backyard where clear water sparkled in a freshly installed swimming pool. To implant it, he speculated, Mrs. K must have spent a sizeable chunk of Dr. Kaplan's life insurance. Although the surrounding soil remained bare in the blazing sun, the pool itself seemed ready to receive hot bodies in its cooling embrace. But Mrs. Kaplan was nowhere to be seen. Instead of reclining at poolside, Loren imagined, she was probably relaxing in her bedroom, in the window of which a small air conditioner, rarely seen in Tocqueville homes, now hummed in place of the former fan.

* * *

All four Temples attended the Austin Avenue Baptist church the following morning. For Loren, Sunday school was the best part. The teacher, a vivacious young woman, seemed bemused rather than appalled at Loren's reluctance to accept the literal truth of every word of the Bible. She explained that if certain passages at first appeared illogical, Christians had to recognize that some portions of God's plan for ignorant humanity remained as yet unrevealed. Diligent study of Holy Scripture would aid Loren, she declared, to understand the purposes of the Almighty. She was so sincere, and so kindly in her responses to his iconoclastic inquiries, that he decided to refrain from questioning her assertions, even those that appeared preposterous when divorced from the context of blind faith.

What bothered Loren most were the contradictions. Mrs. Virginia ("Call me 'Ginnie'") Martin, whose husband was a recently licensed dentist, urged abstinence from strong drink, citing Proverbs 23: 29-35 and Isaiah 5: 22 which Loren verified did indeed condemn the use of intoxicants. Reading further, however, he encountered 1 Timothy 5: 23, which read: "Drink no longer water; but use a little wine for thy stomach's sake and thine often infirmities." When he brought this passage to her attention, Mrs. Martin blushed. Then she stammered: "I can understand your bewilderment, but you have to realize that we mortals cannot always make perfect sense of the Lord's language. We have to rely upon wise educated men like Reverend Pryor to help us understand."

Sure, thought Loren. And Reverend Pryor will doubtless declare that the Bible means what He says it means. End of discussion.

Loren almost questioned Mrs. Martin about the contradiction between Isaiah 2: 4, admonishing the faithful to beat their swords into plowshares, and Joel 3:10, which commanded believers to "beat your plowshares into swords." He decided, however, not to embarrass her further. The good woman meant well and seemed determined to live by the Golden Rule. But Loren suspected that the Bible was full of contradictions and scientific absurdities, if only he were to devote the necessary time to searching its pages for flaws. Probably others had already done this. But he knew better than to ask anyone he knew how to find out. Even his father, whom he suspected could aid in such a quest if he so desired, would probably urge him to focus his intellectual efforts upon more constructive endeavors.

As he was leaving the small classroom where he and a dozen others of high school age had their Sunday morning meetings, Mrs. Martin called him back to her. "I noticed," she said, "that you didn't bring your Bible to class."

"That's because I don't have one," he replied. "I can use my grandfather's Bible at home to look up whatever stuff you ask us to prepare for Sunday school, but my parents don't want me to take it out of the house because it is so old. The covers are loose already."

"You need your own Bible. Every Christian should have one."

I'm not sure I'm a Christian, thought Loren. I certainly don't see how Jesus could have been the only Son of God, except maybe in a symbolic sense. But Mrs. Martin, as nice as she was, probably had her limits when it came to listening to such skepticism. "Yes, Ma'am," he said. "I'll speak to my parents about getting one."

"I don't think that'll be necessary," she said. "I'll see what I can do between now and next Sunday."

"Thank you, Ma'am," replied Loren, feeling foolish.

* * *

Monday was Labor Day. Loren finally got to play tennis with Buzz, who had phoned him the previous evening to suggest that they meet in the early afternoon on one of the public courts located next to the largest Catholic church in Tocqueville. For a while they sprawled on the parched grass at courtside to wait for a couple of girls to complete a pitpat match in the blistering heat. Buzz, looking spiffy in a dazzling white tennis outfit that made his deep tan appear even darker, drew admiring glances from the two teenagers, who tittered nervously whenever they missed a shot, especially if it required one of them to undulate in Buzz's direction to retrieve a ball. Ignoring them, he suggested to Loren that henceforth they avoid both the extreme heat and the competition for court time by playing in the wee hours of the night, when almost everyone else would be asleep.

At first Loren thought this an absurd idea. Then he remembered that he was about to undertake employment that would occupy him until midnight on weeknights. Moreover, he expected to be busy on weekends, practicing or playing baseball with the Stars. But on weeknights; why not? He could make up for the loss of sleep somehow, perhaps by dozing during the day at the high school, if he could manage to sit in the back rows of his classes.

"Sure," he said. "What about one o'clock on Mondays?"

"Tuesdays would be better fer me," said Buzz.

"Tuesdays it is, then. Look, they're leaving."

The two girls were heading for a shiny new Ford roadster parked near the dented truck in which Loren, Buzz, and piles of Lyndon Johnson posters had traveled so many miles together. "How's our man doing?" Loren asked, as Buzz slipped a racket out of its wooden press and popped open a can of new tennis balls with a loud hiss.

"Whut Ah heah," said Buzz, "is that th' state election commission is still studyin' th' returns, particularly those from th' Rio Grande valley." He laughed. "Seems in some precincts thar were mor' people who voted than lived thar. An' people were recorded votin' in exact alphabetical order, wit' th' A's votin' early an' th' W's an' Y's at th' end of th' day. Whut has t' be decided is which candidate wuz th' slickest in gettin' away wit' unverifiable crookedness. They oughta reach uh decision by this time nex' week."

Loren smacked his first serve, trying to hit one of the cracks in the concrete on Buzz's side of the frayed net. "So we'll have a decision, one way or the other, next time we play?" he asked.

Buzz hammered Loren's second serve, hit with lots of topspin, into the net. "Yeah," he said. "Meanwhile Truman is launchin' his presidential campaign t'day an' travelin' through Texas by train all th' rest of this week, wit' Lyndon ridin' along, startin' at El Paso. Ol Coke won' go near Harry."

Loren tried a flat serve down the middle and hit it out. He was still rusty from not having played tennis for over three months. And he felt a twinge in his right shoulder. Better take it easy. "I hope I'll get to see Truman," he said.

"Not likely," responded Buzz. "Once they get t' Dallas, they plan t' swing northeast t' visit Sam Rayburn's home territory. So they won' come near Tocqueville."

"Oh well," said Loren. "I can't vote anyway. Your serve."

They played two sets and Buzz won both easily, 6-1, 6-1. Mopping their faces with damp towels, they headed for their cars. "I'll bring the balls next time," said Loren. "Thanks for the lesson."

Buzz grinned. "Ah kin see that yew haven' played fer uh while," he observed. "Ah'll look fer uh closer match by moonlight."

* * *

As Loren left Shaky in the Temple driveway and headed for the house, he saw Mrs. Kaplan standing in her back yard waving at him through a gap in the intervening hedge. When he reached it he could see that she was wearing a very tight one piece bathing costume. "Come on ovah," she said. "Th' water's fine."

"Can I really?"

"Shore. Whut good is uh new pool if nobody uses it? Yew kin bring yore frens. Only one at uh time, though. Gotta have limits.

"By th' way," she continued, "Ah wanna ask yew if'n yew've heard 'bout some real disturbin' stuff that's floatin' 'round?"

"What stuff?"

"Seems somebody saw sumptin' th' night mah husband hung hisself. An' that assistant D.A. fella is tryin' t' make up his mind whether t' subpoena this supposed witness."

"A witness? No, I haven't heard anything about a witness," said Loren, trying to keep his voice from quavering. "Your husband hung himself in deep darkness, didn't he? How could there be any witnesses?"

Mrs. Kaplan stared at him, her brow furrowed. She started to say something more but then seemed to change her mind. Instead, she gestured invitingly toward the pool. "Unless yew plan t' skinny dip, which is O. K. wit' me, yew'd better git on some shorts."

"Yeah. Right. I'll be just a minute."

Loren hurried into his house and found a pair of shorts, with which he replaced his sweaty tennis togs. Barefooted, carrying a towel, he was leaving through the back door when his mother said from behind him: "Where are you going?"

Startled, he stammered: "Just going out to get a little more sun."

"Don't get burned," she warned, going back into her bedroom. Loren took a roundabout route to Mrs. Kaplan's back yard through the two front yards; so that his mother couldn't see where he was heading. When he arrived at poolside, no one was there. As he looked around for his hostess, she came out the back door, fully dressed, carrying a purse. "Have fun," she called out. "Ah gotta keep an appointment. Ah'll be back this evenin'." In another moment she was in her yellow convertible, backing out of her driveway.

"Damn," Loren muttered. Tentatively he slid into the water at the shallow end. He needed cooling.

CHAPTER 19
DUDE

"Who's th' dude?"

As Loren bounded up the front steps of Tocqueville High School, the first words that reached his ears hit them like the smack of a hostile hand.

Glancing furtively at the scruffy teenagers lounging against the railing and sitting, sneakered feet dangling, on the concrete wall beside the double-doored entrance, he verified his suspicion that the inquiry applied to him. Self-consciously aware of how much his carefully pressed tan slacks and white shirt differed from the torn blue jeans and dirty tee shirts of the grimacing idlers, he felt his armpits begin to flow with nervous perspiration and his face flush. These swarthy adolescents running dirty fingernails through oily black hair obviously viewed him with distaste.

As he dressed that morning in the common warm weather garb of his Illinois prep school, he had not contemplated that what had been suitable for the sons and daughters of Winona millionaires would be inappropriate outerwear in Tocqueville, Texas. Nor did Loren's pale freckled skin, blue eyes, and blonde curly hair blend inconspicuously into the Mexican-Cajun-Italian majority of students in the largest public high school in this sultry corner of the Lone Star state. As the entrance door swung shut behind him, he overheard a parting comment: "Ain't he sumptin'?" It was a bad beginning to his senior year.

Only after entering the crowded halls of the three-story gray building did Loren realize that those who stared as he passed by were not eyeing his apparel, or even his pimply complexion. They were scrutinizing something else.

His shoes.

At Winona Country Day School, both boys and girls were customarily shod in brown and white saddle oxfords. Except for "Keds" and a pair of black patent leather jobs that his mother had purchased for him to wear with a second hand tuxedo to proms and holiday dinner dances, Loren's saddle oxfords were the only footwear he possessed. But they were obviously an exotic item at Tocqueville High School, where canvas sneakers, cowboy boots, or scuffed loafers encased the feet of hundreds of jostling, shouting teenagers thronging the hallways of that institution on the first day of school in September, 1948.

Tentatively navigating the labyrinth of concrete corridors which echoed with the clanging of steel locker doors and the frenzied babble of fellow juveniles, Loren was overcome by a feeling of nostalgia for the cohesive academic family of WCDS. There, he had several bookish friends. And once they discovered his abilities at football and baseball, the jocks, too, had included him in their clannish brotherhood.

The WCDS headmaster, a tweedy sincere man who had said he was impressed by poetry Loren had written in his junior literature class, had called him into his book-filled office and urged him to stay on as a boarding student. A generous scholarship would have continued to pay most of the cost of attending one of the outstanding prep schools in the Middle West, and Loren's father had declared that he thought he could pay the rest. So why had he not lingered for one more year?

He supposed that he had fled Winona out of fear of being too much on his own. But now, as he wandered unhappily through the halls of Tocqueville High School, he thought he should have stayed in Winona.

* * *

Loren's home room teacher turned out to be a boisterous woman in her early thirties named Annabelle Muser. Her desk was located near the door of room 212; so that a student entering the room would immediately encounter the formidable Miz Muser, looking right at him. Confronted by her bold stare, Loren quickly dropped his eyes to take in a single large red rose that protruded from a bud vase in the middle of her desk, and he struggled to keep his voice from quavering as he identified himself and confessed to being a transfer student from Illinois.

He was pleased to be assigned to a desk near the back of the room, next to some tall windows that overlooked the athletic practice fields. He studied Miz Muser as she continued to sign in students. Greeting the ones she already knew with booming good mornings and an occasional guffaw, she appeared thoroughly in command.

As a result of frequent flicks of her pink tongue, Miz Muser's carmine-covered lips glistened liquidly. Her hair, piled into an enormous bun, was jet black, as were her bushy eyebrows. Her skin was clear and creamy, but her high cheekbones were thoroughly rouged. Loren observed that she was not wearing a wedding ring.

Bells had been clamoring in the hall, off and on, for perhaps ten minutes. Loren could see through the open door that the sea of students had thinned to a few stragglers looking anxiously at room numbers. Then one more bell pealed and Miz Muser rose from behind her desk to close the door.

Loren gasped. Now that she was on her feet, he saw that she was a great hulk of womanhood; not fat, just Big. Formidable. Her ruffled white blouse stretched tightly over a bulky bosom. He could see the outline of her brassiere and imagined wickedly what would happen if a strap broke under the strain. Would the class cheer? Or would it emit a shocked gasp? Would Miz "Moose," as Loren decided to dub her, blush and rush to a lady's lounge for repairs? Somehow he doubted that. Rather could he visualize her employing those penetrating black eyes to stare her students down, one by one, until she had cowed the entire class, by the sheer force of her personality, into acceptance of the notion that a loose boob was nothing to get excited about.

Unfortunately, Miz Muser failed to burst her bra during that hour or during any of the many subsequent hours that Loren spent in her classroom, for it turned out that she presided not only over his home room but also over his American History and Civics classes. In a wary way, he learned to like her; for while she frequently chastised other students with biting sarcasm and imaginative punishments when they came to class unprepared or when they otherwise misbehaved, Loren was invariably prepared and always docile. Although he was frequently flustered by her aggressiveness and her embarrassingly personal approach, he soon became a "teacher's pet," a role he had played many times over the years, but not one for which he consciously strived.

Miz Muser was fascinated by government, especially Texas state government. When she taught American history, she took a political and constitutional approach, which was fine with Loren. Her fund of anecdotes seemed inexhaustible. And she was unafraid to repeat stories that Loren thought might even be libelous about Lyndon Johnson and Coke Stevenson.

Beginning with her very first Civics class, she tried to dramatize the U.S. Senate race by writing on her blackboard the daily vote totals for the two candidates as they had been reported by the state election bureau. On the Monday following the August 28 primary, Stevenson led by 210 votes. On Tuesday he was ahead by 430 votes. On Wednesday it was 438 votes, and on Thursday it was 381 votes. On Friday, September 3, however, with late returns from the Rio Grande valley having finally been reported, Johnson suddenly led by 44 ballots out of nearly one million cast. Miz Muser remarked that it seemed strange that one precinct had appeared to give Johnson a 202-1 margin over Stevenson.

On Wednesday, September 8, Miz Muser could hardly wait for the bell to signal the start of Civics class to announce that Johnson's lead, as of the previous evening, had risen to 162 votes, with only five days left before the Texas Democratic Party's executive committee would meet in Fort Worth to decide whether to accept or alter the election bureau's findings. No matter what the executive committee determined, Miz Muser declared, the loser was sure to go to court in an attempt to overturn its ruling. "This election," she asserted, radiating excitement, "will have to be decided by the United States Supreme Court. Th' whole world will be watchin' t' see who'll be th' next Senator from Texas!" Loren, who shared her enthusiasm, was disconcerted to observe that most of his classmates reacted apathetically to her pronouncement. He hoped that their parents were not equally disengaged.

During the same class, Miz Muser read aloud from a full-page advertisement that had appeared in the *Endeavor* the previous afternoon. It accused President Truman of conspiring to destroy private enterprise throughout the United States by instituting bans on racial segregation. Truman, the ad asserted, was trying to force white children to associate with Negro children and submit to the authority of Negro teachers. Darkies would have to be admitted into all hotels, restaurants, theatres, barber shops, beauty salons, colleges, swimming pools, and any other facilities used by the white public. The States' Rights Party of Texas, the ad proclaimed, condemned such efforts by Truman and his backers to turn the United States into a communist society. The States' Rights Party stood instead "for individual liberty and the sovereignty of the states" as essential to the survival of the Republic. "TEXANS," the ad trumpeted, "We Must Unite in the Fight Lest We Forever Lose Freedoms Purchased with the Blood of Our Fathers."

Fortunately for Loren, Miz Muser did not ask his opinion of the States' Rights Party or of its manifesto. Glancing around the room, trying to keep his own countenance expressionless, he saw some students nodding in agreement with what they had just heard. Others appeared puzzled or exhibited indifference, but none appeared bothered by what Loren considered an outrageous pronouncement. To label a society in which Negroes might obtain a few basic human rights "communist," and to equate oppression against Negroes with "individual liberty," sounded like something emanating from Hitler's Germany. And from Miz Muser's approving tone of voice as she read from the States' Rights Party's ad, he feared that she was in full agreement with it.

Happily, the daily quizzes that she inflicted upon her groaning students were entirely drawn from the textbook and did not require any echoes of her own opinionated statements. And since Loren had no trouble quickly assimilating the few pages assigned for each class, he easily answered the quiz questions that appeared to bewilder some of the other students. When his mother inquired why he never seemed to have homework in Civics or American History, Loren assured her that he was doing well in those subjects, as well as in Art and in Journalism, which his father seemed pleased to hear he was taking.

* * *

Adam and Nan Temple had both attended college but both had dropped out before completing their freshman years. Adam had then changed from one type of work to another until he finally found his calling in journalism. Nan had embarked on a career as an actress, which had abruptly ended when she married. From the avidity with which they both encouraged Loren to begin thinking about college, he deduced that both of them regretted not continuing with higher education. Loren himself saw little use for college as preparation for becoming a major league baseball player. But he also realized that the odds against reaching that goal were great, and that if he wanted a rewarding backup career, such as sports writing, he ought to obtain a college degree.

At Tocqueville High School, a senior was allowed to take a year-long course in journalism in place of fourth-year English. Although Loren loved almost all kinds of literature and had always made A's in composition, he hated memorizing rules of grammar and diagramming sentences. Hence he eagerly registered for the senior course in journalism taught by Miz Violet Doonsbury, whose qualifications for teaching the subject he never discovered. She had obviously never worked on a real newspaper. And it was reliably reported by a student who worked in the school office that she had not even graduated from a college. Moreover, in a field that called for a certain toughness, she was a delicate woman, near-sighted behind thick glasses, with a quavering voice that reminded Loren of Eleanor Roosevelt, the widow of the former president.

Miz Doonsbury, it turned out, was high strung and easily provoked into fits of temper, in the course of which she habitually waved the yardstick that she used as a blackboard pointer wildly in the air, flourishing it perilously close to the faces of the students sitting in the front row. If a student failed to give her his full attention, he might suddenly feel the pain of hardwood on his fingers, as she quickly crossed the room and provided evidence that she had many years ago begun her teaching career in a parochial school.

During the very first week of the fall term, she responded to some impolite remarks from an uncouth youth by throwing a chalk covered eraser at him, and then sat pouting and glowering behind her desk, pretending to read, until the bell rang.

V.D. (as she was called behind her back by most of her students) soon discovered that Loren already knew a great deal about journalism. Once she learned that his father was the managing editor of the *Endeavor,* he could do no wrong. Loren tried to be inconspicuous, but it was impossible: V.D. was constantly looking to him for validation of whatever she was telling the other students, cheered by his slightest smile, and troubled by even the hint of a frown.

She seemed to divide her students into two groups: the few favorites, who were quiet, studious and dutiful; and the ignorant troublemakers. The former were constantly flattered and fed easy questions to answer; the latter were suffered in exasperated silence, except when they became boisterous, at which time they would incur the infamous Doonsbury wrath.

Only the favored few were honored by being appointed to editorial positions on the school newspaper or the yearbook, but others might perform mundane duties on those publications for "extra credit," something of which V.D. seemed to have an inexhaustible supply. Consequently, many a marginal student enrolled in one of her two journalism sections, willing to endure her outbursts in order to emerge from the ordeal with an A, or at least a B, instead of risking an F in senior English.

Loren soon concluded that practically all the females in his journalism class had little thought of a future in the profession. For them V.D. had an endless supply of mindless busy work, the completion of which—never mind the quality—guaranteed at least a B in the course. One girl, who sat at a desk directly in front of Loren's, seemed different. Her name, he soon learned, was Mary Beth Carver. She was bouncy, bright-eyed, and built, as he overheard another male admirer say, "like a woman."

On the very first day of the term, as Loren was picking up his books to leave, she turned around, smiled, and said: "Hello. I'm Mary Beth."

Blushing, Loren mumbled his own name and said he was glad to meet her. Before the week was over they were greeting each other like old friends. In Mary Beth's warmth, Loren's shyness soon thawed. She extracted from him the information that he was actually no "Yankee," but had been born in Virginia, and that he had never been north of his birth state until the fifth grade, when he had been unmercifully teased at a school in Michigan for his southern speech and Dixie ways. He brought Mary Beth his most recent Winona CDS yearbook, in which he appeared in the center of a photograph of the football team holding a ball, thus identifying him as team captain. She immediately declared that the Tocqueville High School team was in dire need of his talents and that he should at once go to see the coach.

Accordingly, he devoted part of his lunch period the next day to a search for Coach Reuben Allen and eventually found him in a cramped office in the gymnasium. Allen, a red-faced, white-haired man who must have been pushing sixty, was seated in a swivel chair scribbling X's and O's on pieces of notebook paper. Apparently displeased with Loren for interrupting his tactical planning, he only half-listened to his visitor's question—whether it would be all right belatedly to suit up for football. Then he said that if Loren would report to the football locker room a few minutes before two o'clock, when varsity practice began, he could ask the equipment manager whether he had a uniform that would fit. No inquiry about Loren's past experience or what position he played; no curiosity about his physical condition; and no comment about whether he was even eligible to participate. The pot-bellied impresario obviously wanted to rid himself of this interloper, so that he could resume his solitary meditation.

Nevertheless, Loren sent a note by Mary Beth to his last period Art teacher that he might need to miss class because of school business and, promptly at ten minutes to two, he pushed open the door marked FOOTBALL under the stadium stands and found himself alone in the varsity locker room. There were no players dressing; no equipment managers; not even any lights, until he touched a switch next to the entrance. He found the cage in which were stored pads, cleats and other gridiron paraphernalia, but it was padlocked. Phooey on this, he said to himself. He turned off the light and left.

That evening he read in the *Endeavor* sports section that the THS Purple Panthers had departed that afternoon by bus for Corpus Christi, where they were scheduled to play their first game of the season on Friday evening. It appeared, indeed, that at the very moment he was visiting their locker room, they were on the other side of the stadium boarding their bus, presumably supervised by none other than Coach Allen. Had the man purposely deceived him? Or had he merely had a lapse of memory about where he and his players would be in a couple of hours? Although Loren did not know, he suspected the worst.

* * *

"But Loren," objected Mary Beth, when he told her that his foray into the Panther precincts had been unprofitable, "last year we won only two games, and this year looks like it might be worse. Can't you try again?"

"If Coach Allen wanted me, he would have said so. Anyway, my game is baseball," Loren insisted.

Mary Beth's disappointment was transitory. She was an enthusiast, and so effusive that in a single conversation Loren learned a great deal about her. She had a father who worked at the Wisteria Oil Refinery as a chemical engineer. Her mother was a faithful churchgoer of the Methodist persuasion, who loved to sing in the choir. Mary Beth herself had been voted junior class favorite the previous year, although she was not athletic and only an average student. Her ambition for her life after high school was eventually to get married and have a couple of children and a comfortable home, but first to emulate Brenda Starr, a glamorous girl reporter portrayed in a popular comic strip. She considered her enrollment in Miz Doonsbury's class a beginning to her journalistic career.

When V.D. asked for two volunteers to cover an evening meeting of the school Parent Teacher Association later that week for the Cat Chat, the school paper, Mary Beth startled Loren by announcing that he and she would go. He heard several snickers and saw Miz Doonsbury's eyebrows lift above the rims of her glasses. Nevertheless, she agreed to the assignment. And Loren was elated: somehow he would free himself for a few hours from his night job at the *Endeavor* office in order to enjoy his first date with a Texas lass, whom he yearned to know better. Much better.

CHAPTER 20
HADACOL BOOGIE

Saturday, September 11, was the day on which the Tocqueville Stars were to journey into Louisiana to take on the Bowie Bombers. During the bus ride from Shipper Stadium, Loren sat quietly by himself and stared out the window, listening to the conversations of the other players. Several seemed to be loners like himself. They made little effort, during the three-hour journey along the heavily traveled New Orleans highway, to get to know their new teammates. At lunch in a Bowie restaurant, where the local customers all spoke what sounded like French, and the waitress at Loren's table could hardly be understood, conversation continued desultory.

Loren did not know what to make of such detachment among his new teammates, most of whom appeared to be strangers to each other. Was this remoteness typical of ballplayers passing from amateur to professional status? He had read about animosities between ballplayers: Tinker and Evers, Cobb and Crawford; and even Ruth and Gehrig. And the hazing of rookies, he knew, had been a common practice among pros. With the Stars, however, it was less a matter of unfriendliness than of apathy. There was no enthusiasm whatever. No joshing or rough practical jokes, such as those Loren had encountered among the Scorpions. This was not a team, he thought, but merely a collection of self-centered individuals. He felt unwelcome.

Promptly at three o'clock, the strains of the Star Spangled Banner blasted from a loud speaker on a light pole in center field and the game began. Looking around as he awaited his turn at bat, Loren estimated that there were fewer than two hundred spectators scattered about the unpainted wooden bleachers provided for the Bomber fans. After Jorge Sanchez, the diminutive shortstop for the Stars, bounced weakly to his counterpart on the home team, Loren waited out the pitcher and drew a walk. On first base, he looked to Rand in the third base coach's box for a sign, but the manager kept his hands thrust inside his back pockets and made no eye contact. Sonny Fraser, the beanpole first sacker for the Stars, took a couple of wild swings without connecting and then got lucky. He golfed an inside pitch off his shoetops high and deep into left field. Rounding second base, Loren saw the Bomber left fielder give up on the ball as it bounced into a muddy stream that bubbled along where in more sophisticated surroundings a fence would have been. Two runs. A good beginning.

Running out to third base for the bottom of the first inning and whipping practice throws across the diamond to Fraser, who welcomed them with casual flicks of his roomy mitt, Loren thought how disreputable they all looked—a few like himself clad in complete uniforms reflecting some former affiliation, and the others wearing jeans and tee shirts bearing the names of past sponsors. Most of the

Stars dug into the black dirt in front of their hard wooden bench with spiked shoes, but several wore high topped sneakers. All wore baseball caps, none of which resembled any other. And all, except Loren, incessantly spat, some with huge chaws distorting their cheeks like squirrels carrying nuts and some dripping dark drool from pursed lips down stubbled chins, but all splattering tobacco spit in every direction. Loren tried not to imagine sliding in the stuff, which as the game progressed became particularly plentiful around home plate.

He need not have worried. After the first inning the Bomber pitcher gave up only one more run, which scored on a wild throw from his catcher, who was trying to pick Sanchez off third base. Loren was out twice on infield grounders and a third time on a foul fly, which the Bomber first baseman gloved leaning over the Bowie bench. The home team hurler was far from overpowering but he managed to keep the Stars off balance by constantly changing speeds and moving the ball around on the edges of the strike zone. It was frustrating. As the game entered the bottom of the ninth inning tied at three-all, Loren resolved that if he got up to bat again he would restrain his eagerness and wait for a fat pitch.

Suddenly a commotion broke out in the seats behind the Stars' bench. From his position next to third base, Loren could see two men tussling. One clutched a large brown bottle by the neck, and the other one was trying to wrest it from him. Both were shouting epithets in French. Loren heard something that sounded like "had a call."

"What's that all about?" he asked the Bowie manager, who was grinning in the nearby coach's box.

"Aw, one ol' boy done got d' las bottle uh Hadacol an' d' other one want it real bad."

During the game Loren had noticed that a vendor was selling big bottles of some dark liquid to spectators, mostly males, who seemed to become more animated the more they swigged. He had assumed that the beverage was beer, but it now appeared that it might be a more exotic brew. "What," he inquired, "is had-a-call?"

"Man, dat's th' bestis stuff. Give yew energy. Make yew happy. Yew ain't got it in Texas?"

"I don't know. Maybe. But I never heard of it. Seems people in Tocqueville mostly drink beer."

"Hadacol better. Work faster, too."

Loren believed it. Several additional fans had joined in the struggle to gain possession of the disputed prize. While the players on both teams and the two umpires watched, fascinated, the bottle was finally torn from the grip of its original claimant and immediately tipped up by its new possessor, who only had time for a single glug before it was snatched from his grasp by a barefooted teenager. As this miscreant leaped from the seats and scampered across the infield, pursued by several red-faced men, shouts of encouragement and of derision burst out on all sides.

The juvenile made the mistake of trying to sneak a quick swig of the precious liquid just as he passed the Stars' pitcher, who stuck out a spiked shoe and tripped him. Head over heels the youth tumbled, giving up his hold on the Hadacol bottle as he fell. As a brown puddle spread in the black dirt next to the pitcher's plate, a cry of anguish burst from the thwarted pursuers. At once they gave up their chase and returned dolefully to their seats, while the unsuccessful thief limped away to some unknown destination.

The first Bowie Bomber to bat after the disruption hit a high fly down the left field line, not very deep. Loren joined Sanchez and the left fielder, Robicheaux, a big clumsy guy, in pursuing it. Although it was Robicheaux who yelled "mine, mine," the shortstop had other ideas. As Loren veered away and watched, horrified, Sanchez crashed into his much larger teammate with a loud thump, with the descending sphere bouncing off the resulting tangle into foul territory and rolling into a weedy patch not far from the nearby bayou.

Hustling to retrieve the ball, Loren was about to reach down for it when a scale-encrusted brown head with beady eyes and a flicking tongue rose up out of the thick vegetation less than a foot from his hand. Jumping back, he felt his skin crawl as he stared down at the flat-headed snake, fully as long and almost as thick as a baseball bat. Dimly he heard shouts from his teammates, exhorting him to throw the damn ball. But he wanted no part of the serpent.

Joined by the Stars' center fielder, who had raced over, taken one look, muttered "cotton mouth," and jumped back, Loren slowly walked back toward the Stars' bench, accompanied most of the way by a shaken shortstop and a limping left fielder. The rest of the Stars were already gathering their equipment, inasmuch as the winning run had now scored.

A scowling manager awaited Loren. Shaking his head in disbelief at Loren's explanation, even though it was backed up by the center fielder, Rand led his players aboard the bus, where he took the wheel, ready to transport them back to Tocqueville. From the nearby ballpark, happy music blared from the center field loud speaker. A young bystander told Loren that the tune was called "The Hadacol Boogie."

As Loren waited in line for his turn to climb into the bus, he overheard Robicheaux complain to Sanchez that the latter should have given him precedence in catching the final fly ball.

"Didn' think yew could reach it," retorted the little shortstop.

"Weren't yew afeared yew'd git squished by ol' Roby?" asked another Star, pointing at the still sulking left fielder, who must have weighed almost twice as much as Sanchez.

"Nah," responded the diminutive shortstop. "Size don' count. Hail, Ah once saw uh fuggin' li'l bumble bee chase uh Brahma bull clear 'cross uh pasture."

Loren settled into a seat near the rear of the bus and stared out of the dirty window at the surrounding swamps, as the bus left Bowie heading westward. Soon he saw that someone had left a wrinkled local newspaper on an empty seat across the aisle.

Taking it up, he saw on page one that the Louisiana Democratic party executive committee had removed President Truman's name from the November ballot and substituted the name of Strom Thurmond, the States' Rights Party candidate. The move had been initiated by Judge Leander Perez, the political boss of the delta parishes south of New Orleans and endorsed by the remnants of the infamous Huey

Long political machine. Pretty high-handed stuff, thought Loren. How can such things happen in America?

From the front of the bus, Rand's gravelly voice broke the silence. "We're goin' t' play at home next Sat'day evenin'," he announced, "'gainst th' Southside Scorpions. Th' papers are goin' t' play up th' game as determinin' th' Tocqueville city championship. So be ready t' play better than yew did t'day."

Loren felt a surge of excitement, as he realized that his opportunity for redemption was but a week away. He'd show that damn Bubba a thing or two.

Turning back to the newspaper on his lap, he saw, on an inside page, a large advertisement for Hadacol. The product was described as a "marvelous remedy" for heartburn, gas pains, constipation, indigestion, headaches, and other bodily infirmities, including all weak, rundown feelings. "It matters not how old you are or where you live," the ad asserted, "the B vitamins and minerals in Hadacol will stop your suffering and make you feel wonderful." Satisfied users testified to the efficacy of the elixir, marketed by Louisiana State Senator Dudley J. LeBlanc, "Great Statesman and Fighter for the Rights of the People."

"Amazing," Loren said aloud. Sitting behind him, Sanchez inquired: "Whatcha reading?" Loren turned and handed him the paper. Sanchez looked at it and laughed. "Dat ol' Dudley," he said," is one shrewd fella. He sell dat tonic fer three-fifty uh pint an' it run him 'bout one-tenth dat much t' make it an' 'nother tenth t' advertise it. Dat's uh big profit."

"Doesn't it cost him a lot for all those vitamins and minerals?" asked Loren.

"Whut yew talkin' 'bout? Ten per cent cod liver oil an' ninety per cent alcohol an' nuttin' else, dat's whut Ah heared."

During the rest of the journey home, Loren could not get his mind off the blind faith in the effectiveness of Hadacol expressed by the dozens of regular users quoted in the newspaper. Maybe a snort of the stuff was what he needed to improve his own frame of mind, which at the moment was unaccountably discontented.

* * *

Loren's glum mood was lightened on Monday, when Mary Beth contrived to get him elected as the alternate home room representative to the student council, "in case Ah can't make one of th' meetin's," she said, putting a proprietary hand on his. After she nominated him, one of her girl friends quickly shouted "second," and another one as rapidly moved that nominations cease and that Loren be elected by acclamation, which was done without dissent. This was a tactic with which Loren had previously been unacquainted, but it seemed effective. He would have to remember how it worked.

Also flattering, and even more embarrassing, was Miz Doonsbury's comment, delivered as she was returning the term's first assigned essays to Loren's journalism class, that one of the papers had exhibited a more elegant command of the English language than any she had ever received in over twenty years of teaching; "so vivid; so real! Loren Temple, whar did yew learn t' write like that?"

Startled by the question, since he had assumed that she had been referring to someone else, he stammered: "I don't know. Maybe because I read a lot."

"See, class," said Miz Doonsbury. "Whut have Ah been tellin' yew? Uh good journalist has t' know th' 'mo joost.' That, in French, means th' right word. Exact-aye-munt. Now Ah wan' y'all t' copy th' words Ah've written on th' board." She released a spring holding a large world map down over a portion of the blackboard behind her desk, thus exposing a list of about thirty polysyllabic words, and inspiring groans of dismay throughout the room. "Look 'em up in th' dictionary," Miz Doonsbury exhorted her charges, "an' be prepared t'morra t' be quized on their definitions."

Having ascertained that he knew what the words meant, Loren did not bother to copy them in his notebook. Instead he doodled, drawing stick figures playing baseball, while his classmates reluctantly transcribed the already detested terms assigned to improve their vocabularies.

* * *

That night, when Loren met Buzz under a streetlight near the dark tennis courts located next to the Catholic church on Austin Avenue, he could not help sharing his amusement at Miz Doonsbury's daily word lists. But Buzz shook his head. "Ah think th' ol' gal is tryin' her best t' increase th' odds that uh few barely literate youngsters might be able t' make sumptin' of themselves," he said. "Yew may not need her help, but very few high school kids 'roun' heah have had yore advantages."

Loren protested: "Most of my education has come from reading, which anyone can do."

"Since whut age?"

"I don't know. Maybe four or five. I had a library card in first grade."

"See. That's whut Ah mean. Fer ovah ten years yew've been soakin' up knowledge, an' assimilating th' English language in th' process. But mos' children in Tocqueville nevah read anythang but comic books, unless compelled t' do so by some school teacher, an' then only under protest. Their parents don' care: they don' read either, 'cept maybe newspapers, bits of th' Bible, uh magazine or two, an' if they're really literary, th' *Reader's Digest*."

"That's depressing."

"That's Tocqueville. 'Course there are exceptions, but not many. Yew've been fortunate in yore educational background. Build on it. Don't jus' float along on th' strength of yore head start. Keep readin' an' learnin'."

"Right… Are you ready for tennis?"

"Shore." While conversing they had strolled in the darkness over to a fence behind which was located a single tennis court. Buzz stepped through a gate and dropped a quarter through a slot in a metal box attached to the fence nearby, and floodlights immediately illuminated the area. Knowing that the lights would require another quarter after twenty-five minutes had passed, both players hastened onto the court and began their warmups, stroking a few forehands and backhands and walloping several practice serves.

Loren worried that the loud clopping of gut against fuzz-covered rubber might disturb the sleeping nuns in the adjacent convent, but no lights flashed from the nearby building as they began to play. Buzz was ahead five games to two and about to serve when, suddenly, the floodlights flashed off. In the resulting darkness, enhanced by the abrupt change from brightness to blackness, Loren groped his way to the meter box and deposited a quarter. Then Buzz proceeded to ace him four times with an exaggerated topspin that Loren's eyes, still trying to adjust to the change in lighting, could not pick up.

The second set went faster as Buzz began to hit blistering backhands into the corners, until he had Loren panting and reaching so far for each shot that he could never get his feet set for a proper return. Occasionally Buzz would slice a drop shot barely over the net tape, as Loren grimaced helplessly. A deft half-volley past Loren's lunge, as he charged the net on his opponent's second serve, ended the set at 6-0. The two sweaty players then rushed to gather up the loose balls and clamp their rackets in the wooden presses that kept them from warping, before the lights once more went out.

Afterwards, seated in Buzz's truck, they talked. Loren had read in the *Endeavor* that on the previous evening the Texas Democratic Party's officers had ruled that Lyndon Johnson had defeated Coke Stevenson by 87 votes to become their senatorial nominee. In a chaotic session marked by curses and threats, the members of the party executive committee had balloted 29-28 in favor of Johnson; whereupon those in the minority had promptly stalked out of the smoke-filled room, left the building, and replaced the American flag flying from a tall pole outside with the stars and bars of the Southern Confederacy.

"It looks like the Stevenson people were intending to turn the Texas Democratic Party over to the states' righters," observed Loren. "Then they would have replaced Truman's name on the November ballot with Thurmond's, as was done in Louisiana."

"Right," agreed Buzz. "An' they haven't given up yet. Ah heard on th' radio that they've persuaded uh federal judge t' issue uh restraining order t' prevent th' Democrats from certifying Johnson as their official nominee. Lessen our man kin override th' decision on appeal, Stevenson may emerge th' winner after all."

"What a mess!" exclaimed Loren. "I'm beginning to feel sorry for Johnson."

"Ah'm inclined th' same way. But Lyndon is uh hard man t' pity. Ah 'magine him as uh spoiled brat, manipulated by his Momma till he became an emotionally retarded adult who now uses th' same psychological weapons t' dominate others as were used earlier on 'im. He needs this victory: not only 'cause t' lose wud prolly finish 'im politically, but also t' shore up his fragile ego. If'n he makes it t' the Senate in Washington, Ah predict that he'll be runnin' th' place in no time. But if'n he fails..." Buzz shook his head. "It might kill him."

"He sounds pretty mixed up to me," said Loren. "What about Stevenson?"

"Ol' Coke is a reactionary who belongs back in the las' century operatin' uh slave plantation. But Ah 'magine he don' much care whether he becomes uh senator or goes back t' his ranch. He don' give uh damn whut others think of him or whether he holds any office. Right now he's willin' t' front fer all them fellas who're tryin' t' hold back th' risin' tide of social change. But underneath he really don' care much, 'cause he hisself ain't evah gonna change, an' nobody kin make him.

"Wit' Johnson, it's different. He's uh work in progress. He cud turn out t' be jus' 'nother morally corrupt Dixiecrat. Or he could develop into an honorable

Liberal, carin' more 'bout helpin' people than protectin' plutocrats. Whutever role feeds his ego th' mos'; that's th' one he'll play."

"You talk like you know the man."

"Not personally. But Ah know some people who're close t' him. An' Ah've read reports…" Buzz hesitated. Then, as if he believed he had already divulged too much, he said: "Uh lotta politicians are jus' like Johnson, 'though only uh few have his overwhelming personality. They think th' whole world revolves 'round themselves. Maybe that's whut it takes t' be succcessful at that game."

"Do you really think it's just a game?"

"Uh game wit' flexible rules an' high stakes. An' awesome power fer those who emerge as th' big winnas. Ah'll give yew an example. Whoevah gits elected president in November is gonna have t' make uh big decision durin' his term of office, one that'll drastically affect yore life an' maybe mine, too."

"What's that?"

"Didja see th' story in yore Dad's paper yesterday that th' Koreans are 'bout t' fight uh civil war t' determine whether th' commies in th' North or th' so-called 'democratic' regime in th' South will take ovah th' entire country?"

"No. I didn't read that piece. Probably didn't think it important."

"See if yew kin find it an' read it. Truman calls his foreign policy 'Containment.' That means that if Communism materializes anywhar in th' world, th' United States'll intervene. In uh year or two yew may find yoreself drafted inta th' army; so ol' Harry or sum successor kin say he's holdin' back th' red tide. If not in Korea, then in another godforesaken spot that mos' Americans won' have heared of till their sons an' husbands are sent thar t' fight an' die."

"Do you really think we'll go to war in a place like Korea? Merely because some politicians in Washington don't like a change in government over there?"

"Yup. So be prepared. We're in fer sum real excitement. Crazy stuff… Speakin' of crazy, lookit th' time."

Loren checked his watch. 3:15 in the morning. And he had to be at school by eight. Thanking Buzz for the "lesson," he fired up Shaky and hurried home. But he had trouble getting to sleep. He kept trying to visualize what Korea might be like. The thought that what happened in such a far-away place might threaten his own life made him extremely uneasy.

* * *

In order to escort Mary Beth to the high school Parent Teacher Association meeting on Thursday evening, Loren had to find someone to fill in for him at the newspaper. He persuaded Lois Bankhead, the *Endeavor's* unmarried society editor, to stay late that evening, in order to spell him in the wire room for a two-hour period, 6:30 to 8:30, when little hard news was expected to flow through the teletype machines.

"I have some reading to do," said the accommodating Miz Bankhead, "but you be sure to get back to the office by 8:30; so I can get home in time to feed my cats before their bedtimes."

"Will do," said Loren. "Many thanks."

Emerging from her back door and seeing Shaky parked in the driveway, Mary Beth exclaimed: "Whut have yew done? Yew painted yore car purple! Holy... it looks... swell!"

"Glad you like it. I had a hard time finding the right shade. Seems not too many people are painting their automobiles, or anything else, bright purple."

"Ah should think not... Ah mean, mos' people are not that creative... An' look, yew painted th' entire inside crimson!"

"Yeah. Livens it up, don't you think? Anyway, I hated to drive a car that was all black. Looked like a hearse."

"Wal, it certainly don' now."

Loren kept casting sidelong glances at Mary Beth during the PTA meeting, which was a big bust. The two journalism students, sitting in the first row with pencils poised over their notebooks, had hoped for fireworks. For the president of the local chapter of the Daughters of the American Revolution had been granted a place on the agenda to discuss controversial remarks allegedly made in class by a certain teacher.

"Do you know who the teacher is?" Loren whispered to Mary Beth.

"Miz Muser; who else? She's always playin' devil's advocate. Once or twice every year some dimwit student misinterprets sumthin' she said an' tells uh parent, who complains t' sumone else, distorting th' distortion; an' then Miz Weakley, th' perennial president of th' DAR, decides t' demonstrate her patriotism by makin' an issue outa somethin' that reached her third han'. It's an annual ritual 'tween Miz Muser an' Miz Weakley. Ah see Mr. Simpson, th' president of th' school board, is heah. Yew kin always count on him t' defend his teachers, lessen they're terribly outa line."

"Sounds like a good man."

"Oh, he is. Works at Gulf Electric. Runs th' place."

After a dull discussion of vocational education, the PTA president quickly adjourned the meeting. Fortunately Miz Weakley had not put in an appearance, for Loren had barely enough time to transport Mary Beth back home and rush back to the newspaper office, so that dinner wouldn't be delayed for Miz Bankhead's cats. "If you like, I'll write the story," he offered, as he turned Shaky into Mary Beth's driveway. "It should only take two or three paragraphs, which I can easily produce tonight at the office when the machines are quiet."

"Thanks, Loren," said Mary Beth. "That'll git me t' bed on time, after Ah work on mah history paper. Night." She leaned over the gearshift that protruded from the floor between them and lightly brushed his cheek with her lips. Before he could react, she jumped from the car and, waving and smiling, disappeared inside the house.

That smile! It radiated affection. Loren had never before encountered one like it. For the first time in his life, he thought, he was really in love.

Loren's first impression of Mary Beth had been that she was a bit too voluptuous. But his initial assessment, derived from her habit of wearing baggy blouses and jumpers, or in cool weather, loose sweaters and long, heavy skirts, had been erroneous. He had come to realize that underneath the voluminous outfits that

Mary Beth wore in compliance with the current female fashion, the so-called "New Look," she was actually quite slim. Svelte. Demure. Perfect.

Back at the *Gazette* office, Loren tore loose the pulpy yellow paper containing the night's news from the clattering teletype machines. Attaching the sheets to one another with paper clips by category (national, state, local, feature, and sports), he distributed them to the appropriate desks in the busy news room. While he worked he trembled at the tantalizing thought that some day soon Mary Beth might become more than just a friend.

CHAPTER 21
GRUDGE GAME

On Saturday Loren caught up on his sleep and did not start his chores until after lunch. As he contemplated the forthcoming confrontation between the Stars and the Scorpions, he hoped that he would be able to force his former teammates to rue the day that they had lost his services. His fantasies of revenge, however, melted into moroseness as they were gradually overwhelmed by a fear of failure. A late afternoon nap failed to quiet his nerves, for he dreamed of futility, followed by ridicule from the Scorpions and rejection by the Stars.

That evening, he had hardly made his way into the visitor's clubhouse at Shipper Stadium and begun to pull on a baggy new orange and black Stars uniform, when old Rand ambled around the locker room introducing a newcomer, a beefy redhead named Pete Ostrowski, whom Loren overheard the manager say played a "mean" third base. Then, when the Stars took infield practice, Rand told Ostrowski to take over third base. Loren was sent to the outfield to shag flies with four others. What was going on?

Loren got another surprise when his former team, the Scorpions, began infield practice. A youngster whom the other players called "Cope" began gobbling up grounders at second base. Where was Bubba? Feets was apparently in charge as field manager, for it was the slender Scorpion catcher, already wearing his shin guards, who joined Rand and the umpires at home plate for the ritualistic exchange of lineups.

There was a pause in the proceedings while someone tried to get the ballpark sound system working so that everyone could stand for the music of the Star Spangled Banner. During the delay, Feets wandered over near the Stars dugout. "Hey, Feets," said Loren softly. "What happened to Guidry?"

Startled, Feets looked to see who had spoken. "Howdy, Yank," he said. "Ah didn' know yew were wit' these guys. We gonna kick y'all's asses t'night."

"Maybe. What about Bubba?"

"Wal, nobody knows fer sure. He an' Rose had uh fight an' he went an' quit his job at th' Wisteria works an' tol' Fats he wuzn't gonna be able t' play no more ball fer uh while. They's uh rumor that he's in some kinda trouble wit' th' law. So th' boys done elected me manager."

"That's what they should have done in the first place."

"Thanks. Ah'm doin' mah best. Now Ah gotta git th' guys onto th' field. Good t' see yew, Yank."

"You too."

Loren suddenly became conscious that Rand was addressing the Stars. "...an' now dat our former third baseman is finished fraternizing wit' th' enemy, Ah'll read th' lineup fer t'night's game." It was no surprise to Loren that his name was not among the nine starters. Another opportunity to prove his worth—destroyed by the action of an ignoramus.

The more Loren thought about his latest humiliation, the more he shook with indignation. As the game began, he withdrew to the corner of the dugout farthest away from the manager, who in turn stared gloomily out at the diamond, dribbling tobacco juice down his chin stubble, entirely ignoring Loren. Periodically Rand withdrew into the tunnel leading to the toilet where Loren knew, from remarks by one of the other players, that he had hidden a bottle of bourbon whiskey.

From the very beginning, the Scorpion bats thundered. A. C. Doucet, meanwhile, mowed down the Stars with his spitball and an occasional beanball. Only a three-run homer to left field by Al Robicheaux, the Stars' best hitter, kept the score close. For Loren the game passed in a blur of sound and movement and frustration.

The eighth inning started with A. C. nursing a 5-3 lead, throwing as hard as ever, with the Stars flailing weakly at his offerings. Rand had disappeared. Impulsively, Loren, planning to beg him for a chance to play at least one inning, sought the manager in the tunnel leading to the Stars' clubhouse. He was not there.

The door to the dressing room was open. Loren entered. At first he glimpsed nothing. Then, as he approached the shower room, he spotted Rand sprawled on the concrete floor, eyes shut, clutching an empty whiskey bottle in a gnarled brown hand.

Leaning over the old man and getting a sickening sniff of alcohol, Loren ascertained that the manager was entirely unconscious. Closing the clubhouse door behind him, he hurried back to the dugout.

Emerging into the noise and bright light of the ball field, he checked the scoreboard. The Stars were batting in the top of the ninth, with one out and a runner on second base. Joe Nash, the pitcher, had dropped his warmup jacket on the ground and was ready to bat.

"Hey, Joe," Loren heard himself yelling. "Wait a minute." Clutching the first bat he could reach, he lunged up the dugout steps and hurried onto the field. He could hear murmuring in the stands from the crowd that half-filled the grandstand.

Nash looked curiously at Loren. "Whut's th' matter, Temple?" he asked.

"Rand said I was to bat for you," Loren lied. "He wants Red to throw the final frame."

Joe hesitated, as if disposed to argue. Red Parrish drifted over from the third base coach's box. "Whut's up? he growled.

"Rand got sick," Loren declared. "Too much whiskey. Before he left the dugout, he told me I was to pinch hit for Joe and you were to pitch the ninth."

"Yeah, it's 'bout time," said Parrish. "Joey, yew coach third base an' Ah'll warm up. 'Course we ain't gonna git two runs, nohow," he added sourly.

Joe took Red's place in the third base coach's box, while the home plate umpire yelled: "Stop stallin', ladies. Let's git this game ovah wit'."

Loren took his bludgeon up to home plate. As he stepped into the batter's box, he heard Feet's familiar voice behind his right hip.

"Whut happened t' yew, Yank? Ah'd have thought yew'd be th' big dawg amongst this buncha bushers. Whar yew been?"

Trying to ignore his former teammate, and trying not to look at Masher down at first base, or at Ham chewing his cud at third, or at Bobo scooping up dirt with his big shovel hands at short, Loren rapped his bat on the far edge of home plate and concentrated on the motion of tall, rawhide-tough A. C. Doucet, who was stretching his long arms high above his cap, the ball concealed in his worn glove, his eyes narrowing as he glowered at his former teammate crouched in the batter's box.

Loren felt his muscles quivering. He felt weak, as if he could hardly lift the bat, much less drive the ball for any distance. As he struggled to relax, he watched A. C. drop both hands to his belt buckle, take a quick look at the base runner on second, lift his left foot, and launch the ball with a whip-like motion toward his catcher. Before Loren could move, the ball was in Feets' mitt, and the umpire was bellowing "streee-ike wunn!"

Feets laughed mockingly. "Too fast fer yew, Yank?" he inquired. "Yew wan' Ah should signal fer th' change-up? Jus' uh favor fer an ol' pal, huh?"

Loren knew that even as Feets chattered to the batter he was planning the next pitch and flashing a series of signs designed to keep the runner on second from ascertaining that A. C. was about to throw another fast ball. Glancing toward third base, he saw Ham creeping forward, almost onto the grass. It was his standard tactic against reputedly weak hitters, designed to compensate for his slowness afoot in case the ball was topped or bunted in his direction. If he could catch A. C.'s heater squarely, Loren thought, he could easily drive it past Ham before he could get his glove up to grab it. Grimly, Loren edged forward in the batter's box, practically standing on home plate, digging his spikes into the dirt to get leverage, while he gripped his bat down at the knob so tightly that sweat seemed to ooze between his fingers.

As Loren expected, A. C. fed him an inside fast ball. He concentrated on swinging smoothly, not lunging but bringing the bat around with a compact stroke, hoping to gain power from his wrists as they snapped the stick through the strike zone. The tingle in his arms as he completed the arc of his swing told him that he had met the sphere squarely. The action on the field told him where it had gone.

The runner had his head down and was racing toward third base, being waved around by Joe; and Ham's back was turned as he looked out to where Slick Bangwell was racing toward the left field corner. As Loren scampered toward first, he could not resist the temptation to try to follow the flight of the ball. Finally he located a white spot dropping toward the wall behind Slick, but hooking toward the foul line.

Taking his eyes off the ball in order not to miss first base, he looked out again as soon as his foot had thumped chalk dust from that way station, but the ball had vanished. Apparently, from Slick's dejected posture, it had cleared the fence. At last he had homered! He stumbled slightly in the basepath as he tasted triumph. Then his elation vaporized as he heard the home plate umpire shout: "Foul ball; foul ball!"

Loren's brilliant blast was no more than a long strike.

When he returned to home plate to try again, Feets overflowed with false sympathy. "Too bad, Yank, ol' boy," he crowed. "Yew wuz almos' uh hero. Now yore gonna be uh goat. Tough luck, guy."

Loren knew what was coming. He tried not to show fear. When the bean ball came straight at the bill of his cap, he leaned back from the plate, thrusting the end of his bat into the dirt to keep A. C. from having the satisfaction of seeing him fall to the ground. "Ball one!" shouted the umpire.

Loren could not predict the next pitch. He recalled that A. C. would often follow a bean ball with a round house curve that would appear to start inside, but after driving the hitter back off the plate would dart over the inside corner for a humiliating strike. But the thought flashed into Loren's mind: not this time. For A. C. was an egotist who would want to dispose of this particular batter with flare. He was especially proud of his illegal spit ball, an ideal pitch for the current situation.

Loren watched A. C. closely to see if he moved his hands anywhere near his mouth. Instead, he seemed to be rubbing the ball around inside his glove, where he had at times in the past smeared some grease that could be used to shine one side of the ball and thus provide the means of throwing a sharp drop.

Sneaking a quick look toward third base, Loren noticed that Ham, aware that there were two strikes on the hitter, had retreated well behind the bag. It was time to gamble.

The pitch came in waist high and began to drop sharply. But Loren was prepared. He had crept forward in the batter's box and let his war club droop loosely in his fingers, using only his left hand to thrust the wood at the hurtling sphere. Dropping off the deadened bat with a dull clop, A. C.'s shine ball trickled along the third base line, three feet fair. Caught back on his heels, Ham was helpless. And A. C. had been carried off balance toward first base by his follow-through, so he too was unable to field the bunt. It was Feets who finally chased it down, while the runner slid safely into third base, and Loren crossed first without a throw.

The next batter was Sanchez. Bobo and the second baseman both drifted closer to the center of the diamond at double play depth, mouthing signals to each other behind their gloves. Loren knew Feets would call for a low curve ball, hoping to get the grounder that would end the contest with a twin killing. Tugging on the bill of his cap with his right hand and then touching his left ear with his left hand, Loren flashed the steal sign to the third base coach. With a frown of annoyance, Joe swiped his right hand across the "Stars" lettering on the front of his uniform, "wiping off" the sign. At once, Loren flashed it again.

With a shrug, Joe passed it on to the batter. Just in time. A. C. was already in his windup. Now the little Mexican spread out his stance and took a wild swing to try to bother the Scorpion catcher, as Loren sprinted for second base. "Steal," he heard Bobo yell; and he knew the ape man was on his way to crouch over the base, glove ready for Feets' throw.

With dismay Loren saw that a perfect peg from the catcher had beaten him to the bag by at least six feet. Nevertheless, he hurled himself forward in a vicious hook slide directly into Bobo's tag. Kicking out with the toe of his left foot, he dislodged the ball from the shortstop's glove and onto the ground, far enough away for the base umpire to see it and shout "Safe!"

The other baserunner having scored on Loren's steal, the score was now 5-4 and there was still only one out. Sanchez, however, proceeded to strike out on two shine balls. With the center fielder, a weak hitter, coming up, the rally was in jeopardy. Loren decided to force additional action on the base paths. Taking a dangerously long lead off second base, he tried to induce the Scorpions to call a pickoff play. He watched Feets, and was elated to see the catcher, after flashing a sequence of signs to A. C., briefly drop his right knee to the ground—the signal Loren wanted.

Feets caught the pitchout far enough outside so that the hitter could not have reached it with a fifty-inch stick, but not so far away that he had to delay his snap throw to second base. Again his peg was perfect.

But Loren was not, as expected, scrambling frantically back to the bag. Waiting only long enough to make sure Feets was throwing through, he took off for third base. Knowing that the second baseman would be taking Feets' throw and immediately redirecting it toward Ham at third, Loren ran high, keeping directly in the baseline, hoping that the relay would hit him in his back, not his head. Instead, the ball was thrown high and wide, so that Ham had to leave his base and stretch his pudgy body well into the outfield to reach it. In order to concentrate on snaring it in the webbing of his glove, he had lost sight of Loren, who did not slide but instead hit third base with his left foot on the slope of the inside corner as he headed for home.

Jumping a prone photographer, who had crouched in the baseline to snap an action photo of the expected play at third, and ignoring the screams of Joe Nash—"No, no; come back!"—Loren made for the plate. His imagination pictured Ham turning toward the infield, his eyes bugging as he saw Loren already halfway home, and then making a hurried throw that, with luck, would be off line. Which it was. Feets, trying to block the plate, lunged toward first base to glove Ham's errant throw, enabling Loren to dive headfirst past the catcher and beat the tag by a hair. The umpire's shout of "Safe" could be heard above the excited roar of the crowd, even to the far corners of the stadium.

The score was tied. Loren had dug into the recesses of his memory and reconstructed one of the tricks that the master baserunner of the old Detroit Tigers, Ty Cobb, had liked to play on third basemen in the early years of the century. As for the headlong slide home, that had come from watching Pete Reiser, the daredevil outfielder of the Brooklyn Dodgers. But the cheers of the crowd were all for Loren.

Sitting in the dugout, breathing hard, he savored the compliments of his teammates. "Nice goin', fella," "Way t' go, guy." "Dat took guts; didn' look like yew hadda chance." And A. C., shaken by seeing two runs scored without a hit, walked the next two batters. Then, with the winning run on second base, the Scorpion hurler took a couple of deep breaths and got Al Robicheaux, the Stars' best hitter, to loft a high popup to Masher, retiring the side.

Red Parrish ambled in from the bull pen to pitch the last half of the ninth inning for the visitors. As Dick Peters started out to right field, Loren called him back and told him that Rand had ordered Loren to take over that position. Peters looked around for Rand. Not seeing the manager, he sat down without questioning the command.

In right field Loren watched Duke Daniel blast the first pitch so high in the air that it passed beyond the range of the arc lights into pitch blackness. Fortunately it was hit almost straight up, so there was plenty of time for the infielders to locate it, and for Sanchez, after staggering around and almost tripping over a fielder's glove left behind second base, to make a desperate lunge and capture it in the webbing of his glove.

A.C. then struck out on three curve balls, the last one a foot outside. It looked as if the game might go into extra innings. But the new second baseman, Cope, slashed Red's first pitch safely over second base, and Feets took an inside pitch on his left thigh for a free pass. With the winning run halfway home and Bobo up, the situation looked bad. Loren moved over toward center field for the pull hitter.

After ostentatiously tugging at his crotch, Bobo ignored an outside curve and then lunged at the next offering, lining it over the second baseman's head. Loren knew that with two out Cope would be heading for home with the crack of the bat and that it would take a perfect throw to cut him down. He raced toward short center field, timing his interception of the ball so that he could backhand it at the top of its second bounce, and he used his forward motion to get extra force into his throw. It barely cleared the pitcher's mound and disappeared into the catcher's mitt about a foot above home plate on the third base edge. Cope slid right into it. The catcher held the ball and the side was out. The Stars would have another turn at bat.

In the tenth the visitors hit three grounders in a row. The first two were easy outs, but the third one took an erratic hop and glanced off Bobo's glove onto the outfield grass. It was scored a base hit. Then the number eight hitter struck out on a shine ball that broke down so sharply that it hit on the plate and bounced up over Feets' shoulder and past the umpire to roll all the way to the backstop. Loren's yells from the on-deck circle sped the startled batter safely to first base, while the runner was content to stop at second. And Loren was up.

He felt relaxed and confident. He had forgotten about the unconscious manager in the locker room, and had even forgotten his intense desire to prove that Bubba Guidry and old Rand had both erred in benching him. He knew A.C. would start him off with what was left of his fast ball and he yearned for it.

This time he would not bunt or try for a cheap Texas leaguer over the infield. No tactics. Just swing hard and give it a ride.

The result was a rope that exploded off his bat, heading for the left field corner. Ham speared it entirely by instinct, throwing up his glove in self protection, flinching from the impact, and involuntarily staggering back a step. But he held on. Loren was out. No heroics this time.

As he trotted out to right field, Loren heard the sound of static on the public address system, and then a deep voice say: "Ladies an' Gentlemen. Ah regret t' tell yew that it's twenty-fi' minutes pas' 'leven an' th' law prohibits usin' this stadium after midnight on Sat'day. If'n th' Scorpions fail t' score in their nex' at bat, th' game'll end in uh tie. Please try t' leave th' stadium afore twelve o'clock, at which time th' lights'll be turned off. Thank yew an' good night."

Boos and groans from the crowd were few. Almost everyone had had enough. Although a tie would fail to determine the local champion, that could be settled another time. Throughout the stands people began moving toward the exits.

When Red Parish walked Masher to start the bottom of the tenth, Loren yelled encouragement. "Let him hit it, Babe; you're the one, big guy; let's get two..." His voice sounded strange in the nearly silent stadium.

Slick Bangwell hammered Red's second pitch over the left field wall. The ball was hit so hard that there was never any doubt of its destination. Loren watched it disappear into the darkness, shook his head sadly, and trotted after his teammates toward the dugout. As he stepped down into it he looked up and saw his father escorting his mother up some steps toward an exit sign, with his brother close behind. He would have waved but their backs were turned toward him.

When Loren reached the locker room, several of the Stars had found Rand and propped him up on a bench. The manager kept asking: "Whut hoppened?" He had apparently forgotten why he went to the locker room and seemed to have no curiosity about how the game had gone. No one bothered to tell him.

Loren hurriedly shed his uniform and left it in a pile on the floor. Omitting a shower, and stuffing his spikes, glove, socks, jockstrap, and sliding pads into his old valise, he silently dressed, picked up his bat, muttered "nice game" to several of the other players, and made his escape.

His parents and Tommy were waiting outside. "Too bad about that last at-bat," said Adam. "You almost had a key hit."

"They weren't going to let you play, were they?" asked Nan.

"No."

"What changed their minds?"

"It's complicated. Let's go home. I'm really tired."

CHAPTER 22
FALL FOLLIES

Autumn. The stifling heat began to dissipate as the sun sank in the southern sky. The drop in temperature, however, did little to ease the impact of the oppressive ozone upon the lungs and hearts of Tocquevillians. The worst was when the gulf breezes blew the acrid yellow fumes rising from nearby refineries directly into the city, causing wrinkled noses and stuffed-up sinuses and flutters in the bosom of Loren's mother that sent her gasping to her bed, where she lay, eyes shut, until they subsided.

In Oak Grove where the spacious homes of the wealthy nestled amid the gray beards of Spanish moss dangling from the spreading branches of massive trees, lawn sprinklers ran day and night, and the scent of moist flowers and freshly cut grass fortified the air against the encroachments of refinery fumes. Elsewhere in Tocqueville, people treated the pervasive pollution as unavoidable, resigned themselves to whatever occupations life had thrust upon them, and eagerly sought diversion in the form of Friday night high school football, which as a local attraction rivaled Sunday morning church. Under the bright lights of packed stadiums, uplifted by prayer and the strident strains of loud band music, yelling and bobbing up and down as if possessed, they could temporarily escape the ache of their deep-down desperation.

On Saturday morning, October 2, having stayed overtime at the newspaper to file brief accounts of the local Friday night football games, Loren slept late. He wondered if he could persuade his Mom to flat-top his curly mop of hair like most of the other boys at Tocqueville High School. Unlikely. She liked it long—liked to run her fingers through it, which sometimes led to an admonition to use shampoo the next time he showered. "Confidentially," she would inform him in a stage whisper, "your scalp stinks. You don't want to offend Mary Beth, do you?"

Today after completing his outdoor chores, he would use Lifeboy. He wished he could get rid of the pimples that persistently pocked his face, spotted his shoulders, and itched in the middle of his back where he could not reach them. The more he popped his pores onto the bathroom mirror, the more the diminutive puddings reappeared. He wished he could grow a beard. Enviously he had watched his father strop his sharp straight razor, swirl a little round brush in a pot of Burma Shave, perhaps recall familiar roadside advertisements ("Listen birds/These signs cost money/ So sit a while/ But don't get funny"), and then, after smearing the lower part of his face with the stuff, lean over the sink to scrape the dark stubble from his cheeks and chin. Disconsolately Loren had fingered his own facial hair, as soft as the blond filaments on his forearms, and had yearned for the time when he, too, would require a daily shave.

For Loren's new friend, Tony Sisti, scraping off his chin bristles was already as much of a morning ritual as slicking back his black hair with shiny grease. Loren had encountered Tony at his first P.E. class. Wearing only sweat-soaked shorts, the hairy little guy had been huffing and puffing through a series of flips and feats of body balancing that seemed to strain every muscle to the utmost. He looked fearless and primitive. Shortly after they met he confided in Loren that he intended to become a chemical engineer and make "big bucks." He carried a foot-long slide rule everywhere and disappeared after school to take part in body-building sessions or to participate in something he called "adagio." On weekends, he told Loren proudly, he helped take care of his "daddy's bidness." Since his "daddy" was a member of the notorious Sisti family, reputedly tied in with New Orleans mobsters, Loren was curious about what "bidness," exactly, Tony's father conducted.

When their gym class played flag football, Tony always managed to get himself chosen to Loren's team. He constantly asked about life in the "nawth," which he apparently envisioned as one vast urban ghetto. His effusive enthusiasm, however, allowed Loren little opportunity for more than monosyllables in response to Tony's endless questions.

At times Tony's company was embarrassing. In the school hallways he was prone to stare boldly at passing girls and exclaim appreciatively, when his goggling eyes finally fixed on one with impressive equipment: "Now, dat's uh real fine li'l ass!" Loren would blush and shush and wish he was elsewhere. "She kin put her slippers under mah bed enny time," or "Lookit dat beautiful butt!," Tony would yap, oblivious to the heads turning all around him.

Tony's obsession with the derrieres of decorative damsels, apparently excluding any interest in their other attributes, seemed wonderfully weird. He spoke to Loren of creases, cracks, and crannies; of places bony and buttery; of hidden recesses moist and mobile. Loren found himself trying to visualize such previously unimagined terrain, but his conjectures, given his inability to lay eyes on the empirical evidence, were frustratingly vague.

When he asked Tony whether his extroverted expressions of appreciation weren't extremely hypothetical, given the barriers of clothing between his salacious scrutiny and his ostensible objective, the lascivious little guy grinned and replied: "Ah know whut Ah'm talkin' 'bout. Enny dancer knows how wimmen are made an' when an' whar t' touch 'em."

A dancer? Tony? Loren said: "I thought you were a gymnast."

"An' uh body builder. .But Ah also do adagio." He proudly clenched both his fists and popped out the muscles in his upper arms until they seemed about to burst the seams in his short-sleeved shirt.

"What's ad-dodge-ee-o?"

"Why don' yew cum see fer yoreself? We practice at th' YMCA Saturday evenins' at seven an' Sundays at three."

Loren mulled over the invitation. He knew he would be unable to date Mary Beth on Sunday, which was the day her singing society, the "Lieder Lovelies," had their weekly rehearsals. So he said: "Where is the Y?"

"Down on Front Street, next t' th' Brendon Hotel. Looks like uh warehouse. Yew can't miss it."

"I'll try to be there at three on Sunday," said Loren.

* * *

Neil Gregory, who soon became an even closer friend than Tony, was his opposite. Tall and thin, shy and silent, he was studious without being intellectual. Loren discovered that he was quietly competent about anything that had to do with machines, particularly automobiles.

Loren first encountered Neil one day after school when he was trying unsuccessfully to start Shaky, worried that he would be late for work at the newspaper office if he couldn't get the damn car to run. Leaning over a recalcitrant engine under a gaping hood, wondering which wire did what, he heard a soft voice at his elbow say: "Didja check yore gas supply?"

Loren had not bought gas in over a week, but did not think that could be the problem. "No," he said, "but surely that's not what's wrong."

The slender stranger peered into the driver's compartment to look at the dashboard and asked: "Gas gauge broken?"

"Seems to be," answered Loren. "Makes it hard to know when to buy some."

"Heah's whut yew kin do," said the stranger. Digging in a pocket and taking out a piece of white string, he reached into a second pocket and found there a steel nut, which he tied to the string. Then he unscrewed the gas cap and dropped the nut down inside. After a couple of seconds he withdrew it and pointed to the string. "See," he said, pointing to the string, which was damp only in the vicinity of the nut. "Yore outa gas. Wait."

He ambled over to a restored model A Ford, a beautiful little car with gleaming chrome and polished black paint. Backing his car over next to Shaky, he emerged holding a long rubber tube, which he inserted in his own gas tank. Taking the free end into his mouth he sucked with his eyes closed and his cheeks ballooned out, until with a grunt of disgust he pinched off the end of the tube with his thumb and forefinger, spat twice on the ground, and dropped the open end into Shaky's gas tank. Immediately Loren could hear bubbling, signifying that he was getting gas.

"It's called uh siphon," said the good Samaritan. "Yew don' evah wanna swallow gas, though; it's poison. Mah name's Neil Gregory."

"Loren Temple. I can't thank you enough. I have only a few minutes left to get to my night job. Tell me where and when, and I'll bring you a can of gas."

"Not necessary," said Neil, disengaging the siphon. "That should hold yew fer uh day or two."

"Please," said Loren. "I always pay my debts. Consider it another favor."

"All right. Ah live at 317 Galloway Road. Ah'll be home Saturday afternoon, if'n yew wanna drop by." He looked appraisingly at Shaky. "Maybe we could give this heap uh tuneup."

"Are you a mechanic?" asked Loren.

"Jus' like t' tinker uh little. Maybe Ah'll see yew on Saturday."

* * *

Loren couldn't resist Neil's invitation. Having completed his Saturday morning chores, he drove to the western end of town where he located the Gregory residence nestled in a clump of trees at the end of a long rutted lane. An old tire hung from a large limb to serve as a swing, and beyond it, shielded from the distant neighbors by some shrubbery, three old cars rested next to a small shed which seemed to serve as a workshop.

Spotting a pair of sneakers wiggling under the edge of one of the vehicles, Loren called Neils' name, which elicited grunts and squirms. Eventually Neil emerged, wearing dungarees, a dirty shirt, and a greasy grin. At once he set aside the gallon can of gasoline that Loren had brought him and leaned into Shaky's engine compartment, twisting wrenches on rusty nuts and tugging at writhing wires. As he worked he exuded humms and ahhs from pursed lips under a pallid brow.

"What are you doing?" asked Loren.

"Checkin' yore spark plugs... Yeah. Jus' as Ah thought. Looky here." Neil held out a piece of porcelain topped by a carbon-coated wire. "It's uh wonder that th' thang runs at all."

He disappeared into his shed and Loren heard thumping and clattering. Soon Neil emerged, holding six replacement plugs in greasy hands. "Ah foun' th' right size," he exulted. He bumped around some more under the hood. Then, wiping his hands on an oily rag, he said: "That does it. Start 'er up."

Loren climbed in, turned the key, and pressed the starter button with his left toe. The engine promptly roared with a resonance Loren had not previously heard. Clearly, Neil knew cars.

"Say," he ventured, "do you know anything about steering mechanisms?"

"Whut yew mean?"

"I'm having trouble going around corners. Making turns."

"When did yew las' have th' car lubricated?"

"What's that?"

Neil stared at Loren. Then he said with a faint smile. "Tell yew whut. Take ol' Shaky t' uh filing station wit' uh grease rack—there's uh good one on Austin Avenue not far from th' high school—an' tell 'em t' give 'er uh grease job, which'll cost yew uh couple'a bucks. Yew prolly oughta ask 'em t' change th' oil, too. Uh buck an' uh half. Ah'd do it fer yew, but Ah'm fresh outa thirty weight."

Loren did not know what Neil meant by "thirty weight," but the advice sounded good. So, after arranging a double date with Neil and his girl friend for the following weekend, he drove directly to the recommended gas station and asked the attendant to give him the works. Wondrous strange was the eight-inch thick pillar that rose resolutely up out of the concrete floor to eyeball height holding the heaviness of Loren's singular sedan, while a grouchy guy with a heavy hose thrust its tip here and there around the front axle, knocking crusted mud off little metal nipples, and to the sound of compressed air popping in a nearby pump, fed it grease. "Ah nevah seen uh car so dry," he groused. "Ah oughta charge yew double fer th' lubricant."

He had a similar complaint about the waste oil that he drained from under the engine into a rusty bucket. "Gawd, Ah think yew got deposits in thar from th' dust storms of th' thirties," he said. "Ah could grow me some vegetables in that stuff. Yew better let me change yore filter, too. Ah imagine it's nearly stopped up."

Loren got out of there minus almost eight dollars, but with a new appreciation of automotive maintenance, something about which his father had failed to provide any instruction. Driving home, he discovered that grease made a difference. What had formerly been stubborn steering now responded smoothly to his insistent grip, so much so that when he tried his first turn, the right front tire crashed into a curb. Getting out to inspect the damage, Loren was pleased to see none. Except for a soft brake pedal and the inconvenient shimmy, Shaky now seemed serviceable. Maybe Neil could show him how to repair the brakes and alleviate the shimmy.

* * *

During Loren's post-midnight tennis match on Sunday morning, Buzz resumed his usual political palaver, encouraged by Loren's increasing interest in the subject. On the previous Friday evening, Senator-elect Russell Long of Louisiana had delivered an address at a Tocqueville civic club, which was quoted approvingly in the next day's *Endeavor*. The "Young Kingfish" had proposed a program of federal aid for education, "without strings attached to interfere with the southerner's way of life." When Loren brought this to Buzz's attention, his tennis partner sneered scornfully. Russell Long was "jus' like his daddy," Buzz declared. Better educated, less ruthless, maybe, but nevertheless a fascist.

The same epithet could be used accurately to describe the editor of the *Endeavor*, Loren declared. Hatton had urged his readers to vote for Dewey for President because, he said, President Truman favored "shackling private enterprise and individual freedom," and appealed only to "the passions of fear and hatred." To Hatton, such passions were apparently absent in the deliberations of the Republican-dominated House Un-American Activities Committee. The editor endorsed the demand of its acting chairman (the actual chairman having recently been indicted by a federal grand jury for corruption) for new laws to permit jailing "thousands of American communists" who were allegedly aiding foreign spies to steal atomic secrets and deliver them to the USSR under the noses of officials in the Truman administration.

But Buzz was less interested in the HUAC and its Tocqueville admirers than he was in the outcome of the Texas senatorial contest. Lawyers for Coke Stevenson had petitioned the U.S. Supreme Court to reverse a recent ruling by one of its justices, Hugo Black, that ordered Lyndon Johnson's name to be placed on all November ballots in Texas as the Democratic nominee for the U.S. Senate. Another few days would determine whether Black's order would stand.

The only topic of greater interest to Loren than politics was baseball. Switching the conversation to that subject, he sought sympathy from his companion for the Chicago Cubs, who had finished the season in the cellar for only the second time in their history, while the Boston Braves had easily won the National League pennant. Meanwhile, the Boston Red Sox, pursuing an all-Beantown World Series, trailed the Cleveland Indians by one game, with but a single day left in the American League season.

The hapless Cubs, Buzz consoled Loren, "will rise again." But not with pitchers like Dutch McCall, who had set a team record by losing thirteen straight games. The Bruins were currently as ineffectual as the Tocqueville High School football team, which had lost its third consecutive game, this one by a score of 28-0.

Loren and Buzz sat on the edge of the concrete tennis court slapping at mosquitoes for fully forty-five minutes, trading observations on the state of the western world and big league baseball, before finally switching on the overhead lights to play tennis. While they were still engaged in pre-game practice, Loren impulsively said: "By the way, do you remember that back in August I mentioned a friend of mine who had taken some photos of someone possibly committing a crime?"

"Yeah," said Buzz, whopping a forehand drive with so much topspin that Loren dubbed it into the net. "Whut about 'im?"

"Did I say it was a 'him'? Well, anyway, the photos still haven't surfaced, but this friend now thinks he or she can identify both people involved, even without the pictures."

"How so?"

"Just a lot of little things that form a pattern."

"But still supposition, right? No hard evidence?"

"I suppose so."

"If'n yore askin' whether yore friend oughta go t' th' po-lice wit' whut he—or she—supposes happened, Ah think that if'n Ah were that person Ah would wait t' see whether th' photos turned up. See whut they show; then decide. Th' po-lice kin be purty impatient wit' people who go t' 'em wit' unverifiable speculations 'bout uh supposed crime. They're likely t' question th' motives of th' informant, an' sometimes even consider such uh person uh possible perpetrator. Ah'd let th' matter rest fer now. Les play."

Walking to the backstop at his end of the court, Buzz stripped off his sweater. As he picked up his racket and two fuzzy new balls and prepared to serve, an inscription rippling in green across his white tee shirt read: "SHS Tennis, 1935."

Under the lights, Loren struggled to compete. He was gradually improving, and a dozen games went to duce before the match ended 6-0, 6-2, but Buzz was clearly his superior in all aspects of the game, running his young opponent ragged with deft drives into the corners and with serves sometimes slammed, sometimes sliced, but always difficult to return.

During the second set, Loren won his first serve with a couple of thundering aces down the middle and then actually broke Buzz's serve when the latter uncharacteristically netted a couple of easy returns. With a 2-1 score Loren, encouraged, flipped the ball overhead, hoping for another ace, only to abort his swing when the lights suddenly clicked off, leaving him in total darkness. Fumbling in the shallow pocket of his shorts for a quarter, he felt the coin drop from his fingers and bounce off his sneaker. Drat, he thought, bending over to retrieve it.

Just then there was a sound like a tree branch snapping, and Loren heard a hiss near his head. Frightened, he located the coin and stumbled through the darkness to the light meter. As light once again flooded the court, Loren saw Buzz leaning over his valise. Turning, he held a can of new tennis balls in one hand. "Let's try these," he suggested. "Th' ones we've been usin' are uh bit bare."

"O. K.," replied Loren. "Say, did you hear a strange sound when the lights were off?"

"No."

"Kind of like a loud pop?"

"Ah didn' hear anythang'."

"Hmm." Loren fought the thought that Buzz might have had something in his valise besides new balls—something that he could earlier have transferred from the glove compartment of his truck. As far as Loren knew, hissing snakes did not fly around in the dark, nor did he believe Buzz's hearing so bad that he had not heard the popping sound. Maybe this middle-of-the-night tennis wasn't a good idea. But Buzz...! Loren could hardly imagine danger in that direction. There must be some other explanation.

* * *

At school the following Monday, Loren encountered Tony Sisti in the hall. Slapping Loren familiarly on the back, Tony suggested that he and his current girl friend, whom he described as an adagio dancer with a "cute li'l ass," double date with Loren and Mary Beth at the THS football game on Friday evening. "I can't," said Loren. "I have to work at the newspaper."

"Well, whut 'bout takin' in uh show on Saturday?" inquired Tony.

"I'd like to," responded Loren, "but I've already set up a double date with another couple. Actually," he continued thoughtfully, "I've been having second thoughts about that engagement, too. I've been feeling really tired lately. Schoolwork, the night job, and midnight tennis—it all seems too much."

"Midnight tennis? Who's idea is that?"

"Buzz's." At Tony's puzzled look, Loren added: "Sam Howell. You probably don't know him. Actually, he works for your father."

Tony said: "Howell... Yeah. Ah know who yore talkin' 'bout. Tough guy. An enforcer."

"Buzz?"

"Sure. Whut mah Daddy calls uh problem solver. Came outa th' war wit' uh buncha medals. Served in Europe wit' th' British commandos behin' German lines. Mah Daddy checked on 'im. Knows how t' kill people wit' his bare hands."

"Wow!"

"Afore he went t' work fer Sisti an' Sampson, he wuz over in New Orleans wit' th' mob. Hadda gal; uh red head; some kinda cabaret dancer. They were gonna git hitched, but somethin' happened an' they didn't. Mah Daddy says Buzz won' talk 'bout it. He came t' Tocqueville right after they broke up."

"I didn't know..." Several troubling thoughts flashed through Loren's mind. Mrs. Kaplan had been a dancer in New Orleans before she married her medical man. Could she and her former lover have secretly kept their relationship alive? Could Buzz have been her accomplice the night that Dr. Kaplan died? But Loren was fairly sure that person had shaved legs, like a ballplayer who taped them regularly, and Buzz's legs were hairy. However, considering the nature of this new information, Loren decided that to continue confiding in his tennis partner—even to continue their tennis dates—might be too great a risk.

As soon as school let out on Friday, he phoned the S & S Company to leave a message for Buzz. He had a bad cold, he said; hence he would be unable to play tennis that weekend. He felt guilty about lying to Buzz, who had always appeared to be a protective friend, but the recent occurence on the darkened tennis court was too troubling to ignore. Better safe than sorry.

On Saturday, just as the evening grew gloomy, he steered Shaky, with Neil and his girl friend Sally Spencer in the back seat and Mary Beth in front, into a choice spot near the front of the Crystal drive-in theatre located off the Port Amberley highway. As he hooked the speaker over the driver's side window, he heard Popeye advise Wimpy to abandon burgers and eat spinach instead. Since his companions didn't want popcorn or Coke, Loren decided to skip the concession stand. The car was cozy and the blackness around them was dense. Huge figures of western gun slingers flickered on the screen, firing their weapons endlessly without reloading.

Loren hoped to get in some serious smooching. But Sally was in a chatty mood, and Mary Beth kept the girlish gossip going. Disappointed, Loren concentrated on the movie. When Sally stopped talking to slap a mosquito and ask what Randolph Scott was doing now, Loren thought, resentfully: Scott isn't the only one who's randy. Next time he and Mary Beth came to the Crystal, they would come alone. When the movie ended, Loren, sulking, started to drive away, only to hear Mary Beth ask: "Aren't yew goin' t' unhook th' speaker?"

"Oh." Shaking his head at his stupidity, he returned the device to its proper place; then pulled into a line of vehicles exiting the theatre.

"That wuz fun," said Mary Beth, after they had dropped off Sally and Nile at their homes.

"Yeah," said Loren.

"Yew don' soun' very enthusiastic," she observed.

"I guess I'm selfish, wanting you all to myself," he admitted.

"That's sweet," she said. "We're alone now; so let's drive uh while an' look at th' moon."

At once Loren's mood lightened. Looking up through the windshield at the great glowing globe of the harvest moon, he swung Shaky around, pointing westward toward Houston and accelerated to top speed, almost forty miles per hour. The car's heaterless interior became chilly as a night wind whistled through Loren's window, and Mary Beth, shivering, slid over beside him; whereupon he extended his right arm around her shoulders, touching lightly at first; then tightening his grip until his hand rested just below her bosom. She let her curly head drop onto his shoulder.

On the verge of chancing an additional liberty, Loren hesitated when he became suddenly conscious of a growing glare in his rear view window. It appeared to come from a motorcycle or a car with only one working headlamp, and it was rapidly shortening the distance between the two vehicles. Soon it was virtually attached to his rear bumper. Mary Beth sensed his concern and turned to see what was behind them.

"Uh one-eyed car!" she exclaimed. "Aren't we lucky."

"Why?" asked Loren.

"Surely yew've heard th' ol' saying, 'one-eye means this; it's time fer uh kiss.'"

"No… But I think its a great idea."

Clutching the steering wheel tightly with his left hand, Loren turned toward her upturned face, smooth and pale in the soft moonlight. Her moist lips and tightly shut eyes signified acceptance, erasing his irresolution.

As his own eyes closed, and he felt her breath mingling with his, there came suddenly a terrific jolt that almost wrenched the steering wheel from his hand and slammed his shoulders and Mary Beth's hard against the seat back. Shaky had been bashed from behind.

Looking in the mirror, Loren saw the one-eyed vehicle, clearly the cause of the crash, suddenly swing out to the left and move abreast of Shaky, its driver hunched behind a dirty window. Loren could now see that it was not a car but a pickup truck. It lurched abruptly toward Shaky, its front fender grinding against purple paint, its mass moving Loren's car inexorably toward a deep roadside ditch. Simultaneously, another vehicle emerged from a side road directly ahead and turned toward them, only a few yards away.

Loren brought his right foot down upon Shaky's brake pedal with all the force he could summon, while with the fingers of his right hand he grabbed the back of Mary Beth's collar to prevent her from being thrown forward into the windshield. At first the brake did not engage; then came a grinding sound, a loud screech, and a smell of burning rubber, as the one-eyed pickup hurtled past, veering to the right as its driver averted a head-on crash, while the third vehicle also swerved to its right to the edge of the pavement.

"Mah Gawd!" exclaimed Mary Beth. "That idiot coulda killed us!"

"That may have been his intention," said Loren grimly, his trembling hands tightly gripping the steering wheel.

"Whadaya mean? He rammed us on purpose?"

"Possibly."

"Why?"

"Someone doesn't like me. That's all I can figure."

"Who is it? Can't yew have him arrested?"

"Not without proof. Right now, all I know is that a pickup truck, make and model unknown, license plate numbers unseen, driver unidentified, with a right headlight not working, and maybe a bit of purple paint rubbed into its right front fender, tried to run us off the highway. Not a lot to go on."

"Whut are yew goin' t' do?"

"First—take you home. Then I'm going to…" He hesitated, realizing that he couldn't check the vehicles of the two people he most suspected, Bubba and Buzz, because he had no idea where to find either one. Despite his air of intimacy, Buzz had never revealed to Loren where he lived. And Bubba, since his divorce, had supposedly left town. Therefore all Loren could tell Mary Beth was that he intended to "check on some things."

"Ah'm worried, Loren," she said. "Should yew be goin' out after dark at all, while this person is at large?"

"I'm not going to give up my job at the paper," Loren asserted. "It's valuable experience. I'll keep an eye out for trouble. And we can stay near other people when we're together and stay off lonely highways."

"Aren't yew goin' t' tell yore parents?"

"Not now. For one thing, my mother would worry. And her health is not good. I've got to handle this business myself. So I'd appreciate it if you'd keep what happened tonight to yourself. Treat it as an accident, which it may have been."

"Yew don' believe that."

"Truthfully," said Loren as he drove into Mary Beth's driveway, "I don't know. One thing I do know is that you owe me something."

Unwilling to wait for Loren to open the car door for her, Mary Beth had already alighted. She stepped back up on the running board and asked, pretending ignorance: "Owe yew whut?"

"A smooch. A one-eyed reward. It was your idea."

She smiled. "So it wuz. Tell yew whut. Since mah mother is watchin' us from th' kitchen window—Ah see her peekin' 'round th' blind—Ah'll save yew two fer next weekend."

"I'll settle for that. Don't catch a cold."

"Funny guy." Shielded temporarily from the kitchen window by a large lilac bush, Mary Beth blew him a kiss. As soon as she stepped up on the porch, someone opened the door to let her in.

* * *

On Sunday morning, the Reverend Pryor delivered an especially excruciating sermon, all the more objectionable to Loren because of the minister's repeated references to the "sins" of the Truman administration. Afterwards, Loren felt a strong desire for solitude. A family dinner in the early afternoon did little to ease his malaise.

Looking at his watch, he realized that the Opera House, a program of classical music carried by a New Orleans radio station, had already begun. Shaky's dashboard radio, he had discovered, could pull in distant stations with much greater clarity than any of the radios in the Temple household. So Loren took refuge in his car. Telling Tommy that he would be home by supper time, he drove aimlessly around the neighborhood. Gradually he felt his tenseness from the scare of the previous evening dissipate, as operatic arias filled the car's interior. He decided to swing by the Guidry apartment and see if Rose was there. Maybe she would tell him where he might find her former husband's truck, so that he could see whether it had purple paint on its right front fender.

Turning onto Cypress Avenue, and spotting the house behind which the two Guidrys had lived together so unhappily, he suddenly swerved Shaky behind a parked car and stopped, rapidly pumping his brake pedal to keep from crashing. Less than one hundred feet ahead, an old black pickup truck was parked against the curb. It was apparently a replacement for the maroon one that Rose had repossessed from Bubba. And there was Bubba himself, standing on the front porch of his former landlord's house, talking with someone inside.

Soon Bubba stepped back, scowling, and returned to his truck, which he drove off in the opposite direction from where Loren was parked. Easing Shaky out from his place of concealment, Loren followed, keeping his distance. He was almost sure that Bubba's truck was the one that had tried to run him off the Houston highway. All he needed to verify his assumption was one good look at its right front fender.

Sunday afternoon traffic was heavy on the streets of Tocqueville and also on the road to Timberland. Nevertheless, Loren was able to keep Bubba in sight as he passed the city limits heading northwest. Suddenly Bubba turned onto a dirt road that meandered through a thick stand of pine trees, the same road, Loren realized, on which the Rand house trailer was located. Slowly he steered Shaky through the lingering dust clouds created by his quarry, keeping well back out of sight.

Before reaching the clearing in which the house trailer was parked, Loren pulled off into an aperture in the undergrowth, concealing Shaky behind some bushes out of sight of the road. Then, refraining with difficulty from slapping at the mosquitoes that swarmed about him, stinging his bare arms and neck, he slipped as silently as he could over the forest floor, heading toward the sounds of people arguing.

Peering from behind a big oak tree near the clearing in which Rand's trailer rested, he saw Bubba standing in front of his truck, clenched fists on his hips and a sneer on his face. He was talking to Rose, who Loren now realized must be old Rand's daughter. She stood expressionless in the trailer's door clad in a voluminous bathrobe, her hands thrust deeply into its pockets.

To loud demands by an insistent Bubba that she move back into their former apartment and "gimme 'nother chance," she responded with a caustic cackle. "Not on yer life," she declared. "Ah tole yew Ah nevah wanted t' see yew again an' Ah meant it. Why don' yew git outa heah afore Ah lose mah temper."

"Whut yew gonna do, call yore Daddy?" asked Bubba with a sneer. "He ain' heah. Ah done seen 'im in town parkin' yore truck in front of Eddie's place. He's prolly stinkin' drunk by now. It's jus' yew an' me, Babe."

"Ah said, git!"

"Come on, now. Not afore Ah enjoy whut Ah ain' had fer quite uh spell." With a growing grin, Bubba advanced toward his ex-wife.

Suddenly a pistol appeared in her left hand and she fired it: once, twice, three times. As the reports echoed around them, both Bubba and Loren jumped. Rose had not shot at Bubba, but had instead put three slugs through the cab of his truck. Loren could see ragged holes—two in the driver's door and one in the windshield, from which cracks radiated like a shiny spider's web.

"Th' next un'll be through yore ugly face," declared Rose, pointing the pistol at Bubba.

"All right," he said, subdued. "If'n yore gonna be nasty 'bout it, Ah'm goin'. Yew-know-who has promised me uh job in New Orleans. Ah'll be goin' thar. But not afore Ah settle up wit' yew, yew bitch. An' yore muffafuggin' daddy."

"Ah oughta shoot yew right now," Rose threatened. "Ah could bury yew in th' woods, an' no one would evah find yew."

"Too bad fer yew," retorted Bubba, "there's someone watchin' us, ovah behin' that tree."

"Whut!" Rose looked in Loren's direction, which gave Bubba a chance to run to his truck. Starting it with a roar, he spun the rear wheels in the soft dirt and made his escape.

Dropping the pistol back into her pocket, Rose directed one more curious glance at the spot in the woods where Loren was breathlessly hiding, and then she shook her head and disappeared inside the trailer.

Carefully Loren tiptoed away from the scene of action. Climbing into Shaky, he started the engine as quietly as he could, backed slowly onto the road, and hightailed it toward home. Behind him a muscular young woman, wearing only shorts and a bra, emerged from the woods and stood staring at the dirt where Shaky had left tire tracks that had not been made by a pickup truck.

CHAPTER 23
THE DANCE

Loren was getting increasingly dispirited. He missed the comforting conversations with Buzz, particularly the ones about baseball. Adam, distracted by his heavy workload at the *Endeavor* and by his growing concern for Nan's worsening health, now had little interest in discussing the national game. During Adam's lifetime, his favorite team, the Chicago Cubs, had finished in the National League's first division no less than thirty-three times and had dropped as low as seventh only twice in forty-seven years. In 1948, however, they had dishonored their heritage and deeply offended Adam by sinking to the bottom of the standings. This had occurred only three years after the Cubs had won their tenth pennant and narrowly lost the World Series to the Detroit Tigers. As if they were now beneath his notice, Adam contemptuously dismissed them as the "Dubs." Even Loren's loyalty was wavering.

As for Tommy, he enjoyed playing catch with Loren but otherwise appeared to have no interest in baseball. Music was his passion, and now that he had joined the THS orchestra, he had time for little else. He had given notice that he would soon stop delivering newspapers, so as to sleep as late as possible before stumbling off to school. He was not a morning person, he asserted, and he needed more time to practice his violin and for good ol' bed.

So Loren brooded alone about the latest baseball news. The Indians had won an exciting pennant playoff game with the Red Sox. Lou Boudreau, the Cleveland manager and star shortstop, had socked a pair of homers to seal the victory. Boudreau had also shrewdly neutralized the left-handed power of the Boston slugger, Ted Williams, by crowding the right side of the stadium with five fielders instead of the usual three, leaving only a third baseman and a single outfielder to cover the vast region from the left field line all the way over to right center. Having thus disposed of one Boston team, the Indians had then defeated the National League Braves in the World Series, four games to two, with their ace, Bob Lemon, winning a pair, and the rookie Negro center fielder, Larry Doby, hitting.318 to lead the champions at bat.

Stan Musial (.376) and Ted Williams (.369) had led their respective leagues in batting, with Musial missing the triple crown (BA, HR and RBI) by a single homer, while Joe DiMaggio had pounded out 39 round trippers and had driven in 155 Yankee baserunners to top the junior circuit in both those categories. Hal Newhouser was still the top hurler in the American League, closely followed by Lemon, Bearden and Feller of the Indians, and Raschi, Lopat and Reynolds of the Yankees. On the mound for the slugging Red Sox, Jack Kramer had managed an 18-5 record, but his ERA was 4.35, almost two runs per game higher than

Bearden's. The pitching leaders in the National League were Johnny Sain of the Braves, Harry Brecheen of the Cardinals, and Johnny Schmitz of the Cubs.

Loren amused himself during slack periods at the newspaper office by making up his own all star teams for the season that had ended. In the American League, by position, his team consisted of Lemon and Newhouser, pitchers, and Hegan, Fain, Gordon, Keltner, Boudreau, Williams, DiMaggio, and Henrich as position players—five Indians, two Yankees, and one each from Detroit, Philadelphia and Boston.

Loren's National League all stars consisted of Sain and Brecheen, pitchers, and Cooper, Mize, Robinson, Pafko, Reese, Kiner, Musial and Ennis as position players, with New York, Brooklyn and St. Louis each contributing two, and Boston, Philadelphia, Pittsburgh and Chicago one of the members of the senior circuit dream team.

So much for baseball in 1948, Loren thought. The sports pages of the newspapers were now almost entirely devoted to football, a game that Adam followed closely but one in which Loren no longer had much interest. As a thirteen-year-old freshman at Winona CDS he had tugged on a leather helmet and struggled into shoulder pads and rubber cleated shoes, taking his licks from older boys, some of them veterans returning from military service who cussed and spat and alluded obliquely to experiences too horrible to describe in detail.

By his sophomore year, Loren had made the varsity team, and during his junior season he had excelled as a single wing tailback. But he did not dream about football; he did not pour over publications that recounted its past glories; nor did he imagine that he would ever engage in it again. If it turned out that he could not play baseball professionally, then he would try for a career as a sports writer and satisfy his competitive urges by playing tennis and golf, two athletic occupations well suited to loners.

He was far from ready, however, to abandon his overriding ambition. Almost any professional baseball team, he thought, could use another good pitcher. What he lacked in unusual ability at that position—he did not have the long arms of a flame thrower, or the muscular development needed for consistency in snapping off a succession of sharp curves—he might make up for with smarts and with his natural talent for throwing accurately to any spot in or around the strike zone. What he needed now was to experiment with a variety of grips and twists of the wrist, and an assortment of speeds, to give his mediocre fast ball just enough movement and varied velocity to keep hitters off balance. This would take perseverance. Happily, Tommy enjoyed assisting in such explorations.

Saturday, October 16, was a warm, sunny fall day, ideal for playing catch. After tossing a few warmup pitches to Tommy, who positioned himself in front of the closed garage door, Loren looked for a sign. The wiry little fellow thrust an index finger between his knobby knees. High in the air went Loren's left foot, back stretched his right hand, its fingertips digging into the stitches of a dirty baseball, and then his slender arm flashed forward, his wrist snapping downward to provide a deceptive "hop," just before the ball was supposed to disappear into the spindly receiver's mushy mitt with a satisfying splat.

Except that this time something went wrong.

Horrified, Loren watched the sphere fly high above Tommy's desperate leap, skip diagonally off the inclined garage roof, and smash through a second story window behind Mrs. Kaplan's back fence—into Rose Guidry's garage apartment.

Tommy, whose location had prevented him from observing the disaster, but who had heard glass shatter, looked scared. "What do we do now?" he asked.

Various expedients flashed through Loren's mind. Tell his father when he got home from work? Definitely not. Tell his mother, who was inside preparing supper? No; she would consult his father. Pretend ignorance and innocence and maybe nobody would hold him responsible. Not a chance.

"We have to go over there and apologize and offer to pay for the window," he said.

"We?"

"You aren't going with me?"

"Well," said Tommy. "If you aren't brave enough to go by yourself..."

"Forget it!" Flinging down his glove, Loren strode angrily over to the privet hedge next to Mrs. Kaplan's garage, squeezed through a narrow opening, and made his way to the back fence beyond the spooky building. A few feet away was the white clapboard wall to which was attached the metal staircase that he had climbed once before when he had his disastrous confrontation with Bubba. Hoisting himself over the fence and clattering up the stairs, Loren tapped deferentially on the apartment door. Hearing no sound inside, and hoping that no one was home, he knocked again, louder.

Abruptly, the door opened to a familiar scowl. Rose, minus her pistol. No lipstick or nail polish, no rings on either hand, dark hair chopped short, a man's sleeveless undershirt revealing tufts of underarm hair, lime green shorts, muscular brown legs, and bare feet. All this Loren took in while she was scrutinizing him, doubtless registering curly blond hair, a ruddy complexion, a dirty white T shirt with damp armpits, blue jeans, and scuffed Keds. Then she smiled grimly and beckoned him inside. "Ah wondered whether yew would drop by t' examine yore work," she said. Pointing toward the broken window above the kitchen sink, she said: "Take uh look."

"I'm very sorry," said Loren. "I don't know what happened. Of course I'll pay for the damage."

"That's good t' heah."

"Do you want me to try to find someone to repair it today? Perhaps your husband knows of someone?"

She laughed mirthlessly. "Yew don' wan' mah former husband involved in this," she said.

"What do you want me to do?" he asked.

"Yew might start by helpin' me t' clean up this mess," she said. Reaching into a closet, she took out a metal dustpan and a broom and began sweeping the floor. Loren began carefully picking sharp shards of glass out of the sink, depositing them in a ceramic bowl sitting on the counter nearby. He felt uncomfortable. The room seemed awfully warm for October.

"Heah," she said. "Lemme finish." She took two paper sacks out of the closet, crammed one into the other, and poured the contents of both the bowl and the dustpan into the sack. "Now, young man," she said firmly, "Ah wan' yew t' dispose of this bag in th' trash can downstairs. As fer th' window, Ah've already phoned uh repair man. He'll be heah soon. If'n yew'll jus' put three dollars in an empty bottle next t' th' fence where yew jus' climbed over, Ah'll git it t'morra. All right?"

Loren wanted to ask her some questions, but refrained. "All right. And thank you, very much."

"Not necessary. Mah father wuz uh ball player, as Ah think yew know. So Ah'm aware of whut kin happen, even when uh pitcher has excellent control." She paused, as she realized that she had just let Loren know she had watched him playing catch with Tommy. Then she smiled slightly and added: "Still, Ah would advise pitching in uh different direction from now on."

"Don't worry," Loren said, "I won't let it happen again.

Her smile widened. She reached into a drawer and retrieved a discolored baseball. "Heah." She tossed it to him. "Please remove this evidence of yore erratic control." With this admonition, she turned and disappeared into another room.

After descending the stairs from Rose's apartment, Loren was about to climb back over Mrs. Kaplan's back fence when he noticed that a maroon pickup truck was parked out on Cypress Avenue, near where Bubba's truck had sat earlier. It closely resembled one which Rose's father had driven to a Stars' practice, and which Loren remembered seeing parked behind the Rand trailer. On impulse, he walked out to it and looked at the right front fender. It was badly scratched and dented but showed no purple paint. He examined the headlights. Both had bulbs. Without reaching into the cab and flipping the light switch, he would not be able to tell whether they both worked. Looking back past the main house at the large garage behind it, he could see only a single window through which Rose might be watching, and its shade was drawn and not moving. He decided to chance discovery and reached for the door latch on the driver's side. It would not open. Locked. Again he looked back at Rose's window. This time he seemed to see the shade move slightly. He decided that it was time to return home.

* * *

Besides leaving Loren bleary-eyed five mornings a week from lack of sufficient sleep, his night newspaper job also prevented him from hearing some of the nation's outstanding opera stars sing at the Tocqueville City Auditorium. Patrice Munsel, a coloratura soprano who at the age of twenty-three was a veteran of six seasons at New York's Metropolitan Opera House, performed on Monday evening, October 18, with Mary Beth and her mother present as part of an enthusiastic audience. And a week later, the Wagnerian tenor Lauritz Melchior, widely known as the "Great Dane," whose career at the Met went back at least to 1927, sang pieces from Lohengrin and the Flying Dutchman, as well as Gounod's "Ave Maria."

For Loren, seeing these people in the flesh, particularly Miss Munsel, would have been a glorious experience. Having heard both of them sing on the Saturday afternoon Met opera radio broadcasts, he wished that he could have heard them in person.

Nevertheless, his thralldom to almost a dozen clicking, clanging teletype machines was not without its benefits. For Loren was not only getting a toehold in the newspaper world; he was also enhancing his education in American politics and world affairs. He had begun to read stories about a "crisis" in U.S. relations with the USSR as they filtered through the news services, stories that referred to certain "influential air force generals" urging a "lightning war" against the Soviets, to last, at most, three months, "conducted by small fleets of high speed planes dropping atomic bombs on strategic enemy centers." It seemed obvious to Loren, upon reading such revelations, that the frantic efforts by the Republican members of the HUAC to foment an atomic spy scare, were undertaken in support of the advocates of "preventive" war. Fortunately, Admiral William Leahy, President Truman's principal military adviser, and General Omar Bradley, the army chief of staff, had vigorously opposed the idea. Loren wondered whether, in years to come, assuming that the many crazy people in positions of power did not bring about an atomic war that would destroy western civilization, historians would look back at the chicanery of the despicable Richard Nixon and his HUAC cronies, and wonder why Americans had countenanced their corruption.

Maybe a proliferation of television sets, of which there were already almost half a million in American homes, would enable citizens closely to examine such people as Nixon—to study the movements of their bodies and the expressions on their faces. Anything to help sort out the rascals from the dedicated public servants like Leahy and Bradley. But what would TV watchers make of the British war monger, Winston Churchill, whose "iron curtain" speech had produced so much support for Truman's policy of confrontation with the Soviet Union, and who was still at it. An eight-column banner headline in the *Endeavor,* citing a statement by Churchill, proclaimed on October 9: "Only A-Bomb Will Halt Russia!" It had been Churchill's habit for more than half a century periodically to denounce Russian perfidy and aggressiveness. Now he declared that only the atomic bomb prevented the tyranny of Soviet communism from spreading across continental Europe.

With all of their terrible losses during two world wars, and with a political system that precariously held an aggregation of distinct ethnic societies together by fragile ideological cobwebs (this Loren had learned in civics class in Winona Junior High School), how could the dictatorship of Marshal Stalin, any more than that of Czar Nicolas, keep the USSR from flying apart, absent some external threat or invasion? Leave them alone, Loren thought; don't give them a foreign enemy to draw their people together behind their brutal communist rulers.

The warning delivered on October 12 by the United States representative at the United Nations that his country was arming itself to "stay the heavy hand of Russia's constant drive for world power" would only add to the paranoia of a people who had learned by hard experience to expect invasions at any time across their European border. Truman's executive order issued several days later to strengthen the American military reserves was only apt, Loren thought, to increase Russian fears of imminent aggression on the part of the West. Loren was not afraid of Russian communism. What he feared was being forced by idiotic old men to take part in a "crusade" against it and perhaps become nameless cannon fodder, a victim of the delusions of pigheaded politicians.

* * *

The world seemed to be going mad. Loren sought diversion from his worries about the future in newspaper stories about the eccentricities of ordinary people. He chuckled at the perspicacity of the *Endeavor* reporter who marveled at the ten foot high tomato plant growing behind the Mouton house next door. "A veritable miniature jungle, the wonder of the neighborhood," this investigator had written. The paper had even sent a photographer to provide its readers with a picture of this vegetative miracle, which had for several months supplied tomatoes to more than a dozen families. Loren wondered how eager these people, including his own parents, would have been to bite into the juicy red globes if they knew that he had been slipping next door almost every week night after work, at some risk to his reputation, to douse the plant with piss.

He had commenced this bit of neighborly philanthropy one evening when his bladder was bursting and his brother was locked in the bathroom, apparently constipated, with no indication that the facility would be immediately available. The following evening the same thing had happened, except that this time it was his mother who had just begun her bath when Loren realized that he badly needed relief. It was so easy to step out the kitchen door across the Temple driveway through the sparse shrubbery dividing it from the north side of the Mouton residence, and cut loose. Neither domicile had windows looking directly out upon the scene of action, which meant that Loren's libations were invisible, as long as they were delivered in darkness. What began, then, as an emergency measure, became a covert ceremony—and ultimately, Loren liked to think, a valuable service. The neighbors got succulent fruit; the readers of the newspaper got a mystery to ponder; Mr. Mouton, somewhat to his surprise, gained a local reputation as a consummate agriculturalist; and the Temples saved on their monthly water bills.

* * *

After the high school let out on Friday, October 22, Loren was in the kitchen gulping a glass of milk when the telephone rang. It was Mary Beth, reminding him that he was supposed to pick her up the following evening at seven o'clock to take her to the homecoming dance. Loren was not enthusiastic about going, but Mary Beth was, so he told her with as much good cheer as he could summon that he could hardly wait to escort her to the affair.

The gym was already crowded when they arrived. The polished basketball court reflected the brightness of the electric florescence high above and the radiance of adolescent infatuation below. Upon the hardwood, nervously smiling girls attempted to follow the awkward gyrations of their clutching partners who labored with varying degrees of success to keep time to the bellicose beat of a very loud band.

Every window and door in the building had been opened in order to alleviate the stifling heat, and moths and kindred creatures flapped against the lethal lights. An occasional sizzled victim dropped in an erratic twirl into the commotion below, more than once settling softly upon the tossing curls of an elaborate coiffure. Loren saw one dying moth fully an inch across, its wings still fluttering feebly, slide down inside the coat collar of the student body president, a precious glad-hander, smooth of voice and smooth of step, who danced on, hugging his girl friend, unconscious of the shredding and grinding of the small gauzy body taking place between his expensive jacket and his stiff white shirt.

Loren, who loathed the fellow, was tempted to steer Mary Beth a few feet closer to him, so that he could impart the disconcerting news. But Dandy Donald Wilkins was showing off, taking advantage of a lively waltz to whirl and bend and master his doting date, so that before Loren could say anything, they had both disappeared behind the other dancers.

Besides, the waltz was about to end, which meant that a jitterbug piece would probably follow, and Loren and Mary Beth had an agreement that they would sit out all of the strenuous numbers. In such cases she might leave him wandering aimlessly on the fringes of the dancing, while she bunny hopped with another admirer, it being understood that when the music slowed again, she would steer her partner in Loren's direction; so that he could cut in and resume the slow sway, right-left, right-left, that was his unimaginative but safe way of dancing.

Someone had invented a special step called the "Purple Hop," which had become the unofficial school dance. A couple would hop alternately on each foot, side by side, with their inside arms around each other's backs and their outside hands raised, forefingers pointed at the ceiling to signify that Tocqueville High School was "number one," after which the dancers would swing away from each other, sometimes holding on with the fingers of a single hand, sometimes entirely adrift. Loren thought the whole thing stupid.

But Mary Beth liked to bounce about. When a pasty looking individual with shiny shoes and greasy hair came to fetch her back to the floor, she squeezed Loren's hand and left to join the thundering herd. Loren got himself a Coke and sipped from the small green bottle as he settled himself at the edge of a raucous group, at the center of which Hank Harper, an ugly ruffian who played center on the football team, was reciting dirty limericks. If only, back in Winona, Loren had been able to overcome his adolescent awkwardness and shyness around girls, and had learned to dance properly; then, he thought, he would not be an embarrassment to Mary Beth. He flushed. He...

"Loren!" Mary Beth spoke his name so loudly that he jumped and spilled his Coke on the floor. His reverie broken, he looked around and saw that the musicians had left the bandstand for a break, and that the dancers were lining up at the refreshment tables or chatting together in little groups. Some were drifting out the doors to catch some fresh air, some to smoke.

"What's the matter?" asked Mary Beth. "Your face is red. Are you sick?"

"Naw," replied Loren. "Just a little hot. Let's go outside for a while."

The sidewalk circumscribing the building was crowded with strollers and cigarettes were flashing like fireflies in the front seats of automobiles out in the parking lot. Mary Beth led the way through narrow gaps and alleys among the silent ranks of parked cars, past giggling neckers and silent smoochers, heading in the direction of Shaky. As they passed a topless yellow convertible parked not far from their destination, its doors flew open and two classmates in rumpled sports jackets jumped out, grinning, to block their path. A pair of females with smeared lipstick remained inside the sleek vehicle, fingers patting at disarranged hair, one girl tugging at a strap to get it back over a bare shoulder.

"Hullo, Mary Beth," said the tall crew-cut, looming above them. It was Jimmy Johnson, the best-known athlete at THS and, by reputation, one of the dumbest; nevertheless an unrivaled woman-chaser. Beside him, his bleached blonde hair barely reaching Jimmy's chest, stood "Mouse" Montgomery, his best buddy. They were inseparable; they dated together, attended classes together; and played varsity football, basketball and baseball together. They had been the bane of every teacher who had them in class, because of their boisterousness and obtuseness, while girls waited hopefully for the privilege of going out on double dates with them. Nobody treated females with more familiarity than J. J. and the Mouse. Stalking the halls of THS between their classes like lions patrolling a pride, they pawed, patted, and hugged every good looking girl who passed within reach, alert for "fresh meat," as J. J. would frequently shout exuberantly to his small crony. A few young women shrank from their predatory groping, but it seemed to Loren that still more of them glowed adoringly and lingered longingly, hoping to hear the coveted words of invitation to a ride in the famous yellow convertible. Big Stud and Little Stud, other guys called them enviously. And Loren suspected that similar descriptive language was used by some of the most uninhibited girls.

The fact that the THS football team had suffered its sixth straight defeat the previous evening seemed not to have diminished J. J.'s self-confidence. Crushing Mary Beth in a proprietary hug, he lifted her, struggling, into the air and swung her as if he intended to tumble her into the back seat of the convertible. Meanwhile, the Mouse blocked Loren's path, leering lasciviously.

At first, watching Mary Beth kicking and flailing with clenched fists at J. J.'s broad back, as he hoisted her up over the car door, Loren hesitated, afraid of getting hurt if he intervened. Then, suddenly, he lost all sense of caution. His right fist smashed into Mouse's nose and knocked him flat.

With his sidekick on the ground, J.J. flung Mary Beth onto the front seat of his car, snarled a violent epithet, and swung a big fist at Loren's face. Not only did he miss as Loren ducked away, but he also threw himself off balance, which gave Loren the chance he needed to lash out with his right foot and bury it in J.J.'s crotch.

As the bruiser collapsed, cursing, beside his small companion, Loren hauled Mary Beth out of the yellow convertible. Hurriedly he escorted her past several other cars to where Shaky awaited them, hoping that J.J. and the Mouse were enough incapacitated so that they would not immediately follow.

As soon as he and Mary Beth were safely inside his trusty jalopy, Loren drove it rapidly out onto the nearby highway and headed out of town.

Mary Beth was sobbing. "I wuz so frightened," she sniffed. "Yew cudda been badly hurt."

"Yeah, but I wasn't," observed Loren, trying to sound brave. For, now that the fracas was over, he did feel frightened. He anticipated an occasion in the near future on which J.J. and the Mouse would seek revenge. The thought caused him to quiver with excitement, as did an accompanying thought, one of a more imminent adventure.

Several miles from the Tocqueville city limits, Loren turned Shaky onto a narrow unpaved road that bisected two swampy rice fields. A crescent moon and little sparks of stars glittered in the shallow water, as the car bumped along the levee.

The shell road ended at a wide metal gate. Tony Sisti had told Loren of this place, "one of th' greatest neckin' spots in East Texas." Mary Beth gazed at the gate and said: "Whut now?"

"We park," said Loren. Twisting the steering wheel, first in one direction, and then in the opposite one, he eased Shaky forward to one edge of the road, and then back to the other edge, gradually turning the car around just short of the gate.

"Whut do yew mean, 'park?'" Mary Beth's flirtatious tone of voice suggested she realized that he had brought them to a snuggle spot.

"What I mean," asserted Loren, turning off the ignition and dousing the headlights, "is that it's time to collect the kisses you owe me." Taking her into his arms, he tasted her soft moist lips. She fastened her fingers in his curly hair and lifted her chin, so that his lips slid down her throbbing neck to the soft flesh below. Pressing his face into the cleavage just above the embroidered bodice of her ball gown, Loren forced her back and down, until he lay on top. He could hardly breathe. When he twisted his head for air, he felt against his ear the pulsating of her rapidly beating heart.

Improvising, he nuzzled a throbbing vein in her neck, while he tore at the flimsy straps that crossed her soft shoulders. "Careful of th' dress," she said. "It's expensive." Squirming away from his embrace, she struggled out of her gown, pulling it up over her head and tossing it into the back seat. In Shaky's dim interior Loren reached out for her again, only to encounter a silken slip. It felt as smooth as skin, as he twisted her onto her back, clumsily kissing her neck and face.

Mary Beth wasn't resisting. Emboldened, Loren reached down and began to work her slip up over her thighs. "Don't do that," she protested and began writhing beneath him. But her wiggling only increased his determination to breach her defenses.

At this dangerous moment a peculiar torpor began to overwhelm his ardor. He felt suddenly languid and disconnected images flitted through his agitated mind. One was of a volcanic tropical island thrusting up voluptuously through a surging sea.

The volcano erupted. Inside Loren's tight underpants it spewed its lava. And then the island was no longer rock-hard but had become squishy soft. Loren lay motionless, knowing not what to say or do. He felt no further fever.

Becoming conscious of his sudden lethargy, Mary Beth pushed him off of her and sat up, hugging herself with goose-pimpled arms. "Ah'm cold," she complained. She stared questioningly at him, but he could not answer her unspoken inquiry. He felt entirely inadequate, unable to explain or to resume their encounter.

His sense of purpose had vanished. Half-heartedly he reached for her, but she pulled away. Then she flung open the car door and disappeared into the darkness.

Mary Beth's flight challenged Loren's masculinity. Tearing off his jacket and tie, and then his shoes, socks, trousers and sweat-soaked shirt, he lunged after her. She was trying to climb a fence dividing the roadway from the rice field but had caught her slip on a strand of barbed wire atop the fence. Seeing him rushing toward her, she cried "No, no!" and wrenched herself loose, leaving most of her slip hanging from the fence, as she fell to her knees in the mud on the other side. In the starlight, clad only in her bra and panties and a few rags, she staggered out into the rice paddy, knee-deep in the muck. Loren climbed over the fence in hot pursuit.

A few strides more and he caught her, and they fell together into the muddy water, Mary Beth weeping hysterically. He tried to kiss her lips and encountered mud that smelled like crayfish and frogs. Slime splashed into his eyes.

When he had clawed them clean enough to lift his eyelids, Mary Beth was rising from the mud beside him, only her teeth and the whites of her eyes uncoated by the dark goo, her hair hanging like a rag mop dipped in tar.

As he reached for her once more, he suddenly saw a disconcerting sight. Approaching Shaky from the far side of the closed gate was a swinging light—probably a lantern carried by a farmer coming to investigate.

Lowering his head, Loren hoisted Mary Beth over his right shoulder and staggered back to the fence with his slippery burden, while she kicked and cried and the light moved steadily toward them. Straining, he managed to lift her above the barbed wire that topped the wire mesh and tumble her onto the ground on the other side. When he dove over after her the jolt momentarily stunned him.

Mary Beth was the first to sit up. "Good Gawd, Loren," she sobbed. "Someone's comin'!"

"That's why we're leaving," he answered, lurching to his feet and grabbing her arm. "Come on." As they both climbed into Shaky, the light from the lantern was almost near enough to illuminate the car's rear license plate.

A twist of the ignition key and a stomp on the starter button brought the car's engine to life, and with an ugly grinding of gears as Loren's bare left foot slipped off the clutch before he had completed shifting from first to second, they left the scene in a shower of shell, accompanied by hoarse shouts from behind the lifted lantern.

"Now whut?" inquired Mary Beth, as they drove toward Tocqueville and began to encounter traffic. A huge tractor-trailer swished by, traveling in the opposite direction, and Loren glimpsed a startled face in the cab high above them, as the truck's headlights lit up Shaky's muddy interior and the mire with which its occupants were both covered.

"I have an idea," said Loren. "Here's the turn."

He swung the jalopy onto a side road and soon pulled up beside a shiny white sand trap adjacient to the eleventh green of the municipal golf course. "Hold on a moment," he said. "I need to check the place out." Soon he returned. "Come on," he urged. "We're all set."

Obediently Mary Beth let him take her hand and pull her onto the soft bent grass of the golf green. "Now whut're we doin'?" she asked. "This," said Loren, spraying her with chilly water from a large hose, conveniently coiled next to a nearby spigot. She shrieked from the shock; then caught herself and, gritting her teeth, turned slowly to let the hard cold stream wash every trace of mud from her nearly bare body. Then she ran back to the car while Loren washed himself, his teeth clicking and his knees shaking from the chill. Rejoining Mary Beth, he found that she had wrapped herself in the blanket that she had discovered in the back seat, and he tried to open it, so that he could share.

"Keep yore distance, buster," she warned him.

Loren was startled at the edge on her voice. "What's the matter?" he asked.

"Ah'll tell yew whut's th' matter," she said shrilly. "Every time we try t' go somewhar an' do somethin', Ah git embarrassed an' humiliated an'... an' nuthin' evah goes right." She began sobbing again.

"Aw, come on," pleaded Loren, trying to put a comforting arm around her. "Think how funny it was."

She pulled away. "It wasn' funny at all," she protested. "It wuz awful. Yew don' realize... Yew aren't ready... Ah think we oughta stop datin' fer uh while."

"What?!" Pulling on his pants and shirt, Loren said belligerently: "What do you mean 'stop dating?'"

"Ah'm sayin' we need uh pause in our relationship—time t' think it ovah."

"Damn it!" Loren burst out indignantly. "I couldn't help those interruptions. Damn it!" he shouted again. "I'll show you I can give you all you can handle." He started the car.

"Now whut?" asked an alarmed Mary Beth.

"I'm taking you to a quiet place where we won't be disturbed," announced a determined Loren.

"It's no use," said Mary Beth flatly, reaching out her hand to switch off the ignition. "Please, Loren; take me home."

"No," he said.

"Please... Listen, Loren; we can't do anythin' tonight. It won' work. I'll go wit yew t'morra. Ah promise."

Yielding to her entreaty, he drove her home and let her out there, her prom dress a wrinkled mess, her hair still muddy; and an anxious look on her face as she fled toward the dark house, doubtless hoping not to encounter her mother.

Fortunately for Loren, his parents seemed to be asleep when he arrived home, and he was able to get to bed without any fuss. For a long time he tossed and twisted, trying to make sense out of the events of the evening. Later he dreamed.

His dream, a familiar one, was of Margaret Plummer. Poor Margaret. Not long after he had abandoned her as his box supper companion by climbing out the window of the Winona Women's Club basement, she had been diagnosed with polio. Less than a year later she had died. Loren's recurring nightmare was of Margaret, rigid in an iron lung, crying out his name.

* * *

When Loren awoke on Sunday morning his cheeks were wet with tears. He felt taut and tired all day. When he phoned to ask Mary Beth to go to a movie, she told him that she had a cold and needed to get to bed early. On Monday evening, she was unable to come to the phone. On Tuesday, when he called after school, her mother said coldly that Mary Beth had "gone out wit' friends." Earlier that day he had roamed the halls of the high school, searching for her, and had spotted her at a distance walking with J. J. and the Mouse, J. J.'s arm encircling her waist.

He was crushed. He wanted to ask his mother for advice but was ashamed to admit that Mary Beth had spurned him. He kept telling himself that she was only an ordinary girl, one who for a time had seemed attracted to him, and was now, apparently, looking elsewhere.

As for Margaret, he had treated her abominably. But she had died of infantile paralysis, not of injured feelings. His behavior toward her had been thoughtless but not intentionally cruel. He had left her because he was not attracted to her. Now Mary Beth had left him, probably for the same reason. Wasn't that what he deserved?

Alone in his room Loren lay on his cot and tried to read. But his mind kept dwelling on his frustrated aspirations and on his own bad behavior whenever he allowed the end to justify the means.

CHAPTER 24
THE BIG WOODS

Loren kept trying to catch Mary Beth alone at the high school, to persuade her to resume their relationship, but she was invariably surrounded by girl friends or escorted by male admirers. When he phoned her home, one of her parents or her younger brother always answered and delivered the message that she was not available. Finally, calling her from the newspaper office on Friday evening, he managed to get her to answer the phone when, it appeared, she was eagerly expecting the caller to be someone else.

"Can't we talk," Loren pleaded. "What about getting together for a milkshake tomorrow or Sunday?"

"Sorry," she said. "Ah already have plans fer th' weekend."

"But this is important."

"Not to me."

"How can you be so nice one day and so nasty the next?"

"Yore uh fine one t' talk. In th' time we've gone t'gether, Ah nevah heard an endearing word from yew; not one. No real affection."

"That's not true."

"Yeah, it is. An' th' pitiful thang 'bout yew, Loren, is that yew aren't aware of the barrier that warns everyone 'round yew not t' git too intimate. It's like you're afraid you'll be betrayed. Yore uh good person, an' Ah'd like fer us t' be friends, once yew quit tryin' t' force me t' go further. But anythin' mor' than friendship is impossible, 'cause of yore fear of real feeling."

"You don't understand. Don't you remember being rammed by that one-eyed truck? I think someone is trying to kill me."

"Why would someone wanna do that?"

"I witnessed a crime, and the people who committed it seem to think I can identify them."

"Mah Gawd, Loren. If this is true, why haven' yew gone t' th' po-lice?"

"I can't."

"Why not?"

"I just can't."

"Are yew," she asked, "somehow involved?"

"I haven't done anything criminal. But I took some pictures..."

"Pictures? Do yew mean pictures of uh crime in progress?"

"Yeah. But the film got misplaced. I'm trying to find it. When I do and can see what the photos show, then maybe I can get some help."

There was a long silence on the other end of the line. Loren thought he could hear Mary Beth breathing rapidly. Then she said: "Wal, Loren, Ah kin see that yew have uh problem. All th' more reason fer us not t' be keepin' company. As yore fren, Ah would advise yew t' tell th' po-lice whut yew know an' ask fer protection."

"What if the police are part of the plot?"

"Th' plot?"

"The criminal activity that may have led to the… episode I witnessed."

"Do yew think some of th' po-lice are criminals?"

"I don't know for sure. But it's possible."

"Can't yore parents protect yew?"

"They'd try. But my mother has heart trouble. The worry might kill her. I've got to leave them entirely out of this ugly business."

"Yew seem t' have got yoreself into uh mess. But Ah find it hard t' believe that all this isn't th' product of uh vivid imagination."

"It's not my imagination. You saw the one-eyed truck."

"Yeah. But it might have been only uh drunk or uh case of mistaken identity."

"There have been other…"

"Loren," Mary Beth broke in, "Ah have t' go now. Someun is at th' door, an' mah parents aren't home."

In the newspaper wire room the teletype machines were chattering and another telephone was ringing insistently.

"O. K., I have to go, too" Loren said resignedly. "Will you call me soon?"

"Ah'll give it some thought. Goodbye."

She hung up. Doing likewise, Loren picked up the other phone. An angry voice said: "Took you long enough. Who's this?"

Startled, Loren replied: "Look, I'm very busy. Who's this?"

"This is the publisher of the *Gazette*. Who're you?"

"Don't you know?"

"No!"

"Good," said Loren, hanging up. Going into the wire room to start filing the local high school football scores, he worked in a daze, realizing, after having talked with Mary Beth, that their former relationship was probably irreparable. From now on, he feared, she would be unattainable.

* * *

Driving home shortly after midnight, Loren found himself thinking over what he had told Mary Beth about witnessing a crime. Despite Mrs. K's involvement in that nasty business, he still felt an almost irresistible attraction to her. His association with Mary Beth had helped to keep his thoughts away from his fascinating neighbor. But now…

Speak of the Devil! On arriving home, the first thing Loren saw when he hopped out of Shaky was one of two female figures standing in the darkness on Mrs. K's front porch beckoning to him. Approaching them, he saw that Mrs. K and her sister both wore short bathrobes and apparently nothing else.

"Ah believe you've met Olivia," said Della Kaplan in a syrupy voice. "We wuz wonderin' if'n yew'd like t' join us fore uh beer."

"I'd better not," Loren stammered. "It's late and I need to get some sleep. But thanks anyway."

The dim light escaping through Mrs. K's partly open front door illuminated a striking change of expression on her countenance, from a sly smile to a sullen scowl. "Listen heah," she snarled. "Olivia saw yew climbin' ovah th' back fence th' other day, visitin' Miz Guidry in her apartment. Ah wanna warn yew: stay away from that gal. She's big trouble."

"Trouble? What kind of trouble?"

"Nevah yew mind. Jus' keep clear of 'er. An' don' believe anythin' she mighta tole yew. She's uh complete liar."

"She didn't say anything about you."

"Wal, she'd betta not; an' yew'd betta not, either, 'cause Ah got ways t' shut yew both up, permanently. Yew understan'?"

"I have no intention of seeing Mrs. Guidry again," said Loren. "And I don't know why you're threatening me. I haven't done anything to you."

Mrs. K's grim stare made him shiver. "Jus' keep yore mouf shut, 'specially 'bout mah late husband's death," she warned. "An' maybe nuttin' will happen t' yew." She trailed her silent companion back inside her house and shut the door with a decisive bang.

Trembling, Loren entered his own domicile. The mask is off, he thought. That woman is evil. I wish she'd move somewhere else.

As he tiptoed to his room, trying not to awaken his parents, he felt as frightened as he had ever been in his entire life.

* * *

After sleeping late on Saturday, October 30, Loren was glumly eating breakfast, conscious of his mother's silent scrutiny and resentfully anticipating her curious questions, when he heard the telephone out in the hall ring once, and then his brother's eager "Hello," followed by an unenthusiastic, "Yeah, I'll tell him."

"Loren," Tommy called. "It's for you. Someone named Tony."

Picking up the phone, Loren said: "Hi Tony, what's up?"

"Hey, man. How yew doin'?"

"Pretty well."

"Yew soun' like yew've been visited by one of mah Daddy's enforcers." Tony's laugh was jarring.

"No," said Loren. "I'm just tired. My night job is getting me down. And…" He hesitated. Then he asked: "Do your Dad's 'enforcers' ever bump people's cars, so they'll stop and get beat up, or worse?"

"Ah spose they might do somethin' lak that. Why d' yew ask?"

"Because a pickup truck with only one headlight banged into my rear bumper several nights ago."

"How come?"

"I have no idea."

"Musta been some drunk. Ah wouldn' worry 'bout it. Say, ah've gotta proposition that'll take yore mind offa yore troubles."

"What's that?"

"Ah wan' yew t' come t' mah dance recital t'night. Eight o'clock at th' school auditorium. Th' program'll be ovah by nine an' afterwards we kin go t' a movie. Abbott an' Costello meet Frankenstein. Also Lon Chaney, th' Wolf Man. An' Bela Lagosi as Dracula. Halloween. Lotsa laughs."

"Tony, I'm really not in the mood."

"Whatsa matter? Breakin' up wit' Mary Beth got yew down?"

"How'd you hear about that?"

"Everyone knows yew two ain't t'gether any more. Big deal. Happens alla time. Mary Beth musta had four or five steadies las' year. An' she'll prolly have several mor' by nex' summer. Uh nice gal, but flighty."

"I didn't know."

"Wal, yew bein' new an' all... Listen, yew ain't heared th' best part."

"What's that?"

"Ah done lined us up uh double date. Wit' two hot patooties. Real purty gals from th' dance group. Yew'll drop yore teeth when yew see th' gal Ah got fer yew. Name of Shelley. When mah gal, Sophie, axed her if she'd go out wit' yew, she got real excited. Uh date wit' uh genuine yankee! One wit' curly hair an' blue eyes! That's whut she said. Son, yew can't miss. Say yew'll come."

"Sure, Tony; I'll be there. Thanks a lot." As he hung up the phone, Loren felt better already.

* * *

Curious to know what was involved in Tony's adagio dancing and looking forward to his blind date with the girl named Shelley, Loren arrived early for the recital. To his surprise, it turned out to be a combination of ballet, acrobatics, and bodily exhibitionism, performed to classical recorded music played at a slow tempo. For the males, the main duty seemed to be, as Tony had put it, "throwing gals around." For the girls, dressed in skimpy costumes that revealed their firm figures, the scenario seemed to demand that they alternate between flexing, posturing, and displaying what Tony called some "really smooth moves."

Particularly attractive was a blond gamine who probably weighed no more than ninety pounds, which made it relatively easy for the muscular young men striding about the stage to toss her from one to another. Sheathed in a tight leotard and skimpy skirt, she seemed inexhaustible as she flung her well-developed little body back and forth in time with the music. Loren said a prayer to all his baseball saints, to Lou Gehrig, to Christy Mathewson, to Charlie Hollocher,... Let this girl be the one.

As soon as the performance was over, and the loud clapping from the sparse audience had ended, Tony came down off the stage, still breathing fast and streaming sweat, to introduce a good looking brunette, swarthy like him, and slightly taller. This was Sophie, exhilarated and obviously on good terms with Tony. "Hey," she called to someone on the stage, "come meet yore date."

Loren felt his heartbeat accelerate. Hallelujah! It was indeed the little blonde! She immediately separated herself from the other dancers on stage and, disdaining the nearby steps, leaped over the footlights to land lightly nearby.

"Showoff," said Tony. "Loren, Ah wanna introduce Shelley, th' star of our show."

The object of his effusiveness smiled shyly, her flawless features still rosy from her recent exertions. She looked coyly up at Loren and extended a slim hand. "Nice t' meet yew," she said tremulously. "Pardon mah pantin'. Ah'm still outa breath."

"Loren loves it when uh gal pants fer 'im, don' yew pal?" said Tony.

Loren, speechless, could only shake his head, while both girls laughed. "Tony, yore uh real card," said Shelley. "Uh joker, that is." Loren thought admiringly: a sense of humor, too!

"We gotta go back t' our dressin' rooms t' change," said Sophie. "If'n yew don' mind leavin' yore car wharevah yew parked it, we kin all ride wit' Tony. "Ah hope yew an' Shelley won' mind bein' crammed t'gether in his rumble seat." She winked suggestively.

*   *   *

The movie was fun. The girls giggled and shrieked with laughter at the comic parts, and shut their eyes and squeezed the hands of their dates when things got spooky. Loren briefly thought of Mary Beth and wondered if he should feel guilty, but a sniff of Shelley's heady perfume as she leaned toward him wiped out the thought. Afterwards Sophie said: "It's uh beautiful evenin'. Les go fer uh drive."

"Good idea," said Shelley. "Whut about it, Loren?"

Looking at his watch, which read past eleven-thirty, Loren said: "I have to be home by one a.m. But anything's O. K. until then."

"Away we go!" exclaimed Tony, stepping on the accelerator and heading his car northward out of Tocqueville into the darkness of the hinterland. After a quarter of an hour had passed, Loren realized that they had begun to speed through the ghostly groves of the Big Woods. Beside him in the rumble seat, Shelley shivered. He extended an arm around her shoulders and let his mind wander into the realm of sexual fantasy, wherein he might…

"Loren," inquired Shelley. "Whut're yew thinkin'?"

"Nothing."

"Why don' we?" Shelley started to say… "Whut's th' matter?"

"Hey, Tony," Loren called out, leaning to his left out of the rumble seat, trying to make his voice heard through the driver's window, "doesn't that car behind us have only one headlight?"

"Yeah, yore right," Tony yelled. "An' Sophie knows whut dat means, doncha, gal?"

"Yew'd better keep bot' hands on th' wheel," warned Shelley. "Maybe we oughta… Whut wuz that?"

"He bumped us," exclaimed Loren. "What's wrong with him?"

Thump. Again the vehicle behind them hit their rear bumper, with Loren and Shelley sitting just in front of it, shaken by the impact. Loren looked back to try to identify the assailant, but he could see only a shadowy figure behind the windshield of a pickup truck that had now fallen about two car lengths behind them.

"Here he comes again!" Loren yelled to Tony, as the pursuer began once more to close the gap between the two vehicles. "Can't you outrun him?"

"Ah'm gonna try," bellowed Tony, and the trees beside the road began to zip by, faster and faster, as he floored the accelerator.

At first the single headlight fell far behind, but eventually it began to draw nearer, as both vehicles hurtled dangerously through the darkness. Shelley screamed: "Stop; we're all gonna die!" Loren, rigid with dread, cautioned her to hold on, and assured her that everything would be fine because Tony was a skilled driver. He hoped.

A moment later, Tony tried to negotiate a sharp curve that suddenly loomed up out of the blackness. The right front tire twisted off the pavement onto a low shoulder, while Tony wrestled with the steering wheel, trying to hold the car away from the nearby ditch. Despite his efforts, they tipped over into it and bumped to a stop.

Up on the highway, their pursuer had apparently roared past, but over the rumbling coming from the engine of Tony's car Loren thought he heard brakes screeching and believed that they were still in danger. He pulled Shelley from the rumble seat and called to Tony: "We're going to hide in the woods. Are you coming?"

Helping a shaking Sophie out on her side, Tony replied: "Yew go on. We'll follah. If'n we git separated, meet back heah when th' coast is clear."

Loren headed into the trees, pulling Shelley by the hand. "Not s' fast," she protested. "Ah might trip."

At that moment, the sound of a gun shot echoed in the obscurity around them. Their clothes were being torn by brambles and their faces scratched by tree twigs. Shelley started sobbing. But Loren had an idea. "Listen," he whispered, "do you think you could climb that vine?"

"That vine?" she repeated. "Why?"

"If you can go up it about ten or twelve feet," he said, "and hoist yourself up onto that big branch—see it up there, that big shadowy shape—you can probably go up a little higher and find a comfortable crotch to hide in while I lead whoever's chasing us away from you. Can you do it?"

"Shore Ah kin do it."

"I'll give you a boost." He reached out his arms. She threw her palpitating body against him and brushed his lips with hers. Then she stepped back and shed her skirt. Her bare legs and skimpy panties were barely visible in the darkness. "Ah'm ready," she said. "Hide mah skirt."

He bent down, grabbed her trim ankles, and straightened up, feeling her hands pressing down on his shoulders and her knees sliding up from his thighs to his chest, as he hoisted, and she helped by transferring her hands to the dangling vine. Then, as he stepped back, she wrapped her muscular legs around the wrist-thick vegetative rope and began to struggle monkey-like upward.

Meanwhile, from the direction of the highway, Loren heard someone approaching, snapping twigs and muttering curses, through the woods. "Are you O. K?" he whispered.

"Yeah. Go," she murmured. "Hurry."

Picking up Shelley's skirt, Loren veered off diagonally, moving further from the road but on a path that would allow him eventually to intercept it beyond a curve that they had previously passed. Once Shelley's hiding place was well behind him, he shouted: "Come on, you stupid jerk; see if you can find me before the wolves find you first." Fortunately there were large trees between his pursuer and himself, because his challenge was instantly answered by a pistol shot. The shooter had somehow managed to advance closer than Loren had thought likely, given the darkness between them and his own efforts to minimize the noise produced by his movements. He realized that he'd have to move more rapidly if he wanted to stay safe.

Scuffing a shoe on a stone, he picked it up and hurled it through the trees with all his strength. As soon as it crashed into a copse, the stalker triggered two quick shots, apparently hoping that they would find the unseen fugitive.

During the silence that followed, snorting and snuffling suddenly sounded in a nearby thicket, and two huge hogs bolted through the bracken, shredding it with their tusks, their sharp hooves leaving torn turf behind them as they escaped deeper into the dark woods. There was no reaction from the shooter, who apparently recognized that the commotion was not caused by a human being.

Taking a deep breath, Loren resumed his retreat. Ahead, through an opening in the trees, he glimpsed a stretch of starlit pavement. However, as he dodged through a tangle of brambles, some of which tore his trousers and ripped red ridges in his bare arms, he saw shadowy shapes slithering through the grass between the highway and himself. Several large snakes. Apparently he had stumbled upon a nest of them. Behind him he heard rustling and a grunt of pain, as his pursuer encountered an obstacle.

Hoping he would escape being bitten, Loren plunged ahead, scattering the hissing snakes as he leaped among them and then beyond, trying to minimize contact between his flying feet and the ground. Then he was out on the highway, miraculously unscathed, running toward Tony's car, which he estimated should be parked around a bend a quarter of a mile ahead.

Behind him he heard a shrill yell and two shots, followed by several clicking sounds. The serpents, he hoped, had decided to sink their fangs into his pursuer, which ought to put an end to the chase. Hoping that had happened, he ran on at top speed.

Puffing, he rounded the bend in the road and saw Tony's car just ahead. There was no sign of anyone around. But as he came up to the vehicle and opened the front door on the passenger side, both Shelley and Sophie stepped out of the shadows, scratched and disheveled, but otherwise apparently all right. "Whar's mah skirt?" inquired Shelley.

"I had to hide it in the woods," replied Loren. "It was slowing me down. Maybe we can retrieve it by daylight. Where's Tony?"

"Ah dunno," said Sophie. "We got separated. Ah ducked into uh culvert not far from heah. Tony said he wuz goin' t' try t' surprise whoevah wuz chasin' us."

"That guy had a gun," said Loren. "Didn't you hear the shots? I hope Tony had enough sense not to get too close. I don't believe he did, because whoever it was kept coming after me… unless there were two of them."

"Thar may have been," said Shelley, shivering. "After yew left me, Ah heard someone go past below whar Ah wuz sittin' up in that tree, an' then, uh li'l later, thar was uh pattering soun', almos' like uh big dawg. But it couldn't have been uh dawg, cud it?"

"Probably a wolf," said Loren.

"Surely not," said Sophie. "In Texas?"

"They've been spotted in these woods," said Loren. "Red wolves. Usually several together, though." He shivered. "I wish Tony would come. We need to leave."

At that moment, an indistinct figure emerged from some nearby trees. It was Tony, his clothes ripped and his face scratched, holding something shining in his left hand. It was a pistol.

"Where'd you get the gun?" Loren asked.

"Had it in th' glove compartment," said Tony. "Ah always carry one 'cause some of mah daddy's bidness rivals kin be purty rough. Ah wuz gonna try t' sneak up on whoevah wuz stalkin' us, an' either capture 'im, or plug 'im if Ah had to; but—damn it t' hell—the sonuffabitchin gun wasn' loaded. He thumbed the cylinder and it fell open to reveal six empty chambers. "Ah could kick mahself."

"Well, we know there's at least one stalker out there," said Loren. "Let's scram."

"Right," responded Tony. "If Sophie'll take th' wheel, Ah think th' three of us kin push th' car outa th' ditch."

Soon they were on their way back to Tocqueville. At Loren's suggestion, Shelley sat with Sophie in the relative warmth of the front seat, while he sat alone in the chilly rumble seat, looking back apprehensively for the first few miles to see if someone was following. But no threatening single headlights overtook them, and soon they merged safely into the consoling traffic of the city streets. When they stopped to let Shelley out at her home, they discussed the evening's events and finally agreed that they would keep what had happened a secret for the time being. Their parents would be told only that Tony's car had slid into a ditch and that when they were crossing a farmer's field to go for help, they were all chased into an unfriendly wooden area by an angry bull.

A stupid story, thought Loren. But not as difficult to believe as the truth. Especially when nothing had been seen of the one-eyed truck, once it had passed Tony's car. After offering apologies to his waiting mother for being an hour late, and telling her the agreed-upon cover story, he took off his ruined clothes, smeared some biting orange iodine on his cuts and scratches, and lay gratefully down on his cot. He was suddenly very sleepy. His final thoughts before he descended into dreamland were, first, concern whether Shelley would stick with him after discovering that he was a person pursued; and second, worry whether Tony's gun had really been unloaded when he snatched it from the glove compartment.

* * *

On the following morning Loren awakened to discover that the other Temples had gone to Sunday school without him. Eating his oatmeal, he still felt tired, having been bothered throughout the night by a succession of troubling dreams. Heavy-limbed and defenseless, he had been hunted by a faceless figure whom his every effort to elude proved useless. The identity of his nemesis remained uncertain. At times the shadowy shape resembled Bubba. One it seemed very much like Buzz. Another time it appeared to be Emile. But it could even have been Della Kaplan. Somehow he had to find and develop the missing film. Perhaps then he would know his foe.

* * *

Loren began to worry. Where were the other members of his family? Church usually ended by twelve-fifteen or twelve-thirty at the latest; and it was now almost one-thirty. He was hungry for Sunday dinner. The others must have gone visiting. He had his head inside the refrigerator looking for a snack when the back door swung inward and his father appeared, looking upset. "What's the matter?" Loren asked.

"Your mother is at the Hotel Divin," replied Adam. "She had heart palpitations in church, and Tommy and I rushed her to the nearest hospital. After checking her chest, they admitted her. Tommy's with her now. I came home to fetch her things."

While delivering his account of Nan's difficulty, Adam had entered their bedroom and begun to pull underclothing and nightgowns out of drawers, and a robe and slippers out of the closet, throwing them hurriedly into a large leather suitcase that he dragged from under the bed.

"Anything I can do to help?" asked Loren from the doorway.

"You might come to the hospital about six and relieve me," said Adam. "By that time I'll need to get something to eat. And Tommy has to get to bed, so he won't sleep through his alarm and be late for his paper route. The last time he overslept your mother took irate phone calls for a week afterwards."

"I'll be at the Hotel Divin at six," said Loren. "What room?"

"I can't remember. I think it's 108. Ask at the entrance."

As he watched his father head out to his Hudson to return to the hospital, Loren felt culpable. Ever since being allowed to go out by himself after dark, starting with the beginning of his freshman year in high school when he was only thirteen, his mother had insisted that he return home before she retired to bed. He was supposed to arrive not later than eleven on nights preceding school days and by one a.m. on Saturday and, of course, on nights when he was working at the newspaper office. Nan had not approved of Loren's arrangement to play tennis with Buzz past one in the morning, because it kept her awake even later, but she had reluctantly allowed it and had suffered accordingly.

If any emergency prevented Loren from getting home on time, he was supposed to notify his parents by phone. But last night he had been unable to call. Hence his mother had stayed up, worrying. He had stammered apologies through his closed bedroom door when she had knocked after hearing him tiptoe into the house, but he knew that her weak heart had not been improved by the long wait. He would apologize again when he got to the hospital and vow never again to be out late, even if it meant ridicule from his companions on some future outing.

Meanwhile, he realized that he now had a rare opportunity, with nobody else in the house. Slipping into his parents' bedroom, he began to search for the object that he thought must be, had to be, somewhere among his mother's things. It took only a couple of minutes to locate the errant film canister. It was lying on the floor, between one of the rear legs of his mother's dressing table and the wall behind it, perhaps accidentally pushed into that spot by a blind thrust of the vacuum cleaner. Transferring the stray spool of film to his own room took but a few additional seconds, just as Tommy came through the back door and went directly to the cookie jar in the kitchen, shouting: "Hey, Loren; are you home?"

"Yeah," Loren responded, blowing dust off the precious roll of film and thrusting it under his pillow. "How is Mom?"

"The nuns have her in an oxygen tent."

"That doesn't sound good. Was she breathing all right?"

"Seemed to be. While I was still there the doctor came and gave her a shot. Soon afterwards she went to sleep. Dad said he thought she was all right; so I came home to get some shuteye."

"I'll be going there soon," said Loren. "Meanwhile I need to make a couple of phone calls."

"Before you do, there's something I want to tell you."

"What's that?"

"Do you remember that I decided some time ago that I wanted to be baptized?"

"Yeah."

"Well, you said that you might consider doing it, too. We could both give Mom a great gift if we did it on her birthday, three weeks from today."

"Sounds like an original birthday gift."

"Will you do it?"

Loren thought it over. Then he said: "Sure, I'll go along, if we can get Reverend Pryor to do the dunking on that date."

"It's not a frivolous ceremony, you know."

"I know."

"I asked Dad what he thought," said Tommy. "He said he approved of us doing what *he* had done as a boy, almost forty years ago."

"Then I guess all we need to do is to schedule it with Reverend Pryor. I'll ask Dad to phone him tomorrow."

Loren went into the hall and looked up the number for the Sisti residence. He rang it and asked for Tony, who wasn't home and wasn't expected until late.

"Drat!" Until he could talk to Tony, he couldn't get Shelley's telephone number. He wanted to ask her for a date for the following weekend, just the two of them. Maybe he'd see either Tony or Shelley at school.

* * *

Loren stayed up late that night. He visited his mother in the gloom of the Hotel Divin, where solemn nurses in hooded habits whispered and shushed, and Nan lay propped up on two thick pillows sleeping soundly. Inside the oxygen tent she had some kind of monitor attached to one arm, while from the other a tube extended upward to what looked like a hot water bag hanging on a hook above her prone body. Once, while Loren sat reading, he became aware of a slight movement in the bed and, looking up from his book, saw that his mother's eyes were open, staring at the ceiling. Quickly he went over and took her soft hand in his. She squeezed it and smiled. Through the oxygen tent he could barely hear her faint reassurance: "I'm better. I'm glad you're here."

Tears streaked his cheeks as he said: "Mom, I'm terribly sorry that I came home so late last night. I shouldn't have gone with Tony at that hour. I won't ever be that late again. I promise."

His mother pressed his hand again and said something that sounded like: "Don't worry, Loren. This is not your doing." He fervently wished that were true.

Soon Nan was asleep again. About an hour later Adam arrived. "It's past two," he said. "You go home and get some sleep. Set the alarm; so you won't be late for school. I called Hatton to tell him I probably won't be in tomorrow." He grimaced. "Hatton wanted to come here, but I told him there was nothing he could do and that visitors are discouraged."

Loren closed his book and got up to leave. "Should I come back after school?" he asked.

"No, better go straight to work," Adam said. "I'll see the doctor when he comes by in the morning. If he is encouraging, I might go home for a while and let the nuns handle things. Have they been checking on her regularly tonight?"

"Yes. Every half hour. They look her over, glance at me, and then leave without saying anything."

"They've probably been instructed to let the doctor do all the talking with the patients' families. The head nurse seems competent. She works seven days a week. Imagine that."

Loren couldn't. "Phone me if you need me," he said.

"I will."

* * *

On his way home, Loren took a short cut through a rough factory section of town. Lost in thought about his mother's condition, he did not see the shiny black Lincoln ahead of him suddenly halt for a traffic light. It was too late to pump Shaky's brakes enough to stop short of the other vehicle. He was still hammering away with his right foot and muttering "damn, damn," when his front bumper rammed into the polished chrome protecting the rear end of the Lincoln, rocking both cars for several seconds, until they subsided into an ominous silence.

Loren held tightly to Shaky's steering wheel with sweat-soaked hands. He closed his eyes and hoped he was dreaming. When he opened them, he saw in the shadows of the dimly lighted street a very large man dressed in a dark suit and what looked like black cowboy boots. The man's big bald head gleamed like a globe as he leaned into Loren's window with an angry expression on his pockmarked face.

"Sorry," Loren mumbled. "My brakes... they don't work very well. I need to get them fixed."

The other driver looked for a moment as if he was about to club Loren with one of his clenched fists. Then Loren heard a hiss of breath being expelled. In his rear view mirror there had appeared the headlights of an approaching vehicle. Without a word, the bald man turned away and strode back to his car, got in, and drove away. Soon his car vanished.

Loren shuddered. There had been something terrifying about that monstrous man. The eyes, bulging like marbles, had held no hint of pity for Loren's predicament. Rather had they reflected a disposition to do something terrible to anyone who irritated their owner. Loren had caught a glimpse of brown leather inside a gaping lapel as the man leaned forward. Probably a holster. And there had been someone else in the shiny Lincoln as well, someone slumped on the passenger side of the front seat. Not that the driver had looked as if he would require reinforcements.

As Loren drove home, he was so tense that his very pores seemed to have eyes to peer into the blackness around him, looking for more danger.

* * *

The next day was November 1. After school Loren found a note from his father on the kitchen table informing him that Nan was much improved and was out of the oxygen tent. She was tubeless, too, and eating. The doctor had said she might be able to return home by mid-week.

Gulping milk and chewing on an apple to go with his peanut butter sandwich, Loren quickly leafed through an early edition of the *Endeavor* that had thumped against the front door just as he started to sit down. First he turned to the comics to scan Buck Rogers, Alley Oop, Ozark Ike, Freckles, Kerry Drake, Mickey Finn, Li'l Abner, and his favorite strip, Mark Trail. Then he turned to the front page.

Things looked bad for President Truman. With the election only one day away, and the Republicans estimated to have spent twice as much money as the Democrats, and with over seventy per cent of the nation's newspapers having editorially supported Dewey, the odds seemed overwhelming against Truman's retaining the presidency. This supposition was echoed in all the major public opinion polls, the results of which must be so discouraging to Democrats, Loren thought, that many who would ordinarily cast their ballots for the incumbent president would now not bother to vote.

Locally, the white-haired former judge who was unopposed for re-election to Congress had made a radio speech on Friday night urging his constituents to vote for Truman, but the Endeavor had given his comments much less play than an address delivered at the municipal auditorium on Saturday evening by Strom Thurmond, the States' Rights party candidate for President. Thurmond had derided the "perfidy" of Truman and his "machine and minority dominated Democratic party" for going "all out to destroy and eliminate, now and forever, the cherished traditions of the Southland." According to a spokesman for Thurmond, the South Carolinian was resigned to finishing third in the popular vote nationally, but was confident of carrying the deep South, which would give him enormous bargaining power in the House of Representatives when neither Dewey nor Truman obtained a majority of electoral votes. When the balloting began in the House, Thurmond calculated, a surprising majority of the congressmen would vote for him over either Truman or Dewey, and he would then become President.

Such a scenario was deprecated, however, in Hatton's final pre-election editorial, which flatly predicted an easy victory for Dewey over a "pathetic" Truman, "a political accident as vice president and a political tragedy as president."

Even Lyndon Johnson's hard won victory in the Texas Democratic party primary now seemed in danger of being reversed. His opponent, former Governor Stevenson, had endorsed the Republican candidate, Jack Porter, a Houston oil magnate, and the Republican-dominated Senate in Washington had authorized a special investigation of the Johnson-Stevenson contest, with its operatives already engaged in impounding ballots and election records in at least eight counties. So, thought Loren, even if the U. S. Supreme Court were to let Johnson's victory stand, the Senate itself, if it remained in Republican hands, could still declare the election invalid and prevent Johnson from taking his seat.

In New York City, the recent inaugural address of Dwight Eisenhower as president of Columbia University, in which the general pledged that henceforth the Columbia faculty would "teach the facts of communism," had received wide acclaim. "The truth about communism is, today, an indispensable requirement," Eisenhower had declared, "if the true values of our democratic system are to be properly assessed."

As if this had been a green light, the HUAC had promptly altered the direction of its insidious investigations from atomic spying to "the universities and the threat of 'subversive' forces in higher education," starting with hearings to be held at Columbia University. Political columnist Marquis Childs warned that "Manifestations of thought coercion and guilt by association are developing in a frightening fashion. Fear and suspicion are poisoning the lives of American citizens who have never had the slightest shadow of a thought of disloyalty." Childs warned against "the dangers and disasters of political demagoguery in abolishing our freedoms while pretending to protect our security."

On the foreign front, the news was even more ominous. The fighting between Egypt and the new state of Israel promised soon to involve most of the Arab world. It was likely, Loren thought, that American Jews would try to pressure the Truman administration into taking sides against the Muslims. Meanwhile, Uncle Joe Stalin, the Soviet dictator, was threatening war over control of the former German capital city of Berlin. In the Far East the Chinese communists were in the process of driving the American-backed nationalist war lords into the Yellow Sea, a debacle that had already inspired some Republicans to cry out for American military intervention.

In Korea the Russians had apparently violated an agreement with the United States for a mutual withdrawal of forces by maintaining a strong economic and military presence in the northern portion of that divided nation. Here were four widely separated trouble spots, which individually and collectively, given the recent twists and turns in Truman's foreign policy, his petulant aggressiveness, and his call for the re-militarization of America, threatened to bring on World War III, potentially a caldron that would consume not only many of the surviving soldiers from the second world war, but also a new crop of young men from Loren's own generation.

Loren's future had never looked so ominous. His hopes for a career in baseball were fading. His mother's health was faltering. His yearning for a sexual experience remained unfulfilled. He anticipated serious consequences resulting from his carnal curiosity in photographing the escapades of Mrs. Kaplan. And his desire to avoid the dangers of military service looked increasingly hopeless. Everywhere that he looked for satisfaction, or simply for safety in a perilous world, discouragement and danger stared back, offering only fear and frustration.

Leaving the newspaper open on the kitchen table for his father to find when he came home from the hospital, Loren scraped back his chair and sighed with resignation as he contemplated his last week of work at the newspaper office. One final gloomy glance at an inside page of the *Endeavor*, however, froze him into startled immobility. It couldn't be true. For a second time he read the headline: WISTERIA WORKER SHOOTS SELF, and saw the name underneath it: J. C. Guidry.

Loren felt both sad and relieved as he read the three-paragraph story. While swooping down over the Tocqueville High School campus at sunup on Monday, the pilot of a small plane spraying insecticides to rid the area of mosquitoes had spotted an inert form lying near the football field. He had radioed its position to someone at the airport, who in turn phoned the police. Well before teachers and students began appearing at the school, detectives photographed and searched the area and an ambulance removed the body. Nobody at the school, except the principal, was informed about the incident, until after the *Endeavor* went to press about mid-day.

The deceased had been identified from evidence found on the corpse as Mr. John Charles Guidry, formerly a worker at the Wisteria refinery, but recently self-employed. He had been shot once in the head with a pistol that was found clutched in his left hand. There were powder burns around the wound. Asked to comment, a police spokesman had referred the reporter to Emile Mouton, an assistant district attorney, but Mr. Mouton had refused any comment.

Rising from the kitchen table, his thoughts in turmoil, Loren saw through the window none other than the same Emile Mouton, conversing with his mother in her front yard. Hoping to learn more about Bubba's demise, Loren tore the story out of the paper and took it next door.

Mrs. Mouton had gone back inside and Emile was about to get into his car, when he heard Loren call his name. "I just wanted to ask you about this story in the newspaper," said Loren. "I knew this guy. We played baseball together last summer. Can you tell me anything beyond what has already been reported?"

"So yew were acquainted wit' J. C. Guidry? Whut did yew know 'bout 'im?"

"Well, I haven't seen him since the end of August, but I did hear that he had been divorced from his wife, quit his job, and maybe left town. Someone said he might have gone to New Orleans. But I don't know whether that's true."

"It's true. Whut about th' divorce? Wuz it messy?"

"I believe so. Bubba could be very unpleasant and he seemed to be getting worse."

"We've talked t' th' wife. She doesn't seem very upset 'bout his death."

"Did she tell you he was right-handed?" asked Loren.

Emile favored him with a searching stare. "Yore uh purty clever fellah," he said. "Makes it unlikely that he would shoot hisself in th' left side of his haid; right?"

"That's what I thought when I read the newspaper account."

"An' heah's uh graduate of Southside High electing t' blow his haid off inside th' football stadium of uh rival school. Doesn't make sense, does it?"

"No. If it wasn't suicide, I hope you find the killer."

"We will. By th' way, we're still workin' on Dr. Kaplan's death. Yew don' have any insights t' offer 'bout that so-called suicide, do yew?"

"No. I'm really confused. Before we moved to Tocqueville, I had absolutely no direct experience with death. Now, within several months, two people I have known slightly have died violently, both under suspicious circumstances. It's enough to give a guy the gollywobbles."

"Golly… What?"

"That's what my mother calls bad dreams… nightmares."

"Ah meant t' ask; how is yore mother?"

"Improving, I think. I'm going to stop by the hospital when I get off work about midnight." Loren consulted his wristwatch. "I'm late. I'd better get going. Thanks for talking with me."

"Mah pleasure."

By the time Loren backed Shaky out of the driveway, Emile's car had already departed. The Assistant D. A., thought Loren, was a smart guy. Maybe he would be able to discover the truth about Dr. Kaplan's death without the need for a scared and ashamed sixteen year-old to get involved. At least Bubba would no longer be trying to shoot Loren… Unless, of course, the driver of the one-eyed truck was someone else.

CHAPTER 25

YIPPEE

Tuesday, November 2, was election day. By the time the high school classes ended that afternoon, the temperature had climbed to a balmy eighty-one degrees. Most of the talk among the students at THS centered on the dead guy found the previous morning on the school football field. But there was also considerable concern among the jocks whether the New York Yankees, the parent team of the local Texas League club, would fare well under their newly announced manager, the clownish Casey Stengel. Loren could not imagine what had possessed the Yankee owners to put the future of their famous franchise into the hands of the fifty-seven-year-old rubber-faced former manager of the Brooklyn Dodgers and Boston Bees. Stengel's nine teams had amassed a collective winning percentage of only .435 from 1934 to 1943 and had five times finished seventh, never higher than fifth.

Stengel's playing career, which began in 1912 and lasted fourteen seasons, had been mediocre at best, as he bounced around among Brooklyn, Pittsburgh, Philadelphia, New York and Boston, all in the National League. What must the great Joe DiMaggio, who would now have to call Stengel "Boss," be thinking about this development? Loren had never liked the Yankees, the team that had twice humiliated his beloved Cubs by 4-0 margins in the World Series, first in 1932, and then again in 1938. He hoped Stengel would drag them down to the depths.

By ten o'clock that night, the teletype room at the newspaper office was crowded with onlookers, including personnel from both papers who had abandoned their customary activities or their homes to watch the election returns arriving on the clattering machines. Loren could hardly edge through the curious crowd to tear off pieces of yellow paper for the copy desk of the morning *Gazette*.

President Truman appeared to be holding his own in the eastern states where the polls had already closed. Dewey was carrying New England, Pennsylvania, New Jersey and his own state of New York, but Truman was ahead in Ohio, Virginia, North Carolina, Georgia, Florida, Kentucky and Tennessee. Hence the two candidates were almost even in electoral votes as returns began to arrive from the farm states. "Here's where it'll be decided," pontificated Ward Hatton, who hung over the Associated Press teletype machine so proprietarily that Loren could hardly get his hands on the stories for the *Gazette* that were spewing out of its clicking maw. "Th' farmers of mid-America have been solidly Republican ever since the Civil War," asserted Hatton. "Let Truman have California; even Texas, God forbid. The men in overalls will win it for Dewey."

By midnight, almost time for Loren to leave, the results from the central time zone had arrived. Truman, the cocky little middle westerner, had carried Illinois, Wisconsin, Minnesota, Iowa, Missouri, Arkansas, Oklahoma and Texas, losing only

Michigan and Indiana to Dewey, and Louisiana, Mississippi, Alabama and, of course, South Carolina, to Thurmond, the candidate of the ultra-segregationists.

The election was over. Truman, not Dewey, had captured the "farm vote." No matter what occurred in the voting precincts of the West, the feisty Missourian had been awarded another four years in the White House by a majority of the American people. Loren lingered until he was sure of the result, restraining any show of emotion until Hatton and most of the other journalists had departed. Then he yelled "Yippee!"—which elicited grins from most of the remaining watchers. It was a magical moment.

* * *

On the following afternoon, the eight-column banner headline on the front page of the *Endeavor* which, Loren later learned, had been authored by an elated managing editor while Hatton sulked in his office, read: "Truman Sweeps Into White House As Democrats Nab Control of Congress." It had been an "astounding upset" that had carried into office ten new Democratic senators, including Johnson of Texas, who could now stop worrying about a soon-to-be-extinguished Republican majority in the Senate denying him his seat in that body. The Democrats had also regained control of the House of Representatives, which Loren hoped might lead to the demise of the HUAC, whose Republican chairman, it seemed, was about to be indicted by a federal grand jury for requiring salary kickbacks from his office employees.

Even the election of a Republican named Gerald Ford to the congressional seat in the Michigan district in which Adam Temple had lived as a boy, and which he still considered his favorite place, did not diminish the joy that radiated from Loren's father. "At least that Ford fellow played college football," said Adam. "Maybe that kind of background will give him a feel for working people."

Wishful thinking, thought Loren. He wondered whether his father would have said the same thing about Ford if the newly elected Congressman had not been from central Michigan.

* * *

Nan came home from the hospital the next morning. Sensing something different when he entered the kitchen after school, Loren looked around and spotted her purse on the counter next to the bread box. "Mom!" he yelled, and ran to her bedroom. There she lay, propped up on several pillows, reading a magazine. Smiling, she said: "You might have thought you were rid of me but, as you can see, I'm pretty tough."

"Oh, Mom," quavered Loren. "I'm... I'm glad you're home. That hospital was depressing."

"Oh, it wasn't so bad," said Nan. "The nuns were very conscientious. What they may have lacked in modern techniques, they made up for in attentiveness. Anyway, I made it home. And I plan to stay."

"You've got to take better care of yourself," admonished Loren. "Anything you need done, just tell me. My night job ends on Friday, and I can help you a lot after school."

"Don't promise more than you're able to deliver. Say, look here at this cute little guy." Thrusting her magazine toward Loren, Nan pointed at a photograph that accompanied one of several stories devoted to re-elected Representatives who were expected to be influential in the next session of Congress. A freckled-faced fellow of about forty grinned into the camera. Beside him stood an attractive, intelligent-looking woman holding a baby boy. In front of them was a little girl looking tenderly at the baby. Loren read: "Albert and Pauline Gore of Tennessee, proud parents of Albert, Jr., born on March 31, expect great things from the young man when he gets a little older."

"Aw, Mom," complained Loren. "One baby is pretty much like another. But the daughter—the story doesn't even mention her. Is that fair?"

"No, it's not fair; it's just the way society is. Speaking of girls, how's your love life?"

"Mom!"

"Indelicate of me to put the question that way, I suppose. What I meant was: have you developed a special interest in anyone since you and Mary Beth broke up?"

"Well, there's this one girl..."

"Yes?"

"She's an acrobat."

"Really!"

"Yeah, but I've only had one date with her. That was last Saturday when, you remember, we had car trouble and I made it home very late. Shelley and I got along fine, but the evening was a disaster. She must have been displeased with the experience, because I haven't seen her or heard from her at all since the weekend."

"Shelley. That's a nice name. Can't you phone her?"

"I don't remember her last name. Tony knows it, but I haven't seen him either. He hasn't been in PE class this week."

"What grade is she in?"

"She's a junior, I think, or maybe a sophomore; I'm really not sure."

"Why don't you consult last year's THS yearbook. Neil probably has one. Look for her picture and her last name will be there, too."

"Mom, you're a genius!"

"No, you're the smart one. I'm just a mother who has lived longer. Now, get along; you'll be late for work."

After hugging his mother, Loren went off happily to his job. That night, when he got home, the house was dark and still, except for the rumble of the ceiling fan in the hallway. A comforting quiet. Everything seemed normal again. Loren realized that a portion of the depression that had recently overcome him was owing to his concern for his mother's condition. He wished that he had spoken the words that were on his lips but had remained unspoken—that he loved her. Why were they so hard to say?

* * *

Friday night was Loren's last evening for working in the wire room. He was kept busy answering the phone to record the results of local high school football games and trying to insert the scores into the teletype machine devoted exclusively to state news. This entailed banging the bell every time the device momentarily fell silent, and then hurriedly typing what he needed to transmit before someone else managed to break in. One of the telephone calls that punched through this pandemonium came from Baytown to report that the THS football team had lost its seventh straight game, this one by a score of 33-7. THS had not won a game since mid-season of 1947. Loren was glad he had decided not to try out for the team.

As midnight passed and Saturday came, the stream of news diminished to a trickle, most of it inconsequential. It was time for Loren to leave. As he laid his last few sheets of teletype paper on the copy desk inside the *Gazette* news room, he heard someone call his name from the office of the paper's publisher, Earl Stoner. It was indeed a summons from that gentleman, a Gary Cooper look-alike and man-about-town, whom Adam had called one of the few true journalists on either of the Tocqueville papers.

"I hear this is your last night with us," said Stoner, smiling. "I want to congratulate you for doing an excellent job filling in for Miz Marshall. Your father was right when he told me you were capable. Any time you want a letter of recommendation, I'll be glad to write you one."

"Thank you," said Loren. "I've enjoyed working here." He hesitated, thinking that perhaps there was something else he ought to say. But, no; let sleeping dogs lie. "Well, goodbye." He started out through the door, only to be brought to a halt by Stoner's parting words. "And, Loren, I have to thank you, also, for setting me straight last week about the priorities of a busy journalist, when I phoned to check on a football score."

Loren felt his ears turning red. He tried to think of an appropriate response, but could not. Finally, he said: "Well, thanks for being such an understanding employer." Then he fled. He had a feeling that Stoner and his father would later enjoy a laugh together at his expense, if they had not done so already.

* * *

Earlier that same day Loren had at last reached Shelley Taylor. He had obtained her last name from Tony, who finally showed up, limping badly, in PE class. To Loren's inquiry, Tony answered that he had been stuck at home with a bad infection in his left ankle. Something, perhaps a black widow spider, he said, had bitten him, and the venom had caused serious swelling. Penicillin seemed to have helped reduce the swelling, but Tony would have to sit out flag football for a while. As Loren raced back and forth on the rough turf of the football field, trying to snatch away rags dangling over the buttocks of opposing players, he wondered whether the inflammation in Tony's ankle had really resulted from a snake bite.

At home after school, he consulted the Tocqueville telephone directory and discovered, to his chagrin, that there were at least two dozen Taylors listed.

Eventually he was able to get Tony on the phone in order to obtain Shelley's address: 1115 Peters Street.

William Taylor was the name listed for that address. Loren hopefully dialed the number. Shelley answered. "Hi, Loren," she said. "Ah wuz hopin' it might be yew. Sophie called earlier an' said Ah might be gettin' yore call. Ah bet yew wanna know why Ah wasn't in school las' week."

"Well, yeah," stammered Loren.

"Ah had th' wust case of poison ivy evah," she said. "Uh horrible red rash all ovah mah hands an' legs, even some on mah face an' neck. An' itchy! Ah've been miserable. Used up three bottles of calamine lotion. Sloshed it on till Ah looked like uh weddin' cake wit' pink frostin'."

"I'm really sorry. Where did you run into so much poison ivy?"

"Are yew kiddin'?"

"No, really."

"Do yew 'member that tree Ah climbed?"

"Sure."

"It mus' have been covered wit' poison ivy vines. We couldn't see 'em in th' dark. But after Ah climbed up into th' lower branches, Ah felt some leaves an' said uh prayer that Ah wuz grabbin' Virginia Creepers. No such luck."

"I guess you won't be able to go see a play with me this weekend."

"No way."

"Is there anything I can do for you?"

Silence. Then Shelley said: "From now on keep away from one-eyed pickup trucks."

"I'll certainly try."

"Ah have t' tell yew," she declared, "that even 'though Ah think yore uh nice guy, another episode like th' one las' Sat'day night, an' Ah'm findin' uh fella whose life is less excitin'."

"I understand. I hope I'll see you at school on Monday."

"Me too. Bye." She hung up. Loren resigned himself to an uneventful day at home, reading and listening to the radio. Shelley was a sport. She was only about fifteen, he assumed, but almost as well endowed as... Mrs. Kaplan. The film! Tonight, once he had absolute darkness he would process it to see if he had captured any incriminating images on the night of Dr. Kaplan's demise.

Impatiently he waited for the other Temples to go to bed and for every light to be extinguished. Just before midnight, he set to work in the bathroom to mix his developer in an enameled tray with the correct amount of tepid water, the temperature of which he carefully measured with a thermometer. Pouring the mixture through a glass funnel into a large brown bottle, he then washed out the tray and went through the same procedure with the fixer. Now he was ready for the tricky part.

Turning on a red safelight, he switched off the ceiling light. In the dimness he carefully removed the roll of film from its protective canister and began feeding it into the grooves that surrounded an interior spool that he had earlier removed from his developing tank. It slid in easily, and Loren heaved a sigh of relief, as he reinserted the spool into the tank and screwed on the top.

Next he poured liquid developer into the hole in the lid. Then he inserted an agitator into the same hole, so that he could rotate the spool holding the film, in order to prevent spotting. When his watch told him that twenty-five minutes had passed, he tipped the tank, poured the developer back into the brown bottle; and then filled the tank with tap water, agitating the film for several minutes to be sure that it was thoroughly washed. After pouring the water down the sink drain, he replaced it with acid fixer solution, which he left in the tank for forty-five minutes, to make sure that the negative images that he assumed were now visible on the film would not, in the future, fade and ultimately vanish. He spent that time sitting on the toilet seat, reading a baseball magazine.

In the wee hours of Sunday morning, he opened the tank and withdrew the spool. Removing the film strip, he held it under the cold water tap to rid it of any residue of chemicals and then used a clothespin to hang it from a wire clothes hanger, which he hung on the shower curtain rod, so that it would drip its remaining moisture into the tub and not on the tile floor. After carefully wiping all the surfaces where chemicals might have been spilled, he took a deep breath and held the still dripping film up to the brightly lit electric bulb located above the bathroom mirror.

From several years of experience examining photographic negatives, he could tell that he had captured vivid images of human figures in all eight frames. Tomorrow night he would stay up late again and make some enlargements that would enable him, he hoped, to identify Mrs. K's mysterious companion.

In order to keep the other members of his family ignorant of what he was doing, he carried the dangling film strip into his room and hung it out of sight it in the back of his closet, putting a wad of soiled underwear underneath it to catch the drips. He then put away his equipment and flopped on his cot. Soon he slept.

* * *

At church the following morning, the Reverend Pryor delivered his usual uninspired sermon. After the service he unenthusiastically admitted the two Temple boys to his study to complete plans for their baptisms.

While describing the ritual, he seemed distracted. Once Loren saw him sneak a longing look at a leather golf bag from which protruded a set of expensive-looking clubs. At a few minutes past one o'clock the boys returned home to join Adam and Nan for Sunday dinner, followed in Loren's case by a nap.

Later Loren intended to play catch with Tommy, if his brother could be persuaded to put down his dratted violin for a while. Actually Tommy was getting pretty good on the tricky instrument. He had started taking lessons only three years ago in Winona and he was already second chair in the "fiddle" section, as he termed it, of the THS student orchestra. Moreover, he had his eye on the position of concert master, which would be open the following fall.

But when the white-haired Hungarian who came to the Temple home to give Tommy violin lessons learned that his pupil regularly played catch with a baseball, he voiced violent objections. "No, no!" he exclaimed. "You haff to end dis baseball bidness at once! Now! De fingers; dey mus be protected at all cost!" He wiggled the digits on his own age-spotted left hand. "Dey haff to be fast und flexible; dey cannot be bruised or broken;, ever, ever!"

Tommy seemed amused when he narrated the maestro's admonition. Nevertheless, he now seemed less eager to serve as catcher for his older brother's practice pitches. Late that afternoon, however, he agreed to do so, and once they were out in the driveway, he was his usual peppy self, pounding his mitt with his right hand and exhorting Loren to "put it right in here," as if the old Hungarian had never said a word.

After darkness set in, Loren waited impatiently for Tommy and his parents to retire, so that he could set up his photographic equipment in the bathroom without being interrupted. It was after midnight before the others were all in bed, and by that time Loren was himself yawning uncontrollably. Therefore he was rather relieved to discover that the bottle of print developer that he needed to produce enlargements from his negatives did not contain enough solution to do the job. He would have to purchase more.

CHAPTER 26
THE KICKER

On Monday afternoon, Loren's life once again changed direction. During PE class he called the plays for his flag football team, running, passing, kicking, and occupying the safety position on defense. Not until the hour was almost over did he notice a withered little man wearing a THS baseball cap and a purple jacket watching from a folding chair located near the door to the gym.

Shifting his attention back to the game, Loren prepared to kick off to the other team, something the others had insisted that he do because he was better at it than anyone else. His advantage, he believed, came from his brown and white saddle shoes. Everyone else wore sneakers or took off their cowboy boots and played in their stocking feet. In any case, nobody had recently suggested in his hearing, as Tony had once done, that only girls wore saddle shoes. His abilities had silenced them all.

This particular kickoff was one of Loren's best. It sailed, end over end, from his own forty yard line across the opposition goal line and entirely out of the end zone, so that there was no way to run it back. A bell then sounded from the classroom building, signaling the end of PE. As Loren headed for his art class, he was accosted by the elderly onlooker.

"Ah'm Coach Cooper," the man declared. "How long yew been kickin' thataway?"

"I got into a couple of games as a freshman," replied Loren. "I began kicking regularly for the varsity as a sophomore."

"Not heah. Whar?"

"Winona Country Day. In Illinois."

"Nevah heared of it."

Loren started to retort that he'd never heard of Tocqueville High School either until the previous summer, but instead he contented himself with: "We won most of our games."

"Why ain't yew playin' fer us?"

"I tried. But when I went to see Coach Allen, he acted like he didn't want to be bothered. So I took a job downtown instead."

"Yew work after school?"

"Not anymore. My job ended last Friday."

"So yew could kick fer us."

"I imagine so, if you want me."

"We need someone t' do our place kicking. Our regular kicker hurt his knee several games back. His replacement, uh kid named Montgomery, ain't doin' th' job."

"Mouse?"

"Yeah. Yew know 'im?"

"Not well. He's pretty small."

"Uh li'l squirt. But he's uh battler. Trouble is, he can't seem t' git th' hang of place kickin'. Yew done any playin' 'sides kickin'?"

"Well, I played tailback. Ran and passed."

"Huh. This gits real interestin'. Come wit' me. Practice starts in half an hour. We'll git yew suited up an' git yew uh play book, an' yew kin take uh quick look at it afore it's time t' take th' field."

"What about Coach Allen?"

"Leave 'im t' me. Ah'm th' athletic director, which makes me his boss. Yew'll be our kicker. We got three games left this yeah. If we don' win uh couple, Coach Allen ain't likely t' be back next yeah. So he's gonna be willin' t' try anythin'."

Loren hesitated. "I'm supposed to be in Art class now. I'm already late."

Allen gave him an impatient glare. "D' yew wanna play, or not?"

"I'd like to play."

"Then let's git ovah t' th' locker room. Ah'll fix things wit' Miz Harper. We done bidness wit' her afore. Yew'll git uh good grade: Jus' show up fer ten or fifteen minutes at th' beginnin' of class, an' then she'll let yew leave fer practice."

A peculiar system, thought Loren. He liked his Art teacher, who had already taught him how to do lithographing, and was encouraging him to continue on his own, telling him that he had real talent. But the opportunity to show off his athleticism for Shelley was too tempting. Art would have to wait.

* * *

In the locker room underneath the stadium, Coach Cooper stood over the freckle-faced student equipment manager to make sure that he produced pieces of paraphernalia until Loren was entirely satisfied. He tried on a pair of shoulder pads that promised protection for his collar bones; rejected a pair of bulky hip pads in favor of lighter but harder rib pads; and slid hard rubber thigh pads into the inside slots of uniform pants with cushioned knees, before he pulled them on over an elastic athletic supporter that covered Mister Wiggly with a metal cup. Then he added a plain white sweatshirt, white wool socks, hightopped shoes with hard rubber cleats jutting from their soles, and a hard plastic helmet with elastic netting to hold it a short distance from his head and a chin strap to keep it from being knocked off in a collision. This completed his regalia.

As the locker room began to fill with players, many of whom looked at Loren curiously, Coach Cooper followed Coach Allen into the latter's small sanctum. When they emerged, Allen came directly over to Loren, who was waiting, fully uniformed except for his helmet, seated on a wooden bench.

"Yer name Temple?" Allen asked.

"Yessir."

"Coach Cooper says yew kin place kick."

"Yessir."

"Let's see. Rog, come 'ere."

A half-dressed fellow about Loren's size stood up. "This 'ere's Lane Temple," said Coach Allen. "Ah wan' yew t' take 'im out t' th' south end of th' stadium an' hold fer thirty extra point tries, an' ten field goal attempts each from th' ten, fifteen, twenty and twenty-five yard lines. Git Hulk t' center th' ball t' yew. An' keep track of how many successful kicks Lane makes. When yore finished, come over t' th' practice field an' git t' work on yore regular routine. Got it?"

"O. K., Coach," replied Rog cheerfully. He tugged a purple jersey over his shoulder pads, summoned Hulk Harper, the big all-conference center, to join them, and led Loren through an opening in the stands onto the playing field. Loren wondered if they were traversing the very spot where Bubba's body had been found.

"Whar yew been playin', Lane?" asked Rog curiously.

"I played last year in Illinois. Kicked points and field goals for our team. Coach Cooper asked me to try out."

"Wal, Lane, yew may find out that we play uh mighty tough game heah in Texas."

"My name is Loren. And I don't see how Tocqueville can be too tough with seven straight losses."

"Uh wise guy, huh?"

"No. But where I came from, we won most of our games."

Rog was silent until they reached the center of the field next to the south end zone. Then a gawky guy in gray sweat clothes, apparently a student manager, tossed one of four footballs he had brought along to Hulk, who leaned over it on the two yard line, and Rog went down on one knee some seven yards out. Loren swung his right leg up and down, to loosen it. Then he said: "I'm ready."

He stepped into the first hike, held point down by Rog, and blasted it high over the middle of the cross bar, well beyond the fellow fetching. He then relaxed a bit, concentrating on fundamentals: head down, eyes fixed on a spot slightly below the center of the football, easy swing of the leg, and follow through. He soon lost count of how many times he had kicked the ball through the uprights, but eventually Rog said: "That's thirty. Ah gotta admit, Loren, that yore uh helluffa kicker. Thirty fer thirty. Don' yew evah miss?"

"I'm not supposed to miss."

"Lessee how yew do at field goal range," interjected Hulk, who had begun to show considerable interest in the proceedings.

With Hulk centering the ball from the ten yard line, which entailed a kick of almost thirty yards, Loren was ten for ten. From the fifteen, he was eight for ten, dubbing a couple when he tried too hard to get extra zip into his kicking leg. From the twenty, he was ten for ten again. "Wow!" exclaimed Rog. "All ten! Ah kin hardly wait 'till Friday. Have we got uh surprise fer Port Natchez."

The goal posts looked far away from where Loren stood on the thirty-four yard line, as he began his final series of kicks. Trying too hard, he hooked the first one to the left, and short. The second one hit the cross bar and bounced back. But number three was good and so were five of the next seven. A better than fifty per cent average. Not bad.

"I can do better," said Loren to Coach Allen, when Rog had delivered his report. "I'm out of practice."

"Yew'll git yore practice. Coach Cooper said yew did more than kick on yore high school team."

"Yes. I played tailback in the single-wing formation, and on defense I played safety."

"We use uh T formation. Yew evah play quarterback in th' T?"

"A little. We used it occasionally."

"Do any passin'?"

"Some. I'm not very good at it."

"Let's see." Allen blew his whistle and gathered his squad around him. When he had their attention, he ordered the fullbacks, guards and tackles to hit the blocking sled, and the other backs and ends to line up to catch passes. Hulk would center and "Lane" would take the first turn at quarterback, passing.

"Now, Lane," Allen instructed. "We use uh pro-style offense, wit' th' quarterback either handin' off or droppin' back t' pass. Th' linemen'll try t' form uh pocket t' protect yew; so whut yew do is take 'bout five quick steps straight back, turn 'roun', spot yore receiver, an' throw. Don' worry 'bout pass routes right now. Did Coach Cooper give yew uh play book?"

"Yessir."

"Study it. Ah wan' yew t' have all th' pass routes memorized by Thursday. Think yew kin do that?"

"Yessir."

"Good. Let's git t' work."

Loren awkwardly edged up behind Hulk, who was bent over forward, his huge paws possessively petting the pimpled surface of a scuffed football. Tentatively, Loren thrust his own hands into the opening below Hulk's massive buttocks.

"Lane!" yelled Allen.

Loren jumped.

"Git up close. Poke that top hand right up 'gainst Hulk's nuts; so yew kin feel 'em. When yew wan' th' ball, give 'im a li'l nudge."

"But not too hard," growled Hulk.

"Yessir," mumbled Loren. Feeling foolish, he followed instructions. Mouse Montgomery was the first pass catcher to race downfield about seven or eight yards and then cut across the middle of the field. He made a small target but Loren led him perfectly with a tight spiral that had a slight upward tilt on the front end. Hence it floated, rather than bored, into the clutches of the runty runner, who drew it to his chest without breaking stride.

The same scenario followed when J. J. Johnson lumbered downfield. And a flock of others. After a while Loren found himself asked to throw button hook passes, passes into the flat, and fly passes downfield. He made them look easy. A few were dropped, but not one was off target. Conscious of the growing enthusiasm among his new teammates, he felt himself falling into a pleasant rhythm. Hike; drop back; throw; slide forward to Hulk's hindquarters; and do it again. And again. Long hours practicing with his father during the Winona years were paying off.

Finally, a loud blast of Allen's whistle ended the exercise. "Time fer Stephenson t' throw uh few," he said. "Lane, yew join th' receivers." As Loren fell in behind one of the lines of guys waiting to run out for passes, he overheard Rog whisper to Mouse: "Gawd. 'I'm not very good at it.' Th' sonuffabitch didn't miss uh throw." Mouse merely shook his head. He didn't seem very happy about Loren's performance.

Running out for passes, Loren caught all he could reach. In one instance he was forced to leap for a high throw from Rog and spear it with one hand. Neither Rog nor Mouse, who were apparently the number one and number two quarterbacks on the THS team, regularly threw catchable passes. Rog seemed to think that every situation called for bullet passes, inappropriate for certain fly patterns or short pitchouts, especially since he was frequently off target. And Mouse's passes wobbled, perhaps because he had small hands, and were thrown either too early or too late, which increased the probability of dropped balls or interceptions.

Loren was surprised to see that his skills were so superior to the other two. Maybe he had made a mistake in not going out for football at the beginning of the season. But then he would have missed the opportunity to work at the newspaper office...

Coach Allen's whistle blasted through his reverie. "Ah wan' th' fust an' second stringers t' run through some plays," he shouted. "Lane, yew watch carefully an' try t' figure out whut's happenin'."

As the two teams lined up and the two quarterbacks, in their respective turns, spouted numbers and hut-hutted to initiate the plays, Loren suddenly realized that the first stringers were all wearing purple jerseys and the other players were all wearing white. Looking down at his own white sweatshirt, he wondered whether his performance in practice would produce a change.

* * *

On the following afternoon, Loren discovered that the road to first string status would be treacherous. As practice was beginning, he saw Mouse on tiptoe whispering into J. J.'s ear. At first the big end shook his head; then, as Mouse persisted in what he was saying, J. J. finally nodded, looking grim.

After an hour spent warming up, with Loren place kicking, Coach Allen again ordered a scrimmage, the first team matched against the subs. At first Loren sat and watched. The drill called for the purple shirts to line up on the ten yard line and in four plays or less run or pass for a touchdown. Invariably they succeeded. They were bigger, averaging about 175 pounds in the line and perhaps 155 pounds in the backfield, compared with the white shirts, who looked to be on the average ten or fifteen pounds lighter. Hulk, especially, was a mighty force in the middle, as he blasted wide holes for his backs. Double-teaming him made little difference. And J. J. at right end rarely failed to wipe out the opposing tackle on runs to his side. He was also a capable pass catcher, muscling his way through the defensive backs to gather in Rog's hard throws. Seeing Mouse playing at safety, trying vainly to defend against his tall pal, Loren wanted to laugh. It was ludicrous.

"Lane!"

"Yessir."

"Git in thar an' replace Mouse. See if yew kin stop those passes."

"Right." Tugging on his helmet, Loren ran into the end zone and tapped Mouse on a shoulder pad. "Coach wants you to rest a while," he said. Looking malevolent, Mouse appeared inclined to resist. Then he shrugged and trotted over to the sideline.

The purple shirts broke out of their huddle and took their positions. Loren saw a slight grin on J. J.'s face and suspected that he was about to be tested. He was right. As soon as the ball was snapped, the big fellow came right at Loren. No finesse; just power.

Loren counted to five, giving Rog time to drop back and release, and then flitted in front of J. J. in time to intercept the pass. Speeding toward the nearest sideline and then turning upfield, he froze Rog with a head fake and then entirely eluded him with a crossover step. At midfield he was in the clear, his nearest pursuer ten yards behind, when Coach Allen's whistle called him back.

"That's th' way t' defend 'gainst th' pass," shouted Allen. "How many times have Ah tole yew guys; wait fer th' passer t' commit hisself, an' then go fer th' ball. Now let's try some runnin' plays."

Playing safety, Loren found himself fending off people coming at him from all directions, as he tried to help the other backs plug the gaping holes opened in the second team's line by the purple blockers. J. J. seemed to take a special interest in trying to knock Loren down. Fortunately, he was so clumsy that it was not difficult to fend him off or make him miss entirely. He began cursing Loren, referring to him in an undertone, as he picked himself up after another unsuccessful block, as a "cocksucker" and "muffafugger." Loren laughed in his face, which infuriated him all the more.

Eventually, Coach Allen ordered the varsity to play defense, which gave Loren a chance to see what he could accomplish as a T formation quarterback. His center was no bigger than himself and appeared intimidated by the sight of a crouching Hulk, ready to manhandle him as soon as he delivered the ball into Loren's hands. In the huddle, Loren told his fellow white shirts that since he had not yet had an opportunity to learn all the plays, he would simply describe what he wanted to do and then name a number to signal when the ball should be snapped. "We'll begin with off tackle, to the right side, on three. Left half carries; others block," he whispered.

"That's numba 35," piped up a scrawny fellow who played left guard. "Th' three back through th' five hole."

"Thanks," said Loren. "Hit 'em hard."

As soon as the ball hit his hands, the two lines crashed together with grunts and curses and the usual thumping and scraping sounds. Loren slid to the right and handed the ball off to the left halfback, who was promptly buried under a pile of defenders. Watching, instead of racing to the rear for self-protection, Loren paid the price. From behind someone smashed into him with devastating force, knocking him flat on his face, and then falling on top of him, slamming his helmet with a hard hand; so that his head felt momentarily as if it might explode. "How'd yew like that, yew shitass toadhead?" growled J. J., towering triumphantly over him.

Staggering to his feet and spitting dirt, Loren wobbled back to the huddle, trying to shake off the swirling sensation behind his eyes, hoping that he had not suffered a concussion.

"Are yew all right?" one of his teammates asked.

"Yeah," said Loren grimly. "This time we'll run a pitch-back to the right halfback around left end. On four. And don't anyone else try to block J. J. Leave him for me."

"Yew kin have 'im," he heard the fullback mutter.

The play started as planned, with the guards pulling and Loren faking a handoff to the fullback heading inside left tackle and then tossing the ball back to the right halfback. The left halfback and the two guards bypassed J. J., as they looked for others to block. Just as J.J. reached out his long arms to engulf the ball carrier and throw him for a loss, Loren hit him with a vicious block at shin level, that knocked him head over heels. Behind his interference, the runner burst into the end zone.

Satisfied, Loren got up and went back to call another play. But the others were not huddling. Instead they were solemnly staring past Loren. Turning around, he saw that J. J. was still on the ground, groaning, and Coach Allen was hustling over from the sideline, a worried look on his face.

Soon a cluster of coaches, managers, and purple and white shirts surrounded the prone player, whose moans and curses Loren could distinctly hear over sounds of reassurance and expressions of sympathy.

A student manager ran toward the gym and disappeared inside. Most of the players sat down on the ground and wordlessly waited. A few, including Mouse, remained standing next to where the coaches were quietly talking among themselves. After about twenty minutes, an ambulance appeared at one end of the practice field and a manager rushed to open a gate.

Loren watched while the attendants loaded J. J. onto a stretcher. "Broken leg," he heard one of them tell Coach Allen. When the injured player had disappeared inside the vehicle and had been driven away, Coach Allen gathered the remaining players around him and said: "We've jus' had an accident. Ah saw th' play; it wuz uh clean block. J. J. caught his cleats in th' grass. It coulda happened t' anyone. Summa yew may wanna visit J. J. at Baptis' hospital in uh day or so, as soon as they kin git his leg set an' put it in uh cast. Meanwhile, we've gotta lotta work t' do t' prepare fer Port Natchez. Th' linemen go wit' Coach Crowder ovah yonder; th' backs stay here wit' me. Ah wanna discuss some new plays we're gonna install t'morra."

CHAPTER 27

THE QUARTERBACK

The rest of the week passed uneventfully, with football practice on Friday consisting of one hour of movies, shown in a darkened classroom, during which the coaches pointed out what they called "keys," patterns of behavior by Port Natchez players during a recent game. Loren made mental notes on the tendencies of certain players.

One reason for not going outside on Friday was that by two o'clock the skies were spouting rain. That evening, the field at Port Natchez, a chalk-lined expanse of sodden grass enclosed within shallow bleachers that seated fewer than a thousand spectators, was shrouded in a driving downpour. Loren sat shivering in a yellow slicker on the THS bench while Mouse kicked off pitifully and flubbed his only extra point try, as the two teams struggled to a 7-6 score, Port Natchez in the lead, with only a couple of minutes left in the contest.

Then, trying to run around end on a keeper play, Rog slipped in a puddle near the fifty-yard-line and crashed out-of-bounds into a wooden bench that the Natchez substitutes had moved almost onto the sideline, so that they could better see the action through the curtain of rain. The Purple quarterback did not not get up. From the other side of the field, Loren watched while one of the spectators, apparently a doctor, leaned over the fallen player. Eventually Rog made it to his feet and was helped off the field by a couple of student managers. They escorted him to a car parked behind the bleachers, which carried him away.

Mouse was already throwing a football to one of the other subs, getting ready to replace Rog. Still sitting uncomfortably on the bench, Loren wished that the game was over and he was home.

"Lane!" He saw Coach Allen beckoning.

"Yessir!"

"Go in at quarterback an' try t' get within field goal range. Yore only hope is sideline passes t' stop th' clock. Yew have wun timeout left. Save it as long as yew kin."

Loren ran out onto the field, conscious that Mouse, left behind, was furious. Bent over in the huddle, he said "I want a winged T. Halfbacks, go down and out toward the sidelines. After you catch the ball, be sure to get out of bounds before you are tackled. We've got to stop that clock after every play, or we don't have a chance. You ends, stay in tight to the tackles and block. Give me time to throw. On three. That's it. Break."

As the Purple players trotted foward to their positions, a distant clap of thunder and flash of lightning signaled that the storm, already fierce, was about to intensify. Loren shouted: "Set! One, two, three... and felt the wet ball between his hands. Sliding slightly on the slippery turf, he dropped back, looking toward the left sideline; then, just as an enemy rusher got a heavy hand on his hip, he swiveled and threw a bullet pass to the right halfback, who juggled it and then held on just as he lunged across the right sideline.

First down on the Port Natchez thirty-eight. Again Loren threw to the same receiver, and again the defenders were unable to prevent him from falling out of bounds, just as he was tripped by a tackler. Barely over a minute left, and the ball resting on the twenty-five. Whoever was running the clock for the home team had a lazy hand on the stop switch.

One more throw, thought Loren. This time his primary receiver was well covered; hence he was forced to throw to the other side. It was an accurate pass, but the left halfback dropped it. Second down and about thirty-five seconds left. Loren drew back from the huddle and called to the referee: "Watch me for a time-out signal." The official nodded. He understood.

Again the snap; again the slamming together of the linemen and the squishy sounds of people running. Loren, after faking a sideline pass, suddenly lowered the ball into his right armpit and dashed forward through a crack in the struggling mass of players in front of him, cut sharply toward the middle of the field, dodged one tackler, and was knocked off his feet by a second one. Even as he fell forward to pick up an extra yard, he began yelling "Time out! Time out!" Although the referee's whistle sounded almost immediately, Loren feared that his gamble of trying to improve the position of the ball for a field goal attempt might have taken too much time. But then, looking at the scoreboard clock, he saw that it still showed two seconds left to play.

Running over to the visitor's bench, he asked for a dry towel, so that he could clean his hands of the slime that covered them as a result of his tumble into the mud. "Say, Coach," he asked Allen. "Can I have Mouse as my holder?"

"Whutever yew say, son," said Allen. "Mouse! Go in fer Smitty. Yore gonna hold th' ball fer uh field goal." To Loren he said: "Good luck, young fella."

With a bewildered look, Mouse put on his helmet and accompanied Loren out to the huddle. A short toot from the referee's whistle signaled that the time out was over. "All right, guys," said Loren to his ten teammates. "I've gotta kick it about thirty-five yards, not counting the height of the crossbar. I can do it if you'll hold fast for four seconds. Block like you've never blocked before. Hulk, you've gotta give Mouse a perfect center snap. Let's go!"

Eleven determined Tocquevillians broke from their huddle and lined up in punt formation. Mouse knelt about six yards directly behind Hulk, holding out his hands as a target for the long center snap. When Mouse's fingers wiggled, Hulk delivered him the ball, a nice spiral perfectly placed. Trying to position it for the kick, however, a nervous Mouse let it squirt out of his hands. For a moment Loren stood helpless as he watched Mouse scramble for the errant pigskin, fumble it again, and finally pick it up just as a burly rusher crashed into him, which popped the ball out of his hands into the air, blessedly back to Loren. Snatching it, Loren frantically evaded a brace of Port Natchez tacklers. Others seemed to be all around him, yelling: "Git 'im! Git 'im!"

Seeing an opening, he dashed through it, heading for the sideline, quickly realizing, however, that any chance of running for a score was unlikely to succeed.

There were too many mud-covered red jerseys in the way. A pass was out of the question; none of his teammates had shown the sense to run toward the end zone. There was only one thing left to do. He slid to a stop, swung around to face the goal posts, and with the sound of oncoming footsteps close behind him, let the ball fall, point down, onto a wet but smooth spot in the grass, and drop kicked it with all the strength he could summon from his right leg, end over end, between the goal posts about a foot above the cross bar.

Lying where he had been knocked down by a tardy tackler, Loren heard spectators screaming, red jerseyed players cursing, his own teammates shouting for joy, and the opposing coach protesting loudly to the referee that the play was illegal and the score should not count.

"Naw," replied the zebra-suited official. "It wuz uh legal drop kick. Ah ain't seen wun in twenty-five years, but th' rules allow it." A grin split his wrinkled countenance. "It shore wuz purty."

The girls's locker room in the Port Natchez gym, which had been allocated to the THS team as their dressing room for the game, was alive with elation. It was their first victory in over a year! Coach Allen shook hands with Loren; and several teammates did likewise or slapped him on the back. Even Mouse gave him a grudging grin. Bitsy, the corpulent sports editor of the *Endeavor*, was there, too, and said: "Ah cud tell when yore daddy fust brought yew t' see me, that yew were uh winnah. Ah'm gonna call yew th' hero of th' game in mah story t'morrow."

"Please don't do that, Mr. Mason," pleaded Loren. "I only played a few downs. It was a team effort. Please don't single me out; it'll make the others feel bad."

Bitsy had already turned away to converse with Marvin Crowder, the line coach. Two middle-aged fat fellows bumping bellies.

* * *

The following week passed routinely. Loren's classes were humdrum. Even Miz Muser's facial contortions and vocal pyrotechnics in her home room and in her history class were becoming wearily familiar. At home Loren was too tired following afternoon football practice to concentrate on schoolwork. Fortunately, his three years at Winona CDS had prepared him so well that he was easily able to complete his assignments in the mornings before breakfast.

Despite his heroics at Port Natchez, he still wore a white jersey at football practice, while Mouse quarterbacked the varsity. On Friday, all THS students were released from their classes at noon to participate in a pep rally in the gymnasium. When Loren got there, the bleachers on both sides of the basketball floor were crowded with excited students whipped into a frenzy by waving, bouncing, yelling cheerleaders wearing white sweaters with big purple T's, and reciting such slogans as: "Bust 'em, sock 'em; knock 'em down. We're th' toughest team in this here town."

Asked to speak, Coach Allen discoursed on brotherhood and loyalty, and how it wasn't important whether you won or lost but how you played the game. And then he fell on his knees and clasped his hands before his chest, and offered up a prayer aloud to his "Heavenly Father" to keep the Tocqueville players from harm and let them taste the well-deserved rewards of their dedication and hard work, especially the seniors.

Members of the school band played "Deep in the Heart of Texas," "The Yellow Rose of Texas," and lastly "The Eyes of Texas," at which time everyone stood and many sang. Loren remained silent.

In anticipation of the event, most of the varsity players had worn their purple game jerseys to school, thereby identifying themselves as local notables, objects of awe particularly venerated by susceptible females, even though the team had lost seven straight before the lucky two-point win over Port Natchez. Loren remained inconspicuously seated in the stands when a dozen members of the squad ran out onto the floor and began shouting "Kill, kill, kill…!"

Loren looked around. Student reactions ranged from something resembling religious fervor to stone-faced disapproval by a very few. In the bleachers across the floor he saw Shelley and Sophia, sitting together, both of them radiant with enthusiasm. He did not see Tony or Mary Beth, but he did spot Neil seated not far away, and the two of them exchanged slight smiles signifying: "Whut yew gonna do?" They were trapped in cultural craziness, and there was nothing for a sensible senior to do but sit silently and wait it out.

As the pep rally continued, Loren the Loner sat surrounded by wiggling, waving, shouting schoolmates jumping up and down. He thought about what he had witnessed that morning in math class. His teacher, Mr. Gamble, a seedy guy with a weak chin, a thin mustache and a quavering whine, had oscillated between bravado and obsequiousness when struggling to maintain order in a classroom half full of football players, including Hulk, J. J. and the Mouse. Sitting near the latter two, Loren had noticed that when Gamble passed out the mid-term exams he favored the footballers with extra sheets of paper, dropped on their desks face down. When Loren turned his over, he discovered that it contained the answers to all of the exam questions. As he was pondering whether it would be right to take advantage of this gift, he heard J. J. loudly complain: "Say, whar's mah answer sheet?"

"Shh!" whispered a disconcerted Mr. Gamble, the back of his neck turning rosy over his dandruff-sprinkled jacket. "Yew don' git one 'cause yore hurt an' kin't play no more."

"Whaddya mean, Ah don' git one? Ah always git th' answers."

"Not any more. Principal's orders. Sorry."

"Shee-it. Yew stupid li'l prick. Yore th' one who's gonna be sorry." Leaning on his crutches, J. J. shambled out of the room, amid a shocked silence, which changed to a titter and a few loud laughs from several of the footballers, as Mr. Gamble vainly beat on his desk with a ruler, demanding order.

How long had this been going on? wondered Loren. He recalled how hard it had been for some students at Winona CDS to hold on to their eligibility to participate in varsity athletics, which required at least a C average in rigorous academic subjects. What a difference!

Loren could not see any logical justification for the mindless pep rally, the pandering prayer, and the anti-Christian cries of "kill," all accomplished by the cancelling of classes for the entire student body, in order that a few should receive deference denied the academically able and even the better teachers. He wondered, as he had on so many occasions since June: was this the right environment for him? If not, where would he ever find one?

* * *

The game at Southside High School that evening began with Mouse at quarterback for the purple shirts, while Loren sat on the bench, except for kickoffs and one extra point attempt, which he made easily. Tied 7-7 at halftime, the two teams struggled on approximately equal terms up and down the field until the game was nearly over. Then a green-shirted player slammed into Mouse, as he tried to pass, and a second southsider picked off the errant delivery and ran it all the way across the THS goal line. The score changed to 13-7, with less than two minutes left to play.

Amid the groans and curses from teammates on the bench beside him, and the uproar from the fans of both teams who packed the stadium seats and stood three-deep behind both end zones, Loren watched as Mouse tried to stand and then collapsed back onto the ground. After treatment by the trainer, which consisted largely of a sniff of smelling salts, the bantam quarterback was helped, glassy-eyed, off the field.

Loren had his helmet on when the expected summons came from Coach Allen. "Git us uh score, boy. Do lak yew did at Port Natchez. We're countin' on yew."

Sure, thought Loren. That's why you sat me on the bench. As he ran out to the huddle, he looked at the clock. Scarcely one minute left. "Listen, guys," he said. "We're going to set up a screen of blockers along the sideline to try for a long runback. When the kickoff comes, watch to see which side of the field it heads toward; then set up your screen on that side. Try to keep the sideline clear of green shirts. I'll take left safety; Rick take the other side. Whoever gets the ball, take it as far as you can, but don't get tackled before you get out of bounds. We have no more time outs. Watch for an on-side kick. Fall on it; don't try to pick it up and run with it. And then we'll have to line up at once and throw a hail Mary pass, or we won't have time for any play at all."

The kickoff went to the other side, dropping into Rick's hands on the sixteen yard line. He promptly fumbled it and was barely able to retrieve it and make the sideline before being buried under a bunch of Greenies.

Time for only one play, Loren realized. During practices he had seen Hunk, horsing around, throw the ball for prodigious distances, sometimes as far as seventy yards. Now the time had come to give the big fellow a chance to be a hero.

Just as Loren was about to call the play, Mouse burst into the huddle. "Yore out, Rick," he said excitedly to the right halfback. His face alight with enthusiasm, he said: "Coach wants me at quarterback an' Lane at wingback fer uh hail Mary pass. Let's..."

"Wait a minute," Loren blurted out. "It's almost eighty yards to the goal line. You can't throw the ball half that far. There'll be Greenies all around me, with forty yards to go."

"But coach said..."

"Forget it. You play wingback and go straight down the middle toward the Greenie goalposts. Billy, you play center, and Hulk, you replace Rick at right half. When I take the snap from Billy, on four, Hulk drift over toward the sideline like you don't know what's going on, and be sure to stay well behind me. I'll wait as long as I can before being tackled and then throw you a lateral. Take your time... and then throw the ball as far as you can toward the Greenie goal posts. Mouse should be there. I'll try to get downfield, too, to help. Everyone else block like hell! Break."

They rushed into punt formation. Loren visualized Coach Allen on the sideline wondering what was going on. When the center snap came, he watched his linemen, elbows up, doing their best to hold back the snarling, clawing, charging Greenies, and he waited until the dike collapsed and arms were reaching out for him,... at which time he swiveled and hurled a long lateral pass over to Hunk, near the sideline. Not even waiting to see whether the big guy caught it, he burst through the clearing congestion, and raced downfield. As he neared the thirty, he saw Mouse converging from the right (what took him so long?) and then looked back over his shoulder just in time to see Hulk heave the ball over a leaping lineman, a super throw that would challenge either Mouse or Loren to reach it.

There were only two Greenies in the area when the ball settled into Loren's reaching hands, as he sped across the twenty, but they were uncomfortably close. A sudden swerve left one of them cursing on the ground, but the second one hit Loren with a diving tackle at the ankles and he felt himself falling.

Mouse was puffing about two yards behind him. Just before Loren hit the ground he was able to shovel the ball to his tiny teammate. For a long moment Mouse stood still, holding the ball while more Greenies thundered toward him. With the wind knocked out of him, Loren gasped "Move, Mouse!" Then, with a sudden gleeful grin, Mouse started sprinting toward the goal. As he crossed the ten yard line, he looked back and observed that the nearest panting opponent was well behind him. He started to dance. Lifting his knees and twirling and waving the ball around in one small hand, he yelled in a squeaky treble: "Greenies, Weenies,...!"

Damn it, thought Loren. Cut the crap and get the ball over the goal.

Then came the disaster. As Mouse danced over the two yard line, the ball flew out of his hand and landed back by the five, flipping around like a fish out of water, as a pop-eyed Mouse scrambled to recapture it, and several excited green shirts converged on the same spot.

Mouse got there first. Snatching up the ball, he took a couple of strides, and then disappeared under several brawny southsiders, with the ball popping out of the pile to be joyfully downed on the one-yard line by a fourth Greenie.

* * *

In the locker room afterwards, Coach Allen threw a tantrum. To Mouse, who was crying, he directed such epithets as "stupid cocksucker" and "shitbrain." Denting several steel lockers with angry kicks and petulant punches with a right hand that Loren thought would probably be swollen by morning, he exclaimed: "Ah dunno why Ah wanna coach yew fuggers; yew drive me crazy." He slammed his way out of the room, banging the door behind him.

Hulk, hunched over trying to disentangle a knotted shoelace, muttered: "Maybe th' bastard won' have t' worry 'bout us next yeah. Ah hear th' school board is gonna give 'im th' ax."

Mouse sniffled: "Ah'd lak t' give 'im th' ax all right, on his fat neck."

"Cum on, Mouse," said Hulk. "Coach is right. Yew fucked up."

"But he ain't s'pposed t' curse me," whined Mouse. "Ah wish J. J. wuz heah. He'd shore belted him wun."

"Fergit it," rumbled Hulk. "We got wun more game. Let's concentrate on next Thursday. Thanksgiving. Th' last time 'roun' fer us seniors."

"Good man, Hulk," said Loren. And got out of there.

CHAPTER 28

THE BAPTISM

At ten a.m. on Saturday Loren and Tommy met with with Pastor Pryor to discuss the arrangements for their baptism the next day. Afterwards, dropping Tommy at home, Loren drove downtown to purchase photographic paper and chemicals, so that he could make enlargements of his Kaplan pictures late that night, after his movie date with Shelley. Evening shadows were starting to shroud Tocqueville when he finally found the Taylor domicile, after having driven around for almost an hour peering at street signs and house numbers in the city's most affluent sector.

As Loren left Shaky and started toward Shelley's front door, it opened and she came out to meet him. She was dressed very much as a Winona CDS girl would have been, in an ankle-length long sleeved green and brown checked jumper over a crisp white blouse with a pointed collar. Although she seemed surprised by the sight of an all-purple car, she appeared gratified that Loren hurried to open Shaky's passenger door for her and seemed even more pleased when he asked her if she'd like to see the movie "Son of the Bride of Frankenstein" at the Casino Theater, with Basil Rathborne, Boris Karloff and Bela Lugosi. "Ah love scary movies," she said.

When they arrived at the theater, Loren was worried by the sign in the ticket-seller's window that said all children under sixteen had to be accompanied by a parent. However, no one objected when he paid eighty cents for the two of them, and they walked inside. She shook her head when he asked her if she wanted anything to eat or drink, and waved to an usher, who immediately stepped away from two elderly people arguing about where they should sit, and led them down a long aisle, eventually pointing his small flashlight at two empty seats, front and center. As they sat down, the movie's opening credits were running. Despite Loren's tardiness in picking Shelley up, they hadn't missed any of the feature.

As soon as they were seated, she whispered: "Were yew nervous outside 'cause yew thought Ah might not be sixteen?"

"No, I...," Loren started to say. Then he confessed: "Yes, I guess so."

"Rest easy. Ah turned seventeen las' month. Ah may be small but Ah'm not as young as Ah appear. Ah hadda miss uh yeah of elementary school 'cause of bein' sickly. That's why Ah got into gymnastics, in order t' build up mah body."

"I see," said Loren. "A great body, too." Then he blushed.

The movie was indeed scary. But when Loren reached for Shelley's hand to assure her of his protective presence, she smiled at him, not frightened at all. Leaving the theater, they agreed that the movie was inferior to previous Frankenstein flicks, and that it was time for Hollywood to find fresh material.

As Loren drove Shelley home, she asked whether he had heard about a controversy involving her English teacher, a Miss Staley, who had objected to the emphasis on athletics over academics at THS. Before her astounded students, she had condemned the principal, George Barclay, for budgeting twice as much money for movies of the football games as had been allocated for library books during the entire year. One of the students had immediately gone to the principal with an account of the incident, and Shelley, along with several others, had been summoned to the office to verify the story.

"Whut else could Ah do?" she asked Loren. "Ah hadda tell th' truth. Miss Staley wuz angry. An' th' school does spend much more on athletics than on academics; everyone knows that. Doesn't she have th' right t' speak her mind?"

"I should think so," said Loren.

"Mr. Barclay doesn't think so. He's asked th' school board t' fire her."

"No!"

"Yeah. They've called uh special meetin' fer Monday evening at seven o'clock. It's t' be at th' school auditorium. Ah'm supposed t' be there as uh possible witness. Ah wish Ah could say or do somethin' t' help Miss Staley, but Ah don' think they'll allow it."

"Do you want me to go with you?"

"No. Yore on th' football team. Better yew stay out of it."

It was almost eleven when Loren delivered Shelley to her home, where she insisted on leaving him at the car and going inside by herself. "I don' wanna disturb th' others," she declared.

Why didn't she want him to meet any of the other members of her family?

After Shelley was safely inside and the front porch light turned off, he backed Shaky down the long driveway and began the twenty-minute trip home. As he drove, he considered the situation. On the way home from the theater, Shelley, unlike Mary Beth, had kept plenty of space between Loren and herself. Although she had thanked him warmly for the movie, she had also turned down his invitation to take her somewhere for a burger and a shake, pleading fatigue. Truly, she had looked tired, with dark circles showing under her violet eyes, and a slight slump showing in her posture as she made her way indoors. Perhaps she had not fully recovered from her ordeal in the big woods.

Loren feared, however, that her distance resulted less from not feeling well than from an aversion to him personally—to his pimples, to his not being a local boy, or to something he might have said or done, to which she had taken offense. Like a frustrated predator who had returned from an unsuccessful hunt, devoid of prey, he arrived home glum and undone.

He had undressed and collapsed onto his cot before he remembered that this was the night on which he had planned to make photographic enlargements from the Kaplan filmstrip. It was almost midnight and he was very sleepy. To carry out his plan would keep him up at least another three hours. I've waited this long, he told himself; I guess I can wait a day or two longer. Soon he slept.

*   *   *

Nan's forty-first birthday began with Tommy, still in his pajamas, taking orange juice, tepid tea, and slightly burned buttered toast on a tray to her bed. Pretending to be displeased that the boys had excluded him from this special service, Adam was placated with a plate of scrambled eggs and fried bacon, cooked by Loren. When Nan passed by the kitchen on her way to the bathroom to begin getting ready for Sunday school and church, she peered dubiously at the grease-splattered stove.

During Sunday school, Loren wondered whether he ought not to forego becoming a member of the church. His pretty young teacher had won him over more by her sincerity and her apparently unconscious sexuality than by the attraction of her lessons, which persistently maintained that all the members of the church should do "God's will," as delivered to them by their pastor.

Preachers like Pryor, Loren thought, preyed on the gullible and the fearful. They spewed statements of doubtful authenticity, which they called "the Word of God." Faith in "the Word," they asserted, was an essential component of Christianity; without it, people like Loren would wind up in hell.

Maybe so, he thought. But I refuse to be emotionally manipulated. Am I religious? Yes, I believe I am. For one thing, I'm awed at the miracle of life. In this I feel kinship with others. But, somehow, when people band together in sects and in churches, they seem to emphasize their differences from others, rather than their common spirituality.

In the new Bible that Loren had recently received from his Sunday school teacher, he had discovered words of wisdom and inspiration. But he also knew about instances when men who claimed special authority to say what scripture meant had taken Biblical passages out of context, or distorted them entirely, to authenticate terrible injustices. He had recently read an account of a lynching that had taken place in Tocqueville several years before. It had been excused, and even praised, in local pulpits, as a just expression of God's terrible wrath against sin. Loren wondered what Jesus would think, should he materialize in East Texas as some people seemed to think would soon happen, if he witnessed the barbarism and duplicity performed in his name by so-called Christians.

Uneasy at the thought that allowing the Reverend Pryor to baptize him would be an act of hypocrisy, Loren almost decided not to do it. But his brother was counting on him to participate in the ceremony, and his mother and father would be disappointed if he backed out now. So he followed two other young men up to the baptismal font, and was in turn followed by a very nervous Tommy.

Standing silently near the small square pool that would purify the participants in the baptismal ritual, Loren waited and watched the two non-Temples, one after the other, step down into waist-deep water where Reverend Pryor awaited them. Intoning the words, "Upon yore profession of faith in th' Lord Jesus Christ, Ah baptize yew in th' name of th' Father, an' th' Son, an' th' Holy Spirit," Pastor Pryor pushed them under the water and momentarily held them there, before raising them in their sodden Sunday suits to a standing position, after which they proudly mounted the steps and left by a rear door, puddles forming on the floor behind them.

Loren had no difficulty with his part of the ritual. When he felt Pastor Pryor's clammy hands on his shoulders, he held his breath and went under, feeling no more holy after being immersed than he had felt previous to the experience. As he stepped out of the water, he still hoped that a sense of something spiritual would possess him. He wanted the sacrament in which he had demonstrated his love for his mother to mark an important passage in his life. Instead, the ritual ended in absurdity.

As he was about to pass dripping through the rear door, a strange sound behind him caused him to turn around. He saw his brother, a look of sheer panic on his face, struggling with the Reverend Pryor, who was trying to push him under the water. The little fellow seemed to fear being drowned.

Water was splashing out of the font in all directions, and Loren heard Pastor Pryor growl: "Stop resistin', you li'l prick." But Tommy fought harder, frightened but determined to stay above the surface.

"Goddam yew; git under thar," snarled the pious preacher, his expression furious and his suit coat pulled halfway off, as a desperate Tommy grabbed anything he could reach to keep from going under. "Screw yew, yew li'l cocksucker," muttered God's messenger, as he endeavored to immerse his young suppliant.

Finally, Tommy yielded to a thorough dunking. For a fearful moment Loren thought that Reverend Pryor was going to teach his brother an ultimate spiritual lesson by drowning him. Whatever the pastor's intention, Tommy managed eventually to surge out of the water and stagger away from the sacramental scene, while most of the church members looked distressed, a few hid amused expressions behind their hands, and several could not contain their laughter.

In the robing room, an infuriated Pastor Pryor pulled off his galoshes in tight-lipped silence and treated the boys to the spectacle of a man of the cloth as naked as a plucked chicken while he changed to dry clothes. By the time that an amused Loren and a distressed Tommy had done likewise, the irreverent reverend, as Loren now thought of him, was entering the pulpit to deliver his Sunday sermon.

The two boys decided to give the occasion a miss. "Lord knows what he'll say," Loren speculated, as they waited together beside the Hudson for their parents to rejoin them. "His theme will probably be the impossibility of a thirteen-year-old walking on water."

Tommy was not amused.

CHAPTER 29
THE MASSACRE

When Loren entered the locker room to dress for football practice on Monday afternoon, he found a purple jersey hanging in his locker. At last he had become a starter. He realized, however, that entering a game late in the final quarter and improvising a handful of desperation plays was not the same thing as trying to carry out Coach Allen's "game plan" derived from many pages of plays filling a thick loose-leaf folder. Theoretically, each play committed to that compilation ought to produce a touchdown every time it was called. If only each X did his job, then the O's would be unable to cope.

Unfortunately, Loren realized, those little X's, from Coach Allen's frustrated perspective, symbolized awkward youngsters who gave him migraines by invariably botching their assignments. Whether the curly-haired yankee called Lane could bring about an overall improvement, Loren imagined Coach Allen asking himself, was uncertain. Smart and sound on fundamentals, "Lane" had not yet had time to learn the strengths and weaknesses of the other players and how best to utilize each one, and they had not yet developed the confidence in his leadership needed for him to be truly effective.

Coach Allen worked the boys hard that Monday afternoon, and again on Tuesday, concentrating on a passing attack and a blitzing defense, tactics that offered the only chance of competing with the Port Amberley Leopards, who were reputed to be bigger and stronger than the Tocqueville guys at almost every position. For this reason, Loren guessed, Coach Allen had decided not to include any game movies involving the Leopards in his Wednesday practice session, which he called for 8:30 a.m., even though it would require all the boys on the squad to miss their morning classes. When one teacher had protested, Loren heard that Coach Allen had asked her rhetorically: "Whut is more important; yore fifty minutes dealing wit' sumptin' that has no practical application in th' real world, or our preparation fer uh game that'll draw three thousand people t' our stadium?"

The teacher in question, Mary Staley, was unlikely to appreciate hearing that her subject, English, had no practical value. Loren could not understand the vehemence with which Principal George Barclay, according to rumor, had insisted that the school board terminate Miss Staley's teaching contract, despite her fourteen years of devoted service. He knew that she had begun teaching at Tocqueville High School well before Barclay, whose inability to produce winning football teams at another institution had led to his promotion to assistant principal, and in due course to the top spot at THS. So many coaches, having failed as teachers, were then given authoritarian power over others who had succeeded in the same line of work. What a way to run an educational system!

Loren surmised that Mary Staley's hearing before the school board would be a mere formality, with the verdict a foregone conclusion. But rumor had it that she intended, nevertheless, to make her case as best she could, even though she had the reputation of being a quiet, shy person outside the classroom, except on rare occasions when she became indignant at some gross injustice. Well, was not her own situation such an instance? Loren envisioned her planning her presentation while she selected a tasteful conservative outfit to wear to the star chamber proceeding.

* * *

When the school board met at seven, at least a dozen of Miss Staley's students, including Shelley, were sitting near the front of the school auditorium. Well behind them, Loren sat alone, curious to see what would happen. Up on the stage, Mr. Barclay had been joined at a long table by four middle-aged men and one elderly woman, who represented the school board. Miss Staley, seated well apart from her judges, began with a statement in which she spoke of her years of frustration having to provide her own supplies or do without, while the school library budget, already pathetic, dwindled. Meanwhile, the athletic coaches were not only allocated the lion's share of the funds budgeted annually for THS, but also, owing to Principal Barclay's personal priorities, were periodically allowed to divert money that had originally been budgeted for academic programs to their own use.

"Do yew dispute Mr. Barclay's authority t' decide when, where an' how t' spend the school's money?" asked one male board member in a hostile tone of voice.

"No, Sir; I do not. He clearly has the authority. But I differ at times with the way he exercises it. I believe that it is my right as a citizen in a free country to do so."

"Perhaps." said another board member. "But yew expressed those views t' yore students—t' uh captive audience."

"I do not expect my students to endorse my opinions on matters not directly within my area of academic expertise," replied Miss Staley. "And I certainly do not test or grade them on whether they share my opinions. But if I am unable adequately to teach English because my department is deprived of money even for chalk with which to write on the blackboard, and if I cannot adequately teach reading because there are not enough dilapidated volumes in the library appropriate for my courses, then I think the students have a right to know what is going on."

The woman member of the board spoke. "Being uh new member of this body," she declared, "yore infraction seems clear t' me. Yew've been insubordinate t' Mr. Barclay, an' we therefore can't hardly avoid goin' ahead t' severely punish yew."

"Dangling participle; double negative; split infinitive…," muttered the object of her accusation.

"Whut did yew say, Miss Staley?" inquired one of the men.

"Nothing important… You may have noticed that some of my students are here. Perhaps you would wish to inquire of them whether they believe my teaching to be deficient."

"That won' be necessary," said one of the men, who appeared to be in charge. "Th' issue is not whether yew are uh competent teacher—Ah have no doubt that yew are—but whether yew have publicly expressed opinions at variance wit' school policy. Do yew have anythin' more t' say devoted strictly t' that issue?"

"No, Sir."

Suddenly a loud baritone voice sounded from the rear of the auditorium. A well dressed man of about fifty had risen to his feet. "Are we to conclude, gentlemen and lady," he said, "that you intend to vote to dismiss this good woman, whom you admit is perfectly competent to perform her duties, because on a single occasion she expressed her frustration with practices that undermined her ability adequately to do her job? Are we expected to approve an action that will publicly endorse failure over success? I speak of Coach Allen, whose teams at Tocqueville High School have thus far won only five games while losing forty-four. In any other occupation, the successful employee, Miz Staley, would be promoted and given more money to work with, while the failure, Mr. Allen, would be fired or at least demoted. You people have peculiar values, I must say."

"Who're yew, Sir?" indignantly inquired the chairman.

"I am a parent who has two children enrolled in this school," said the commentator.

"Wal, yew have no business intervening in our proceedings."

"Oh, but I do. You are a public body, and this hearing, as I'm sure you know, is required by law to be open to the public. Any citizen may address the board if he or she can show a Texas driver's license. As a journalist, I contemplate writing an article in which I shall discuss the status of a teacher's constitutional rights at Tocqueville High School. Furthermore, I shall highlight the lack of judgment of members of the school board in persecuting this poor woman. She has dedicated her life to educating your youngsters. Now you intend to fire her for having spoken out against gross mismanagement on the part of certain school officials."

"Now wait uh minute," protested one of the male board members, who had thus far remained silent. "We ain't persecuting nobody."

"Glad to hear it," said the outspoken parent, sitting down.

After an awkward pause, the chairman called for a motion. Silence ensued, finally broken by the board member who had denied any attempt to persecute. "Ah move," he said, "that we tell Miz Staley t' stop criticizing Mr. Barclay in her classes, an' that we then adjourn." Another board member immediately called out: "Second." The chairman called for the ayes and nays, and the vote was three to one, the dissident being the woman board member, who was scowling her disapproval.

Once they realized what had happened, most of the high school girls in the audience gleefully gathered around Miss Staley to extend their congratulations. Loren swiveled in his seat to see how the articulate gentleman, whose strong statements had turned the tide, was reacting to the outcome. But he had disappeared.

* * *

After Loren had spoken a few words of support to Shelley and her friends and had shaken hands with Miss Staley, who seemed stunned by what had happened, he returned home to find his father sitting in his armchair, sucking on a lemon drop and reading a magazine.

"That was quite a performance you put on," Loren said. "I was impressed."

"Liked it, did you?" said Adam, looking smug. "I hadn't planned to say anything. But there I was, blatting away."

"I wouldn't call it blatting."

"I hope they don't realize that I made up that part about the Texas driver's license. I took a chance that there weren't any learned lawyers around."

Loren laughed. "Present company excluded, the only learned person at that meeting was Miss Staley. And she seemed a bit bewildered."

"Yes, well, she's worth a dozen of your coaches, with their big salaries, expense accounts, loaner cars, booster slush funds, and speaker's fees for spouting homilies to morons."

"To be fair," said Loren, "I can think of coaches, like the ones at Winona CDS, who were well worth their pay."

"Oh, sure. Especially at the college level. Rockne at Notre Dame; Stagg at Chicago; Crisler at Michigan; men like that. Character builders who stressed academics as well as winning football.

"When I covered sports for the New York *Post*, and later for the *Times*, and was sports editor of the Washington *Post* and three other papers in the South, I met plenty of college coaches who were both superb teachers and well-educated gentlemen, real role models for their players. They recognized that their young men would be folk heroes for only a short while. In the long run it would be what they learned in English, history, math and science that would determine their success in life. Just think: one minute a player is invincible—hundreds, maybe even thousands of people cheering, even praying, for him—and then, wham, a serious injury, and that's the end of football. Or he plays through a succession of minor injuries until he graduates or is bumped aside by someone even better. He has a long life yet to live. What does he have to fall back on? Texans need to re-order their priorities."

"Yeah. But football can be fun."

"I know how much fun it is. I played it when I was your age, and I've followed football all my life. But when people are eager to subsidize teams with public money and think nothing of buying costly tickets to weekend games, while at the same time they are unwilling to spend what is minimally needed for adequate educational facilities and teacher salaries, then we can hardly call ourselves a civilization. Our values are sadly misplaced."

* * *

On Wednesday morning, the THS footballers, minus their pads and helmets, ran through plays on the practice field, and then trooped over to a weedy field near the railroad tracks to join in a noisy pep rally, with many parents and other adults joining the high school students to cheer and chant around a huge bonfire. Looking on, Loren considered what his father had said and done. Despite an intensity of expression that sometimes gave listeners to his diatribes the feeling that he was overstating his case, Adam had a generous, idealistic heart and a tendency to take up his cudgel for people who seemed unable to defend their own interests. Like his political hero, Franklin Roosevelt, he cared about underprivileged and victimized people, even if his personal prejudices and his lack of tact in social situations limited his effectiveness in befriending them. This, Loren had come to realize, was why Adam preferred to fight his battles with the written word rather than in person. It must have taken a considerable effort for him to get out of his comfortable armchair, surrounded by his books and periodicals, go to the school board meeting, and then speak out. His son was proud of him.

* * *

Late that night, Loren finally got around to the task of making photographic enlargements of the Kaplan negatives. Would they supply the answer to the crucial question: who was Mrs. Kaplan's mysterious lover and accomplice the night her husband died? As the first eight-by-ten sheet of white photo paper darkened in the developer, Loren suddenly had an idea: once he identified Mrs. K's mysterious visitor, maybe he should make it known that any further assaults or harassment would immediately result in a packet of pictures being transmitted to Emile Mouton. Surely the person who drove the one-eyed truck could discern that it was not in Loren's interest to reveal his peeping tom activity and that he would prefer to keep his pictures private. Whether an arrangement could be worked out, however, probably rested on the content of the fateful film.

So Loren watched closely, fascinated, as images slowly grew distinct on each enlargement. Mrs. Kaplan and her husband were easy to identify in each picture in which they appeared. The features of the outsider, however, remained disappointingly obscure. The face was turned away, or the lighting was bad, or movement had blurred that portion of the picture. Only the next-to-last photo, taken while Mrs. Kaplan and her friend were hoisting her husband in the garage, revealed enough to cause Loren to believe that if he isolated that small portion of the picture that contained the mysterious visitor's face, scarcely more than a dot on the negative, and inserted a more powerful lens in his enlarger to blow it up to a much larger size, he might be able to tell who it was. He was just screwing in the replacement lens when his mother tapped on the bathroom door. "Loren," she said, "it's two a.m. and you have a game tomorrow. It's past time to get some sleep."

"I only have about fifteen minutes left to go," replied Loren.

"No," said Nan firmly. "It's time to stop... now! You can tie up the bathroom some other night. Right now I need to use it."

"O. K., I hear you," said Loren. Quickly he disengaged the Kaplan film strip from the enlarger, rolled it up, and slid it into a canister. Rinsing the final enlargement under the cold water tap, he slid it into a folded newspaper, so that it would be concealed from his mother's curious observation. The other damp enlargements were already well wrapped.

Pouring chemical solutions into brown bottles, and making sure that his photo paper was encased in a heavy cardboard box to prevent any light from reaching it, he called out to his impatient mother: "I'm hurrying; just a couple of moments more." Snapping off the red safelight, turning on the bathroom ceiling light, and gathering up his clandestine photographs, he unlocked the door.

"Let me move my stuff out of your way," he told his mother, who was still standing wearily in the hall in her robe and slippers. "Then the bathroom's yours."

"I didn't know you had taken any pictures recently," said Nan. "Can I see them?"

"Oh, they're still wet and have to be kept wrapped up," said Loren glibly. "Anyway, they're just some old baseball shots from Wrigley Field. I told Neil and Tony I'd make some copies for them. Nothing you'd care about."

While he removed his equipment from the bathroom, Loren was conscious of his mother's intent stare. Fortunately, she refrained from interrogating him. As soon as the bathroom door closed behind her, Loren quietly carried his enlargements outdoors, slipping surreptitiously through the chilly darkness to a dingy shed located behind the Temple garage, a place that had been used by some previous resident as a chicken coop. Shining a flashlight on a wire that stretched from one side of the shed to the other, he used clothes pins to hang up his enlargements, so they might thoroughly dry without curling or sticking to some foreign object. Later he would find an even more secure spot in which to store them. Right now, he believed, they were safe from interlopers.

Returning to his room and sitting impatiently on his cot, he eventually heard Nan pass by his door on her way back to her own room, where he hoped she would soon sleep. An exciting idea had entered his mind while he was removing his enlargements and equipment from the bathroom. Even though he hadn't absolutely identified Mrs. K's confederate, he suspected who it was and he thought he knew how to obtain evidence that would help to prove or disprove his assumption. Although it was now past two-thirty in the morning, he believed that he would be unable to sleep until he had found out if he was right.

* * *

Trying to push Shaky silently along the driveway, while steering through the car's window, proved impossible until he remembered to release the emergency brake. Then it was easy. Once out in the street, he started the engine and drove across town to Southside High School, where he parked in the shadows next to the Greenie gym. He had to rattle four different doors before one of them opened and allowed him to tiptoe down a long hall past a half dozen classrooms to the vicinity of the main entrance, where the school office was located.

Behind a glass partition that divided the school secretary's desk from the vestibule, someone had left a single light burning. It dimly illuminated steel filing cabinets and shelves holding reference works, piles of manuals and periodicals and, at the very bottom, a row of school yearbooks. But the door that would provide access to these riches was locked.

Determined not to be thwarted, Loren reached up and gripped the top of the intervening partition and pulled himself up until he was able to get his elbows and chest over it, and then one leg over it as well. The rest was no problem, except that when he dropped to the floor inside the office he accidentally bumped a metal waste basket, which made a loud noise as it crashed over on its side, spilling cigarette stubs, crumpled facial tissues, and other bits of paper onto the linoleum floor. Hurriedly, Loren began to scoop up the debris, in order to restore it to the uprighted waste basket, but he had not yet finished doing so when he suddenly became aware of footsteps hurrying down the hall toward him. He barely had time to dive under the secretary's desk, when the beam of a flashlight lit up the wall behind him, resting momentarily upon an autographed framed picture of Martin Dies, the witch hunting congressman who had once represented the Tocqueville area in Washington, and then moving like a prying eye about the room.

From his uncomfortable refuge, Loren was unable to see who the newcomer was, but he prayed that it was not the school secretary or one of her assistants, or—God, let it not be the principal! Then the doorknob rattled and he felt a sensation in his chest like his heart ceasing to beat. But the lock held. Muttering something unintelligible, the investigator departed, whistling tunelessly as he passed down the hall. Loren could now see that it was a colored man in overalls, probably the school janitor. He must have seen the tiny bit of trash left on the floor next to the waste basket. Perhaps he had gone to fetch a door key, so that he could clean it up before people arriving for work encountered it, although it was unlikely that anyone would do so before Monday. In any case, it was time for Loren to leave.

Quickly he scurried over to the book shelves, located the school yearbook for 1934-1935, and clambered back over the glass partition, dropping with a slight thump onto the floor on the other side. Hastening down the hallway, he heard a shout: "Hey, yew; stop!" It must be the janitor, he thought. I can't let him see my face. He ran as fast as he could toward the door through which he had entered the building, hoping desperately that his pursuer, whom he could hear running after him, had not in the meantime locked it. Fortunately, it burst open at his first thrust, and it took only another moment for him to pile into Shaky and roar away with his lights off into the empty streets of South Tocqueville. After traveling two blocks, he slowed the car, turned on its headlights, and carefully drove under the twenty-five mile an hour speed limit the rest of the way home.

Safely back in his bedroom, he intended to take a look inside the stolen yearbook, but the sound of his parents' bedroom door opening led him quickly to snap off his beside lamp, and with his booty thrust down between his cot and the wall behind it, he pretended to be asleep. Six hours later, at nine-thirty in the morning, he discovered that pretence had become actuality.

* * *

What finally got a groggy Loren off his cot and out of his bedroom on Thanksgiving morning was a knock on his door by Tommy, who informed him that some girl who called herself "Shirley" was on the phone.

"Hello," Loren mumbled into the instrument, vaguely conscious that he was still too sleepy to be completely understandable.

"Loren, is that yew?" asked Shelley.

"Yeah. I was up most of the night; so bear with me. I'm trying to wake up."

"Ah'm sorry. Ah didn' think yew'd still be sleepin' at this hour."

"What's on your mind?"

"Loren, Ah hope yew don' mind, but Ah need t' cancel our date fer this evenin', an' also t' beg off yore parents' invitation t' come t' yore house fer Thanksgiving dinner after th' game."

"You do? Why?"

His disappointment must have been apparent at the other end of the line. "Listen, Loren," she said. "This has nuthin' t' do wit' mah attitude t'ward yew. Ah like yew uh lot; really Ah do. But... Ah have t' confess somethin'. Uh former boy friend of mine, an older guy, jus' got home from college fer th' vacation, an' he called an' wanted me t' go out wit' him. An' since he's only goin' t' be home fer two or three days, Ah didn' have th' heart t' say no. Ah hope yew understand."

"Oh, sure. Have a nice time. Call me when you feel like it." He hung up. He understood, all right. Another girl friend, come and gone.

As if his distress had radiated far and wide like a telepathic lament, the phone rang before he left the hallway. Of all people, it was Mary Beth, asking if she could come by to talk with him.

"I guess so," he said. "But I have to be at school by eleven, and I haven't had breakfast yet; so better make it snappy."

"Ah'll be right there," she said.

He was chewing his oatmeal when Mary Beth knocked on the outside kitchen door.

"Hi, Loren," she said with her irresistible smile. "'Member me?"

"How could I forget?"

"Ah hope we're still friends."

"Sure."

"Even though Ah know yore goin' out wit' Shelley Taylor. Ah wanted t' bring yew this gift fer yore birthday." She handed Loren a small flat box that looked like it held a tie or perhaps a couple of handkerchiefs.

"Go on; open it," she said.

"But my birthday is not until tomorrow."

"Ah won' be heah t'morrah. Ah have t' go t' Houston t' spend th' rest of th' vacation wit' mah uncle an' his family. So won' yew oblige me an' let me see whether you like whut Ah brought yew?"

"Sure," said Loren. Tearing off the silver wrapping paper and gold ribbon that decorated it, he opened the box to reveal a white silk scarf which, when he spread it out, showed his initials stenciled on it in purple. "Say," he said. "That's really neat!"

"Do yew really think so?"

"Yes, I do. Thank you, very much. That was really thoughtful of you."

"It's not as much as yew deserve. An' yew prolly shouldn' wear it when yew go out wit' Shelley."

"I may not be dating Shelley anymore," he said.

"Really? From whut Ah've been hearin'; yew two're an item."

"Don't believe everything you hear," said Loren. "How's J. J?"

"Don' believe everythang Yew heah," replied Mary Beth. "Ah only wanted t' be seen wit' him 'round school t' make yew jealous. Ah nevah went out wit' him."

"What?"

"That's right. He kept askin' me, but Ah alluz had an excuse. Ah did date uh couple of other guys, but nothin' serious. One thang Ah verified: they weren't in yore league."

"What league am I in?"

"Th' Big league," she said. "An' yew really fixed J. J. Wobbling 'round th' school on crutches, only bragging 'bout hisself four or five times uh day, 'stead uh th' usual dozen or so. That's like humility fer anyone else."

They both laughed. Loren glanced at his watch. "I'm really sorry," he said, "but I have to leave right away. Coach Allen gets very angry if we're late."

"Ah understand," she said. "Beat those Leopards!"

He smiled grimly. "Not likely," he declared. "But I'll play as well as I can."

Starting up Shaky, he saw his mother standing with Mary Beth on the side porch, both waving goodbye. His brother came out of the garage, holding his violin and bow in his left hand, and gave him a thumbs up sign. And he knew that his father, who was still at the newspaper office, would soon be home to take Nan and Tommy to the game. He no longer felt tired. He felt good.

* * *

The game against Port Amberley was a massacre. Even a majority of the fans who packed Purple Stadium seemed to be waving yellow and black pennants and pompoms and cheering for the visiting Leopards. Although Loren sent the initial kickoff almost to the opposition goal line, the receiver followed a wedge of interference straight up the middle of the field to daylight, after which he ran unmolested for six points. From that moment, the Purples waged an uphill battle.

There was no subtlety to the Leopard attack. It was pure power: classic single wing "student body right" off-tackle rampages by a tailback as large as the Tocqueville tackles, running behind ruthless blocking that cleared a wide path like a mowing machine moving through a hay field. As for the Tocqueville offense, Loren at first tried a ground game, but he soon gave up after both he and his fullback were repeatedly buried under masses of Leopard tacklers before they could even get started. Then, when he tried to pass, he had a terrible time getting rid of the ball over furiously charging linemen who seemed to surge through his blockers as if they were made of cardboard.

When Loren did manage to get the ball to a receiver, the guy almost invariably dropped it, probably from fear of an imminent bone-crushing tackle. At halftime the score was 28-0. The Tocqueville team had gained a minus twenty-seven yards on the ground and completed only three short passes out of sixteen attempts.

Just before the two teams went under the stands for their twenty-minute break, Loren was hit hard trying to lateral the ball to the left halfback and, as he went down, his tackler clubbed him on the back of the neck between his helmet and his shoulder pads, causing a pulse of blinding pain to shoot through his head, as he lay with his face buried in the torn turf. "How'd yew like that, yew li'l sissy?" rumbled the big lineman who had made the hit. As he raised up, he pushed Loren's face further into the sod.

On the way to the locker room Loren wiped tears from his cheeks with bruised hands. He was so furious that he could hardly think straight. Wordlessly he slumped on a bench while the coaches circulated among the battered gladiators, offering encouragement, but realizing that this was not a time for unrealistic bluster or the voicing of unwarranted expectations. Just before they were due to return to the field for the second half, Coach Allen asked for a moment of silence, during which Loren could dimly hear a band out on the field playing Dixie, and could imagine the Confederate flag proudly fluttering beside the Stars and Stripes over the scoreboard at the south end of the stadium, as the fans, with not a Negro among them, stood respectfully to honor the anthem.

Then Coach Allen prayed aloud for the Savior to protect his players from injury and to give them opportunities somehow to restore their honor. Loren was too tired and too angry to critique the prayer, except to conclude that it was pretty pathetic. When the head coach said, unenthusiastically, "Go git 'em, Lane," as the players straggled out the locker room door, Loren merely nodded.

By the time the Leopard kickoff rose into the air, coming end over end right at him, Loren had worked himself into a veritable frenzy. Not even conscious of catching the ball, he accelerated toward a mass of intermingling, butting, tumbling players at about the twenty-five yard line, saw a seam, and went for it. A grimacing guy in a yellow and black shirt reached for him and Loren slammed right through his arms. Another one loomed up before him, and he veered slightly and slammed the heel of his hand into the tackler's face and left him cursing on the turf.. When two more converged on him, he crashed into them both with all his strength, dragging them along behind him until another, and then another, piled on and finally brought him down.

As he got to his feet, he noticed that he had almost made midfield. In the huddle he called for a quarterback option play, which was designed to provide him an opportunity to pitch out to the halfback, to pass upfield to one of several potential receivers, or to run the ball himself. He ran, dodging and breaking tackles, as he cut back against the grain, forcing the defensive backs also to reverse direction. Straining for the sideline, he found himself trapped by three opponents, who were closing in from as many directions. Lowering his head, he ran right over the first one; knocked the second one flat with a vicious stiff arm; and then fell over the third one out of bounds.

The referee positioned the ball on the Leopard twenty yard line. In the huddle, with his teammates staring at him as if he were some kind of freak, he called for a pass. "Hold 'em," he spat at his linemen. When he dropped back to throw, he saw with satisfaction that they were fighting their hearts out, battling the much larger Leopards with everything they had. The developing scene downfield resembled the view through a kaleidoscope: yellow and black and purple and white flickering on a sea of green under a bright blue sky, against a multicolored background of shouting spectators. Seeing purple about to enter the end zone, Loren launched a hard spiral and then concentrated upon evading a large lineman who was charging at him like a mad bull, completely hiding the action downfield.

By the time Loren was able to obtain an unobstructed look, the whistle had blown and a zebra shirt was bringing the ball back. "What happened?" he asked Hulk, who was standing despondently nearby.

"It wuz uh perfect pass," said the center. "Right in his hands. Joe jus' dropped it."

On the next play, Hulk himself failed to block his counterpart, who came storming through to hit the fullback just as Loren was handing him the ball, which of course produced a fumble and a Leopard recovery.

And so the game continued, with almost everything the Purples tried failing, and almost everything the Leopard behemoths attempted succeeding. Loren carried the ball like a trapped tiger, refusing to go down until hit over and over by tackler after tackler. On defense, he repeatedly slashed in from his safety position to fight off blockers and bring down the ball carrier. But it was all to no avail. The final score was 41-0.

Some of the Purple players were crying as they limped wearily off the field; several were cursing in bitter frustration; but most were simply glad that the carnage had finally ceased. Showering and dressing quickly, they shook hands, one by one, with each other, and with the coaches and managers, and quietly departed, most of them in small soundless groups, and a few, like Loren, alone.

* * *

As Loren passed underneath the stadium toward the afternoon sunshine, a small figure clad in a hooded sweatshirt, blue jeans and sneakers, with a blue bandana covering all of its face except the eyes, thrust a piece of paper into his hand and then disappeared behind a concrete pillar.

"What's this?" asked Loren. "Who are you?" He tried to follow, but whoever it was had vanished.

He scrutinized the scrap of paper. It said: "We have to talk. We each have something the other one wants. Park your car outside Davis's drugstore at 9 p.m. Be alone. Tell no one. When you see a headlight blinking, follow."

* * *

As soon as he arrived home, Loren slipped surreptitiously back to the small shed behind the Temple garage to take a quick look at the enlargements he had hung there. He wanted to compare what he had seen of the eyebrows of the mysterious messenger with the eyebrows of Della's accomplice in the disposal of her husband.

The photos were gone! Someone had stolen them! Not anyone in his family, or he would have been quizzed about them by now. Who, then? He feared the worst.

* * *

At Thanksgiving dinner, which featured sugar glazed ham cooked in pineapple juice, Loren was morose and uncommunicative. His parents, he thought, assumed that he was brooding about the game and respected his silence. His father refrained from an analysis of the contest, and his mother only once expressed her concern about a purple bruise that now blemished one of his cheekbones. Even Tommy confined his comments to his own activities and those of his friends.

As Loren left the table, planning to go lie down for a while, his mother said: "Oh, son; I forgot to tell you; before she left today, Mary Beth hinted that if you were not too tired, she'd like to see you this evening. You look pretty worn out to me. Shall I call her and tell her she'd better wait until next week?"

"No," said Loren. "I'll do it. Thanks for letting me know."

As he dialed Mary Beth's number, he speculated about the identity of the person who had summoned him to meet that evening. Was the author of the message the one who had delivered it? The driver of the one-eyed truck? Would it be safe to go alone? He had seen Emile arrive next door to spend the rest of Thanksgiving day with his parents and sisters. Should he show him the note? If he did that, though, the entire story—about his peeping and taking the photos, especially—might become public knowledge. He would be ruined.

"Hullo. Hullo. Is anyone there?" inquired Mary Beth.

"Sorry," said Loren. "I was distracted. It's Loren. I'm really beat up from today's game, and I didn't get much sleep last night, and I also think I might be coming down with a cold; so I wonder if it would be all right if we got together whenever you return from Houston?"

"Ah wuz afraid," she said, "that yew'd be feelin' low, after that disappointing game. But yew played great. Mah father an' mother were both cheering fer yew."

"Thanks. I tried. But we were outmatched."

"Th' others were. Yew weren't. Anyway, whut Ah think we should do is fer me t' stay heah while mah parents an' brother go ovah t' Houston t'morra mornin'. Ah'll tell them that Ah need t' work on mah school assignments, an' t' give mah love t' Uncle Tom an' so forth. It won' be uh problem. Meanwhile yew kin git yore beauty sleep, an' t'morra, whenevah yew've got 'nough rest, come on ovah an' we'll visit."

Loren's urges stirred within him. She hadn't said, "We'll talk." She had said "visit," in an otherwise empty house, with bedrooms. "Sure," he stammered. "That sounds fine. I'll call when I'm ready to come." As he hung up, he thought he heard her whisper something like "Me, too," but he was probably mistaken.

*   *   *

"I think I'll go lie down," Loren announced to his mother, who was stacking dirty dishes on the kitchen counter. "I'm really worn out."

"All right, dear," she said. "Are you going out tonight?"

"For a little while," he said. "But I shouldn't be out late."

Once in his room, with the door locked, he retrieved the stolen SHS yearbook and began leafing through it. Among individual pictures of members of that year's graduating class, he found four people with whom he had become acquainted: John Charles Guidry, Delilah Sue Guidry (Della was Bubba's sister; that was a surprise!), Sam Houston Howell, and Rose Robicheaux Rand. There they all were, easily recognizable, looking fresh-faced and innocent, and ready to take on the world. Except, possibly, for Bubba, whose expression was, characteristically, more of a glower than a grin.

Further along, among the group photos, Loren verified that Rose and Della had been two of the senior cheerleaders, while Buzz appeared among the members of the tennis team, and Bubba, looking belligerent, was on the baseball squad.

But the most evocative image appeared among the advertisements near the back of the book. In a photograph occupying one-quarter of a page, the "fabulous foursome," as the caption called them, stood arm-in-arm, all four, even Bubba, smiling broadly at the camera, and all four wearing Southside High School letter sweaters. From the possessive way that Buzz was hugging Della, and that Bubba was embracing Rose, any observer might have concluded that they were very close friends.

So that was the way it was, thought Loren. Bubba and Rose had commenced an unhappy marriage which produced no children. But what had happened between Buzz and Della? He knew that she had gone to New Orleans where she had been a cabaret performer, and Buzz had gone off to college, also in New Orleans, the only one of the four to do so. Then what? Had Buzz come back to Tocqueville and surreptitiously resumed his relationship with Della, until the two of them murdered her husband? Or rather, had Bubba answered a plea from his sister to do away with Dr. K? Or had someone else been involved? The yearbook provided no answers to such questions, but close study of several of the pictures devoted especially to eyebrows hinted at the truth. Loren hoped that his impending meeting with the driver of the one-eyed truck would definitively answer the question: who was Della's lover and companion in crime?

CHAPTER 30
HADES

By the time that Loren reached Davis's drug store, the street in front of it was shrouded in darkness. Thick clouds concealed the moon and the stars. There was little traffic, so that when a maroon pickup truck approached from the direction of downtown, it was momentarily the only other vehicle in sight.

A single headlight flashed off and then on again as the truck passed by. Loren could dimly see that the driver wore a baseball cap and that there appeared to be no passenger. He swung Shaky into a U turn and followed.

His guide led the way out to the Houston highway and then, after several miles, turned southward. Loren then realized that they were heading for Hades, which was what local teenagers called the Pricklepeak oil field. There, within some four hundred acres, over two thousand rotting wooden and rusting steel derricks straddled squeaking, thumping, groaning pumps. Flames like huge torches spewed endlessly into the night sky, casting an eerie flickering yellow light over several square miles of desolate terrain.

In the *Endeavor* Loren had read that a state regulatory agency had filed a brief in federal court against the operators of this and many other oil fields in Texas for annually wasting over one hundred billion cubic feet of natural gas by burning it off, a practice that had continued for half a century. During a cold snap the previous winter, schools and businesses had been closed for several days owing to lack of heat, while only a short distance away enough natural gas to heat a city the size of New York was being burned off. But oil men ruled Texas; hence the unconscionable squandering of valuable energy continued as the sky over Pricklepeak glowed nightly, illuminated by the flickering flames.

From Slick and several schoolmates, Loren had heard stories about Hades as an environment that could break down the resistance of even a determined virgin. "Man," Slick had once said, "that gal may seem uh dry well, but wit' th' magic of Hades us ol' roughnecks know how t' wiggle dat drill up an' down til' she gushes." Tony, too, had advised Loren that if he ever wanted to get to the bottom of the mystery of girlhood, he should take his date out to Hades and all would be revealed.

Now, however, Loren sensed that he was about to face danger, not desire, in that hypnotic spot. Perhaps on some future night he might return to probe the puzzle that had thus far resisted his earnest inquiries.

But what was he thinking? Faced with a moment of truth, he was lost in fantasy. Up ahead the maroon truck had halted and its lights had gone out. Its driver was waving him forward. He pulled up close behind and got out. The driver took off her hat. It was Rose Guidry.

"I thought it might be you," he said.

"Ah'll bet. Climb in an' let's git down t' bidness." Loren opened the truck's passenger door and got in beside her.

She continued: "Ah'll tell yew whut yew wanna know 'bout certain events that took place nex' door t' yore house, if'n yew'll give me whut Ah wan'. Agreed?"

"I guess so."

"Not good enough. Say: 'Ah know so.'"

"I know so."

"All right," Rose said. "Whut do yew know 'bout Dr. Kaplan's death?"

"Well, I know that it wasn't suicide."

"How so?"

"From the way that he was hanging. The knot in the rope was on the wrong side of his neck. Also the bucket that he supposedly stood on was dented on its side, not as it should have been, on its bottom. Also, I saw the radio in Mrs. Kaplan's trash."

Rose stared at him, wide-eyed. "Yew are one smart guy. Maybe yew've guessed th' rest. Fust of all, evah since she moved back t' Tocqueville from New Orleans, Della and Ah have been lovers..."

"You!" cried Loren.

"Of course. Who else?"

"But..., lovers. I mean..."

"Loren, haven't yew evah heard of lesbians?"

"No. Not really."

"Yew've certainly had uh sheltered life. Yew've heard of homosexuality, haven't yew?"

"Yes. Dr. Kaplan..."

"So yew knew 'bout that, did yew?"

"I'm afraid so."

"Wal, if'n men kin have sex wit' other men, or like Dr. Kaplan, wit' boys, why can't women have th' same kinda relationship wit' women?"

"I suppose that makes sense."

"'Course it does. That's why Della an' Ah were gettin' t'gether whenevah we could git free from our husbands. Fortunately, Dr. Kaplan wuz frequently outta town, an' Della managed t' git me some capsules t' put inta Bubba's beer on Friday nights, so he'd be knocked out till mornin'.

"Th' night that Dr. Kaplan died wuz one of those nights. As soon as Bubba wuz asleep, Ah went ovah th' fence in th' dark like Ah alluz done, an' slipped inside through th' back door. Ah foun' Della cryin'. Her slimy husband had sneaked back t' surprise her an' had forced hisself on her an' then tol' her he wuz goin' t' take uh bath. We could heah 'im splashin' roun' in th' tub, along wit' some music comin' from uh radio.

"Della wuz gonna teach 'im uh lesson. She went t' his room, grabbed uh leather belt, an' burst into th' bath room wit' th' intention of whippin' th' daylights outta 'im. As she swung th' belt, Ah saw 'im try t' rise up outta th' tub, but he slipped an' fell toward th' wall, grabbin' at it t' catch hisself, an' in doin' so he knocked th' radio off its shelf, an' it fell into th' water.

"Either it electrocuted 'im instantly or produced uh heart attack that killed 'im. It also blew out th' lights, an' Della had t' feel her way inta th' kitchen t' git uh flashlight, so that we could check t' see if'n he wuz still alive. Which he wasn't."

"So you had to figure out what to do next," said Loren.

"Exactly."

"And you decided that you would try to make his death appear to be suicide by hanging."

"It seemed like th' best thing t' do. We hauled 'im t' th' garage an' Della foun' some rope. An' we hung 'im."

"What about Bubba?"

"Ah, mah late husband. Whut 'bout th' deah departed?"

"How did you kill him?"

"So yew don' buy th' suicide story thar, either?"

"No."

"Wal, yore right. But Ah didn' kill 'im. He wuz pesterin' me, tryin' t' git me t' call off th' divorce afore it became final, which wuz bad 'nough. But then he became violent an' threatenin'—said that if'n he couldn't have me back he'd tell th' cops that he had overheard me say to Della on the telephone that me an' her had killed her husband fer th' insurance money. An' he woulda done it.

"When Ah tol' Della whut Bubba had said he'd do, she phoned someone she knew in New Orleans, who sent muscle t' Tocqueville t' persuade Bubba t' keep quiet. When th' guy showed up, Bubba wuz purty drunk. He tol' 'im he wuz gonna blab everythin'—that no damn wimmen wuz gonna shut 'im up. Then he pulled uh knife—an' got hisself shot. The shooter phoned me that evening at mah Dad's an' asked whut t' do wit' th' body. Ah tole 'im th' fust thang that came into mah mind.

"Ah also suggested that he wipe th' gun clean of finger prints an' leave it beside Bubba; so that his death would look like uh suicide. An' he said t' me: 'Lady, Ah done already thoughta that. Yew don' have t' tell me mah bidness.'

"Anyway, after he hung up Ah have t' admit that Ah cried. But not fer long. Bubba wuz uh bastard."

"I agree with you there," said Loren.

"Thar wuz one near miss," continued Rose. "Big Claude, th' New Orleans guy, was on his way t' dump Bubba, when someone rear-ended his car. He thought he had been discovered an' wuz ready t' shoot th' driver of th' other car, when he discovered that it wuz jus' uh kid drivin' uh jalopy wit' bad brakes. Th' kid wuz obviously scared an' unaware that th' mobster had uh body in th' front seat. So th' guy decided that uh single killin' wuz 'nough fer one evenin', an' he drove on."

Loren shuddered.

Rose continued: "Speakin' 'bout rear-endin', Ah guess yew know it wuz Della who borrowed mah truck an' bumped yew one night on th' highway—tryin' t' scare yew, so that when she tried t' find out how much yew knew 'bout whut wuz goin' on, yew'd be 'fraid not t' tell 'er everythin'. But then she heard that Buzz wuz protectin' yew, an' she decided t' leave yew alone.

"Della an' me may have covered up uh few thangs, but we ain't murderers. We got raw deals from our husbands, both of whom turned out t' be real jerks, an' when we wanted t' be free of them, they wouldn' let us go. It wuz their own behavior that did them in, not us… Now let me tell yew whut Ah wan' from yew."

Oh, oh, thought Loren. Here it comes. "I already know," he said. "The pictures."

"Ah already got th' pictures. Lookin' out mah winder late one night Ah done seen yew sneak 'em inta yore li'l shed. While yew wuz playin' football, Ah wuz confiscatin' 'em. Now Ah need th' negatives. An' Ah also wan' th' baseball Ah gave yew when yew visited mah apartment. Ah thought it wuz th' one ah picked up off th' floor after it smashed through mah winder. But it turned out that th' one Ah gave yew was one that mah daddy done give me when Ah wuz uh li'l gal. Hal Newhouser hisself done give it t' 'im in uh Detroit Tiger trainin' camp. Ah've treasured it evah since."

"You must be a real baseball fan," said Loren.

"Yeah. Ah inherited it. By th' way, Ah oughta tell yew that mah Daddy thinks yew have uh lotta potential as uh ballplayer. He hadda force yew off th' Stars, even though he didn' wanna do it."

"Why?"

"He'd learned that yew worked wit' Buzz fer Marco Sisti. He thought they'd planted yew on th' Stars t' gather information that might endanger his life, an' mine."

"I can't understand why he would think that."

"Yew have t' realize that mah Daddy knows some things that he wishes he didn't, goin' back t' his younger years ovah in Louisiana when he briefly wurked for uh rival of Cato Sisti's. He succeeded in baseball an' left that bunch behind. But Marco has tried several times t' persuade 'im t' divulge whut he knows; so as t' give th' Sisti mob an edge on their competition. But mah father knows that if'n he talks, he's as good as daid. So he won' do it. Th' pressure has got 'im drinkin' uh lot mor' than he should."

"So I saw. Of course you can have your baseball back," said Loren. "I'll go get it."

"An' th' negatives of yore sneaky pictures. Has anyone else seen 'em?"

"Just me."

He saw her eyes shift from his face to the glove compartment located in front of where he was sitting. What was in it? He could guess. He slid forward in his seat and leaned one elbow on the dashboard directly over the spot at which she had briefly stared. He said: "You don't have to worry. I won't give the negatives to anyone else."

"Loren," she said firmly, "Yew'd betta not. Ah'm uh desperate woman." She moved across the seat toward him and said: "Ah spose yew wan' somethin' in return."

"Well, I…"

"Yew're uh handsome young man. Ah imagine yew've had sex wit' lotsa girls. Yew mus' be real hot stuff, huh?"

"No, I don't… I never really did it."

"Yew've nevah had sex… wit' anyone?"

"Not unless kissing counts."

"That's amazin'. Tell yew whut Ah'm gonna do. Ah'm gonna give yew th' thrill of yore life, an' then yore goin' t' give me whut Ah wan'. Deal?"

"But..."

"No buts. Here, lemme unbutton yore shirt." She leaned forward and soon exposed his bare chest, which she caused to tingle by running her fingernails back and forth across it. She then reached down for his fly and he felt and heard the zipper slide downward. His belt buckle was next, and then she asked him to lift up, so that she could remove his trousers. When he did so, she also took off his shorts.

He felt very vulnerable, naked from his belly down to his socks, his most private part protruding shamefully, as Rose divested herself of her denim shirt. There was hardly any light in the truck cab, but it was enough to show the concentration on Rose's face as she slid off her blue jeans and enough to highlight the hollows and protrusions packed provocatively into her skimpy undergarments.

"Come on," she implored, leaning forward. "Kiss me."

Tentatively, he reached both arms around her. With his fingertips he explored the vertical rigidity of her spine and then the soft warm flesh that sheathed her ribs and especially her hips. She pressed herself against him and her mouth clamped down on his, her wet tongue forcing itself into his mouth.

She forced him backwards, feeling with one hand between his thighs for his manhood. And the kissing continued, until he could hardly breathe.

She was the aggressor; he was the novice. At first he felt frightened; tentative; and weak. But the fire of her passion ignited his own, and he began to tighten his embrace and to crush his hungry lips against hers, until she, too, started gasping for air. Then, suddenly, as he was fumbling at her undergarments, he sensed her reaching behind him, heard the glove compartment door pop open, and then felt a hard object pressing against the back of his head.

"Yeah, it's mah gun," she said. "Th' same one yew saw me use on Bubba's truck when he came t' Daddy's trailer t' try t' intimidate me. Quite uh sight, wasn' it, li'l Rose backin' down big Bubba?"

Loren dared not move a muscle. "What are you going to do?" he asked.

"Lessen yew try somethin' foolish," she said, "Ah won' shoot yew. But Ah'm gonna stick t' yew like glue till yew give me yore negatives, alla them, plus mah baseball."

She slid back away from him, her pistol unwavering; her exhilaration revealed by the marble-like bulges in her bra, pointing at him like auxiliary weapons. Loren, too, remained stiff with excitement, which she noticed, and laughed.

"Yew really wan' it, don' yew?" she observed.

He didn't respond. "It" was the right word. Not her.

"Ah'm sorry Ah can't accommodate yew," she said. "Ah led yew on so Ah could git th' gun. We wimmen are quite willin' t' use sex to git whut we wan', 'though whut we really wan' is love. Yew males don' mind pretendin' love fer us, when all yew really wan' is sex. Ah'll git mah sex an' mah love elsewhar, thank yew. Let's go fetch those pictures."

At that moment the entire interior of the truck cab was illuminated by bright headlights aimed from a vehicle that had apparently been parked, for how long Loren didn't know, in the deep shadows only a few yards away. Loren's open shirt and lipstick-covered mouth, and the gun gleaming in Rose's fist, were as well lit as if they were on stage.

A deep voice, one familiar to Loren, seared through the darkness. "Drop th' gun, Rose. An' git down outa yore truck wit' yore hands held high."

Rose turned pale. The hand in which she held the pistol began to shake so hard that Loren was afraid the thing would go off. She whispered: "Ah've gotta git outta heah." Then she suddenly fell back against the driver's door. Poking the pistol through the open window, she fired a fusillade at the other vehicle. Both headlights winked out amid the sound of shattering glass and a hissing that suggested a punctured radiator. From the blinded vehicle there was no return fire.

Reaching a trembling hand for the ignition key, Rose brought her truck to life with a loud roar, and with the rear wheels spinning, and the back end fishtailing, she steered it at an ever-increasing speed toward the main highway.

Looking back through the rear window, Loren spotted a dark shape, silhouetted against the flares of Hades, pursuing them. "Looks like he's gaining on us," he told Rose.

Grimly gripping the wheel, she said: "Maybe Ah done killed his coolin' system, which oughta slow him down some." She laughed harshly. "An' Ah sure as hell shot out his lights."

"Listen," said Loren. "I have an idea. Up ahead, turn right."

She stared suspiciously. Then she shrugged. The truck rocked, its tires spewing shells, as she made the turn. Almost at once its single headlight picked out a narrow one-way bridge spanning a small stream directly ahead.

"As soon as we're across," Loren suggested, "turn off your lights."

The truck's tires thumped on the rough boards as they thundered across the bridge, the handrails on both sides almost touching metal. As soon as they were past the structure, Rose doused her lights and they were immediately rolling along in complete darkness, the flames of the oil field now behind them, and a heavy cloudbank continuing to obliterate the moon and the stars. Worried about getting stuck in a ditch with an angry gunman in pursuit, Rose slowed her truck to a crawl.

Back at the bridge, the sound of a rasping crash echoed through the night, followed by such a silence that Loren could only hear the throbbing of Rose's truck engine, the crunching noise of its tires on the shell road, the croaking of distant frogs, and his own heavy breathing. "I think we're safe now," he said.

"Ah gotta thank yew," she replied. "How did yew know 'bout th' bridge?"

"One of my friends drove me around one day. I have a good memory for geography."

"Ah'll say."

"Now I think you should take me back to my car, and then I'll go get you those negatives."

"How kin Ah trust yew?"

"You have no choice. Your pistol is empty; I counted six shots back there. And the negatives, as far as I am concerned, are hot potatoes. I'll be glad to get rid of them."

She thought for a moment. Then she said: "How do Ah git back t' yore car?"

"Turn left up ahead," he directed. "Then go about two miles and go left again."

She followed his instructions and in ten minutes they were back beside Shaky. Alighting from the truck, Loren said: "I'm going home to get the negatives. I'll also fetch your baseball. Meet me at Jake's Hog House at... (he glanced at his watch)... at eleven-thirty. If I don't show up by midnight, look for me in front of Davis's drug store at eight tomorrow morning. O. K?"

"Yeah. Ah hope fer both our sakes that yew won' change yore mind."

"No way. The stuff is all yours. As my father would say, all I want now is peace and quiet, and very little of that."

She laughed. "Loren," she said, "Ah wish yew were 'bout ten years older. An' female. She reached out both hands and pulled his face to hers. This time her kiss was not aggressive; it was affectionate.

* * *

Shaky was not capable of much speed. It took Loren a lot longer to make his way back to Tocqueville then it would have taken Rose's truck. Nervously, he kept looking in his rear view mirror to see whether someone was following.

He slowed down to bump over some railroad tracks. Around him were the dark shapes of industrial buildings, closed for the holidays. Not another vehicle was in sight.

Suddenly a pickup truck lacking lights, its horn sounding, its tires churning, and steam rising from its hood, darted out of an alley, and squealed to a stop directly in front of Shaky, forcing Loren to stop. Out of the truck stepped Buzz "Whar is she, Loren?" he called out.

"Who?"

"Yew know who. Rose."

"I don't know where she is."

Buzz approached. Spreading his elbows on Shaky's window sill, he said: "Turn off yore ignition an' hand me th' key."

Loren did as instructed.

"Now listen, Loren," Buzz continued. "Rose is uh dangerous woman. She may have killed both Dr. Kaplan an' her former husband, Bubba Guidry."

Startled, Loren asked: "What makes you think that?"

"Mrs. Kaplan has tol' us th' entire story. She came home from visitin' uh lady fren' an' discovered that her husban' had encountered Rose, who had broken inta their house lookin' fer drugs. She had managed t' knock 'im unconscious an' then hang 'im jus' afore Della—Mrs. Kaplan—arrived. Rose then threatened t' tell th' police that she'd looked outa 'er kitchen window an' seen Della murder Dr. Kaplan unless Della went along wit' th' idea of a suicide. Della was scared. She agreed. Later, however, she had second thoughts an' decided to tell Emile whut really happened."

"And you believe what Mrs. Kaplan told you?"

"Ah've known Della fer years. Ahm purty shore she's tellin' th' truth."

"I think that you're the one who's not telling the truth," said Loren. "I think you and Mrs. Kaplan are collaborators—in what and why, I don't know. But I do know that she was your high school girl friend. For a while I even believed that you were her lover, but I guess that what you have with her is really more of a business arrangement. Maybe involving drugs. Who is that in your truck; your hit man, Big Claude?"

Loren was stalling, hoping to keep Buzz talking until another car came along, at which time he hoped to be able to think of some way to escape. He could see a bulge under Buzz's jacket at his left armpit and wondered how long it would be before he brought out the gun.

Buzz seemed surprised by Loren's expostulations. Then he laughed. "Ah'm prouda yew," he said. "Somehow, yew've discovered mor' than Ah wudda thought possible. Keep at it an' yew'll make uh great detective. But yew've made one big mistake."

"What's that?"

Buzz turned and waved at his truck. The passenger immediately climbed out and walked toward them. It was Emile.

"Hello, Loren," he said. He turned toward Buzz. "Ah spose yew've decided t' tell 'im. Ah hope he can keep his mouf shut."

"Oh, Ah'll vouch fer Loren," declared Buzz. "Ah know 'im well. Ah thought he'd come t' know me, too, but Ah s'pose Ah wuz too secretive 'bout mah work."

"What work?" asked a bewildered Loren.

"Buzz is operatin' under covah," said Emile, "helpin' us t' crack open th' rackets of th' Sisti organization. It's still centered in New Orleans, but now it's gettin' established in Tocqueville, too."

"But how could you get away with it?" Loren asked Buzz. "Surely Mr. Sisti would find you out, sooner or later?"

"That's right," said Buzz. "But Marco has agreed t' cooperate t' save his own skin, an' to git revenge on his father, Cato, an' th' other two brothers. Some ol' scores t' settle. No honor among thieves, even in th' same family."

Emile said: "Th' New Orleans feds put out uh story that they had fired Buzz from th' bureau fer unspecified acts of corruption. He disappeared fer uh while into th' underworld, till he arrived heah, supposedly t' work fer Marco, but really t' watch 'im an' protect 'im, while we gathered evidence that we hope will destroy th' power of uh huge hunka of organized crime along th' Gulf coast."

"Wow!" exclaimed Loren. "And Dr. Kaplan and his wife were both part of the rackets, probably involved with drugs."

Emile nodded. "Bubba too," added Buzz. "An' we think prolly Rose. She an' Della were extremely close, until recently when Della took up wit' uh young woman named Olivia."

"Do you mean Della's younger sister?"

Emile laughed. "She ain't exactly a sister," he declared.

"Oh," said an abashed Loren. "I wonder if Rose knows about her… Anyway, I can believe Bubba was involved with the mob. But not Rose. I know she didn't murder anyone."

"Why d' yew say that?" asked Buzz.

"She told me what happened," asserted Loren. "And I already had enough information, acquired independently, to confirm what she said.

"Dr. Kaplan's death was an accident. He was drunk and knocked a radio that he was playing on a shelf above his tub into his bath water. He had a bad heart. Either he was electrocuted or he had a heart attack that killed him. Mrs. Kaplan got scared, I think mainly because any investigation of her husband's death would reveal her mob ties. So she persuaded Rose who had come by for a love visit, to help her make it seem like suicide. But they could not have hanged him if he had not already been dead. And there were no signs on his body of a struggle or of him being hit with anything."

"This kid's amazin'," said Emile. "Ah could tell th' hangin' wuz faked, but Ah nevah imagined how Kaplan really died."

"An' Bubba;" asked Buzz, "whut 'bout 'im?

"Something to do with his mob employers," said Loren. "I'm not sure what. But Rose told me that Mrs. Kaplan knew the guy who killed him and tried to make it look like suicide. He had told her all about it."

"Big Claude!" exclaimed Buzz. "Della knew 'im in New Orleans. Ah shoulda guessed."

"It all makes sense," admitted Emile. "Loren, do yew think yew kin get in touch wit' Rose an' ask her t' please supply us with uh deposition. Assumin' her story is true, we'll furnish her wit' immunity from prosecution."

"I don't know where she is," said Loren. "But she might get in touch with me. If she does, I'll tell her what you said."

Buzz looked at his watch. "Gettin' on t'ward midnight," he observed. "Loren, isn't it already past yore curfew?"

"Way past," sighed Loren.

"Wal, go on home an' git some sleep," said Buzz. "We'll talk more, later. O. K?"

"O. K.," said Loren, much relieved.

"One mor' thang," warned Emile. "Not uh word t' anyone, not even yore parents, 'bout any of this. Whoevah yew tell will automatically be in danger. Th' people we're after are, among other things, murderers. Buzz's life is in danger every day. So is mine. We've gotta keep mum—th' three of us."

"I'll say nothing," said Loren. "I don't want any more trouble."

"Good," said Emile. "Mah best t' yore folks." Buzz tossed Loren his car keys and the two men re-entered Buzz's truck and drove away. Loren wondered how they could safely navigate with a perforated radiator and no headlights. He saw Emile holding a flashlight out his window.

Once he was home, Loren leaped from Shaky and hurried to his room. Taking the envelope containing the Kaplan negatives from underneath his rag rug and the Newhouser baseball from a dresser drawer, he was just re-entering Shaky when his mother called from the kitchen door. "Loren! Where are you going at this time of night?"

"I forgot to give Mary Beth something that belongs to her. She needs it badly. I'll be right back."

"Can't it wait until tomorrow?"

"No. Sorry. Gotta go."

He gunned Shaky in reverse out onto the street, and broke the speed limit all the way to Jake's, aware that the restaurant's doors were usually locked at midnight and that all of the patrons would probably be cleared out by now, almost twelve-fifteen. About two blocks from that establishment, he passed Rose's truck, departing. Honking his horn, he made a U turn and pursued her. She heard him and pulled over to the curb. Stopping behind her, he jumped out and ran to climb into the passenger seat beside her. Breathing hard, he apologized for being late, as he handed over the baseball and the envelope containing the film. "My neighbor, the assistant district attorney, stopped me and wanted to chat," he said. "I didn't want him to think there was anything unusual going on; so I waited him out. Anyway, you've got what you want."

"Thank yew, Loren. Ah wuz worried that yew weren't goin' t' keep yore word."

"I always do. Or try to. There is one thing more I'd like to know."

"Whut's that?"

"One night when I was playing tennis very late with a friend, someone apparently took a shot at me. Do you think you might know who it was?"

"Someone shot at yew? That seems strange." She thought a moment. Then she asked: "Who were yew playin' wit'?"

"Sam Howell."

"Buzz?"

"Yes."

"That s'plains it. When did this happen?"

"Early last month. The first or second, something like that. A Saturday night; very late."

Rose laughed. "Do yew know anythang 'bout Buzz?" she asked. "Whut he does fer uh livin'?"

"We worked together in Johnson's Senate campaign."

"Who employed 'im?"

"Mr. Sisti. I believe his first name is Marco."

"Exactly. Marco Sisti is th' son of one of th' mos' feared mob bosses in th' country. An' Buzz works fer 'im as an enforcer."

"How do you know this?"

"From Della, who wuz Buzz's girl fren till he went away t' college. She's been keepin' up wit' his movements. Lately, she seems t' think he's got hisself in big trouble."

"What kind of trouble?"

"She didn' say."

"Well, what would Buzz's work have to do with our tennis sessions? He always acted like a regular guy around me."

"Oh, Buzz kin be charmin'. But he's as tough as uh live oak. Yew said thar wuz only one shot?"

"Yes."

"I'll bet th' shooter wuz scared stiff an' ran away immediately."

"Do you mean he was aiming at Buzz and not at me?"

"Ah'd bet on it."

Loren gave the matter a moment's consideration. He remembered Buzz reaching into his valise, probably not replacing a gun, as Loren had feared, but starting to take one out to return fire. "For a while," he said to Rose, "I suspected that Buzz might have tried to shoot me."

She laughed. "Not likely," she said. "Ah imagine it wuz Big Claude tryin' t' carry out a contract on Buzz." She thought a moment. "Or could it have been...? Naw, she wouldn'... Ah don' believe she would..."

Something that she had thought of disturbed Rose profoundly. "If that's all," she said, "Ah'd better go."

"One thing more," said Loren. "I happen to know that Emile Mouton is still investigating Dr. Kaplan's death and that of your former husband. He wants to talk to you. It seems that Mrs. Kaplan told him in the presence of a woman calling herself her sister, who is now living with her, that you were responsible for the deaths of both men. It might be a good idea to try to clear yourself with Emile. I think he'd believe you."

Rose frowned, staring blankly through the windshield. Then she asked: "Are yew sure 'bout this? 'Bout Della livin' wit' 'nother woman?"

"I'm afraid so."

"Ah see. Ah wondered who that wuz answerin' th' phone sayin' Della wuzn't home. Ah thought it wuz uh housekeeper an' that Della had prolly gone t' New Orleans. Damn 'er! Ah thought she loved me."

Loren could think of nothing consoling to say. Rose was tough. And smart. But her world had collapsed. "I wish I could help," he said.

She laid a hand on his arm. "Yew already have," she said. "Now Ah think its time fer me t' disappear. Don' worry; Ah'll be fine. Goodbye."

She drove off. Loren went home.

* * *

When he awakened late on the morning of Friday November 26, he sat stupefied on the edge of his cot. Gradually the frightening fantasies that had flitted through his troubled dreams evaporated and he returned to reality. It was his seventeenth birthday. One more year to go before he was draft bait. How would he spend the precious time?

It was well past time for breakfast, so he settled for tomato soup, two peanut butter sandwiches, and a large glass of milk. Then he went into the small study, where his mother was paying bills, sticking three-cent stamps on envelopes. She gave him a wan smile.

"Say, Mom," he said. "I'm sorry I was out so late last night. But I had to speak to..."

"Loren," she broke in, "I hope you're not going to tell me that you had to speak to Mary Beth, because she already phoned this morning to say she missed seeing you yesterday evening. She would like you to call her."

Feeling a revealing blush creeping up his neck toward his cheeks, Loren quickly said: "No, it was Buzz. I had to take him some stuff that I mistakenly ran off with when we played tennis together."

"I see. Is there anything else you'd like…?"

At that moment the phone out in the hall began to ring. "I'll get it," said Loren.

It was Sophie, responding to his hurried request when they passed in the hall at school on Wednesday, that she phone him.

"Hey, Sophie," he said. "I was wondering if you knew why Tony seems to be avoiding me. Every time I've seen him recently, he slips away without saying anything."

"Ah think he's embarrassed," she said.

"Why?"

"Ah shouldn' be talkin' 'bout it," she said. "Please promise yew won' tell Tony."

"I won't."

"Wal, he's 'shamed 'bout whut he did that night in th' big woods."

"What are you talking about?"

"Tony knew yew were 'fraid of one-eyed trucks; so he arranged wit' uh guy he knew t' foller us wit' one headlight disconnected an' give us uh li'l bump. An' then he purposely ditched his car, an' tol' us t' run into th' woods. Ah didn' know till afterwards that it wuz one of his damn practical jokes. He nearly scared me t' death. When Ah tole Shelley 'bout it, she said she'd like t' kill 'im."

"But someone *was* shooting at us."

"Naw, that wuz Tony; shootin' into th' air. He alluz keeps uh gun in his glove compartment, 'cause he sometimes has t' work fer his daddy 'round some purty tough people."

"What happened to the guy in the other vehicle?"

"Once we hit th' ditch, he figured he'd done whut Tony wanted; so he drove home." She paused. Then she said: "Anyway, Tony paid uh stiff price fer his dumb joke. He got bit by a snake. After he let yew an' Shelley out, Ah hadda go wit' 'im t' th' 'mergency room. We wuz thar three hours. His leg wuz swollen up real bad.

"After Ah saw he wuz gonna be O. K., Ah tole 'im it served 'im right fer tryin' t' scare us that way. He said he wuz terrible sorry, an' he'd nevah do anythin' like that again."

"He'd better not," said Loren. "Tell Tony I forgive him. But no more practical jokes." He hung up.

Someone was knocking on the front door. He went to see who it was. Nan, coming out of the study, joined him. On the front porch, dressed in a short-sleeved white shirt, neatly creased brown slacks, and well-shined shoes, stood Buzz. "Hello," he said. "May Ah come in?"

"Sure," said Loren, standing aside.

Entering, Buzz smiled at Nan. "Good day, Mrs. Temple," he said. "Ah've been wantin' t' meet yew. Mah name is Sam Howell. Ah'm yore son's former partner in crime, which is prolly whut helpin' Lyndon Johnson git 'lected t' th' Senate 'mounts to." They shook hands.

"Nice to meet you at last," she said. "I believe Loren has referred to you as "Buzz." Is that what you like to be called?"

"Yes, ma'am. Buzz th' fuzz." He took a card from his wallet and showed it to her. Her eyes widened. "My, my," she exclaimed. "I had no idea."

"Ah'd like yew t' keep it uh secret," Buzz cautioned. "Loren knows. But please don' tell anyone else."

"Don't tell what?" asked Adam, who had entered the house through the back door, so quietly that they had not heard him. "I had to park out front," he said. "Someone's truck is in the driveway."

"It's mine," said Buzz. "Ah 'pologize. Ah hadn' planned t' stay fer mor' than uh minute." He extended his hand. "Sam Howell."

"Mr. Howell," acknowledged Adam, shaking hands. "Loren's friend. Say, you might be interested in this; I know Loren will." He opened an early edition of the *Endeavor* to an interior page and pointed to a picture. Loren looked, as did Nan and Buzz. In the yard in front of a nondescript brick house, were several hand-lettered signs all reading "For Sale." Underneath, a caption identified the owner of the house as Calvin Allen, Tocqueville High School's football coach, who was considerably upset at how someone had defaced his front lawn.

"It didn't take the fans long to express their disappointment at yesterday's debacle," observed Adam. "Still think you'd like to be a coach or manager, Loren?"

"Mr. Allen isn't a very good coach," said Loren. "But it's sad to think how his wife and children must feel. That's ugly stuff."

"Sneaky, too," said Nan. "I don't approve of people sneaking around." She looked directly at Buzz, as if daring him to disagree. He returned her stare and gave her a big grin. After a moment she smiled back. "If you aren't too busy, Buzz," she said, "perhaps you'll eat supper with us. My husband and I would like to get better acquainted with you. Is six o'clock all right?"

"Thank yew, ma'am," replied Buzz. "Ah'd like that very much. An' in th' meantime Ah think Ah owe it t' Loren, t' come clean 'bout sum thangs Ah've concealed from 'im since we became acquainted." He turned toward Loren. "Ah have Cokes an' cookies waitin' fer us at mah place," he said. "How 'bout we take uh run ovah thar. Maybe Ah can answer yore questions; at least sum of 'em."

And I'll bet that you have some for me, thought Loren. Nevertheless, he responded: "That'd be great. Let's go."

To Adam, who seemed a bit disconcerted, Buzz said: "Uh pleasure t' meet yew, Suh. Ah'm lookin' forward t' dinin' wit' yew this evenin'."

* * *

When they climbed into Buzz's truck, they encountered Rose, seated inside. "Ah've been waitin' fer yew two," she said. "Ah wan' yew both t' go wit' me t' see Emile. Ah phoned 'im. He'll be waitin' fer us in his office. An' Ah also phoned Della an' gave 'er uh piece uh mah mind. Th' bitch!"

"Ah hope yew didn' tell Della that yore turnin' 'er in," said Buzz.

"Naw," replied Rose. "Ah ain't no fool. But Ah spose she could tell sumptin' wuz up, 'cause Ah wuz purty mad."

"Wal," said Buzz, "she'd have to find out eventually that yew'd wised up about 'er. Wit' yore help we kin git this whole business settled. An' rid Tocqueville of two mob molls in th' process. Once Della an' Olivia are called afore uh grand jury,

Ah believe they'll leave town at once an' disappear forevah. Have yew brought th' photos and negatives?"

"Yeah." Rose showed him a large manila envelope.

To Loren's unspoken question, Buzz said: "Neither of yew need t' worry that these pictures will evah be seen by anyone 'sides us an' Emile. Th' mere threat t' show them t' th' grand jury'll do th' job. Yew can count on it."

"Ah hope so," said Rose. "Ah can't leave town right now 'cause mah Daddy is in real bad shape. He needs me t' stay wit' 'im."

"We'll keep yore involvement confidential," said Buzz soothingly.

As they traveled in Buzz's partly repaired truck in the direction of downtown Tocqueville, they passed the Episcopal Church. On a glass-covered bulletin board located near the sidewalk appeared a message in large letters. Loren read: "Nothing in life is to be feared. It is only to be understood. Marie Curie." Slumping against the locked door on the familiar hard seat, he sighed. His two companions would soon make everything right. And once he had mailed the stolen yearbook back to Southside High School, he would have met all his own obligations. He felt as if a dam had collapsed inside him...

Breaking the silence, Buzz said: "Guess we're in fer uh wait."

In front of them red lights had begun to blink beside a railroad crossing. As they drew near, they could see the huge headlight of a locomotive less than one hundred yards up the track and hear the warning blast of its horn. Buzz braked to a stop less than a car's length from the shining rails, and they settled back, resigned to watching a long line of box cars rumble past.

Suddenly, Buzz sat up straight. "Whut th' hail!" he shouted, staring into the rear view mirror. Loren turned and looked behind them. An opulent yellow convertible with its top down, driven by a red-haired woman all three of them knew, was approaching from behind them very fast, far too fast to stop before it ploughed into their rear bumper. On Della's face was a diabolical grin...

* * *

What happened next was cataclysmic. The truck's sudden surge as Buzz floored the accelerator; Rose's screams; the ear-splitting wail emanating from the smoking, thundering monster that hurled itself savagely upon them; and the neck-cracking thump of the locomotive's cow-catcher against the rear of the truck that spun it off the rails and onto the concrete surface of a nearby filling station, where it narrowly missed crashing into a gas pump before thudding to a rocking stop against a deserted office.

Loren, shivering, fingered a bruised elbow and gave thanks to a benevolent Providence. Rose slowly pulled herself up from the floorboards, a thin trickle of blood running down her forehead. And Buzz continued to clutch the steering wheel, as if trying to prevent it escaping from his white-knuckled grip.

They were alive! Buzz's quick thinking had saved them from certain destruction when Della had attempted to ram them onto the track in front of the massive iron engine. But what about Della? Loren jumped onto the ground on wobbling legs and staggered around the twisted truck bed that had once carried piles of Lyndon Johnson's campaign signs. Behind him came Rose and then Buzz. A long line of box cars, flat cars, cattle cars and tank cars continued to rattle past until finally there appeared a red caboose. On the rear platform stood a man wearing overalls and a striped cap, who stared curiously at them as the train, already slowing down in response to an evident attempt by the engineer to bring it to a stop, nevertheless continued forward.

At first Loren saw no sign of Della's convertible. It seemed to have vanished. "Where could she be?" he inquired aloud. "Look," said Rose. She pointed a short distance down the tracks. A grotesque heap of mutilated yellow metal lay in a patch of weeds a few feet from the rails, an orange tongue of flame licking at a collapsed tire. In the distance Loren heard the sounds of sirens. As they grew louder he sensed movement beside him and turned to see Buzz offering Rose a cigarette lighter. Nodding, she flipped its lid and touched the resulting flame to the packet that she had carried from the truck. It took hardly more than a moment for the large brown envelope to dissolve into gray ashes, which were at once blown away by a gentle breeze, as if they were the last remnants of Loren's youth.

ABOUT THE AUTHOR

Norman Ferris, a life-long devotee of the Chicago Cubs, played high school, college and semipro baseball. He is currently Professor Emeritus of History at Middle Tennessee State University. An authority on the diplomacy and statesmanship of the American Civil War, he authored *The Trent Affair* (1977), which received a Pulitzer Prize nomination. *Yank* is his first work of fiction. He lives on a farm near Murfreesboro, Tennessee with his wife, Kathleen, and assorted animals.

During the Korean War Ferris enlisted in the U.S. Navy and after a year of foreign duty spent over two years as the youngest military officer working for the Chairman of the Joint Chiefs of Staff in the Pentagon. He then earned a law degree and a Ph.D. in history at Emory University, following which he had a distinguished academic career that included service as Chair of the Tennessee Board of Regents Faculty Sub-Council, Chair of the National Assembly of State Conferences of the American Association of University Professors, and Chair of the Tennessee Humanities Council. In 1997 he left the classroom to devote himself fully to fiction writing and to service as a local political party activist.

Printed in the United States
5865